Praise for Anna Castle's *Murder by Misrule*

Murder by Misrule was selected as one of Kirkus Review's Best Indie Books of 2014.

"Castle's characters brim with zest and real feeling... Though the plot keeps the pages turning, the characters, major and minor, and the well-wrought historical details will make readers want to linger in the 16th century. A laugh-out loud mystery that will delight fans of the genre." — Kirkus, starred review

"*Murder by Misrule* is a delightful debut with characters that leap off the page, especially the brilliant if unwilling detective Francis Bacon and his street smart man Tom Clarady. Elizabeth Tudor rules, but Anna Castle triumphs." — Karen Harper, NY Times best-selling author of *The Queen's Governess*

"Well-researched... *Murder by Misrule* is also enormously entertaining; a mystery shot through with a series of misadventures, misunderstandings, and mendacity worthy of a Shakespearian comedy." — M. Louisa Locke, author of the Victorian San Francisco Mystery Series

"Castle's period research is thorough but unobtrusive, and her delight in the clashing personalities of her crime-fighting duo is palpable: this is the winning fictional odd couple of the year, with Bacon's near-omniscience being effectively grounded by Clarady's street smarts. The book builds effectively to its climax, and a last-minute revelation that is particularly well-handled, but readers will most appreciate the wry humor. An extremely promising debut." — Steve Donoghue, Historical Novel Society

"Historical mystery readers take note: *Murder by Misrule* is a wonderful example of Elizabethan times brought to life...a blend of Sherlock Holmes and history." — D. Donovan, eBook Reviewer, Midwest Book Review

"I love when I love a book! *Murder by Misrule* by Anna Castle was a fantastic read. Overall, I really liked this story and highly recommend it." — Book Nerds

Praise for *Death by Disputation*

Death by Disputation won the 2015 Chaucer Awards First In Category Award for the Elizabethan/Tudor period.

"Castle's style shines ... as she weaves a complex web of scenarios and firmly centers them in Elizabethan culture and times." — D. Donovan, eBook Reviewer, Midwest Book Review

" I would recommend *Death by Disputation* to any fan of historical mysteries, or to anyone interested in what went on in Elizabethan England outside the royal court." — E. Stephenson, Historical Novel Society

"Accurate historical details, page turning plot, bodacious, lovable and believable characters, gorgeous depictions and bewitching use of language will transfer you through time and space back to Elizabethan England." — Edi's Book Lighthouse

"This second book in the Francis Bacon mystery series is as strong as the first. At times bawdy and rowdy, at times thought-provoking ... Castle weaves religious-political intrigue, murder mystery, and Tom's colorful friendships and love life into a tightly-paced plot." — Amber Foxx, Indies Who Publish Everywhere

Praise for *The Widows Guild*

"As in Castle's earlier book, Murder by Misrule, she brings the Elizabethan world wonderfully to life, and if Francis Bacon himself seems a bit overshadowed at times in this novel, it's because the great, fun creation of the Widow's Guild itself easily steals the spotlight.
Strongly recommended." — Editor's Choice, Historical Novel Society.

"Fans of historical mysteries will find this book just as captivating and well-done as the rest in a highly recommended read brimming with action and captivating scenarios." — D. Donovan, Senior Book Reviewer, Midwest Book Review.

Praise for *Publish and Perish*

Won an Honorable Mention for Mysteries in Library Journal's 2017 Indie Ebook Awards!

"In this aptly titled fourth book in the Francis Bacon series, Castle combines her impressive knowledge of English religion and politics during the period with masterly creativity. The result is a lively, clever story that will leave mystery fans delighted.—Emilie Hancock, Mount Pleasant Regional Lib., SC, for Library Journal.

Also by Anna Castle

The Francis Bacon Mystery Series
Murder by Misrule
Death by Disputation
The Widow's Guild
Publish and Perish
Let Slip the Dogs

The Professor & Mrs. Moriarty Mystery Series
Moriarty Meets His Match
Moriarty Takes His Medicine
Moriarty Brings Down the House

The Lost Hat, Texas Mystery Series
Black & White & Dead All Over
Flash Memory

MURDER BY MISRULE

A Francis Bacon Mystery — Book 1

ANNA CASTLE

Murder by Misrule
A Francis Bacon Mystery — #1

Print Edition | June 2014
Discover more works by Anna Castle at www.annacastle.com

ISBN-10: 0986413097
ISBN-13: 978-0-9864130-9-4
Produced in the United States of America

ACKNOWLEDGMENTS

A warm and hearty thank you goes out to everyone who supported me through the writing of this book, especially through the seemingly endless editing process. The book is the better for the wise counsel of my fellow Capitol Crime Writers: Russell Ashworth, Jerry Cavin, Will Chandler, Donna Daniel, K.P. Gresham, David Hansard, and Julie Rinaldi. It was further improved by the sharp eyes of my agent, Pamela Ahearn. Editor Jennifer Quinlan of Historical Editorial provided that all-important final polish.

I also wholeheartedly thank the Sisters in Crime Guppies group PressQuest for giving me the courage and support to venture forth into publication. Extra thanks are due to my role models Kaye George, Diane Vallere, and Susan Schreyer. Without you, this book might never have existed.

For my parents Carmen and Dale, who keep on making things possible for me

ONE

Westminster, 19 November 1586

A sudden roar startled Francis Bacon out of his thoughts, making him jump, his shoes actually leaving the ground. He glanced to either side, hoping no one had seen him. Of course, the street was empty. The roar came from the cheers rising from the tiltyard where all of London celebrated Queen's Day with jousting and pageants. The world and its wife were there today, including everyone who mattered at court. Everyone, therefore, except him.

He didn't know why he'd come down to Westminster. He should have stayed in his chambers at Gray's, reading in the blissful peace of the deserted inn. He needed exercise, he'd said to himself. Stretch his legs, catch a breath of air. Once he was out, he'd thought he might drop by Burghley House in hopes of gaining a moment with his uncle, the Lord Treasurer and Her Majesty's most indispensable counselor. He knew His Lordship would not be at the tiltyard. He rarely took time off from work and disliked noisy spectacles. Francis didn't much care for them either. Sweaty people, filthy grounds, ear-splitting roars like the one that had just startled him. Dreadful. He shuddered to think of it.

His uncle had refused to see him. The secretary offered a transparent excuse about heaps of letters and an aching head. One did not need the deductive gifts of a Bacon to recognize that he was *persona non grata* at Burghley House as well. All he'd done was have an idea — a perfectly reasonable idea for reforming the English common law — and mention it here and there. He was born to have ideas, he'd been told as much from infancy. But his proposal had created a bit of a stir. The queen didn't like controversy among her courtiers, so she'd banished him until further notice. The punishment far exceeded the crime, but to whom might one complain?

On a sort of self-flagellatory whim, he walked down the Strand to Whitehall, thinking of popping up to his friend Henry Percy's to borrow a book. He changed his mind on the very threshold, wavering two steps forward, two back, taking another slow step forward. Then he turned and walked quickly away with downcast eyes. He knew, and everyone would know he knew, that banishment from court meant no visiting of friends who were visiting at court. What had he been thinking? He'd taken a risk just passing through the King Street Gate.

He should go back to his chambers at once and stay there. He walked swiftly past the palace and turned into the Privy Garden to get off the main street. If German tourists were allowed to stroll here at their pleasure, then surely so should he be. He inhaled deeply as he hurried through the maze of tall yews, appreciating their wholesome fragrance to bolster his courage until he reached the narrow street on the other side. Now he was officially outside the palace grounds. Safe. Francis exhaled a sigh of relief and directed his steps toward the Westminster wharf. He'd catch a wherry back to the Temple Stair and avoid the whole palace area until he had been restored to the queen's good graces.

The lanes south of the palace formed another maze, with narrow alleys winding between tightly-packed houses, darkened by the overhanging upper stories. The short

November day was drawing down. Rows of puffball clouds streamed across the sky, casting confusing shadows across the timbered walls. But Francis knew Westminster like he knew his Bible. He could walk it blindfolded.

He turned a sharp corner and stumbled onto a soft mass. Backing up, looking down, a gasp of horror choked his throat. The mass was a man, dead, sprawled across the middle of the lane in a pool of wet dirt. Wet with blood, which Francis had walked right into. If he'd been paying attention, he would have smelled it first: the tang of fresh blood was unmistakable. He backed off a few paces and checked his boots, a thoughtless act he immediately repented. The poor man, whoever he was, deserved his first consideration.

Francis took a few breaths, patting himself on the chest to calm his heart, his gaze averted toward the pink plaster wall beside him. He'd been to funerals, but he'd never seen a corpse, much less nearly trampled one in the open street. He steeled himself to take another look. He avoided the face at first, easing himself into the odious duty. He noted a doublet of excellent cloth and a figured Spanish belt. The clothes were rich: this man had been a gentleman.

Ah, worse! The garment he'd thought was a cloak was in fact a robe: black, with two velvet welts on each wide sleeve. Those stripes told him the man had been a barrister.

There was no help for it now; odds were high he knew him. Francis took two gingerly steps closer and shifted his gaze to the face. *Ah, mercy! What have we come to?* The body in the lane was Tobias Smythson, an ancient of Gray's Inn, Francis's own Inn of Court. He not only knew him, he knew him well.

Smythson had been Francis's tutor when he'd first arrived at Gray's back in 1579, an eighteen-year-old boy newly bereft of his father. He'd been disoriented and miserable, facing an uncertain future. Kindly, wise Tobias Smythson had taken him under his wing. He'd guided his

3

studies without those annoying little jokes about the speed with which his pupil mastered each subject. He'd introduced him to judges at all the courts. Francis wouldn't say it had been a convivial relationship — they weren't close in the way of real fathers and sons — but it had been comfortable, productive, and most welcome in those difficult early days. In a few years, it became obvious to them both that Francis had no further need for a tutor. Although they saw one another less frequently, they remained on amicable terms.

Now, here his old tutor lay, dead in the street. How could such a thing have happened? What was he doing here on such a day? A barrister would have a hundred reasons to visit Westminster on an ordinary day. But why today, a holiday? Smythson was no fonder of the Queen's Day crowds than his uncle and himself.

Fortunately, it wasn't Francis Bacon's job to solve that mystery. He should call the coroner now, or, considering the proximity of the palace, the Captain of the Queen's Guard, Sir Walter Ralegh. He took three strides back toward King Street before he caught himself. He had been forbidden to speak to any courtier at any time on any subject. The queen's temper was unpredictable. She might well be incensed to see him approaching the tiltyard gallery even under these extraordinary circumstances.

A flash of anger creased his brow. Really, the situation was preposterous! By rights, as the son of the late Lord Keeper of the Great Seal, he ought to have a personal attendant at all times who could be sent hither and yon with messages. Then he remembered that he did have one, after a manner of speaking: the upstart son of a privateer who had been foisted upon him in exchange for the payment of an unfortunate accumulation of debt. Thomas Clarady was sure to be at the tournament, getting drunk with his friends. Francis jogged up to King Street and whistled for a boy to summon him. Thanks to the superfluity of population in the capital, there were always boys eager to earn a farthing or two. Since Clarady was undoubtedly dressed like a carnival clown, he ought to be easy enough to find.

TWO

Queen's Day was the most glorious day so far in all of Tom's nineteen years. He and his fellow law students had skipped chapel and dined early in a Holborn ordinary to make sure they arrived at the Whitehall tiltyard in time to claim choice positions at the rail. They'd just watched the Earl of Cumberland fling the Queen's Champion clear off his horse in a masterful display of jousting prowess. Now the Earl of Essex was performing a pastoral pageant, complete with Hermits, Shepherds, and Wild Men.

Tom tried to listen to the earl's poetry, but his eyes kept shifting toward the magnificent personages seated near the queen in the gallery overlooking the yard. He felt a bit of a bumpkin not knowing which was who, but in fairness, he'd only been in London since Michaelmas. Today alone, he'd seen two earls and Captain Sir Walter Ralegh, who sat astride a silver stallion below the gallery, guarding the queen.

Not a bad start for a newcomer. By this time next year, he'd know them all. And some of them might know him.

Someone important could notice him today. Such things happened. He knew he looked gallant in his emerald velvet and canary silk, his short beard trimmed to perfection. Tom stood tall and squared his shoulders. He drew in a deep breath to swell his chest, inhaling aromas of dust, spilt wine, and horseshit. He set his fist on his hip to draw attention to the coiled hilt of his new rapier. The pose pushed back the drape of the sleeveless black gown that declared him a law student at one of the prestigious Inns of Court.

He had truly arrived at the center of the world, in his rightful role as a gentleman, new-feathered though he might be. These robes proved his status. They also got him in nearly everywhere. Nobody minded law students poking in to see what was happening. The robes were as good as a letter of marque.

Thirty minutes later, Tom's pose had wilted. His tummy was rumbling, his head was wobbly, and they were nearly out of wine. The young Earl of Essex, dressed as an Old Knight, stood alone on the platform beside a taffeta shrub, intoning a polymetrical paean to solitariness. The other players were long gone. Tom knew that a love of poetry was one of the marks of a gentleman, but he had to struggle to pay attention.

"This meter has too many feet," he muttered. "Makes my brains itch."

That earned a chuckle from his diminutive friend Trumpet. "It's that bumpity French style: bum, tee rum, tee rumpty rumpity REEDLE dum."

Trumpet, properly known as Allen Trumpington, claimed to be seventeen, but Tom thought fifteen nearer the mark. The boy had black hair and green eyes that tilted up at the corners, pixie-like. He had a tragic wisp of a moustache of which he was perversely proud, often patting it as if to make it grow. The other students at Gray's Inn teased him about his stature and his love of study but scrupulously avoided mention of that pitiful moustache.

Every man was entitled to his illusions.

The earl ended his last alexandrine verse with a flourish and a bow. Applause rose from the crowd. The queen sent a silken scarf by way of a footman to reward her courtier.

Tom passed the wineskin to Trumpet, who shook it, frowned, and passed it on to Stephen.

"Why are you giving this to me?" Stephen reached over Trumpet's shoulder to hand it back to Tom. "Get some more, Tom. Before the next tourney starts."

Tom rolled his eyes at the tone of command. He wasn't Stephen's retainer anymore. He was Francis Bacon's much-avoided, semi-pseudo-apprentice. But he wouldn't mind another skinful of wine himself. He looked about for a vendor.

Stephen Delabere was the eldest son of the seventh Earl of Dorchester. He had sandy hair and amber eyes. His chin was too narrow and his nose was too sharp, but he was handsome enough for a lord. Years ago, Tom's father had lent Lord Dorchester a large sum on absurd terms to buy Tom's way into a noble household. Captain Valentine Clarady was a privateer and proud to serve queen and country by raiding Spanish ships, but he wanted more for his only son. So Tom had left the rambling manor on the Dorset coast where he had grown up surrounded by adoring sisters and aunts and guests from all the Seven Seas: merchants and sailors with parrots and adventurous lords. Even blackamoors with rings in their noses. The earl's household had paled by comparison, but Tom made the best of it. He quickly learned to manage the malleable Stephen so as to let his noble master-*cum*-playmate shine while he quietly got what he wanted.

"Didn't you like the earl's poetry?" Stephen asked, a trifle worried. "I thought it was rather fine."

"The poetry was magnificent," Tom assured him. "I loved the poetry. Except for the meter. That meter made me dizzy."

"The meter was a bit strained," Stephen said. "But some of the lines were good. 'Envy's snaky eye'? That was brilliant." He narrowed his eyes and lips and thrust his head forward, trying to look snaky. It made him look drunker. "Nor envy's sssssnaky—"

Trumpet talked right over him. "I kept hoping the Wild Men would come back and trounce those pribbling Hermits."

"I hated the Hermits," Tom said. "For one thing, if they're so devoted to hermitation, why do they go about in a group?"

That got a laugh from Ben, who had watched the whole performance with the abstracted gaze he wore when puzzling out some legal jim-jammery. Benjamin Whitt was taller than Tom and Stephen by a good three inches and older by two years. He had dark eyes and a long face, like a melancholy hound. He always wore brown on brown with dabs of beige. You would look at him and think, "What a sad, dull fellow!"

And you would be wrong.

"It was an allegory," Ben said. "The Wild Men show our savage side: Man as Beast. The Hermits illustrate the virtues of solitary contemplation. The Shepherds exemplify the pacifying nature of, er, Nature. The deeper message—"

"Hang the deeper message!" Tom crowed. "I wanted a sword fight." He glanced up at the courtiers in the gallery and struck an oratorical pose. "I submit to you that shepherds and savages, while all very well in their way, do not belong in a tourney. They are not justly joustly. Not—"

He was interrupted by a small, scruffy boy, who had somehow materialized in front of the rail to tug at Tom's yellow silk sleeve.

"Stop that." Tom twitched his sleeve away from the urchin's dirty hand. "Be off with you!"

The boy stood his ground. "I've a message for Thomas Clarady. That's you, ain't it?"

"Who wants to know?"

"Your master sent me. Francis Bacon, he said he was. He wants you, quicker than quick, no matter how drunk you be. I'm to show you where and get another ha'penny. He said, 'Tell him not to quibble.'" The boy did a fair impression of Bacon's precise enunciation. "What's quibbling, master? Some lawyer trick?"

Tom growled under his breath. He had half a mind to say no, but Bacon could have him tossed out on his ear whenever he pleased. His father was at sea again and wouldn't learn about it for months, by which time the damage might be unfixable.

He was spared the indignity of obedience by Ben, who admired Francis Bacon beyond all comprehension. "We'd best go at once," he said. "He could be in trouble."

"If he's fallen into the Fleet, you're fishing him out." The Fleet River was the sewer of west London. "He's probably just short of coin for a wherry."

They grabbed the other lads and began working their way through the crowd toward the gate. They followed the boy down King Street to a side street, down an alley, and into a lane lined on both sides with tall houses. At the juncture, Francis Bacon paced back and forth, clasping his hands tensely at his breast.

* * *

The boy was sent back for Captain Ralegh. Bacon relayed his instructions through Ben and then slipped away with one last sorrowful glance at Mr. Smythson's body. The lads were left to stand guard.

The lads moved toward the body as if drawn by a string, bending forward to peer down at it. His eyes stared at nothing, open to the gray sky. His lips still snarled, teeth bared, as if he had died shouting curses at his attacker.

Not a quiet death.

Pity and disgust knotted together in Tom's belly. Sudden death was always ugly yet somehow fascinating. He couldn't look away.

They didn't have long to wait. A ringing voice cried, "Hold them here! Block the way!" Then Sir Walter Ralegh rounded the corner on his silver stallion. The Earl of Cumberland was close behind him. He positioned his mount to block the lane. Sir Walter glanced at the lads and down at the corpus as he rode carefully past. He turned his steed to block the farther end.

Ralegh dismounted and handed his reins to Stephen, who happened to be closest. Stephen recoiled, offended. Tom nipped in and neatly twitched the reins into his own hand to forestall an outburst. Stephen's prickly temper could not abide such minor slights. One of Tom's jobs had been averting these little conflicts, which tended to make Stephen look petulant rather than lordly.

Trumpet edged him aside to snatch the reins, holding them as if they were relics of immense holiness. Ralegh was his hero.

"Do you know this man?" Ralegh asked them, eyeing their student robes.

"Yes, sir, Captain Ralegh." Tom bowed. "He's our tutor, or he was. Mr. Tobias Smythson, an Ancient of Gray's Inn."

"A lawyer," Ralegh said. "May God rest his soul." He waved the lads back and paced around the body, careful to avoid the swathe of bloodied mud surrounding the torso. He shook his head and spoke to Lord Cumberland. "Well, he's plainly dead. It's equally plain that he was murdered. I judge there was a struggle: witness his face and the state of his garments."

The barrister's robes were wrenched about, twisted on his body, and smeared with mud along the sides as though he had writhed and fought beneath his attacker. One outstretched arm displayed the velvet welts on his sleeve that proclaimed his profession. He'd argue no more cases in Westminster now.

Captain Ralegh drew his rapier and used it to lift aside the edges of the robes to reveal the gray doublet underneath. "He's been stabbed, more than once judging by the quantity of blood. See these slashes? And here's bombast, pulled loose by the knife." He pointed with the tip of his sword at a straggle of horsehair, sodden with blood.

Somehow that tiny detail was more horrible than the whole. Tom grimaced, turned aside, and blew a sour breath from his mouth. Then he remembered the company he was in and schooled himself to turn back. He didn't want these powerful men to think him a coward.

"More must wait until the body is washed," Ralegh said. "But look at this." He raised cut strands of leather on the edge of his blade. "Purse strings. Four of them. Two purses taken."

"A thief, then," Cumberland said.

"Perhaps."

Ralegh contemplated the body, lips pursed, hand on hip. He was resplendent, a tall, straight figure in silver and white, gleaming in the dusky shadows. Tom glanced at Stephen, who was studying Ralegh's costume as if composing instructions for his tailor. The satin melon hose still held their graceful bell-like shape. The radiant white plumes rose unwilted from his hat as if pulled aloft by a call from heaven. The monochromatic effect of the silver and white was striking. Dramatic but not gaudy.

Tom suddenly felt like a juggler at a fair. Or a beacon: he should be stood upon a cliff for ships to steer by. The green was well enough, but the yellow was far too bright. And the carnation garters were too much; he'd known it in his heart when he'd put them on.

Ralegh pointed with his sword at Smythson's hands, which bore two gold rings, one set with a carved black stone. "Was our thief too fastidious to steal the rings from his victim's fingers?"

Cumberland shrugged. "Perhaps he was disturbed. Or feared to be."

Ralegh scowled at the crowd gathering beyond Cumberland's copper stallion. "I told that boy to block the way." Then he scanned the area around the body. "Had the man no hat?"

Tom spotted a crumpled object at the foot of a house and went pick it up. It was a gray capotain hat with a pewter brooch stuck in the crown. He dusted it off and handed it to Ralegh with a small bow.

Ralegh acknowledged the offering with a short smile. Then his eyes caught on Tom's earring. "That's an exceptional pearl."

"Thank you, sir." Tom touched the item: a large golden pearl dangling from a gold wire in his left ear. He always wore it. For luck, and to remind him where he came from. "My father brought it back from the South Seas."

"He sailed with Drake?" Ralegh looked impressed.

"Yes, sir," Tom said with pride. It wasn't often that his father's vocation brought him credit rather than the reverse.

Cumberland snapped his fingers. "You're Valentine Clarady's son, I'd wager my horse on it. You're the very spit of him. And I've seen him wear the twin of that pearl myself."

"So have I," Ralegh said. "I remember him now." Then he frowned as he took another look at Tom's robes. The expression on his face, though fleeting, spoke loud as a hiss to Tom: *How does a sailor's son get himself admitted to an Inn of Court?*

Ralegh shook his head and cast a world-weary smile at Cumberland. "Oh, to be free to sail where you will instead of languishing in the stuffy chambers of the court!"

Cumberland chuckled sardonically and started to respond when a spindle-shanked man in pink chamlet edged past his restive mount.

13

"Captain Ralegh," he said, bowing deeply. "I am William Danby, the Queen's Coroner. I've brought a cart." He gestured behind him. Tom spotted the long ears of a donkey poking up above the crowd that had gathered a few yards behind Lord Cumberland's stallion.

"Good," Ralegh said. "We'll want that presently."

"Who is the—"

"A lawyer of Gray's Inn," Ralegh answered. "He's been murdered. By a thief, most likely, although there are elements inconsistent with that theory."

Tom heard a murmur run through the crowd. *Murder. A lawyer. A lawyer's been killed.*

The coroner muttered some pietistic phrase and stooped to draw down Mr. Smythson's eyelids. Tom exhaled a breath of relief, although until that moment he'd not been aware of how much those staring eyes unsettled him. The coroner's assistant spread a discolored blanket over the body and the whole crowd sighed as one.

Ralegh turned to inspect the other end of the lane. There was nothing to see but his own horse and Trumpet, still faithfully holding the reins. Ralegh granted him a smile, which the boy returned with an expression equally fraught with terror and delight.

Ralegh tilted his head back and scanned the houses on either side. Most of the windows were shuttered and the few that were open were empty. He turned full circle, plumes dancing as his gaze traveled up to the rooflines and down to the dirt. As he turned back to the coroner, Tom caught a flutter of motion inside a window on the first floor of the house just beyond the protected section.

Ralegh returned his attention to the coroner. "There doesn't seem to be anything useful to see here." He nodded toward Tom. "These lads say they were pupils of the dead man. They may know something."

Stephen stepped up. "By your leave, Captain Ralegh, we know very little, but that little I am most willing to impart. I pray you'll allow me to present myself. I am Lord Stephen Delabere, eldest son of the Earl of Dorchester. I first met Mr. Smythson in September, upon entering Gray's Inn, the which Society I joined to learn something of the law. Not that I intend to become a barrister. Naturally not! But to be a man of parts . . . I'm sure *you* understand."

Tom winced inwardly, recognizing the onset of a spate of Stephen-prattle. This could go on forever. He was seldom interrupted, thanks to his title, but no one actually listened.

He saw Ralegh's eyes glaze over and decided to investigate the glimpse of motion he'd caught in that upper-story window. Winking at Trumpet as he slipped past Ralegh's horse, he walked a few yards with his eyes on the ground, hands behind his back, pretending to look for tracks in the neatly raked dirt. Then he quickly spun about and looked up, straight into the face of an angel.

His heart turned over in his chest. He felt light-headed, weightless, as if his feet had come adrift from the earth. She wasn't really an angel, of course. He knew that with the scrap of his mind still capable of reason. An angel would float on a wisp of cloud or descend in a beam of light, not stand in an oak-framed window with a kerchief on her head.

She was without question the most beautiful woman he had ever seen. Her face was smooth and pale as new ivory. Her hair shone like spun gold, so fair he knew that her deep-set eyes must be as blue as Indian sapphires. Her lips were as red as garnets, plump and full of sensual promise.

"*O, angela luminosa!*" Tom clasped his hands to his breast in a fervent gesture.

She frowned at him — an enchanting frown, the frown of an elfin queen. She waved a slender hand in an unambiguous gesture: *Go away!*

Tom shot a glance toward the others to confirm that their view was blocked by Ralegh's horse. He smiled up at the angel and swept his flat black cap from his head, bending forward in a full court bow, right leg extended, toe pointed. He was glad now for the yellow silk stockings and the green velvet slippers, and even gladder that his legs were well shaped.

The angel frowned again but less severely. Her frown held a touch of melancholy. Perhaps she was lonely. He knew he could win her if he could find a way up to her room.

"Tom!" Trumpet called. "Where are you?"

The angel smiled down at him and Tom's breath caught in his throat. She shook her head, pressed a finger to her lips, and disappeared into the depths of her chamber.

Tom called to her again in a hoarse whisper. "*Revertere ad mi, Angela!*" Somehow Latin seemed appropriate for an angel.

Stephen, Ben, and Trumpet filed around Ralegh's horse. "Captain Ralegh wants us to hurry back to Gray's to inform the benchers of what has happened." The benchers were the committee of senior men who governed Gray's Inn. Stephen spoke with urgent determination, as though preparing to lay down his life for the mission. Tom doubted the sacrifice would be necessary since they had walked from Westminster to Gray's nearly every day for the past two and a half months without incident.

"What were you looking at?" Trumpet asked.

"I've seen an angel," Tom announced. "I'm in love."

"Oh, not again." Stephen groaned.

"How can you fall in love at the scene of a bloody murder?" Trumpet demanded.

Tom shrugged, grinning, helpless. "Love goes by haps. Cupid takes you where he will."

Ben rolled his eyes. "We'd best hurry, *Signor Amore*, if we're going to be the first ones home with the news."

Tom followed the others down the lane, his feet moving at their own direction, his mind filled with the image of his angel's pouty lips and deep-set eyes.

"Who would murder poor Mr. Smythson?" Trumpet asked.

"A thief," Stephen said. "Or a madman."

"I always liked him," Tom said, wrenching his thoughts back to earthly matters. "He was fair. He never tried to catch you out with tricky cases when he knew you were hungover." Smythson had been a decent tutor, firm yet patient, even with Stephen. Tom offered that thought as a silent prayer, hoping it would count in the man's favor when he faced his Maker.

THREE

Francis Bacon entered the hall for dinner on Friday, his stomach roiling with a turbulent mix of anticipation, curiosity, and dread. Lord Burghley was joining the men of Gray's Inn to honor the late Tobias Smythson. Francis had not seen his powerful uncle since his banishment from court. He fully intended to take this opportunity to induce a favorable impression. Yet he wondered why his uncle was here. He hadn't come last month after Serjeant Oldthwaite had died peacefully in his bed. He should think his uncle would prefer to let Smythson's death by violence fade quietly into the past rather than draw attention to its rebuke of the government's ability to keep the streets safe.

Perhaps he meant to leverage men's fears of bodily harm to gain compliance with some new regulation. Or take the opportunity to issue some pronouncement from the queen about watchfulness and duty in these troublous times. That was the most likely explanation.

He hoped his uncle hadn't come to see for himself whether Francis was keeping his word and comporting himself correctly, repairing the rifts he'd inadvertently torn in the fabric of the Society. He was trying, genuinely trying. He didn't need to be monitored.

He braced himself for the crowded room ahead. He normally dined in his chambers, having received special permission from the bench on account of his delicate health. But he always felt a thrill of pride, a sense of ownership, on entering the building. His father had been instrumental in its remodeling. One entered at the bottom of the long hall. Passing through the screen, one's eyes and spirits rose to the soaring hammerbeam roof. Stained-glass windows graced the upper walls on all four sides, admitting enough light, even on a dismal day like today, to obviate the need for candles at the midday meal. Many panes displayed the coat of arms of distinguished members of the Society.

Francis always glanced toward the Bacon arms. The family motto was *mediocria firma*: moderate things are surest. The message helped to ground him when his ebullient imagination went spiraling up into the clouds.

The motto and seal had been chosen by his pragmatic father, Nicholas Bacon, who had died unexpectedly after falling asleep by an open window after a heavy meal. Francis had been recalled from his educational sojourn in the French ambassador's household to find himself fatherless and penniless, his mother battling like fury against his elder stepbrothers over the will. The future he had been anticipating crumbled to ashes like a burnt letter. He had always believed he would join his father in due course as a sort of privy clerk, learning to handle the reins of government at firsthand. His cousin Robert Cecil was being groomed in just that way by Lord Burghley.

After his father's death, he'd hoped at least to be granted some modest post, as clerk in one of the lesser courts, for example. That would be suitable at this stage. He didn't expect to rise all on a sudden, by sheer force of personality. He was no Ralegh. He would have to work his way up. But a young man needed a father to place his feet on the rungs before he could start to climb. In his clumsy efforts to raise himself, he had offended the queen and his lord uncle, so they had taken the ladder away altogether. He might as well have been exiled to the Baltic lands.

Men's voices filled the hall like the roar of the surf on a rocky coast. Francis found it both soporific and mildly alarming, as if his mind were being dulled when he most needed to have his wits about him. He walked between the long tables where the students and junior barristers sat, skirting the round hearth in the center of the room. The tables were full already. He was late.

Two tables stood at the far end of the hall, perpendicular to the rest. The lower one was reserved for the Grand Company of Ancients — the senior barristers. This was where Francis sat. The upper table, raised on a dais, was for the benchers, the dozen or so gentlemen who governed the Society.

Francis's feet slowed as he scanned the benchers' table. His uncle was seated already; that was unfortunate. Francis had meant to arrive first and be found sitting at his ease among the other ancients, flourishing in his professional setting. Spiteful gossip, provoked by his rapid rise through the ranks at Gray's, had reached the court and contributed to the controversy that had gotten him banned. Lord Burghley had summoned Francis to his office and advised him to amend his manners and learn how better to ingratiate himself with his fellow Graysians.

Francis shuddered, remembering that humiliating interview. He'd felt like a schoolboy. He could only be grateful that he hadn't been obliged to lower his hose for a caning. If only His Lordship could have entered the hall to find him laughing, engaged in some lively discussion with his messmates, visibly a welcome dinner companion . . .

He'd spoiled that chance by arriving late.

Ah, well. *Non nocet.* He could explain that he had been studying and lost track of the time, which was the simple truth. Nothing need be said about having fallen asleep in the middle of the morning.

Francis hesitated as he approached his table. Should he walk up to the dais to greet his uncle privately, or simply bow — a half bow? — and take his seat? Navigating the subtle shoals of etiquette was agonizing. Too much, and one risked scorn for obsequiousness; too little, and one caused offense.

He caught his uncle's eye and ventured a smile. Burghley crooked his fingers, gesturing him forward. Francis's heart leapt. Perhaps the queen had relented and decided that a sufficient term of punishment had elapsed. Certainly, he'd learned his lesson. He was quite ready to reform.

He flashed a grin at his messmates as he passed them, lightly leaping up the step to the dais. He nodded greetings to the seated benchers as he walked around to stand behind his uncle in the center seat.

"My Lord Burghley." Francis bowed from the waist. "How fares my gracious uncle on this day?"

"Good afternoon, Nephew." William Cecil acknowledged the bow with a tilt of his head.

He'd said "nephew" instead of calling him by name. Did he mean to emphasize the family relationship, here, in the presence of the benchers? That would be an aid to him, a friendly gesture, reminding them of his close connection to the highest levels. After his father died, Francis had hoped that his uncle would step in and take a father's role in helping him forward.

His hopes had foundered. True, his uncle had helped him to pass the bar early and win a provisional, non-voting seat on the bench. He'd been advanced well ahead of his peers. But his uncle seemed determined to keep him boxed up at Gray's Inn. Francis knew where the problem lay: Burghley feared competition for his son. If Francis were allowed full scope for his abilities, he might surpass his younger cousin. That could never be allowed.

Francis suppressed his nervous excitement. Over-eagerness was one of the charges against him. They exchanged a few words of trivial family news. The horn blew to announce the first remove. Before he could slip back to his seat, Burghley caught his sleeve. Francis bent to hear the murmured instructions: "I'd like a private word before I leave."

"As you wish, my lord."

Francis took his customary seat, girding himself for some chaffing. His messmates were George Humphries, who sat on his right; James Shiveley, directly across; and Nathaniel Welbeck, seated on James's left. Welbeck and Humphries had been among those who'd grumbled loudest about his early advancement. Arrogance, abuse of privileges, unsociability: these charges had added fuel to the conflagration of his schemes at court. Their hostility was one of the reasons he preferred to exercise his new privileges and dine in his chambers.

Welbeck's dark eyes glittered with derision as he said, "Bacon, what a pleasant surprise! You ought to have given us some warning. Poor Humphries will have to tighten his belt without your portion to fill out his plate."

Humphries frowned in embarrassment. An unfortunate expression: it drew down his wiry eyebrows, which, given the tufts of hair in his pointed ears, gave his face a goatish expression. The homely fellow was no match for Welbeck's teasing. Perhaps that was why he could usually be found one step behind, snickering and adding a jab or two of his own.

Welbeck wasn't finished. "Perhaps not altogether a surprise, though, eh?" He cast a meaningful glance toward Lord Burghley then leaned forward to whisper conspiratorially. "Mustn't let the old man think we're slacking. Hiding in our chambers, snacking from a tray." He wagged an admonitory finger. "Won't do, won't do."

Francis refused to be goaded. He was determined to show his uncle that he could live harmoniously with his fellows in spite of all that had passed. He merely said, "Naturally, I wished to join the Society in honoring Tobias Smythson. This is a solemn occasion."

James Shiveley said, "Solemn, indeed. Poor Smythson. May God preserve him. I suppose that's why your uncle's here. I had no idea Smythson was so well connected." Shiveley had a tonsure of red hair and a freckled complexion that gave him a trustworthy mien.

"Nor had I," Francis admitted. "Although some of his clients had affairs that reached into high places."

"Sir Amias Rolleston." Welbeck nodded sagely. Sir Amias was as litigious as he was wealthy. He'd employed Smythson as chief counsel for his endless series of property suits.

Humphries leaned forward and hissed across the table. "I hear he's suing Lady Rich for unrecovered debts."

"Is he?" Francis was impressed. *Née* Penelope Devereux, Lady Rich was the sister of the Earl of Essex and the wife of one of England's wealthiest men. "I had no idea Rolleston's affairs extended into such lofty circles."

"You see, Bacon," Welbeck said, "one learns many things when one troubles oneself to dine in commons." He tore a piece from his loaf of bread and chewed it as if displaying his masticatory prowess. Welbeck was handsome in spite of a long, spondulate nose. He had a convivial manner that drew men — especially shallow, striving men — into his circle. Francis found him irritating beyond tolerance but was determined to repress that reaction in public.

"I had a most interesting conversation with Sir Amias at Westminster this morning." Shiveley treated his messmates to a satisfied smirk.

"You did what?" Welbeck glared at him. "You poacher!"

Humphries shook his head, jowls wobbling. "It's too soon! It's unseemly! It's not fair! Smythson hasn't even been buried."

Shiveley shrugged, unchastened. "I could hardly refuse to speak with the man. Sir Amias has so many suits in play he can scarce afford a period of mourning for his counselor. He needs constant, ready, *expert* advice." That last was delivered with a pointed glare at Humphries, who frowned at the slight to his abilities.

Francis thought Shiveley was stooping to bait a man whose gifts were so limited. But neither had he any sympathy for Humphries. A man should know his own worth: his weaknesses as well as his strengths. Humphries was one of the more marginal members of Gray's Inn. He dined in commons every day, thereby maintaining his place in the Society, but his cases were limited to minor disputes among tradesmen. He had barely squeaked past the bar and more nearly resembled a pettifogging attorney than an ancient of Gray's.

"Did he choose you to replace Smythson?" Humphries asked, a tremble in his voice.

Shiveley deflected the question with a flick of his fingers. "We found ourselves much in agreement."

Welbeck's retort was mercifully forestalled by the appearance of the servers. The discussion of Rolleston's affairs ceased as dishes of green pottage, eggs in mustard, conger eels in souse, and turbot pie were set upon the table. The men served themselves with the economy of interaction engendered by long familiarity.

They ate in silence for a while. Francis picked at his pie, eschewing the eel altogether. His stomach was jumpy with the tension of his uncle's request for a private conversation. What could he want from him? Would it be good news or bad?

He was startled from his thoughts by Shiveley's voice. "What are you reading, Bacon?" His messmate nodded at the book beside his plate.

Francis briefly laid a hand on the leather cover. Why had he brought it? He wouldn't dream of reading through the meal in his uncle's presence. "It's a new work by Giambattista Della Porta, the Italian polymath. A treatise on natural magic." He shrugged as if reading obscure scientific works were as commonplace as playing at bowls.

Francis savored the look of incomprehension on Welbeck's face for a moment then realized that he'd left Shiveley blinking like a cornered hare. He should have lied and mentioned another author — Seneca, Rabelais — anything that would stimulate conversation instead of killing it dead. Another social misstep. He'd cut Shiveley's friendly gesture short.

Welbeck gamely picked up the thread. "Isn't that a little *catholic* for your tastes, Bacon? Or are you planning to use magic to rationalize the whole of the English common law?"

Humphries tittered.

Francis forced his lips into a bland smile. "*Scientia est potentia*: knowledge is power."

"Doesn't seem to work that way for you, though, does it?" Welbeck smiled nastily. He'd won that round. Francis only hoped his uncle hadn't been watching.

The dishes from the final course were removed and the cloth withdrawn. Francis felt somewhat overstuffed. The savor of the too-sharp mustard sauce lingered unwholesomely in his gastric passages. He always ate too much in hall. He'd pay for this indulgence with a restless night.

A rustle of motion rose through the hall as men shifted on their benches, repositioning themselves for the after-dinner speeches. The noise subsided as Treasurer Avery Fogg stood up from the bencher's table and raised his hands. Servers scurried through the rows of tables, placing an earthenware cup of wine before each member.

"Gentlemen." Fogg's deep voice filled the hall. "The bench would like to raise a toast in remembrance of Mr. Tobias Smythson. Then I have a few words about pending matters." He waited until everyone had a cup. "To our dear departed colleague, adversary, tutor, and friend. May God rest your soul in heaven."

Two hundred voices echoed, "God rest you."

Sir Avery nodded. "We will miss Mr. Smythson, each and every one of us, individually and collectively as a society of professional men. He served our Society ably through the years in any office that was asked of him. His tireless and competent practice of the law reflected well upon us all."

Francis suppressed a chuckle. *Tireless and competent* was faint praise. Had Smythson and Fogg crossed quills as opposing counsels for some important lawsuit, resulting in Fogg's comeuppance?

"It will take many men to fill the shoes of a Tobias Smythson."

This time Francis wasn't the only one struggling to contain his response. Sputters of laughter escaped from the lower tables. Fogg frowned repressively, his thick black brows drawing together.

"Many men," Fogg repeated in booming tones that set the iron candelabra ringing. "Tobias Smythson was closely involved with all of us, in one way or another, over the years. Some of us had our differences with him. There may have been some encroachments."

Francis raised an eyebrow toward James Shiveley, who shrugged. Fogg had built his career on property law. Perhaps it was natural for him to think of all relationships in terms of trespass and assignments.

He wondered if any attempt had been made to apprehend the murderer. Gossip at Gray's, according to his servant, had it that Smythson was struck down by a cutpurse. A clumsy, aggressive thief, then. Usually, you only realized you'd been robbed when you reached for your purse to pay the vendor and found dangling strings instead.

Fogg rambled on. Finally, his voice rose to a crescendo. "Let the past be buried. When we think now of Tobias

Smythson, let us remember the best of the lawyer and of the man." He raised his cup to signal another toast. "One last consideration." He had to raise his voice to compete with the increasing restlessness of his audience. "Mr. Smythson was slated to Read this Lent vacation. As a man, he can never be replaced; as a Reader, he must be. The bench will meet to choose a new Reader during the coming week." He glanced down at Francis. "These meetings will be for voting members only."

As a provisionary bencher, Francis was allowed to attend meetings and contribute to discussions, but he was not eligible to vote. It was a reasonable compromise between his obvious ability and his much-objected-to youth. Benchers were expected to be "the chiefest and best learned" of the senior barristers. Francis was only twenty-five. His learning could not be faulted. Time would remedy the latter failing.

He nodded at Fogg to signal his understanding. His eyes flicked toward his uncle, whose gaze remained fixed on his goblet. Would it hurt him so much to offer Francis one small gesture of familial accord? On a more positive note, he didn't seem to be monitoring Francis's behavior. He blinked the idea away, smiling to himself. He mustn't allow this spot of trouble to make him overly suspicious. It was absurd to imagine his busy uncle taking the time to eavesdrop on Francis's dinner conversations.

Fogg resumed his seat. Several benchers turned toward him, elbows on the table, and began speaking in low, urgent voices. Doubtless they had views on the thorny question of when and where to meet. That debate could take an hour in itself.

Francis felt a tingle of excitement. He was an obvious choice for the Lent Reader, having already been admitted to the bench with provisional status. One must Read to earn a voting seat. And only full benchers were chosen for judgeships, the lucrative pinnacle of the legal profession.

He had dreamed of devoting himself to the reformation of the tangled and obfuscated English legal code, but his efforts to pursue that dream had ended in humiliating failure. Being chosen for the Lent Reading would give him a chance to prove himself in a fresh venue. A different ladder to success than the one he had envisioned, but he'd be starting on a higher rung.

Reading constituted a week-long public display of scholarship and oratorical skill, giving a man an opportunity to display his abilities before an audience that included members of the nobility, especially the more scholarly peers like the Earl of Essex. Readers were expected to deliver lucid expositions of historically important statutes in a series of set speeches and formal debates. Readings were challenging on all levels: intellectually, physically, emotionally, and financially.

Reading wasn't cheap. Most Readers bought new clothes for themselves and livery for their assistants. They were obliged to host a dinner during the week and a supper on the last day for the whole Society and their distinguished guests. The costs were substantial, which was part of their function. They formed a barrier to admission, ensuring that only men of status and sufficiency would participate in the governance of the Society.

Francis sipped his claret and turned his attention to his messmates, who were his most likely competitors.

If one counted only years in commons, George Humphries was first in line. He had been called to the bar twelve years ago and had made clear his desire to advance, but he was unpopular. Apart from Welbeck, who tolerated him as a sycophantic sidekick, he had no friends. His father had squandered the family estate in unfounded suits, leaving his son nearly penniless. If he were a lawyer of exceptional acuity, these faults might be overlooked, but he was below the mean in all regards.

Nathaniel Welbeck was a far better candidate. He was a decade senior to Francis: a ripe and ready thirty-six years old. His connections were excellent, his late sister having married the Earl of Orford. He was well dressed, well-spoken, and popular among both barristers and students. He tended to be short of funds, although that condition seemed to be mitigated of late.

James Shiveley was on a par with Welbeck in terms of seniority. Devoted to Gray's, he took genuine pleasure in the moots and bolts and other training exercises. His family was respectable and he had recently inherited a tidy estate. Shiveley was one of those indispensable middling sorts of people who do most of the work in any organization.

Francis wasn't worried — much — about any of them. His abilities surpassed his competitors' as the sun's light surpassed the moon's. He was young; that would count against him. His chief concern was the expense. He'd have to borrow the money against his brother Anthony's estate unless Captain Clarady could be persuaded to fund the event. Perhaps if he promised the son some visible, yet unimportant, role . . .

The benchers' talk droned on. Under normal circumstances, Francis would excuse himself and leave. With his uncle here, it would be impolitic. Perhaps he wanted to sound him out about being chosen as Reader on such short notice. He might want him to decline in order to advance a man owed a favor. Or perhaps he wanted him to accept to forestall someone owed a setback. Lord Burghley was a long-range thinker; his motives were not always identifiable in the immediate context.

The prospect of presenting a week-long lecture on a significant statute with barely two months of preparation was not one of unmitigated joy. On the one hand, accepting would show that Francis was willing to leap gallantly into the breach for the betterment of Gray's. On the other hand, declining would allow him to do a more considered job on a later occasion. He wanted his first Reading to be remembered.

He began mentally reviewing the Henrician statutes relating to advowsons and annuities. Suddenly, he realized that everyone else was rising. He got to his feet and bowed to his uncle, who had apparently been trying to catch his eye.

"Walk with me, Nephew."

"My lord."

They strolled the length of the hall, Francis a pace behind of necessity as much as courtesy, owing to the narrowness of the aisles between the tables. They reached the screen and filed through the door into the yard. They walked slowly toward the gatehouse, beyond which Lord Burghley's coach awaited him.

"How may I serve you, my lord?" Francis shivered. He would have brought a cloak to dinner if he'd known he would be lingering out of doors on such a bitter day.

"It's about Tobias Smythson." Burghley seemed not to notice Francis's discomfort. He glanced about, saw they were alone, and stopped near the chapel wall.

"We are all deeply grieved." Francis tucked his hands under his armpits and painted a portrait of attention on his face. He was determined to appear humble and amenable to anything his uncle should propose.

Burghley blinked away the platitude. "Smythson was assisting me with enquiries into the conduct of some of Gray's members."

"What manner of conduct, my lord?"

"I have received intelligences concerning covert Catholic activities at Gray's Inn. Someone here is facilitating the importation of missionaries and subversive literature into England."

"One hears these rumors, yet I myself have observed no evidence of such activities." Francis deemed it irrelevant to add that he rarely left his chambers except to go book shopping.

"The Jesuits are subtle and trained in secrecy," Burghley said. "Many of their supporters are from old Catholic families here in England. Men who are well placed and even well liked. Their machinations are not easy to discover until after the damage is done."

Francis considered the proposition. "I suppose it is possible, especially for some of the members who have a large clientele. One might not notice the particulars of any given visitor or parcel delivery. One has one's own work, of course. I dine so seldom in hall, you see, what with my studies and my health—"

"Yes, yes. I know. Your mother keeps me well informed about the state of your digestion."

Francis winced. His mother did rather tend to overstate her cases.

"The issue at hand," Burghley said, "is that Smythson was looking into these matters on my behalf. He sent me a message intimating that he had news of a significant nature. He was coming to see me on the day he died to deliver proofs. I do not believe his death was coincident upon a simple act of thievery. I suspect he was deliberately murdered to prevent him from meeting with me."

Francis was shocked. "Too bold, surely, to murder a man of the law on the queen's doorstep?"

Burghley shook his head. His square beard glistened with fine droplets of rain. "These are perilous times, Nephew. Perilous in the extreme. Now that Mary Stuart has been brought to trial, the Catholic element in England is in a desperate moil."

"I warned you about overly harsh measures against the religious factions." Francis tried not to sound peevish, but really, every point in the letter he'd written to the queen on this topic two years ago had been amply borne out by subsequent events and yet he had not received so much as a simple thanks for his efforts.

"You did. As did others."

Not a word of acknowledgement. Francis repressed a sigh and wriggled his toes in his boots to make sure they were still unfrozen. "The Queen of Scots was condemned to death by the nearly unanimous vote of both the lords who tried her case and the House of Commons. Once she's gone, the conspiracies around her will die too."

"I doubt me they will ever die, not fully. The Catholic faction can always find another distant relative of royalty to bear their futile hopes." Lord Burghley's weary expression showed every line of his thirty-and-more years in the queen's service. "We do not yet even have a date for the execution. And while the Stuart woman lives, her admirers will continue to conspire."

"I suppose the queen is reluctant to order the death of an anointed monarch."

"It is a practice of which she strongly disapproves, in general." Burghley allowed himself the shadow of a smile. "The central point here, Nephew, is that Tobias Smythson was murdered for political reasons. The murderer must be apprehended and whatever plot he is forwarding must be foiled."

"If it can be." Francis smiled noncommittally. "Was there evidence of any kind? On the body or nearby?" He hadn't thought to look. He'd scurried away from the scene before any courtiers could arrive.

"Nothing conclusive. I'll have the coroner's report sent to you. The body should also be delivered here shortly."

"Here? To me?"

"Yes, Nephew. I'm giving this job to you."

Francis detected an odd glint in the back of his uncle's eyes and understood that the position was uncontested. Perceived, in other words, as a difficult and probably hopeless task. Yet still better than utter banishment. He'd take it. Besides, Tobias Smythson deserved justice.

"I accept. Willingly. Smythson was a friend; I don't have many of those."

Burghley's expression was unreadable. "I believe Smythson was carrying a letter for me. It was not on his body, but an ordinary thief would have no reason to take it."

"But a conspirator would. I understand." Francis's mind whirred. How could a man investigate the cause of an event days after the event occurred? "*Evidentia, testimonium.* What there is must be found. Although I doubt there will be anything material. Witnesses, there may be. The people who live along that street could be questioned. Have they been?"

"No. Nothing has been done. I am outwardly supporting the assumption of theft as a cover for the real investigation. But I must know what's happening at Gray's. We can't allow the Inns of Court to be corrupted. They are England's schools of government, as much as of the law."

"Indeed."

"I trust that you will not disappoint me." Burghley held his eyes to ensure that his meaning was fully communicated. "This is an opportunity to do the queen a service and regain her favor."

Francis felt a trickle of hope. "May I trust that I'll be reinstated when I succeed?"

"*If* you succeed. The conspirator has been thus far untraceable." His uncle allowed himself a smile. "Find me Smythson's murderer and I believe I can at least assure you of an invitation to dinner on Christmas Eve."

Everyone who mattered attended on the queen on Christmas Eve. Such an invitation would announce to the whole court that he had been restored to favor. Francis bowed low to hide the tears that sprang unexpectedly into his eyes. "Her Majesty is most gracious. As is my lord uncle. I will do all that can be done."

Burghley gave an almost inaudible chuckle. "Be careful, Nephew. These are desperate times. I should greatly mislike being obliged to inform your mother of your demise."

FOUR

Francis spent the remainder of the day in bed, covered with extra blankets. His servant administered an hourly dose of a tonic efficacious against chill. He constructed a list of tasks that might be undertaken in pursuit of Smythson's killer but otherwise did next to nothing. He felt it too risky to descend to the hall for supper.

On Saturday morning, having successfully warded off an ague or worse, he begged a master key from the butler and let himself into Smythson's rooms in Colby's Building on the west side of Coney Court. Smythson's set, like Francis's, were on the most desirable first floor: above the dust and bustle of the yard but with only one flight of stairs to climb.

The chambers were typical. One entered directly from the landing into the outer room, which was furnished as a study-*cum*-consultation chamber with a desk, a pair of high-backed chairs, and a few chests of various sizes. A wide window overlooking the courtyard let in adequate light for daytime work, and a pair of candelabras on the desk supported nighttime labors. A set of shelves leaning against the paneled wall held a collection of books. Francis wondered if Smythson's heirs could be persuaded to donate them to Gray's library as a commemorative gift.

As he ran his fingers lightly across the spines of the books, noting their titles on the surface of his thoughts, his deeper mind reviewed the status of Smythson's heirs. The butler had told him there were two: a son and a daughter, both grown, married, and living in Hertfordshire. They had not yet had time to respond to the messages sent yesterday. The butler also said that Treasurer Fogg had visited Smythson's chambers yesterday to look for a will. Smythson had expressed a wish to be buried at St. Clement Danes Church on the Strand. The burial was scheduled for Sunday, hoping that his children would be able to arrive by then. It was cold; he would keep.

The coroner's report described the number and nature of the wounds inflicted on Smythson's body in explicit detail. Francis was shocked anew by the degree of violence. The coroner surmised that the killer had been under the influence of rage or panic or other such passion. He was surely correct; no man in full possession of himself could perform such a deed.

Francis considered the idea that Smythson had been murdered by his children for their inheritance and dismissed it at once. As his tutor, Smythson had drilled him in learning exercises, both privately and in the hall. Aiming for verisimilitude, he had not been gentle. Francis had watched him argue many cases in the Westminster courts. He could not pretend to have plumbed the depths of the man's nature, but he had an adequate sense of his qualities. Smythson had been melancholic: cold and dry, inclined to a mild irritability, sometimes overly punctilious. Not the type to inspire a furious hatred in his offspring.

Besides, there were simpler ways to kill one's relations in the privacy of one's country estate. Why risk an attack in a public street mere yards from Whitehall?

Francis sifted through the papers on Smythson's desk and then explored the desk itself to be sure there were no hidden compartments. He found nothing of use. Another set of shelves held stacks of commonplace books, dozens of them. He moved toward them with delight. They must go all the way back to Smythson's student days. Francis would have these removed to his chambers at once. He would peruse them to ensure that they contained nothing that might embarrass their author and then transfer them to the library.

He slipped the last volume from the shelf and opened it. Near the end, he found notes that might relate to Smythson's investigations for Burghley. They were written in a cryptic Latin. That language was no obstacle to Francis; nor would it have been for any other member of Gray's. The last page held the words *subvectio, libellus,* and *moneta*; the symbol XII-◗, and a final note: BH QD 4. This last Francis readily interpreted as "Burghley House, Queen's Day, four o'clock," although had he not already been apprised of Smythson's intentions, he might have found the meaning impenetrable.

Subvectio meant delivery or conveyance. *Libellus* meant something written: a notebook, an essay, a petition, a pamphlet. Smythson could hardly have chosen a term more vague. *Moneta* meant money. For the conveyance of documents?

The numeral was probably a month. Twelve meant December. The symbol next to it could be read as a half moon. That put the delivery, if such it was, at about mid-December. Was this what Smythson had discovered? If so, it was slender help since it failed to say where the putative delivery would take place. It could be in someone's chambers or out in the broad fields behind the Inn. Or it could be in a dockside tavern or the aisle of St. Paul's Cathedral, for all anyone could say.

If he knew *who*, he might be able to deduce *where*. But not the reverse, interestingly. Places were more general than persons. For a moment, the insight into methods of reasoning captured his whole attention. Then he realized that he already knew *who* with the same degree of specificity as the *wheres* he had posited. "A member of Gray's Inn" was at least as large a class as "a dockside tavern." A form of inconsistent comparison; he chided himself for the obvious error.

He sighed and returned to his inspection of the room. He opened the largest chest and discovered that its contents had already been disturbed. Writing instruments were tumbled about: an ink bottle turned on its side, a sheaf of new quills bent by a heavy box. Fogg must have made this mess when searching for the will. Francis emptied the chest, careful not to get ink on his cuffs, setting the objects on the floor. No locked boxes, no false bottom. No cash. He quickly searched the smaller chests: nothing. Doubtless, Fogg had removed what money there was to the safekeeping of the Pipe Office.

He replaced everything neatly and stood with his hands on his hips, surveying the room. He could see nothing that would aid in his investigation. He blew out an exasperated breath and crossed to the inner chamber.

This room was more sparsely furnished than the study, although its furnishings were of the highest quality. A bed with green woolen tester and curtains stood against the north wall. Opposite were a single chair, a close-stool, and a tall oaken cupboard carved with the likeness of Smythson and a woman Francis assumed to be his late wife. The room contained no paper of any kind, not even by the close-stool. Smythson had preferred moss to wipe his bottom, as Francis did himself.

He looked under the pillows and beneath the bed. He thought about raising the top mattress to be sure nothing was hidden beneath, but a tentative tug proved it to be quite heavy. No good would be served by wrenching a shoulder.

Smythson wouldn't have engaged in such strenuous exercise either. Francis decided to stipulate the absence of documents between the mattresses; in which case, his work was done.

He sat on the bed, kicking his heels into the fringe of the coverlet. He'd wasted the better part of an hour in energetic labor with nothing to show for it but a few cryptic notes in a commonplace book. He could imagine the disdain with which his uncle would greet such a paltry result.

A member of Gray's might possibly be planning to receive a delivery of letters or pamphlets or memoranda on the day of the December half moon. Pamphlets were the most likely, produced by the Jesuits in Rheims and Rome. A nasty business. Those things were a pernicious nuisance, aimed less at converting Protestants than at inflaming the ardor of covert Catholics in England. They riled people and encouraged them to oppose the queen's sensible middle way through the nation's religious troubles. These foolish controversies disrupted whole communities, separating neighbor from neighbor, friend from friend, sometimes even husband from wife.

Francis hated to think of his fellows at Gray's being involved in such wickedness. Men of the law should be rational above all things. That delivery, if he had correctly interpreted Smythson's note, must be intercepted.

The note was frustratingly vague. Gray's had nearly three hundred and fifty members, although some of those were honorific, like his uncle and his cousin. Others, like his step-brothers, seldom came to London. A fair percentage were *visus in villa*, living in private homes or inns. Even assuming that the conspirator was currently resident at Gray's, he still had two hundred suspects.

He frowned. His uncle might be committing a logical fallacy in assuming that because Smythson was investigating Catholic conspiracies, a Catholic conspirator killed him. The murder could have been motivated by personal reasons rather than political. *Cum hoc ergo propter hoc:* with this, therefore because of this. It was a sophomoric error.

He doubted, however, that his uncle would be pleased to receive instruction in dialectic in lieu of a solution. Even Francis could recognize the arrogance in that. He heaved a heartfelt sigh. What had he come to? Snooping through a colleague's chambers, hoping for obvious evidence of criminal activity. He had sunk to the level of a parish constable.

All because he had dared to dream an outsized dream. He had asked to be named Special Assistant to the Attorney General with a five-year commission to review and revise the English legal code. He presented his first book, *Twenty-Five Maxims of the Law*, written in both English and Law French, as proof of his abilities. He'd asked for a modest salary of four hundred pounds per annum, with two clerks. An ambitious proposal, certainly, but arrogant? He still could not comprehend that charge. He was young, yes, but his gifts were evident. His parents had taught him not to disguise his God-given talents with false modesty, but to exercise them for the benefit of society. If his manner tended to be reserved, it was through fault of bashfulness, not pride.

Apparently the distinction between a lack of false modesty and arrogance was one he had yet to master.

Lord Burghley had promised to present the proposal to the queen in spite of his skepticism. The queen had predictably balked at the expense. Francis had been prepared to negotiate the terms, but she rejected the whole enterprise out of hand. This was not the time, he was far too young, he had never argued a case in court, he failed to understand the politics of such sweeping reforms.

He should have taken no for an answer. Instead, he'd allowed himself to be driven on by the power of his vision. He had written letters — too many letters — to every courtier with whom he had the slightest connection. Some, like Sir Francis Walsingham, had answered him kindly, honoring the memory of his father. Others had rebuked him sharply for his presumption.

Francis moaned and buried his face in his hands, remembering the day he'd cornered Sir Christopher Hatton after the French ambassador's dinner. He'd vexed the poor man for nearly half an hour, stammering forth the details of his plan point by agonizing point.

He'd thought himself so sophisticated, so wise in the ways of the court. He'd had no idea. His proposal stirred up a hornet's nest, zestfully pursued by one faction, fiercely opposed by another, creating an angry buzz that eventually stung the queen herself. She stamped out the conflict in a fine display of Tudor temper, banishing Francis from court and barring him from writing any letters to any courtier on any subject whatsoever until further notice. He was lucky that she allowed him to remain at Gray's instead of sending him home to his mother.

All roads to greatness led through the royal court. Until he could earn his restoration, he was nobody: a man with no prospects, no future. His ambitions were left unsatisfied while his destiny languished unfulfilled.

His uncle had thrown him one slender rope. He must grab hold of it and follow it as best he could. He gazed out the window, seeking solace from the autumnal landscape. He feared the mystery would prove unsolvable. How could he uncover the truth? What could he do, one man alone?

FIVE

Saturday morning after breakfast, Tom, Ben, and Stephen loitered in the yard, waiting for Trumpet. The three older lads lodged together in the Gallery, a tall, sagging building across from the hall. The old place was practically crumbling into the ground — roofs leaked, windows stuck or wouldn't close, a moldy smell seeped from the walls — but Tom felt lucky to be there. When he'd first arrived in September, Bacon had housed him above the stables, like one of the servants. He'd seated him at the clerks' table in hall too. Tom had written to his father at once. Captain Valentine Clarady, too canny to settle all of Bacon's debts before getting his money's worth, stopped payments and sent a crisp word through their chain of connections. Suddenly, room was found for Tom in Ben's chambers. With the subtle sense of irony characteristic of Bacon's sense of humor, he found them a third chum: Stephen Delabere.

No matter. Tom had gained admittance to the biggest and best of the four prestigious Inns of Court at the ideal age of nineteen and he would by God stay in until he rose to the top. Or found something better.

Trumpet had missed chapel, which was nothing strange, and breakfast, which was. He lodged with his uncle, Nathaniel Welbeck, who evidently didn't care if the boy flouted the compulsory chapel rule. Being the nephew of an earl, Trumpet had obviously been indulged all his life.

He could be counted on to go along with Tom's schemes, though, no matter how risky or irregular they might be.

"Let's go roust him," Tom said. "It's not fair for him to sleep all morning."

They walked around the Gallery to Coney Court and spied Trumpet hurrying across the yard, wrapping his cloak around his shoulders.

"You missed chapel again," Ben scolded.

"Nobody woke me, so I slept." Trumpet yawned hugely.

"We'll wake you in future," Tom promised. "Mr. Whitt here doesn't approve of slug-a-beds."

Ben frowned, although Tom had meant it as a compliment. He admired Ben more than anyone he knew, after his father.

Benjamin Whitt, age twenty-one, was the second son of a middling Suffolk gentleman. His family had high hopes for their investment in Ben's education, for which they were mortgaging a dangerous proportion of their lands. Tom believed it was a safer bet than most speculations. Ben lived to study and had wits to spare. He remembered everything he read and most of what he heard. He could analyze and synthesize simultaneously and at speed. Tom and Trumpet had bet that Ben would be Chief Justice of the Queen's Bench by the age of forty.

"Are we off to Westminster, then?" Trumpet asked. "Let's watch the Queen's Bench today."

"Westminster, yes; courts, no," Tom said. "Let's go find the house where I saw my *angela*. We can think of some excuse to get inside."

Trumpet rolled his eyes. "It's too cold for a wild goose chase. How about the Court of Requests? We haven't been there for a while."

"No courts," Tom said. "We're free. Let's have some fun. Let's go out to the fields and practice shooting my new pistols."

His father had sent him a pair of German-made wheel lock pistols taken from a Spanish grandee. Pistols weren't especially useful for a student of the law, but then, Tom's father was a privateer. Had he sent him a book, Tom would have hoist the messenger on the point of his knife and demanded to know what had become of Captain Clarady.

"Too drizzly," Trumpet said, snugging his chin into his cloak. "The gunpowder will be damp. Let's go get some pies. My treat."

Tom pretended to be shocked. "What's the occasion?"

Trumpet shrugged. "My uncle's been feeling generous lately."

"Ho for hot pie!" They paused beside the gatehouse, out of the traffic in the yard. Many men were hurrying toward Westminster to argue cases or observe court proceedings; others were returning to their chambers from the hall to spend the morning studying or writing briefs. Most of them wore the long black robes that marked their status. They looked like busy, important gentlemen. Men of the world. And now Tom was one of them.

Stephen glared at his fellows, his narrow lips pressed together in a stubborn line. "No. No pistols. No pies. No courts. We have to find a new tutor. A good one. Else my father will send his steward up to arrange matters and we'll get someone dreadful."

Tom shuddered at the thought. Stephen's father was a Nonconformist and very strict. And a strict tutor would put a damper on their London lives. Fencing, dancing, music, Italian: acquiring these arts of courtesy was the main purpose of enrolling at an Inn of Court. Clever lads picked up a smattering of history and philosophy — the intellectual trappings of a gentleman — with enough law to keep the neighbors from robbing you blind. Stephen's father expected his heir to gain the social polish of London without having any of the actual fun.

On the other hand, Tom was no longer under any obligation to Lord Dorchester or his heir. He could cut loose, hire any tutor he pleased. Or no tutor, for that matter. On the third hand, however, he was not likely to learn much law without help. It wasn't like university: there were no introductory texts, designed to guide the student in baby steps towards mastery. You got thrown straight into the deep, dark sea of the Year Books, which were case reports written in Law French, which was a deranged, unreadable mishmash of Old French and Latin with the odd lump of English bobbing up like uncooked fat in a sour stew. Sort of like the pidgin he'd learned on his father's ship last year, which seemed a mix of every language with a coast. They used it everywhere that sailors put in to shore. But you picked that up phrase by useful phrase: things like "Bring us more wine" and "How much for the whole night?"

He doubted anyone had ever bargained for a whore in Law French. He absolutely needed a tutor. Also, on the fourth and final hand, the best way for him to get ahead at Gray's Inn was to gad about with a lord. He needed Stephen too, at least for a while.

"Fine," Tom said. "We'll find a tutor. And then we'll go eat pies."

Ben said, "We need someone Lord Dorchester will approve."

"Not a Puritan," Trumpet said. "I beg you."

"And not a Catholic," Tom said. "Then *my* father would object. We Claradys are patriots. We hate Catholics worse than the slithering, slimy sea snakes they resemble. We need a solid middle-way man."

"Someone expert in the law," Ben said.

"Someone who's good at explaining things," Trumpet said.

"Someone with connections at court," Stephen said. "We could do better than Smythson in that regard."

Ben stared across the yard and grinned. "Who is the foremost, up-and-coming legal mind at Gray's?"

The other three shrugged, their faces asking, *How should we know?*

He pointed his chin across the yard at Bacon's Building. It looked the same as it always did: turd-brown timbers crossing puke-colored plaster. Two stories, slate roof, brick chimneys, big windows.

"We give up," Trumpet said. "What are we looking at?"

"Bacon's Building," Ben said. "Home of Mr. Francis Bacon." He laughed. "And behold the man himself."

A slight figure emerged from the door and paused on the patch of pavement, blinking at the gray morning.

"I wouldn't call him the *foremost* legal mind," Trumpet quibbled. "Except by his own estimation, maybe. My uncle says he's too arrogant by half."

"If he is, he deserves to be." Ben turned to Tom. "I suspect he'd welcome the fees."

Tom snorted. "I'm sure he would! But he won't take us. He doesn't like to work."

"He's young," Stephen said. "He might understand that we can't study *all* the time."

Ben said, "He may be the youngest man ever called to the bar. He was only twenty-two."

"He's barely twenty-five now," Trumpet said. "It's a scandal, how quickly he's been advanced. Uncle Nat calls him 'the infant barrister.' He thinks—"

"We could at least ask him," Ben urged.

Trumpet shrugged. "I'm not objecting to Bacon as a tutor. I don't believe that he is the foremost legal mind of our generation, that's all."

"Fine," Ben said. "I'm willing to expunge the superlative. Now, how shall we approach him? He can be a little awkward to talk to."

"Simple," Stephen said. "We send Tom." He grinned his savviest man-of-the-world grin, the one that dropped barmaids fainting into his lap. Tom remembered the rainy day he and Stephen had practiced those grins in front of Lady Dorchester's mirror. "I've heard that Francis Bacon is susceptible to a handsome face."

"I've heard that too," Trumpet said. "My uncle told me—"

Tom groaned. "No, no, no! He doesn't like me."

"Of course he likes you," Ben said. "He recommended you for admittance."

Tom pursed his lips but held his peace. The lads didn't know about the bargain Captain Clarady had struck with Mr. Bacon, and he hoped they never would. He wanted people to think he'd been recommended on his merits. "Steenie should ask. He'd never refuse a lord."

"Me!" Stephen's voice nearly squeaked. "What would I say? I can't ask him. Tom has to do it."

"We'll all go," Ben said. "Tom will speak first." He shrugged. "You're the boldest. And the handsomest. Besides, it's your father who will be paying his fees."

True enough on all counts. Tom made no bones about his looks. He'd gotten used to extra attention from tradesmen's daughters and music masters and matrons who dodged across dangerous thoroughfares to ask directions specifically of him. Often, the Clarady looks were an advantage. But sometimes they provoked envy and sharp little stabs in the back. Quick wits and sharp ears were more reliable in the long run.

They navigated their way through the press of men toward their quarry. Francis Bacon was a man of medium height and slender build, with softly curled brown hair. He was dressed entirely in black — the true black, so expensive to maintain — save for ruffs of snowiest cambric at the neck and wrists. He was watching them cross the yard with an air of expectation.

They stopped two feet away and stood in a line. Tom bowed from the waist. Straightening, he offered his very best smile, the one that displayed his dimple. "I pray your indulgence, Mr. Bacon. We crave a moment of your time."

Bacon's eyes rested briefly on Tom's earring then scanned the other lads until he found Stephen. He smiled warmly, tilting his head. "Lord Stephen."

Stephen flashed a tense smile.

Tom forged ahead. "We were wondering if you might consider thinking about becoming our new tutor since, as you may know, Mr. Smythson has, uh . . ."

"Deceased," Bacon said. "Yes, I know. A terrible tragedy." He seemed genuinely grieved.

The lads bowed their heads somberly to show how respectful they were to their tutor. Tom cast up a glance to see the effect they were having and caught Bacon's knowing eye. He grinned sheepishly. "We really do need a tutor, Mr. Bacon. Lord Stephen's father is very firm on that point."

"The Earl of Dorchester," Bacon said softly.

"We're very little trouble," Ben said. "I can help Stephen and Tom with the elementary exercises and Trumpet practically teaches himself."

Bacon accepted the information with a catlike blink of his amber eyes. His gaze traveled from one lad to the other as if weighing their several qualities. He smiled slightly, more to himself than to them, then addressed Tom's earring. He had the unnerving trick of not quite looking at you when he spoke. "I have considered thinking about possibly becoming your tutor."

Tom drew a breath to thank him, but Bacon stopped him with an upraised finger.

"I decided that I was willing, so I thought about it."

Tom realized he was joking and swallowed a groan. At least the joke was in English. Smythson had sometimes tickled himself pink with obscure Latin puns.

Bacon went on, "The result of my thinking is the conclusion that I will accept the position. On the same terms as Mr. Smythson — plus ten percent — shall we say?"

"Yes, sir. Thank you, sir." Tom bowed low to hide his expression. The terms were exorbitant, but why bargain? Captain Clarady had returned from Drake's globe-circling voyage with enough treasure to found his own Inn of Court. He would gladly spend his last silver penny to turn his only son into a gentleman. And the fees might help bind Bacon to Tom's success at Gray's.

The other lads added their thanks. Bacon received them calmly. Then he arranged himself in a comfortable stance and said, with a mischievous glint in his eyes, "Let's see what you know."

SIX

"My brain feels like it's been emptied by a giant bilge pump." Tom pressed his hands against his head and groaned.

Stephen crossed his eyes and staggered toward him. "Do I know you, good fellow? I fear my wits are gone."

They gaped at each other, goggle-eyed, tongues lolling.

Ben frowned at them. "I found it extremely stimulating. What a mind! Although I thought I had a better grasp of novel disseisin. I've got to read more, that's all there is to it." He looked about him anxiously, as if searching for a law book in the graveled yard.

"You did better than me," Trumpet said. "I sounded like a perfect idiot. I'd start off well enough, but then he'd tangle me up in contingencies and I'd hear myself babbling nonsense."

"He doesn't like your uncle," Tom said. "Did you notice? His nose would twitch every time you mentioned him. That's why he was so hard on you."

"I'm hungry," Ben announced. "I feel like I've run a mile at full gallop. Shall we try our luck in the buttery?"

"After," Tom said. "We don't want to examine Mr. Smythson's corpus on a full stomach."

Ben made a sour face. "True."

Bacon had subjected them to a grueling impromptu examination. Having exhausted their knowledge of the law, he had abruptly changed tack. "Now I'm going to set you a practicum." Then he'd bounced off to fetch the key to the vestry.

The lads were to help him discover who killed Mr. Smythson. Their first step was to examine the body, which had been delivered early that morning from Whitehall. Bacon had made it seem like a murder investigation was a normal part of their studies, but Tom could tell by the startled expression on Ben's face that it was quite out of the ordinary.

Bacon jogged down the steps of the hall bearing a large iron key. "Gentlemen." He walked quickly past them, clearly expecting them to follow.

Tom couldn't make up his mind about Francis Bacon. He had drilled them mercilessly for the better part of an hour, yet Tom had gotten not a whiff of malice nor a whisper of contempt when they flubbed an answer. He simply wanted to know what they knew and had extracted the information with maximum efficiency.

Bacon unlocked the door to the vestry. This was little more than a storeroom, barely ten feet wide, containing one old cupboard and a single chest. Nothing more was needed nowadays since they'd done away with the egregious trappings of popery. It smelled of dust and pennyroyal with something less aromatic underneath.

The center of the room was occupied by the body of Mr. Smythson, laid upon a trestle table and covered with a fresh white sheet. The lads ranged themselves around the table with Bacon standing at the head.

"He looks bigger than he did standing up." Ben spoke in a loud whisper.

"I was going to say smaller," Trumpet whispered back. "Or rather, shorter from end to end, but rounder in the middle."

"That's what I meant."

"It's an odd effect, isn't it?" Bacon spoke at a normal volume. "Something to do with perspective."

Trumpet gestured at the sheet covering Smythson's face. "Shall we . . ."

"Yes," Bacon said. "Please proceed, Mr. Trumpington."

Trumpet drew in a breath, took hold of a corner of the sheet, and flipped it back, exposing the body to the waist. The lads gasped in unison. Tom had expected more stink. The room was cold, though; cold enough to see his breath. Cold enough to stave off rot.

The lads fell silent, waiting, while Bacon stood gazing at Smythson's waxy face. His mouth was twisted with disgust, but his hazel eyes were dark with sorrow.

"He was my tutor too," he said finally. "Did you know that?"

They shook their heads.

"Only seven years ago." He smiled sadly. "Seems like a lifetime."

Another long pause. Then he shook himself slightly and drew a long breath. He looked at the lads again with his customary brightness of eye. "We owe him a debt, all of us here. Let us do our job well and bring his murderer to justice."

Tom and Ben murmured, "Amen." It seemed appropriate.

"What do we observe?" Bacon asked.

Tom, as usual, answered first. "He looks dead."

Stephen snorted.

"I believe his status has been fully established," Bacon said, with a quirk of his lips.

Tom said, "I mean, he doesn't look as if he were sleeping, like people say. He looks cold. Lifeless."

"He looks murdered," Trumpet said. "He must have been stabbed a dozen times. Look at all the wounds."

He reached a hand out as if to touch one of the pale red slashes on Smythson's chest.

"Don't touch him!" Stephen cried.

"Why not? I didn't kill him." Trumpet screwed his eyes shut and set his hand flat on the body. He peeked with one eye, as if half-afraid the wounds might start to flow with fresh blood in accordance with the ancient superstition. *Murder will out*, the crones intoned. The corpse will bleed afresh under the hands of the murderer.

"Well, that's one suspect eliminated," Bacon said dryly. Turning to Ben, he asked, "Mr. Whitt, would you care to present?"

Ben folded his hands behind his back and began a circuit of the body. Like any good lawyer, he thought best while pacing. "First, we must ascertain how the victim met his end."

"Um." Tom raised his hand. "I believe he was stabbed repeatedly. This is suggested by the multiple knife wounds visible upon his torso."

"But," Ben said, "was stabbing in fact the cause of death? He might have been stabbed and then strangled so that his death was actually caused by the strangling."

"That's true," Trumpet said. He gestured formally, using both open hands, toward the neck. "But there are no marks on his neck. Hence, no strangling."

"Why are there so many wounds?" Tom asked. "And look, some of them are barely pricks, while others are deep and bruised all around. Like the killer drove in the knife right up to the hilt."

"Captain Ralegh said the murderer was a cutpurse," Stephen said.

"No," Trumpet said. "That was Lord Cumberland. Captain Ralegh said, 'Perhaps.'"

"Sir Walter disputes the official story?" Bacon frowned. "I hadn't heard that."

The lads shrugged at him. Tom thought one "perhaps" was slender evidence of dispute, but then, he wasn't a lawyer yet. "Why would a cutpurse stab a man so many times? If all I want is your purse, why wouldn't I just cut the strings and run away? Look here." He walked around the table and sidled up behind Stephen. "You be the victim."

Stephen gazed up at the rough-beamed ceiling, whistling tunelessly, pretending to be an easy mark.

"Here's my knife," Tom said, drawing his own from its sheath on his belt. "All I have to do is whisk your robes aside and slice." He demonstrated. "Ouch." He'd pricked his finger. He resheathed his knife and sucked on the wound.

"I believe real cutpurses wear horn covers on their thumbs," Ben said. He had a weakness for lurid ballads and broadsheets — the bloodier, the better — and knew many odd facts about the ways of the underworld.

"That's a useful item." Bacon smiled at him. Ben blushed — just a flash, but Tom noticed. *Oh, ho! Sits the wind in that quarter?*

"Maybe Smythson's thief didn't have one," Stephen said. "Maybe Smythson caught him in the act and grabbed his hand, like this." He grabbed Tom's knife hand.

"But then how can I stab you?" Tom said.

"Maybe he grabbed the other hand," Trumpet said. "He was frightened; he might easily have made a mistake."

Stephen switched to the other hand.

"Now I want to escape," Tom said, "but you won't let go of me."

"I'm going to take you to the constable," Stephen said, dropping his voice to Smythson's register.

"No, no!" Tom cried. He raised his knife hand and pretended to stab at Stephen. Stephen twisted his head from side to side, pretending to be in agony. Then they both stopped and stared at each other.

"Why don't I let go and run away?" Stephen said.

"Then I could run away too," Tom said. "Why do I stand and stab you, over and over?"

They turned to stare at Bacon, who smiled grimly. "That does appear to be the central question."

"He was muddy," Ben said. "Remember? His robes were all twisted, like he'd struggled lying on his back. That's why he couldn't run away. The thief knocked him down."

"But why didn't *I* run?" Tom said. "I mean the thief. He had the purse. He could disappear into Westminster before Mr. Smythson got to his feet."

They all fell silent, thinking.

"You hate me," Stephen said abruptly.

"No, I don't." Tom was nonplussed. "I get irritated sometimes and I didn't much like the way your family treated me, but—"

Stephen's lips disappeared into a thin line. "I meant *the thief* hated Mr. Smythson."

"Ay, me." Tom clapped a hand to his cheek and frowned a mock apology.

"Who could hate him?" Trumpet asked. "He was only a stodgy old lawyer."

Bacon said, "He wasn't always old. And he was a skilled and learned barrister. Suppose some man who lost a vital case due to Smythson's counsel harbored a deep grudge against him. Finding him alone in that deserted lane, his anger might have broken loose like a sudden storm."

"What about the purse, then?" Tom asked. "The strings were cut. A purse was stolen."

"Two purses, according to the coroner's report," Bacon said.

"I remember," Ben said. "Captain Ralegh found two sets of cut strings."

"Why would he have two purses?" Trumpet asked. "Most men carry only one, don't they? They tuck their other oddments into their pockets."

"One for himself and one for a payment, perhaps?" Tom said. "He might have been on his way to his tailor's."

"On Queen's Day?" Trumpet scoffed.

"We can imagine many reasons." Bacon's tone was as chilly as the air in the little room.

Tom felt squelched. He tried another tack. "He would have been bloody, the thief. He must have been well splattered. Wouldn't someone have noticed?"

Trumpet shook his head. "If his clothes were dark, he could turn his cloak inside out and hold it tight around him until he got home. If no one bumped right up against him . . ."

"He'd still have a bloody doublet to dispose of," Tom said. "Or have washed. Some laundress somewhere knows who our man is, I'll wager."

Bacon looked at him sharply, as though Tom had given him an idea. Whatever it was, he kept it to himself.

"If we had any notion of who the man was, we might be able to find her." Ben shrugged. "But we can hardly question every laundress in Middlesex." He gestured at the sheet. He and Trumpet each took a corner and drew it up over Smythson's face once more. "I fear we'll never know."

Tom wondered what else was in that coroner's report. He also wondered why Bacon had been so quick to squash his payment idea. He had a niggling sense their tutor was holding something back.

SEVEN

"This is it," Tom said, pointing up at a window on the first floor of a four-story house.

"No, it isn't," Trumpet said. "The house on the other side was more of a pinkish color. I remember because it made such a striking background to Captain Ralegh's silver and white costume."

"I remember that too," Stephen said.

The lads were rambling through the maze of lanes south of Whitehall on their way home from Westminster Hall, where they'd been observing the proceedings of the Court of Common Pleas. They were looking for the spot where Tobias Smythson had been murdered, *as per* Bacon's instructions. He had told them to return to the scene to elicit all available evidence, whether material, in the form of objects on the ground, or testimonial, in the form of statements from witnesses. Tom was hoping for one particular witness.

"I should think I would remember the place where I first saw my one true love," Tom said. "It was an important moment for me after all."

Stephen and Trumpet snickered. Tom felt affronted, as a gentleman should when the sincerity of his ardor is doubted. Although in fairness, he had similarly sworn his undying love only a month ago, after chancing to sit beside Lady Elizabeth Throckmorton at the theater. He'd written three sonnets to her beauty and dreamt about her for a fortnight.

This was different; he couldn't explain how. He hadn't been able to think of anything but his angel for the whole past week. It had nearly affected his appetite. He'd spent every idle moment planning what he'd say to her when he found her. Today was the day: he could feel it in his bones. He was so sure that he'd stuck an ostrich plume in his best hat in spite of his friends' jeers and Gray's rules about finery. Otherwise, he and the lads wore leather jerkins and everyday slops since they were going on from here direct to their dancing lesson.

Ben walked ahead, studying the ground. He paused every few steps to shift a bit of mud with the toe of his boot. He stopped a dozen yards down the lane and raised his hands, gesturing as if establishing the position of invisible figures. He called back, "This is it!" They trotted down the lane to where he stood.

Tom looked up. "This window looks the same as the other one."

Ben nodded. "These houses were probably built at the same time by the same builder. But that house —" he turned to point across the lane "— is pink. And there's this." He pointed his toe at a clump of mud. "I'm fairly certain that's blood. The worst of it must have been removed."

"Ugh," Tom said. "Poor Mr. Smythson."

"God rest him," the others intoned.

Stephen said, "What are we supposed to be looking at?" He'd been carping and whining throughout their search. Tom wished he would go on ahead, if he didn't want to help. Who was stopping him?

"Whatever is unusual, I suppose," Ben said.

They turned in slow circles. Tom tried to observe with his full perceptive capacity, as Bacon had instructed them, but saw nothing more than walls and windows and sanded earth. The whole area around Whitehall had been swept clean for Queen's Day and there hadn't been time for fresh rubbish to pile up.

"I hope we can find the knife," Trumpet said.

"Surely the thief would have kept it," Stephen said.

"We don't know that it was a thief," Ben said. "My impression is that Mr. Bacon thinks it wasn't."

"He's holding something back," Tom said. "I'm sure of it." He shot a meaningful glance at Ben, who only shrugged.

"Why doesn't he tell us what he wants us to find?" Stephen said. "Why be so cursed mysterious?"

"To prevent our results from being contaminated by *a priori* assumptions." Ben had been thoroughly seduced by Bacon's novel approach to natural philosophy. At least, he claimed it was the philosophy.

"We should look for witnesses," Tom said. "My angel might have seen something."

"She may well have," Ben said, "but she doesn't seem to be at home today."

The window where she had stood was shuttered.

"She could be inside," Tom said. "It's nippy; she wouldn't want the window open. She could be standing there, combing her golden tresses, right on the other side of that wall." He gazed up at the window, raising his arms before him as if in supplication.

"Here it comes," Stephen warned.

Tom lifted his voice in song. He would call his angel to him with poetry and music. He chose the song they'd learned last week from their Italian master, which happened to be apt.

"From heaven an angel upon radiant wings,
New lighted on that shore so fresh and fair . . ."

The other lads joined in. They had an Italian lesson that afternoon; they might as well practice. They made a balanced quartet. Tom and Stephen had the best voices and were both tenors, although Stephen's range was slightly greater. Trumpet's normal voice was mediocre but he could produce a surprisingly sweet falsetto. Ben had a round and fruity basso.

They sang clearly, lightening the dreary morning, enjoying the effect of their voices echoing against the plaster walls.

"To which, so doom'd, my faithful footstep clings:
Alone and friendless, when she found me there,
Of gold and silk a finely-woven net,
Where lay my path, 'mid seeming flowers she set:
Thus was I caught, and, for such sweet light shone
From out her eyes, I soon forgot to moan."

They came to the end of the song. The window before them remained shut. But someone behind them clapped loudly. They turned to see a wrinkled crone leaning out of a window on the first floor of the pink house.

"Beeyootiful!" She grinned toothlessly down at them. "But why're ye singing to an empty window, good sirs, when ye've got me?"

Tom bowed, which brought on a raucous cackle.

Ben muttered indistinctly, trying not to move his lips, "We may have another witness."

Trumpet called up to her, "We're looking for a woman who was here last week, Goodwife. In the window across from yours. A young woman with blond hair?"

"Oh, *her!*" The crone's mouth turned down in a frightful grimace, making her look so like a gargoyle that Tom flinched. "She's not there now. They're at court, this hour."

Tom's heart leapt: his angel was noble if she was at court. Then it sank again: she was beyond his reach. He sighed. He would have to love her from afar. More romantic, if less satisfying.

Ben spoke up. "Were you here last week, Goodwife, when the lawyer was killed?"

"Nor was I, curse the luck! The most exciting thing to happen 'neath this window in all my years and it happens right when I'm having my mug o' ale!"

"Do you normally sit at this window, then?" Ben asked.

"*Normally?* I allus sits here, sir, if that's what you mean. I was only out for a quarter of an hour. Half, might be. Never longer."

Ben smiled up at her, nodding, speaking to the others out of the corner of his mouth. "We need to interview her. She may have seen the killer earlier." The words came out in a sort of squashed creak.

"Why're ye talking so queer?" She craned her withered neck to see them better.

The boys closed ranks, smiling up at her.

"What did you say?" Trumpet spoke out of the corner of his mouth.

Stephen, a gifted mimic, repeated Ben's words in the same suppressed squeak. "We need to interview her."

"Just ask her," Tom urged, poking Ben in the side.

The crone watched their byplay with sharp attention. "You gentlemen is as good as a mummery show. Sing me another o' them songs."

"If you'll let us come up, we will," Ben said.

"Come ahead, fine sirs." She flapped her hand. "I always welcome tasty young gentlemen into my chamber." She burst into a torrent of cackling, rocking back and forth, clutching the oak frame of the window. Tom hesitated briefly; they might be safer questioning her from the street.

The lads found an alley that led them onto King Street. They realized that they were retracing the route they'd taken on the fatal day and kept their eyes skinned for bits of material evidence. Nothing presented itself. Bacon had suggested footprints, but both lane and alley had been thoroughly trampled by three horses and a curious mob.

They counted houses back to the one the old woman occupied and entered a doorway under a sign that read *The Janus Face*. Inside, they were dazzled by an array of silks and taffetas and sarcenets in a rainbow of hues. Gowns and doublets of all kinds hung about the room.

The lads were so amazed by the finery that it was several moments before they noticed a short man of middle years standing before them with a crabbed look on his round face. "If you're from the Middle Temple," he said, eyes raking their student robes, "your costumes aren't ready. I told you December fifteenth and not one day earlier."

"We're from Gray's," Trumpet said.

"Gray's won't be done till day before Christmas Eve. Every year, you expect a miracle, putting in your orders at the last minute. Well, you'll not get one this year neither. You can't get quality workmanship at a moment's notice."

"We're not here for costumes," Ben said.

"What costumes?" Stephen asked. Tom grabbed his arm and pointed at a turban in gleaming purple silk topped with a spray of white plumes. Stephen drew in a delighted breath. They exchanged excited grins. This would be their first Christmas in London, and they meant to enjoy every minute of it. Feasts, plays, gaming, masques, music; dancing, dancing, and more dancing. They had been practicing their leaps for *la volta* for weeks.

Tom winced as Ben trod heavily upon his foot. "We'd like to speak with someone upstairs," Ben said. "A woman at the window?"

The costumer groaned. "My grandmother, you mean. She's been flirting with you, hasn't she? I pray you, good sirs, kindly ignore her."

"We'd like to visit her, Tailor," Ben said. "Only for a moment. We're investigating a murder that was committed here last week."

"Oh, the murder! I heard all about it, that evening when I got home. I was at the pageant, you see, in the tents doing the last minute fittings, so I missed all the excitement."

"Your grandmother may have been a witness," Ben started, but the costumer was shaking his head vigorously.

"Forgive me, sir, but that she wasn't. She was having her mug of ale. She takes it at the same time every day. She didn't see a thing. She's been moaning about it ever since."

"She might have seen someone in the lane a few minutes before or after," Trumpet said.

"Or she might know who was at the window across the way," Tom put in.

The costumer rubbed the back of his neck. "I suppose she might. She'd only have been away a few minutes. She knows better than to linger gossiping over her mug at this season." He regarded his worktable, heaped high with fancy stuffs, and sighed the heartfelt sigh of a man who would earn a year's wages in two months of heroic labor. "It's only going to get worse between now and Twelfth Night."

He directed the lads to the stairs at the back of the house. "I can tell you this, young masters. If she says she saw something, that something was there. There's nothing wrong with her *eyes*."

They mounted the narrow stairs in a single file.

"I don't like the way he said that last bit," Tom said. "The way he emphasized her *eyes*."

"Like there might be something wrong with the rest of her," Ben said.

Trumpet half turned on the first landing. "Like her wits, do you think?"

"A witless witness," Stephen said.

63

"Oh, that's good," Tom said. "That's really good."

"Witless witness?" Stephen hummed a rhythm under his breath. "How about this:

The morning sun shall bear me witness,
Thy something beauty strikes me witless."

"Sparkling," Trumpet suggested. "Thy sparkling beauty. To go with morning sun."

"Too shallow," Ben said. "A sparkling beauty would be superficial only. The loved one should have depth of character as well."

They reached a square landing that allowed access to two chambers. Ben knocked on the door to the rear one.

It opened immediately. Tom had to look straight down to greet the tiny woman before him. She grinned up at them, displaying her nearly toothless gums. "Here are my pretty gentlemen," she crooned. "Welcome to my forest."

Tom crossed the threshold into a dream. The crone's chamber seemed indeed to be more forest than house. Row upon row of leaves sewn of gossamer and silk hung on wire-strung racks that covered all four walls, saving only the window and the door. The leaves, in every hue of green and yellow and brown, rustled as they shifted in the breeze from the open window.

"How do they rustle?" Tom asked in wonder. "They sound so real."

The crone burst into a peal of laughter. "Them's the taffeta. Crispy, they are. I've a specialty in foliage, I do, since I was a wee slip. I sewed leaves for Queen Catherine's wedding masque, I did."

Tom racked his brains to remember who Queen Catherine was. Trumpet got it first. "You don't mean Great Harry's last wife?"

"That's her." She clapped her hands, pleased with her surprise.

Tom blinked at her, both repelled and bemused. This tiny sorceress had survived three monarchs.

Ben said, "Goodwife, we want to ask you a question or two about the events in the lane below on Queen's Day."

"First another song, good sirs. You promised." She folded her hands across her apron and tilted her head, ready to listen.

The boys consulted together in whispers. They decided to give her a round of "The Holly and the Ivy." Everyone liked it and they might as well practice since it was bound to be called for during the coming Christmas season.

The old woman listened raptly. When they finished, she loosed a long, gargling sigh. "Beeyoootiful!"

Ben returned to the matter at hand. "Did you see anyone in the lane that day?"

She cackled. "I saw you. And you and you and you." She pointed at each of the boys in turn. "I saw Captain Ralegh and the one with the suns. Which one is he?"

"The Earl of Cumberland," Tom said. "The Celestial Knight."

"That's him. He don't get his garb from us."

"We mean before, Goodwife," Trumpet said. "Before the barrister was murdered."

"Hmm." The crone's gaze shot to the window with a sharp gleam of malice. Tom felt a stab of fear for his angel. Had they drawn a witch's envy toward her?

She trotted to the window and clambered up on a high stool. She settled herself in what was obviously her accustomed position to show them how well she could see the lane below. The boys moved to stand around her so they could follow her gaze. She reached out a wizened hand and squeezed Tom's buttock. She clucked her tongue wickedly as he shifted back a step.

"I saw a barrister," she told them. "Them's the ones with the velvet stripes on their sleeves. Two welts: that's a barrister. I know my robes. Whether 't was the one as was killed, I couldn't say. He was up at the top of the lane, see there? Coming through the arch."

Tom twisted to look without placing his body within reach of her hands.

"Was he alone?" Trumpet asked.

She nodded. "Alone, alone-oh. Running as fast as he could with his arms a-pumping and his gown a-flapping."

"Why was he running?"

"Why? To escape the Wild Men, of course."

"Who?"

"The Wild Men." She cackled at their confusion. "Two of 'em. From the pageant, good sirs. Wearing my leaves. I'd know 'em a mile away."

"Essex's pageant," Stephen said. "They'll be his men, then."

"Why were they chasing the barrister?" Tom asked.

"I don't know, good sirs." She sniffed. "You might ask that girl you was a-singing to."

"How—"

"What did I say? I saw you leering up at her. I can put one and one together and come up with two, old as I am. She was a-standing in the winder where she worked when you found her. Watching the street like she shouldn't 'a been." Never mind that she'd been doing the same.

"Where she worked? What sort of work?" Tom feared the worst. Had he fallen in love with a strumpet? *Again?*

"She's a limner, good sir. Didn't you know?"

A limner was a painter of the miniature portraits that were so fashionable these days. She was a craftswoman, then; not noble at all. She was beneath him now that he was a member of the Inns of Court. He would have the advantage in wooing her. Something about her elfin smile told him he would need every advantage he could muster.

"Do you know her name, Goodwife?" Tom asked.

"Nor I don't," the old witch said. "How could I? We never spoke. I only ever saw her working by the window, for the light, the same as me."

"Does she live there, too?"

Another long peal of cackles. "Live there, her? That house is for the rich. Fine lords and ladies that come to see the queen."

"Whose portrait was she painting?" Ben asked. "Did you ever see the sitter?"

"Oh, yes. I've an interest, y'know, in the court. 'Twas young Lady Rich. Born a Devereux, she was." She saw their skeptical faces and nodded. "Oh, yes. She's the spit of her mother. I used to get out, y'know, when I was young. Used to be me, going to court to do the fittings. I know who's who, or at least who was."

EIGHT

The bell at St. Margaret's tolled the third quarter. Nearly ten o'clock! Tom and his friends had to hurry. The dancing master was French and a fiend for punctuality. As they stripped down to their shirtsleeves for an hour of vigorous exercise, Trumpet said, "We're going to have to speak with Lady Rich."

Ben grimaced. Stephen drew a hissing breath between clenched teeth.

Tom asked, "What? Do you think she'll refuse to see us?"

"Don't you know who she is?" Stephen goggled at Tom as if he were an idiot. "She's Stella, you buffoon. *The* Stella. From the sonnets of *Astrophel and Stella*?"

Tom's breath caught in his throat. He had forgotten. *Lady Rich* sounded like a matronly personage, wide of girth and wobbly of jowl. Instead, she was none other than the beauteous Penelope Devereux, renowned throughout Europe as the object of the late Sir Philip Sidney's unrequited love, made immortal by his poetry. Catching a glimpse of the glorious Stella had been high on his list of desires when he first came to London.

But to meet her, face to face, speak words to her, and hear her voice in answer? It was beyond imagining.

"God's teeth," Tom said. "She'll never receive us. We're nithings. We're worms."

"Speak for yourself," Stephen huffed.

"She might," Ben said. "It's little enough to ask. One brief question: What is the name of your limner?"

"Any favor from a courtier is significant," Trumpet said. "We'll have to bring a gift." He spoke grimly, as if facing a quest worthy of a Ralegh or a Drake.

Tom frowned. "Something symbolical, don't you think? Like a perfect rose?" He knew he'd be paying for it from his dwindling allowance.

"A perfect rose in late November would be more miraculous than symbolical," Ben said.

Tom racked his brains for a gift that was in season, not too horribly expensive, and suitable for one of the kingdom's premier ladies. He came up empty.

"What about Mr. Bacon?" Stephen said. "His connections at court are the main reason we chose him as our tutor."

Ben frowned. "One of the reasons. But yes, certainly we should ask him. We should make a full report."

Dance practice went well, considering how preoccupied they were by the Lady Rich problem. Soon they'd be ready to start rehearsing in their performance costumes. *La volta* was challenging enough in everyday clothes. Stiffly padded formal doublets and upper stocks added another whole level of difficulty.

After their lesson, at Tom's insistence, they went back to the house near the murder scene to look for the limner. The woman who opened the door claimed to have no knowledge of any such person. She'd seen no portrait painting or signs of such. She and her husband had recently arrived from Warwickshire to seek permission to travel to the Low Countries to visit her husband's relations. She pointed out that the house wasn't terribly comfortable and suggested that a lady of Penelope Rich's standing might have moved to better chambers inside the palace proper. Tom felt thoroughly deflated. His angel could be anywhere by this time.

They barely made it back to Gray's in time for dinner at noon. The meal was followed by the usual two hours of case-putting, in which the students learned to think on their feet. Nathaniel Welbeck put Ben on the spot in front of the whole assembly, skewering him with precedents concerning a hypothetical case that pitted the claims of a bastard son against a legitimate minor daughter.

Ben, stammering and blushing, blurted out a completely irrelevant maxim. Welbeck turned to sneer at Francis Bacon, who had lately begun dining in commons. "It appears that Mr. Whitt's knowledge of the law is waning rather than waxing under his new tutelage."

NINE

Francis Bacon watched Benjamin Whitt stalk stiff-backed and red-faced out of the hall. He sympathized with the man. It wasn't fair for the ancients to play out their conflicts through the students. Whitt had borne himself well in the face of Welbeck's unjust attack. He may not have proved his case, but he'd shown himself to be a man of character.

Later, when Francis went up to his chambers, he found Thomas Clarady and Allen Trumpington struggling up the stairs, their arms heaped with pillows, blankets, a sack of sweet buns, and a basket of quills and commonplace books. Clarady had a lute slung over one shoulder and a large jug hanging from the other.

Francis greeted them with a raised eyebrow.

Clarady said, "Ben refuses to leave the library until he constructs an argument to answer Mr. Welbeck. We're going to help him."

Francis surveyed their supplies. "Why the lute?"

"He'll have to sleep sometime. I thought music would help."

Francis applauded their devotion to their friend and admired Whitt's dedication to study. He felt a surge of pride in his pupils and hoped they would succeed. He would enjoy watching Whitt put Welbeck's nose out of joint.

It wasn't until after he had settled at his desk to peruse his list of investigatory tasks that he realized his whole team of under-investigators was now firmly encamped in the library.

* * *

The first puzzle Francis had to solve was how to request an interview with Lady Rich for his pupils without writing her a letter. She wouldn't speak directly to his servant and he had little faith in the fidelity of a message passed through a chain of underlings.

He drummed his fingers on the desk. It was just his luck that the only two threads he had to follow ran through prominent courtiers! Why couldn't the witnesses be oyster-sellers or wherrymen? Asking lords for favors was ticklish enough in the best of circumstances. Asking them without being seen to ask was nigh impossible.

Was it an accident that his threads led to this particular brother and sister? Francis fervently hoped so. If he turned up evidence that either the Earl of Essex or Lady Rich were involved in Smythson's murder, he resolved to drop his partial results in his uncle's lap without further ado and retire to his mother's house in Gorhambury. He was in no position to prosecute the nobility.

That thought raised his temperature in spite of the cool of his fireless chamber. He fanned himself with a sheet of paper. Their involvement was unlikely after all. The Devereux were society's darlings. Odds were high that they would make an appearance in any matter of importance, sooner or later.

Francis closed his eyes and calmed himself by willing his mind to think about nothing. He heard birds twittering nearby and the crunch of gravel as men strode across the yard below. He smelled the bitter tang of his ink and a soft undersmell of ashes from the hearth. He inhaled deeply then exhaled and opened his eyes.

He had his solution. The muddling of messages as they passed through many mouths would serve him well in this instance. It was best that Lady Rich know as little as possible about the true errand of his emissaries, lest she refuse to see them. She would know, of course, about his exile from court. He hoped that she would find an oblique request arriving by way of her stable boy intriguing enough to grant.

* * *

When Francis next emerged from his chambers, he learned that Whitt's heroic study session had become the main topic of the Society. Bets were being placed on the outcome. Every day, one of the senior barristers dropped by the library to see how the lads were coming along. Some, like Treasurer Fogg, leaned in the doorway recounting rambling anecdotes about past victories in court. Others, like James Shiveley, brought apples and cheese and explanations so elementary even the privateer's son rolled his eyes.

It occurred to Francis that he might be able to use these visits to pursue one of his leads. Someone at Gray's had presumably arranged for the delivery of seditious pamphlets at the next half moon. Perhaps he could elicit some telling reaction — shock, guilt, dismay — by posing an unexpected question.

One day he heard Nathaniel Welbeck's voice across the hall. The man had the audacity to stand within his hearing and give his pupils a false definition of the assize of mort d'ancestor. Intolerable! However, his meddling did give Francis the right to drop in his own pennyworth of advice. He had scrupulously stayed out of it hitherto.

He strolled casually across the landing. Humphries, to his lack of surprise, was there as well. He greeted the lads and corrected Welbeck's misleading information. Then, to demonstrate his recognition that the rules had changed, he delivered a brief but cogent explanation of the principles underlying the restoration of dispossessed property. Whitt nodded rapidly, his eyes burning as if a prior argument were being vindicated. Trumpington scribbled down every word. Even Clarady's face shone as if the light of understanding had finally dawned. Their reactions were gratifying, but he enjoyed Welbeck's disgruntlement and Humphries's dumbstruck expression even more.

Pretending to depart, Francis turned toward the door. He asked over his shoulder, as if he'd just remembered it, "Does anyone by any chance know when the moon will next be at the half? I don't seem to have an almanac handy."

Welbeck blinked at him for a long moment, silent for once. Then he said, "I thought you collected the things. You must have dozens."

"In a dozen languages," Humphries sneered. He seemed to think he had delivered a crushing insult.

Neither of them seemed much interested in the date or alarmed by his question. Undaunted, he tried the same trick two or three more times until he realized that his pupils were studying him with concern for his sanity furrowing their brows.

* * *

On Friday, Francis sought out the laundress in her domain. The question of the blood on the murderer's doublet nagged at him. There must have been a lot of it, especially on the sleeves and cuffs. The killer might have given the clothes away, but a costume suitable for Queen's Day would have cost a pretty penny. Worth salvaging. If the murderer was resident at Gray's, he might have sent the clothes to the Inn's laundress.

The laundry was a stone outbuilding beyond the kitchens. An enormous kettle bubbled over a huge bed of coals. Two roughly-dressed but very clean boys stood on blocks of wood, taking turns stirring a mass of linens in the kettle. The laundress was a woman of middle years who had the hatchet face of an angry Turk and arms as brawny as a blacksmith.

She regarded him with a deep frown as he approached. He knew she was remembering his foray into alchemical studies last summer, which had resulted in an unspeakable mess.

He asked her if she had seen any clothing with unexpected quantities of blood on it shortly after Queen's Day.

"How much blood d'ye expect?" she asked. He couldn't fault her astuteness.

His efforts to describe the probable extent of splattering transformed her frown into a suspicious scowl. "What have you been up to now, Mr. Bacon?"

"Nothing, nothing, I assure you. The clothes in question are not mine." He cast frantically about for an excuse. "Em, er, it was a colleague. An experiment, you might call it, involving poultry—"

She held up a beefy hand to stop him. "T'ain't my job to know, sir." She scratched her chin, which was adorned with three coarse hairs. "Blood, now. I don't recall it, and ye'd think I would. Nasty business, blood. The devil to get out. It'll never come white again, howsoever long ye boil it. But I don't do all the washing, mind. There's many who think they'll get better in Holborn."

"As I feared." How many women took in laundry between here and Westminster? A dozen at least as regular work. And what hard-pressed goodwife would turn down a shilling in exchange for her silence?

Francis smiled and prepared to take his leave, but she wasn't finished. "Queen's Day, though. T'weren't blood, sir, but there was a mess of sopping clothes left for me that night. Seems a boatload of yon gentlemen went into the Thames after the pageant. Drunk as porpoises, sir, is what I heard."

"Porpoises," Francis echoed, wondering where she had learned the word. Some ballad, probably. He hadn't heard about a wherry accident, but then he'd avoided all mention of the Queen's Day festivities, having been barred from enjoying them. Could the murderer have engineered that tumble as an excuse to wash away the signs of his crime in the murky waters of the Thames? He'd have to be a crafty opportunist. And worse, a gentleman of Gray's.

He pressed a halfpenny into her palm and started to walk away. Then he turned back and gave her another one. She really had done a Herculean job of getting all the mustard out of his velvet curtains.

* * *

By Sunday he had explored every path that he could follow without his assistants. Except for one.

He skipped chapel for the first time in seven years, praying that his mother would never come to hear of it. He spent a hair-raising half hour sneaking into every staircase and running up and down on tiptoe, straining his ears to catch the murmur of chanting and sniffing at gaps under doors for the scent of incense.

He was in constant dread lest someone see him. For several horrible minutes, he'd been forced to crouch in a dark corner on a second-floor landing, trembling, heart in mouth, while Sir Christopher Yelverton lumbered up to his rooms on the first floor.

What in the name of a merciful God would he say if he were caught? The last thing he needed was for irrational prying and spying to be added to the list of charges against him. And for all the risk to his reputation, he'd learned nothing. It had been a foolish idea. The conspirator, if such existed, was more likely to consort with his co-religionists after supper, when men strolled freely about the Inn visiting one another.

He needed to discover who could have known about Smythson's intelligence work. He could try some delicate probing among his colleagues during meals, braving the harm to his digestion. At this point, alas, his best hope was that his under-investigators, once Whitt's honor had been restored, would be able to turn something up.

TEN

On the topmost floor of a narrow house in the parish of Saint Martin's Le Grand in the City of London, Clara Goossens sat before her window burning ivory to make black paint. A chill breeze lifted the acrid smoke harmlessly above the rooftops. A small brazier supplied enough heat to keep her hands from growing stiff.

The room was small, just large enough for her sparse possessions. A bed with a straw mattress, two plain chests, the table under the window where she sat. The stool she sat upon. The brazier. Two woolen blankets, a set of linens, and a few household items were all she'd salvaged from her mother's meager estate. She had earned her fine court clothes with her brush. The tools of her trade were her father's legacy: an easel that folded so she could carry it through the streets and the many-drawered writing desk that held her pigments, oils, and brushes.

That was all she owned and all she needed. She was free: that was the main thing.

Except for the nightmares.

She lifted the piece of burnt ivory with a pair of tongs and set it in the mortar to cool. While she waited, she turned again to study the sketch she had made on Queen's Day. Her critical eye approved the vitality of its fluid lines even as she flinched from the horrible event depicted: a murderer in an open robe with velvet welts on the sleeves knelt over his victim, grinning with exultation. The sketch was charcoal, but she could see the colors in her mind's eye: black robe against sandy earth, blood made redder by the pinkish wall behind.

She had dreamt that scene over and over again in the past two weeks. The nightmare churned up old fears she had thought long laid to rest. Even her new patron had commented on the dark circles beneath her eyes. That was bad; the merest breath of scandal could damage her reputation and destroy her livelihood. Ladies at court wanted nothing unlovely to sully their lives.

Clara feared the nightmare would continue until she did something to banish it. She should do something to relieve her conscience.

But what could she do?

She'd returned to work in that same chamber the next morning, hoping and fearing for news about the murder. She'd had no need for subterfuge; the court was abuzz with speculation. No one had any idea who the killer was. They didn't even know he was another barrister.

Clara said nothing that day since Lady Rich had been impatient for her portrait and she feared to lose her fee. Those three pounds would keep her for months. The next day, again she said nothing, fearing they would wonder why she hadn't spoken earlier. She finished the portrait that day and had no excuse to go back on Monday.

Now it was far too late to come forward, but the guilt of her silence consumed her. If she kept silent, the man with the evil grin might escape without punishment. He could kill again and again, having discovered that he liked it and there was no penalty. Each of those lives would weigh upon her soul.

She shuddered and tossed the sketch aside. She took her pestle and began to grind the ivory, carefully, so as not to spill any of the expensive powder. Black was in fashion; she would need lots of black paint and she daren't raise her fees. Not yet, anyway. With a good report from Lady Rich, perhaps one day soon.

Her mind was still caught on the brambles of her predicament. What was a sketch? Not proof of anything. She was an artist; she might have imagined the whole scene. Or so a judge would say. Perhaps she hated lawyers, they would say, perhaps she held a grudge. She didn't, but many people did. She was a foreigner; they would never believe her. And then they might wonder what sort of game she was playing and poke their long English noses into her past.

Here in England, strangers were tolerated only to the extent that they kept themselves out of trouble. Murder was trouble of the very worst kind. People would say she should have screamed at the man, she should have stopped him. She should have run fast for the watchman or anyone who could help instead of sketching merrily away while a man was stabbed to death before her eyes.

She had thought to bear witness by sketching. She was skilled at her trade. She could draw faster than she could run. But they would accuse her of complicity. They would question her about herself. Who was she? Why had she come to London?

She'd be exposed. And worse, she'd be expelled from England and sent back to Antwerp, where Caspar would find her.

She couldn't show her sketch to a judge or the Captain of the Guard or to anyone in authority. But if she never told anyone she would go mad with the pounding of that horrible image in her mind. She might never sleep another night through. And she would be damned for all eternity if the murderer killed again.

She had to tell.

She couldn't tell.

She was trapped.

She heaved a sigh laden with fear and worry. Then she rose and found a clean bottle with a sound cork and a funnel. She returned to her stool and began to transfer the fine black powder carefully from the mortar to the bottle.

Concentrating on the task calmed her. Perhaps she could tell someone not exactly in authority but close to it. A sympathetic person who might help her climb out of this thorny thicket. Another image arose in her mind: the face of the young man who had gazed up at her and spoken the words, *"O angela luminosa!"*

She laughed softly and felt the tension slip from her shoulders. *Tom,* his friend had called him. He reminded her of her father. Although their features were not at all alike, Tom's face held the same open expression, bespeaking a generosity of spirit and frankness of feeling that she admired but could never allow herself to share.

She corked the bottle firmly and placed it in a drawer of her writing desk.

Tom. A plain name. A friendly name. She wondered what his surname was, who his family were. He'd worn the sleeveless black robe of a law student over his elegant holiday clothes. He and his friends had been helping the lords to examine the body. Perhaps they had known the murdered man.

Clara shuddered and forced her mind back to the fair youth who had stood beneath her window. He had fallen in love with her right before her eyes. He had been ready to fall in love, he saw a woman he liked, and whoop, hey! In he fell.

That was like her father too. Johannes Vanderporne had always been ready to meet the world, wrap his arm around its shoulders, and invite it home for supper. He had been a student of Pieter Brueghel the Elder in his youth and had gone on to become a sought-after painter of portraits. Their home had been a comfortable disorder of paint and canvasses, apprentices and clients, with artists visiting from all across Europe.

Clara had been the only child to follow in her father's craft. She learned to make pencils and paints, how to stretch a canvas, how to draw, how to arrange a sitting client. Sharing a talent and a love of art, Clara and Johannes had been closer than most fathers and daughters. His world had been her world. Then he died, killed by his own recklessness. Stumbling home from a party late at night instead of sleeping in the stable with the other benighted guests, he fell into a ditch swollen with rain and drowned. A carter fished him out the next morning.

Her world collapsed in the space of a week. Johannes left his family a pile of debts secured by uncollected fees. Few of his clients had the decency to pay their bills, and the family had no money to hire lawyers to sue them. They sold everything except the paint box and easel that Clara refused to part with. Clara's mother had gone to work in a brewery, taking in mending to occupy her evenings. She'd worked herself into an early grave.

Now Clara never looked too far ahead. She knew how quickly disaster could lay waste to a life. She was safe and mostly content, and that was enough. She didn't need handsome young gentlemen singing under her window.

She wouldn't mind a friend, though. Perhaps Tom could give her sketch to the authorities without risking her direct involvement.

Clara cleaned her hands on a scrap of linen. She pulled her easel over to the window and clipped a fresh sheet of paper onto it. If she drew Tom's face, the act of making lines, of rubbing in shadows, might help her decide whether he could be trusted. She closed her eyes for a moment to summon his image then opened them and began to sketch. His face was almost rectangular, with a strongly rounded chin. His brows and mouth formed straight lines, framing his well-formed nose and his wide-set eyes. She thought in some moods he might look severe, but she doubted such moods came upon him often. He was a man of choleric humor: made for sunshine, laughter, and good fellowship. After he spoke his words of love, he had smiled at her, showing a dimple in his cheek that melted her heart.

She would like to see that dimple again and bask in the warmth of his open smile. She rose from her stool to walk around the easel, studying her drawing from various angles. It was a good face. A trustworthy face.

Clara decided that if she ever saw Tom again, she would show him the sketch she'd made of the murderer. Then she sighed and smiled sadly to herself as she rolled up his portrait. She wasn't likely to see the golden-haired youth again.

ELEVEN

Francis Bacon had a quiet word with Sir Avery Fogg before supper. The meal was tench in jelly, onions boiled with sugar and raisins, and eggs in broth. He gave most of his share to George Humphries. After the cloth was withdrawn, Fogg rose and announced the case to be put: a rematch between Benjamin Whitt and Nathaniel Welbeck in the matter of the bastard's inheritance.

Whitt stood in the aisle between the long tables. He had an array of papers laid ready on the oak that Allen Trumpington and Thomas Clarady sifted briskly through when called upon, presenting him with the relevant note at the critical moment. They sat on the edges of their respective benches, leaning forward, ready to support their spokesman. Lord Stephen leaned back with his arms crossed to signal his nonparticipation. Francis was surprised to observe that it was Clarady who supplied the needed term — twice — when Whitt stumbled on a phrase in Law French.

After his pupils had thoroughly demolished Welbeck's defense and received the thundering applause they deserved, Francis summoned the under butler to order a jug of malmsey for his pupils and another for his messmates. Their astonished response to his largesse was not altogether flattering.

Humphries remarked, with a characteristic lack of civility, "If we were benchers, we would never have to pay." To Francis's best knowledge, Humphries had never treated his messmates to wine.

Welbeck accepted a cup with ill grace. "Perhaps they should nominate your new pupil for Reader. He's old enough. About your age, isn't he, Bacon?" He laughed heartily at his own joke. Humphries snickered along with him.

Francis gave him a withering look.

Shiveley said, "They're a fine group of men, Bacon. A credit to our Society."

"I wanted to honor them." Francis raised his cup. "To the queen, to England, and the future of Gray's Inn!"

The others followed suit. An innocuous enough toast, and the wine was not half-bad.

"I also wanted to share a cup or two with my messmates in remembrance of Tobias Smythson," Francis added. "I find myself thinking about him often since his death."

"To Smythson!" Shiveley raised his cup and they drank again.

Francis let a silence develop as each man savored the wine and relaxed into the familiar mellowness of the hall on a dark autumn evening. Men's voices rumbled in the background. Yellow candlelight reflected on the oak paneling. A servant fed the fire from a basket of staves. Most members would pass the hours before bedtime here in warmth and fellowship. A group in one corner was reading through the play to be performed before the queen on Christmas Eve. They'd chosen *The Misfortunes of Arthur* by Graysian Thomas Hughes. Francis was charged with devising the masque for the interlude— a tribute to his talents. He'd hardly given it a thought, however, being occupied with more serious matters. He couldn't give it up now, though, without risking more censure for being unreliable and lacking holiday spirit. He ought to be grateful they allowed him this small involvement in the court's festivities. He could write the masque even if he couldn't watch it be performed.

"Who's getting Smythson's chambers?" Welbeck asked, breaking the comfortable silence.

"It's not decided," Shiveley said. "I myself have put in a bid."

Chambers were typically leased for long periods. When the lessee died, the chambers reverted to the lessor, which in this case was the bench. Since the Inn was desperately overcrowded, desirable chambers such as Smythson's were hotly contested.

"Have you?" Welbeck's eyes glittered. "So have I."

Humphries grinned suddenly, hunching his shoulders with a private joke, but said nothing.

Francis wasn't interested in the question of chambers. He already inhabited the best lodgings at Gray's, courtesy of his father. He supposed that Smythson's rooms would go to whomever had the most compelling combination of seniority, influence, and cash. Since Treasurer Fogg was, he believed, the last of the benchers with third-floor rooms, Smythson's first-floor address would most probably soon be his.

He let that topic die. A short time later, he asked, as though the thought had arrived in train with other matters, "What do you suppose Fogg meant about 'encroachments' in his eulogy? Did he and Smythson ever oppose one another in court?"

"Not in court." Welbeck smirked. "In *courting*. Something *you* wouldn't understand."

"Why not?" Francis asked, puzzled.

"A matter of the heart, Bacon." Welbeck patted himself on the chest. "A conflict *de amore*. In short, a woman."

"Ah. The Widow Sprye." Francis enjoyed the look of thwarted malice on Welbeck's face. "I merely thought the subject too *inurbanus* for a eulogy." Absurd how people assumed that simply because Francis declined to spend his leisure time chasing prostitutes around the city that he was wholly ignorant of the earthier passions.

Everyone knew that Avery Fogg was involved in an *affaire de coeur* with Mrs. Anabel Sprye, proprietress of the Antelope Inn in Holborn. She was well-endowed in every sense of the word: voluptuous, influential, and rich. Fogg's wife had died many years ago; his children were grown. He was free to court handsome widows by the dozen, if he so desired. The widow in question seemed not averse to his attentions. Fogg was more often to be found in her well-ordered establishment than in his own chambers.

"Smythson was courting Mrs. Sprye?" Shiveley asked. "I never heard that. I don't believe it either. He wasn't the type. He was too—"

"Cold? Limp? Lacking the sensual spark?" Welbeck prompted. Humphries guffawed loudly. Shiveley frowned at his lack of delicacy.

Francis reviewed his memories of Smythson in the last month or two. He had noticed, now that he was reminded of it, greater attention to grooming than had been customary for the man. Thrice-weekly visits to the barber instead of once; a fashionable new hat that accorded ill with his outdated doublet. Francis suspected that he would have better advanced his cause with Mrs. Sprye if he had spent the money on a set of leather-bound Year Books. She knew more about the law than many a judge in Westminster.

"It's not implausible," Francis said. "Men his age often conceive a longing for the comforts of a woman's care."

Welbeck barked a laugh. "A woman's care! How delicately you put things, Bacon. As if he had developed a passion for possets and broidered cushions for his gouty knees."

"Possets!" Humphries chortled. "A man with Smythson's money could have possets brought to him in bed around the clock."

Welbeck helped himself to another cup of wine. "I suspect Smythson's interest in the delectable Widow Sprye had less to do with her personal charms and more to do with the influence of the Andromache Society."

Francis laughed. He might well be right. His mother was a member, along with her sister, Lady Russell, and a dozen equally formidable women. The Andromache Society was a group of widows who met once a month for a private dinner at the Antelope. Their collective influence at court surpassed that of any courtier other than his lord uncle or the Earl of Leicester. Rumor had it that no man could attain a judgeship without their approval.

"He wanted her influence, not her favors." Francis nodded. "Surely Mrs. Sprye is too wise a bird to allow herself to be netted for such unflattering purposes?"

Welbeck said, "She's a woman, isn't she? She was probably stringing Smythson along to keep old Foggy on his toes."

Francis wondered if that was a mixed metaphor. The French puppets, called *marionettes*, were made to dance by pulling on strings. They did seem to dance on their toes. Not strictly mixed, then, but still not a pleasing turn of phrase.

"Disgraceful," Shiveley said. He was entering into his middle years and had lived a bachelor life. He tended toward the prudish. "Think of the example it sets the young students." He nodded toward the table where Whitt and his friends were playing primero.

"Yes," Welbeck said, affecting an expression of concern. "Because none of those round dogs has ever wooed a wench under false pretenses." That elicited a fresh snicker from Humphries, who was unlikely ever to have wooed any female under any pretenses whatsoever. "My nephew tells me that Delabere and Clarady have left a trail of broken hearts through every bawdy house from Westminster to Smithfield."

Francis smiled serenely at the intended slight to his pupils. Their extracurricular activities were no concern of his. The money for the wine had been well spent. Fogg's temper was notorious and the man was as territorial as a mastiff. Jealousy was one of the commonest motives for murder. It might well inspire the sort of frenzy that had left its marks on Smythson's body.

He must pay a call on Mrs. Sprye. Why would a woman of her wit and influence tolerate the clumsy courting of Tobias Smythson?

TWELVE

Saturday dawned clear and cold with a sharp breeze from the east. The lads warmed a basin of water at the fire in their chambers and washed and dressed with especial care. They were going to court this morning to meet with Lady Rich. Even Ben had brushed his "best brown" doublet and hose until they were almost furry. Tom loaned him a pewter brooch for his hat but could do nothing about the drabness of the overall theme. Well, Ben could stand at the back. They needn't all be peacocks.

They met Trumpet in the yard and exchanged a round of compliments. Tom was wearing his best clothes, the green velvet peasecod doublet and short melon hose with the yellow silk linings and stockings. He had wanted to buckle on a pistol opposite his rapier, but Stephen had declared it one touch too many.

Stephen was never wrong about fashion. He glowed in orange-tawny satin with linings of saffron sarcenet. His ruffs and cuffs were trimmed in a full inch of cobweb lace. Naturally, he also wore his sword. As a lord, he had a right to it.

Trumpet was bright, as usual, in scarlet and cream. He favored the longer galligaskins, imagining they made him look taller. They really just made him look old-fashioned. He wore a wide-brimmed hat with a long, drapey feather that kept falling across his brow.

Tom had found a fan at the White Bear in Cheapside made of iridescent peacock feathers set in a carved cherry wood handle. Even Lady Rich might not wholly scorn it. He'd had it wrapped in gauze and now carried it tenderly in his hands. He had been keeping his eyes open for golden-haired angels everywhere they went and had even startled a few women by leaping in front of them with his hands clasped in supplication. Alas, none had proved to be his angel. He fervently hoped that Lady Rich would help them find her.

They entered Whitehall Palace through the Court Gate. The distinctive aroma of the court struck them at once: the civet and rose perfumes of the courtiers; the lavender and rosemary strewn among the rushes on the floor; and underneath it all, the rank stink of overused privies.

They were met at the entrance to the Great Hall by a gentleman wearing a ruff so wide and so stiff that he was forced to turn his whole torso in order to look to the side. The visual effect of the lacy frame was striking, but it must be desperately uncomfortable. Tom preferred his own ruff, four inches of softly pleated cambric. It finished his costume elegantly without bunching up under his beard or prickling the back of his neck.

Stephen introduced himself with his full titles. He informed the chamberer, in haughty tones marred by only the slightest quaver, that they had come to court by invitation for an audience with Lady Rich. The other lads stood one step behind him.

The chamberer studied them with narrowed eyes, as if calculating the cost of their garments. He then performed a finely calibrated quarter-bow to Stephen, bending neatly at the hips. He led them at a brisk pace out into the courtyard, across the Preaching Place, through an arch, up a stair, and into a wide gallery running above the Privy Garden. The walls between the tall windows were hung with gold and silver brocade that gleamed in the weak December sun. The ceiling was painted blue with silver stars. The floor was covered with plaited mats that cushioned the sound of their footfalls. Men and women stood or strolled about the gallery in small groups, dressed in the uttermost finery, murmuring in low voices as they watched each other watch each other.

"Wait here, my lord." The chamberer gestured at a section of untenanted wall and minced away. Tom was glad to have time to absorb the exalted surroundings before meeting the goddess Stella.

"Have you been here before?" Trumpet murmured to Stephen. He allowed his feather to obscure half his face, as if sheltering in its protective cover.

"Never." Stephen echoed the hushed tone. "I was presented to the queen at Longleat on one of Her Majesty's progresses. My father hates to come to court. He says it's nothing but sin and wastefulness." He sighed, gazing wistfully at the elegant persons arranged through the gallery. Some of their costumes were worth more than a knight's annual income. "This is much better than Longleat."

"This is real." Tom was awed by the whole experience: the chamberer with his fantastical ruff, the gilt brocades, the haughty courtiers, the woven mats. "This is Whitehall, *camerades*. The center of the world. This is where history is made."

The others nodded their wholehearted agreement. They stood together in silence, soaking up the radiance.

Stephen stood ramrod straight with his shoulders squared and his chest thrust forward to emphasize the lines of his padded doublet. He lifted his chin in a gesture Tom thought of as the "Chin of the Earl." He tapped a beribboned foot nervously as he pretended to be unimpressed.

Tom tried to adopt a nonchalant pose, with his left fist set on his hip behind the hilt of his sword. He hoped they looked like men with vital intelligence from faraway places and not like students on an errand for their tutor.

Three young ladies-in-waiting clustered together by the centermost window, whispering behind their hands and giggling as they shot glances in the lads' direction. They were as cute as bunnies, all round and wiggly, about fifteen years old — Trumpet's age. They were dressed identically in silver and white.

Tom was engaged in a winking match with one of them when Stephen whispered, "Look sharp!" He tilted his head toward the staircase.

Tom saw Sir Walter Ralegh's head rising, rising, as the man himself mounted to the topmost step. Two Ralegh sightings in one month! His sisters would never believe him.

Today, Captain Ralegh was dressed for the outdoors in a leather jerkin and tall boots. Perhaps he had come to accompany the queen on a hunt. She would surely not wish to squander such a fine day inside. He strode down the gallery with a loose, confident grace, as if he owned the palace and everyone in it. Lions walked like that, prowling the avenues of their bosky kingdoms.

The trio of maids stood on their toes, fairly quivering in excitement. Ralegh's eyes turning toward them as he walked. One of the maids risked a smile. He flashed her a grin so feral and so masculine even Tom felt a thrill.

It was too much for the maiden. Her eyes fluttered up as she fainted backward with a high-pitched sigh, bearing her companions down with her. Their farthingales bounced from side to side, ballooning up from the slender figures lying prostrate on the floor, revealing the sensible red wool petticoats beneath. The two unfainted ones struggled vainly to right themselves.

Tom wanted to help them, but Ralegh was approaching. He bowed, making a leg, and offered up a tentative smile. Ralegh passed him by without a flicker of recognition.

Tom swallowed his disappointment and went to help the maids. Stephen and Ben set the fainted girl's farthingale aside like a fallen log. Then they lifted an unfainted one to her feet by grasping her firmly under the armpits and hoisting her straight into the air, letting her skirts swing free so they could land her at a level. Ben tugged her doublet straight while Trumpet gave the rear of her skirt a quick dusting. They repeated the process for the other girl.

Tom got an excellent view of the interior of a fashionable lady's nether garments as he knelt to help the fainted girl, who raised up on her elbows, blinking herself back to the world.

"Forgive me." He reached for her hand. "I know it's not the time. But are you using metal bands in your farthingale instead of canes?"

She growled at him, outraged.

Stephen and Ben bent to apply their maiden-raising method once again. "Possibly not the best time to exercise our perceptive capacities," Ben remarked.

Tom shrugged. "I have three sisters in Dorset." He grinned apologetically at the maid, displaying his dimple. "They count on me to keep them abreast of changes in fashion."

The girl glowered at him as she found her feet. She huffed and she grumbled, but she gave him the name of her mercer.

The chamberer returned. He shot a repressive glare at the maidens as he beckoned Stephen forward. The others fell in behind as he walked erectly up the gallery, glancing neither right nor left. They turned a corner into an older part of the building where the ceiling was lower and the floor changed levels every few yards for no apparent purpose. Here courtiers stood in nooks and recesses, conversing in tight whispers. Eyes darted suspiciously at them as they passed.

They arrived, finally, at a wide recess backed by a narrow slit of a window. A young woman with burnished hair and flashing dark eyes perched upon an invisible seat, her skirts spread wide around her.

Stella!

The chamberer bowed to her and vanished. Lady Rich's overgown was black taffeta embroidered with gold thread. A string of gold beads outlined a deep slash in her voluminous sleeves, which revealed a lining of gold and white floral-figured silk. Her ruff was as wide as the chamberer's, trimmed with inches of delicate lace. She was exquisite. Her features were fine; her brow clear and high. Her mouth was round and slightly tensed, as though she were preparing to tell you something that she knew you would not like to hear.

Stephen performed a full court bow, sweeping off his hat, extending his pointed toe, and touching his forehead to his knee. The others followed suit.

"Lord Stephen." The lady's voice was mellifluous, like honeyed wine from the sun-drenched Canaries. "Have we met?"

"No, my lady." Stephen stood to face her, peer to peer. His father outranked her husband after all. Never mind that his father was a religious zealot who never left Dorsetshire and her brother was the rising favorite of the queen. "May I say that I have long desired to meet the renowned and magnificent Stella of the sonnets? And now that I have, I understand the vain impostance of mere words. The futility—" He stopped abruptly, clamping his lips together in a pained grimace.

Lady Rich made a small humming sound, like a soft coo. Tom kept his face pressed to his knee, although he could feel the blood draining into his head and was finding it difficult to breathe. He waited until he saw Trumpet right himself before straightening. As he stepped discreetly to one side of the recess, Lady Rich scanned him up and down with a look so hot it lit a fuse of alarm that raced up his spine and exploded in his brain.

He had come expecting a dove and had encountered a tigress.

He could feel his ears pressing back into his skull and struggled to maintain his calm. He flicked a glance at Trumpet, whose down-turned face was almost covered by the feather in his hat. Stephen seemed bedazzled, swaying slightly from side to side. Ben stood as stiff as a statue, his cheeks as red as oxblood.

The lady seemed pleased by their responses. "I was intrigued by the message my steward received from your tutor. What question could inspire him to such reckless subterfuge?"

Reckless subterfuge? Hadn't Bacon just written her a note in the usual fashion? There were definitely things he wasn't telling his assistants about this Smythson business.

The lady was waiting for an answer. Tom poked Stephen in the ribs then snapped back into his impassive pose.

Stephen inhaled sharply. "Reckless, yes, thank you, my lady. I wonder too, my lady. But first, I pray you'll accept a small token—" He snapped his fingers several times. Tom handed him the fan.

Lady Rich unwrapped it, passing the gauze to the gentlewoman who stood beside her. This woman was dressed in dark gray with a plain collar and cuffs. She stood with her hands folded at her waist and had the abstracted air of a person who does not speak a single word of English.

"A fan." Lady Rich twitched her lips. "It's a routine gift, but perhaps Marguerite will like it." She passed it to her waiting woman without a glance at either woman or fan. Tom felt a pang: half a sovereign gone, with so little result.

"And now your question." It was a command.

"Yes, my lady," Stephen said. "We are assisting Mr. Bacon in his investigation of the death of Barrister Smythson. Perhaps you —"

"The lawyer? The one that died on Queen's Day?" She sounded affronted, as if Smythson had deliberately spoiled her holiday. "No one could talk of anything else for the whole evening. It was boring."

"Yes, my lady," Stephen said. "Excruciatingly boring. I myself can scarcely bear to speak of it."

"What have lawyers to do with me?" She said the word *lawyers* as one might speak of vermin that had died in one's servants' quarters.

"Yes, my lady. I mean nothing, of course. I mean, of course, nothing. To do with you. The idea is unthinkable. I have no interest in lawyers either. Who would? One spends the obligatory year at an Inn of Court, for the polish, you know. A smattering of this and that. My father thinks it wise. Your own brother — well. Naturally, I far prefer hunting and dancing, the theater and, er—"

He broke off and flashed a glance at his friends for support. Trumpet's feather bobbed as the boy stared straight down at his feet. Ben made a gurgling noise deep in his throat.

Tom took a step forward and bowed again from the waist. He tilted his face toward Lady Rich in a pose more complex than anything his dancing master had ever inflicted on him and said, "My lady, we are informed that you were having a portrait painted that day, in a chamber near the fateful spot."

"In the morning. I attended the tournament in the afternoon."

"Yes, my lady. We were so fortunate as to glimpse you sitting in the gallery with the queen." She closed her eyes in a slow blink, accepting the tribute.

Tom righted himself and strove to breathe normally. "Yes, my lady. Your limner remained in the chamber. I later saw her at the window. We would like to speak with her, if we can find her."

"My *limner?* This was worth risking the queen's wrath?" Her interest in their visit was extinguished like a candle flame in a gust of wind.

"Yes, my lady. Or, well, no, I don't know about the wrath. But I beg you, my gracious lady, would you be so kind as to tell us her name?"

Her eyes went flat. "Why would I want to know that?"

* * *

They had almost regained the top of the stairs and a clear shot to fresh air and freedom when Lady Rich's waiting woman caught up with them. She spoke in rapid French, which Trumpet, astonishingly, seemed to understand. The boy listened with an ear cocked, face averted, as if concentrating on catching every syllable. The others could do nothing but stand and wait. Tom and Stephen had had French lessons in Lord Dorchester's household, but their skills were no match for a fluent speaker. Law French sounded like English tied in knots and hung upside down in a high wind. Real French was altogether different.

When the woman left, Trumpet translated. "She said, let's see: 'My mistress says to tell your master she also can be indirect. Of course she knows the name of the limner she sat with for so many weeks. She is a Fleming, a widow, called Clara Goossens.'"

She pronounced it the way the Frenchwoman had: *Clahrah Goozenz.* It sounded foreign, smooth, like clean pebbles in the mouth. Trumpet chuckled. "She didn't seem to know we were here about the murder. She added, 'Her fees are very reasonable, but he should make haste because the limner will certainly raise them when my mistress's portrait becomes admired.'"

THIRTEEN

They found their way out of the gallery and back to the courtyard without any further mishaps with important personages. Ben breathed a sigh of relief. "So that was the famous Stella."

Trumpet said, "What do you think of your goddess now that you've seen her up close?"

"She's magnificent," Stephen said, but he didn't sound convinced.

"She's terrifying," Tom said. "She raised the hair on the back of my neck just by looking at me. And Captain Ralegh didn't even remember us." Trumpet offered him a sympathetic pout.

Ben clapped Stephen on the shoulder. "If they're all like that, my lord, your father may have the right idea about court."

They walked through the gateway and stepped into an impromptu parade. Term had ended. The law courts at Westminster were closed for the Christmas vacation. It was time for the men of the law to play.

Church bells clanged, filling the air with joyous noise. The street before them thronged with lawyers: students throwing their flat caps in the air; barristers in black robes, kicking up their heels to display parti-colored stockings; serjeants in gowns tufted with silk and velvet. They formed a veritable river of lawyers, like a school of trout heading for the sea. The lads laughed at a trio of portly judges dressed in ankle-length gowns of murrey with snug white coifs tied under their chins. They'd linked arms and were pacing a stately *cinque pas* down the center of the street.

"Hey ho!" Tom shouted, throwing his cap in the air. "We're free!"

Five full weeks until the start of Hilary Term. Five glorious weeks of Christmastide in London, during which all students were obliged by the rules of Gray's Inn to remain in commons with nothing to do but amuse themselves. The lads joined the stream heading north, past Charing Cross and onto the Strand. The crowd thinned as members of the legal community filtered into taverns along the way. Tom and his friends took the shortcut across the fields.

The queue into the hall for dinner was longer and rowdier than usual since men who usually dined in their London homes had come to celebrate the end of term. The lads worked their way to their usual seats at the top of the second table.

Tom flapped his napkin open and eyed the expanse of pristine linen. He sniffed the air. Even a whiff of food would be welcome. He wondered what the cooks would give them for the end-of-term feast. Saturday was a fish day, but even so, there might be venison or beaver. Although in truth, he could eat his own weight in stockfish today. Talking to famous ladies was hungry work. "I'm ravenous."

"Me too," Stephen said. He pinched a morsel from the loaf of bread set in the center of his plate.

"Best pace yourselves," Ben said. "There's bound to be lots of announcements today."

"What's to announce?" Tom asked. "Term is over."

Ben started to answer, but Treasurer Fogg stood up from the center of the bencher's table and raised his hands for silence. The murmuring ceased at once. Everyone was eager to get past the prologue and on to the meat.

The treasurer smiled down at them. "Welcome, Gentlemen, members of the Society of Gray's Inn, the largest and most illustrious of our Inns of Court!"

Cheering and applause.

"I promise to be brief."

He broke his promise. He began at the beginning, reminding them of the origins of the Inn. He rehashed famous cases and sketched the biographies of prominent members. Tom could feel the strength drain from his body, sapping his attention. Soon all he could hear was the growling of his own belly.

The hall grew noisy as men shifted on benches and shuffled their feet in the rushes on the floor. Fingernails tapped on wooden plates, coughs rose up in one corner and traveled across the hall. Tom could see servers peeking impatiently around the screen. A group of students under the south windows were tossing wisps of rushes at one another in open warfare. Trumpet slumped on his bench with his eyes glazed as if under a spell. Stephen finished his loaf and started stealing pinches from Tom's. Tom slapped his hand and moved his loaf to the far side of his plate.

"Gentlemen, please!" Treasurer Fogg bellowed. "Two last announcements and then the feast may begin."

"Thank God," Ben muttered. Tom grinned. Ben normally had a boundless appetite for words.

"First," Fogg said, "as you know, we benchers have the sorrowful duty of naming a Reader to take the place of the lately departed Tobias Smythson. May God rest his soul in peace."

An echoing murmur arose from the tables.

"After due consideration, we have determined that the next Lent Reader will be Mr. James Shiveley." A tall, long-limbed, red-headed man stood and made a bow.

Tom lifted his hands, ready to applaud, when cries arose from the ancients' table.

"What?"

"Not so!"

"Unfair, unfair!"

Two senior barristers sprang to their feet, waving their hands, remonstrating. Others remained seated but raised their voices toward the benchers' table on the dais. Francis Bacon looked as though he'd been slapped.

Tom leaned across the table toward Ben. "What's wrong? Don't they like Mr. Shiveley?"

Ben shrugged. "I was expecting them to name Mr. Bacon. I think he was too."

One of the ancients slapped his palm on the table and shouted, "No, sir! I must protest!"

Trumpet flinched. "My uncle thinks he should have been next. He's talked of nothing else all week."

Mr. Humphries lumbered to his feet. "If I may speak, Mr. Treasurer, I would like to point out that I myself am senior to all of these men and that, unlike some I might name, I have never failed of continuance in commons."

"Only because you can't afford to eat elsewhere," someone sneered.

Humphries flushed and sputtered, struggling for a retort.

"You should be content that we chose any of you ancients," Treasurer Fogg said. "Were we not shorthanded, we would more properly nominate a bencher for the Lent Reading."

"One named Avery Fogg, I suppose." Nathaniel Welbeck rose from his seat.

More cries of protest broke out. Even Bacon leaned forward, gesturing with a long, pale hand to emphasize a point that couldn't be heard over the cacophony of voices. Fogg stepped down from the dais to shake his finger in Welbeck's empurpled face.

Trumpet groaned and lowered his forehead to his empty plate. "We'll never get any food."

"I don't understand why they're so upset," Tom said. "What's so important about being a Reader?"

"It's essential," Trumpet said, sitting up again. "It's the next-to-last step on the climb to a judgeship."

Ben said, "Here's how it works. We're students, yes?" The others nodded. "Six years after we enroll, we are eligible to pass the bar, subject to the approval of the bench. Five years after that, if we behave ourselves, we are allowed to argue cases in the Westminster courts."

"Eleven years!" Tom was horrified. "We'll be old men!" He'd expected to become a barrister in two or three years. Five, at the outside. As long as he lived at Gray's, he had the right to wear the robes that proclaimed him a member of an Inn of Court: undeniably a gentleman. But someday he would surely want to live somewhere else. If he were a barrister, his status would be assured. If he weren't, who would he be?

Ben grinned at his dismay but mistook the cause. His worries were the opposite of Tom's: he had breeding but no money. "It's not that bad. We can write wills, advise about investments, counsel persons considering a suit at law. A man can earn a handsome living without ever passing the bar. At any rate, once you pass, you're eligible to Read. But then you have to wait your turn."

"Readership is a bottleneck," Trumpet said. "That's why there's so much contention. They can call a dozen men to the bar at once, but only two can Read in a year."

"Luckily," Ben said, "not everyone wants to Read. A man can do very well managing the legal affairs of his own county or maintaining a London practice. But you have to Read if you want to be a bencher at your Inn, and you have to be a bencher if you want to be a judge."

"And then you have to wear one of those idiotic little coifs," Tom said, startling a blurt of laughter from Stephen. "Did you see those three this morning?" They hummed a galliard, mimicking the dancing judges with their fingers on the tabletop.

The fracas at the ancients' table was winding down. Bacon had settled once again into his habitual slouch and was picking discreetly at his bread. Treasurer Fogg returned to the dais and raised his arms, gesturing for silence. "I thank you for your patience, Gentlemen, and beg you to forbear a minute longer while we turn to a happier theme. We must elect a leader for the season that is now upon us."

Tom groaned. "Can't we eat first?"

Fogg donned an impish smile that sat unnaturally on his stout cheeks. "Christmastide is here. We need revels; we need dancing; we need gaiety. We need a leader to guide us toward those timeless ends. In short, we need a Prince of Purpoole!"

Cheers shook the roof beams as caps flew into the air. This was the real signal for the end of term: the election of a Court of Misrule to devise the festivities that would occupy the Society until Lent.

"Have we any nominations?" Fogg cried.

Ben leapt to his feet. "We have, Mr. Treasurer. None better. One of our newest members is the scion of one of our oldest families: Lord Stephen Delabere, son and heir of the seventh Earl of Dorchester."

Tom and Trumpet pounded cupped palms together. A howl of disappointment sounded from one of the other tables, but Stephen was the ranking member of the new students. There really was no contest.

Treasurer Fogg bowed low, extending a surprisingly well-formed leg. "My Prince, I salute you. May we be informed of the composition of your court tonight at supper?"

Stephen stood and granted him a regal nod. "You may be so informed after dinner, Mr. Treasurer. *If* we ever get to eat."

Laughter ensued. Servers, who must have been faint with the postponement of their own dinner, dashed out from behind the screen with jugs and platters and trays before Treasurer Fogg could once again open his mouth.

* * *

The boys conferred as they devoured courses of stuffed mackerel, salad, spinach flan, and almond leech. By the time the cloths were withdrawn, they were ready.

Stephen walked up to the dais and spoke quietly for a moment with the benchers. They nodded at him and settled themselves comfortably with cups of wine. He stood with admirable poise in front of the whole assembly. "Esteemed members of Gray's Inn: I am honored to be elected as your prince. I promise that I will serve you to the utmost of my abilities."

Cheers and cries of "Long live the Prince!" followed.

"Now I will announce my court. First, I am informed that I must select a member of the bench as my Counselor in Chief. Since provisionary benchers are allowed, I appoint Mr. Francis Bacon as my Mr. of Revels."

That startled a laugh from Bacon, who had apparently only been half listening. For a moment, he looked like a boy, still a student with a taste for fun. Tom liked him for it.

"Next, I must have a Lord Treasurer, a man who can be trusted to manage the enormous sums of money needed to make my reign memorable. I name Benjamin Whitt to hold my princedom's monies, for that he himself have none."

Cries of sympathy mixed with the laughter as Ben rose to stand beside his prince.

"Since we are under constant threat of invasion and affront from members of those outposts of villainy, Lincoln's Inn and the Middle Temple—"

Boos and hisses rose from the audience as the names of their rival Inns of Court were mentioned. The Inner Temple was, by long tradition, an ally of Gray's.

Stephen held up his hands for silence. "We require a bold and intimidating Captain of the Guard. I name Allen Trumpington to be my shield of strength, for that he himself have none."

Trumpet bounded up to the dais and paced back and forth, glaring fiercely at the ancients. Tom laughed out loud. It was like appointing a kitten to guard the bears.

"Last and least," Stephen said. "In these perilous times, a wise ruler retains a minister to warn him of machinations at home and abroad. I name Thomas Clarady to be my Master of Intelligences, for that —" He stopped and gave the audience a meaningful look.

As one, the Society chorused "He himself have none!"

Stephen made a clowning face at Tom, who was well pleased with his post. Everyone knew that the real Master Intelligencer, Sir Francis Walsingham, had over and again saved England from those milk-livered, pox-marked Catholic conspirators. The position was one of the most important in the kingdom.

Stephen raised his arms high and shouted, "Let the revels begin!" He waved a hand at the minstrel gallery over the screen and music filled the hall.

FOURTEEN

Night settled into the corners of an alehouse by the docks in Vlissingen. The alewife threw a handful of sticks on the fire, the only light in the low-ceilinged room. Flickering shadows improved the scene, masking the smoky grime that smeared the long table and highlighting the dingy white of the alewife's partlet. Rough straw covered the floor and rougher men sprawled across the benches.

Caspar von Ruppa waved his mug. The alewife shook her head at him. "No more for you. Food first."

"I'll drink my supper, woman." He pounded his mug on the table, startling his companion out of slumber with a wet snort. He'd dropped his head to his arms after only three mugs. Caspar had kept on drinking.

What else was there to do while they waited for the wind to change? A job in England was all very well, but they didn't get paid until they started work and they couldn't start work until they got to the estate and they couldn't get to the bloody estate until the wind shifted to the bloody east so they could get across the bloody French Ocean to Ramsgate and up the bloody Thames.

"More!" Caspar pounded his mug on the table again. The alewife shrugged her fat shoulders and obliged him. His gaze followed her broad backside as she swung her hips to avoid the groping hands of another customer.

The alehouse door swung open, letting in a cold draft. Wind from the west: it stank of frustration. A man clothed from head to toe in plush black velvet ducked under the lintel and stood blinking in the firelight. He scanned the room, upper lip twisted in disgust. Caspar had stopped noticing the smell of the place hours ago.

The man's gaze fell on Caspar, studying him, head tilted to one side. "Caspar von Ruppa? The stone carver?"

"Who says I am?" The man was dressed like a wealthy Dutch burgher, but he spoke with the lisping accent of a Spaniard. The sound burned Caspar's ears, but he would listen nevertheless. He might have a job to offer that didn't depend on the godforsaken wind.

The man smiled, a thin smile under a thin moustache. "Your apprentices, down by the ship, told me to look for a man 'the size and color of a block of limestone, but with a broken nose.' An apt description."

Caspar frowned and scratched his short gray beard. He'd give the cheeky bastards the back of his hand when he was done drinking. "What do you want?"

"To make a proposition. Care for a walk?"

"I'd rather drink."

"My proposition is not for everyone to hear."

Caspar drained his draft in four noisy gulps. He slapped the empty mug on the table and belched open-mouthed. The Spaniard closed his eyes as if pained. He was probably used to courtly Spanish manners. He must have quite a proposition to bring him down to the docks. Maybe he had lots of silver *reales* to go with it.

Caspar stood for the first time in hours. He wobbled on his stiff knee, grunting, and supported himself with a heavy hand pressed hard against his snoring companion's back. He got his weight balanced over his two feet and shook his knee out.

The Spaniard gestured at the door with a mocking bow. Caspar squared his shoulders and strode carefully across the room. They walked out into a brackish breeze. It reeked of fish and dockside refuse and yet was fresher than the fusty air inside the alehouse. The chill slapped Caspar's cheeks, sobering him up. Now he'd have to start again from scratch.

The Spaniard pulled a handkerchief from his pocket and held it to his nose. Caspar caught a whiff of lavender and sneered. Stinks never bothered him.

"I hear you're a man who likes money," the Spaniard said.

"Are there men who don't?"

The Spaniard ignored the question. "You did a favor for my colleague last year, carrying some items into England for him along with your tools."

"Ah, that kind of proposition," Caspar said. Now he understood. He would bet half his pay that the Spaniard wore a silver cross under that fancy ruff and had a rosary hidden inside those well-padded trunk hose. "What do you want me to carry this time?"

The Spaniard smiled. "Only a few sheets of paper."

"Paper with words on it, I'll wager."

Well-dressed Spaniards who recruited in alehouses were unlikely to be smuggling lace. Those sheets of paper were probably religious pamphlets, illegal in England and dangerous to transport.

The Spaniard shrugged, one of those Latin shrugs that carried a whole conversation. "We wouldn't need you to deliver sheets of blank paper." He stopped abruptly and gripped Caspar's arm with fingers like iron cables. "These papers are important. You must understand that. They must be delivered on time. They are vital to the future of Europe."

"So important as that?" Caspar doubted these papers were anything more than the usual nonsense, but Catholics loved conspiracies. Everything they did was a matter of eternal life or death. Why anyone would care about someone else's afterlife was a mystery to him.

The Spaniard's dark eyes glittered in the moonlight. "The English have strayed from the path of God. Like errant sheep, they must be brought back into the fold. They've even forgotten how to worship. These pamphlets will teach them, remind them. They are holy lessons to guide them back to the truth."

Caspar said nothing. He remembered the lesson the Spanish had taught the good citizens of Antwerp ten years ago. They called it the Spanish Fury: three days of horror while raging *tercios* sacked the city. Seven thousand Flemish Protestants had learned their lesson that week. Had they gone to heaven or to hell? The English should be grateful to be receiving papers instead of soldiers. Maybe they would be better pupils. He didn't care, as long as he got paid.

They reached the ship that would carry Caspar, his apprentices, and his tools to London, where they would transfer to a boat going upriver. Caspar was looking forward to a few days in the English capitol, mainly for the beer, but also for a personal errand. A friend had caught a glimpse of his wife on the street there recently. Dear little Clara: she'd run away from him. He wanted her back. Perhaps he would teach his errant sheep a little lesson.

The Spaniard snapped his fingers and a man materialized from the shadows rolling a cart, followed by another with a torch. On the cart were six square bundles wrapped in hemp and tied with coarse twine. The carter untied one of the bundles to reveal a block of arebescato marble that shone like captured moonlight.

Caspar's heart beat faster at the sight. He loved fine stone. He often gave himself up to drink between jobs, but when he was working, he was one of the finest stone carvers in the Low Countries. No one sculpted a more regal lion, and his gryphons were prized from Rouen to York.

"This is the first half of your payment," the Spaniard said. "The second half will be paid in silver, on delivery."

Caspar nodded. Those small blocks of Italian marble were worth a year's wages. With them, he could carve a pair of fireplace piers that would so dazzle their patron he'd pay double without so much as a blink. He started conjuring figures worthy of such stone.

"Where do I take these stacks of important papers?"

"Do you know a place west of London by the name of Gray's Inn?"

FIFTEEN

Rain spattered against the windowpanes. Francis Bacon held the letter he was reading toward the window to try to catch more of the dim light. His brother's crabbed and much-abbreviated script was difficult enough in full sun; he'd go blind trying to decipher it under these conditions. His servant, Pinnock, knelt beside the hearth, stirring the embers under a fresh-laid faggot.

Francis felt restless. He needed a walk, weather notwithstanding. He wouldn't mind a roaring blaze maintained at someone else's expense and a hot cup of hippocras. It was only ten of the clock. Perhaps he could kill two birds with one stone. More, if his shot was lucky.

He spoke to the boy. "Don't build up the fire on my account."

"Sir?"

"I'm going out."

"*In this?*" Pinnock's voice squeaked with incredulity.

Francis wrapped himself in a thick cloak and hood and tramped the short distance to Holborn. The Antelope Inn was a hollow rectangle, three stories tall, longer than it was wide. On a dark day such as this, the walls glowed whitely. Yellow firelight danced in the diamond panes of the windows fronting the tavern, enticing to a man with raindrops speckling his lashes.

The painted sign creaked over the arched entrance to the courtyard. Rain cackled on the gravel, which looked as if it had been churned up by a tournament. The place seemed desolate in spite of the fire-lit windows. Most of the guests — spillover from the Inns of Court — had moved out that morning, going home to their families for the mesne vacation.

All to the good. Francis wanted a quiet chat with the proprietress.

He pushed through the door into the tavern and felt instantly suffused with warmth. He noted the confined space, with all the doors and windows closed and the roaring fire generating heat. One of the things he often pondered, in between other thoughts, was the exact nature of the Form of Heat. Air was not warm in and of itself, unlike fire or the rays of the sun. Out of doors, exposed to the exhalations of the earth and other influences, air was variable, impossible to examine. In a confined space, however, one might control the experiment. He had thought of using air captured in earthen jugs. But perhaps Mrs. Sprye would lend him her taproom for an afternoon of philosophical inquiry?

He half turned to go out again to revisit the contrast between the unfettered air, which was cold and wet, and the cloistered air within, which was warm and dry. But then he realized that Mrs. Sprye had noticed him and was even now rising to greet him.

He froze where he stood, torn between the desire to investigate and the fear of seeming foolish.

"Mr. Bacon? Are you coming or going?" Mrs. Sprye walked toward him. She wore a fitted gown of red worsted over a dark pink kirtle banded in black. Her brown hair was tucked into a netted caul, topped by a stiff linen cap. A partlet of lawn veiled her ample décolletage. Her hands were lifted in welcome.

The matter was decided.

Francis smiled, offering no explanation in answer to her raised eyebrows. He knew she wouldn't press. He had always liked her for that. He scanned the room, hoping no one less forbearant had seen him dithering on the threshold. Luckily, it was nearly empty. Two men sat by the inner wall reviewing a long rolled document. The barmaid perched on a stool behind the counter at the back, polishing pewter cups. Mrs. Sprye had been sitting alone at her accustomed table in the far corner, writing.

"Dolly, come take Mr. Bacon's cloak."

The maid hopped off her stool and hurried forward to accept the weight of wet wool as Francis shrugged it off his shoulders. She hung it in the nook behind the fireplace to dry.

"Thank you," Francis said. She giggled at him.

"Stop that giggling, you silly girl," Mrs. Sprye scolded. "Mr. Bacon doesn't care for such foolishness."

"I don't mind," he said. Dolly giggled again.

"You'll want something hot, I'll wager. Dolly, let's have a nice cup of mulled wine for Mr. Bacon. Quick, now! And one for me too, while you're about it."

"Yes, Madam." Dolly bobbed a curtsy and scurried through a door behind the counter.

"Come sit beside the fire," Mrs. Sprye said. "I'm astonished you trudged all the way here on such a foul morning. I would have expected every lawyer in London to be sleeping the day away today."

Francis sighed the sigh of a man with many burdens. "Alas, there is always work."

"And how is your brother Anthony?"

Francis drew in a sharp breath. Mrs. Sprye knew more than she ought about Anthony's intelligence work in France and about his own role in editing and decrypting his brother's letters. Anthony was ostensibly stranded in southern France by his fickle health, but his covert brief was to observe and analyze the political situation. He was well connected and friendly with both Protestants and Catholics. He sent relatively transparent reports directly to the Earl of Leicester and Secretary of State Walsingham.

He sent the more sensitive details to his brother to interpret and transmit appropriately. Francis's work was unpaid, unthanked, and now made more difficult by his recent gaffe at court.

Lady Bacon must have been indiscreet with the Andromache Society. Francis bit his lip and met Mrs. Sprye's gaze with a level look that asked her not to probe. "Well enough. He loves Montaubon. He may never come home."

She smiled to show her understanding of the unspoken request then clucked her tongue like a simple gossip. "He will if your mother has anything to say about it."

Francis shrugged. They both knew that the power of maternal influence attenuated over long distances.

He waited until his hostess had seated herself and then chose a stool that placed his back at an oblique angle to the fire. He would be warm, but not overflushed.

Dolly returned with her fixings on a tray. She set her long-handled pipkin at the edge of the fire and began to mix spices, honey, and slices of fruit. Francis inhaled the scents of cinnamon, anise, and warming claret and sighed again, contentedly. This was what he'd wanted.

While they waited for their drinks, Francis and Mrs. Sprye chatted about gardening, a diversion they both enjoyed. They were not especially close friends, but they had known each other since Francis had first come to Gray's. Each had taken the measure of the other, adding it up to mutual liking augmented by mutual respect. Francis found Mrs. Sprye to be a more comfortable co-conversant than most women he knew. She accepted him as he was rather than regarding him as a block of clay to be molded or a pear tree to be trained against a wall.

When the wine was hot, Dolly filled two pewter goblets, served them, and took her tray back to the kitchen. Francis blew across the top of his drink to cool it. He hated to burn his tongue. He caught Mrs. Sprye's expression of patient expectation. The time had come.

"I have a question for you," he said. "Perhaps two."

"I thought you might. Your boy is perfectly capable of making hippocras."

"Not as good as yours."

She accepted the compliment with a tilt of her head.

"I've been tasked with examining the circumstances of Tobias Smythson's death."

"By your uncle, I presume."

Francis merely raised his eyebrows.

"I thought poor Toby was murdered by a cutpurse."

"The question remains open. My uncle's concern is that some of Smythson's less public activities might have been a factor."

"That his spying got him killed, you mean," Mrs. Sprye had little patience for the circumlocutions of political discourse.

"Yes." Since he could be direct as well, Francis added, "He should not have told you about that."

"He asked me to watch my guests for covert activities and keep him informed. Informed! As if I would allow Jesuits to hide under my beds or secret masses to be chanted in my rooms! Do you think I want my queen murdered by popish scalamanders?" Indignation glowed in her cheeks.

"Did Smythson uncover any such activities at Gray's?"

"I think he did, but he wouldn't tell me what. Or, more importantly, who." Her hazel eyes sparkled. "I like to think he was concerned for my safety, but it's more likely that he feared censure from Lord Burghley for lack of discretion."

Francis let his admiration for both the insight and the sparkle show. "I'm sure concern for you played the larger role."

"Now you're flattering me, which means you haven't yet learned what you came to ask."

116

He nodded, hesitated, and took another sip of wine. "In all honesty, I don't know how to begin."

Her laughter rose in a musical trill. "Ah, Mr. Bacon! If that's the case, I think I can guess your question. You're wondering about the nature of my friendship with Tobias."

"I am, Mrs. Sprye. And thank you."

She sighed and chafed her cup between her palms. "Let us say that Tobias discovered in himself an attraction to some of my less tangible attributes."

That was opaque yet candid. Francis admired her verbal agility. She knew, in other words, that Smythson was seeking influence rather than romance.

He pretended to study her, like a man appraising a work of art. "Yet the tangible attributes are so appealing. Your shining hair, for instance."

She batted her lashes at him. "My flashing eyes."

"Your Venus figure and your Athenaic wit."

Another trill of laughter. She beamed at him. "Mr. Bacon, you astonish me. Dare I imagine that I've acquired another suitor?" She snapped her fingers over her head, signaling Dolly for more wine.

"My mother would be horrified," Francis said, leaning forward confidentially.

"Not quite the demure young baroness she imagines for you."

"Not quite. But I believe you would be the superior companion." His mother persisted in urging him toward marriage, preferably noble, although even she was beginning to realize that his tastes ran more to lords than ladies. Though he wouldn't say no to a baroness with money.

Dolly returned with fresh supplies to make another round of drinks. Dogging her footsteps with a scowl darkening his brow was Treasurer Avery Fogg.

"What's going on here?" He stood before the table, dominating it with his bulk, his fists planted on his hips.

He glared down at Francis. "What do you think you're up to?"

Francis blanched. He loathed physical confrontations. Fortunately, he was not undefended.

Mrs. Sprye swatted at Fogg's arm as if batting away an intrusive but beloved dog. "Fie, Sir Avery! What do you mean by this bluster?" She tugged one of his fists away from his hip. He resisted long enough to let her feel his strength and then allowed her to capture his hand. "Am I not allowed to have a quiet conversation with an old friend?"

"Doesn't sound like a friendly conversation to me," Fogg said. "'Venus figure and Athenaic wit?' Sounds more like courtship."

He stared daggers at Francis, who tucked himself well back on his stool. That bumped him against the lush-figured Dolly where she knelt beside the fire with her pipkin. So he pulled himself up very straight and folded his hands in his lap. Then he feared that the gesture might be misconstrued as coverage and refolded them on the tabletop. Fogg watched all of this with pursed lips and narrowed eyes.

"Stop it this minute, Sir Avery," Mrs. Sprye said. "You're frightening the boy."

Francis closed his eyes to shut out the humiliation. How had he gotten himself into this situation? He'd gotten confirmation, of a sort, that someone was smuggling Catholic literature to or through Gray's, but he hadn't managed to learn who, specifically, Smythson had suspected.

At least he had learned from unbearable personal experience how easily Avery Fogg's jealous temper was inflamed.

SIXTEEN

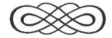

Monday morning was the first real day of vacation and Tom meant to enjoy it to the full. They'd slept until daylight — nearly eight o'clock at this time of year — although the morning was darkened by an icy drizzle. They'd even skipped chapel on Ben's assurance that the benchers would be lenient during the season of Misrule. Tom's plan was to sit by the fire until dinnertime, composing a love song for Clara.

Sunday had not been restful in the least. After breakfast, the lads had gone with the men of Gray's to the burial service for Mr. Smythson. His children arrived from somewhere and went straight away again with most of Smythson's chattels. He'd left his books to the Gray's Inn library, excepting a few gifts to special friends. He left Ben a copy of Sir John Fortescue's *De Laudibus Legum Angliae,* bound in kidskin with gilt lettering. Ben was so surprised and flattered he could scarcely set the thing aside long enough to eat.

"I never would have imagined," Ben said, over and over, until the others started singing it back to him, in harmony.

Tom was glad that his friend had received some recognition. He deserved it more than anyone. He was also, if he was honest, a shade jealous. Nobody seemed to think Tom was good at anything except being handsome, which was scarcely to his credit. He privately believed that he was a fair student when he put his mind to it. He could argue a case with conviction and dash, if the matter wasn't too abstruse and Ben had quizzed him in advance. He had an ear for languages and he wasn't too shabby at rhetoric. He had a knack for persuasion.

He wished now that he had stayed at Cambridge to take his degree. He only lacked two terms. It would have meant missing that glorious year aboard his father's ship, but he needed all the honors he could get.

They spent Sunday afternoon helping other Graysians pack up their moveables for the end-of-term migration. Barristers with no desire to become benchers left without a qualm. Many students preferred to pay the fine for being out of commons and spend the holidays at home. Some men were moving to better chambers. Fully half the Society left on Sunday. A deep silence descended.

High up on the fourth floor, with icy rain clattering against the windows, the lads' chambers felt like a secret hideaway atop a Castle Dour. The crackling fire created a pool of warmth and light. Tom sat on a low stool before the hearth, working on a song about a limner conjuring her dream lover by painting his image. He wore only the long woolen shirt that he always pulled on when he tumbled out of bed. He stretched one bare leg toward the fire, drawing up the other to support his lute. His feet sported a pair of leather slippers so soft with age they showed the imprint of each individual toe. His uncombed curls were partly covered by a densely embroidered, long-tailed cap. As the only son in a household with three sisters, two maiden aunts, a doting mother, and a one-legged boatswain, Tom's linens tended to be richly decorated.

Ben sat to the right of the fire on a low-backed chair. He was dressed in a shirt and a pair of oft-mended breeches, with a dingy shawl draped around his shoulders and a pair of woolly stockings rumpled around his ankles. He leaned forward to toast hunks of dark bread stuffed with thin slices of hard cheese. Every now and then a drip of melted cheese hissed into the fire, sending up a tangy scent. A jug of small ale warmed on the hearthstone, adding a peaty aroma.

If there was a pleasanter way to pass a rainy morning, Tom did not know what it was.

Stephen stood by the window, sipping from a pewter cup. He had managed to get into most of the parts of his costume for the day but hadn't yet troubled to tie up all the laces. He gazed down into the rainy court with a surly look on his face.

Tom strummed his lute strings and hummed his tune. "I wish I could think of a word that rhymes with limner."

Stephen looked over his shoulder. "I don't know why you bother. She's a tradeswoman. She'll either be too prim to sleep with you or she'll fall on her back for half a shilling. Either way, you won't need music."

Ben clucked his tongue but wisely stayed out of it. Tom contented himself with a glower and a curled lip.

He had shared a bed with Stephen for the better part of the past seven years and could read his moods like a ha'penny broadsheet. Stephen was grumpy because he felt thwarted by the rain. He had little tolerance for thwarting because he believed that his father's rigid rules kept him from entering his proper sphere in life. Which was true, perfectly true. His father kept him on a very short leash.

The real problem was that Stephen was too weak-willed either to confront his father or to do what he wanted and take the consequences. The earl was a hundred miles away, for the love of a generous God! If it weren't for Tom's coaxings, Stephen would never go anywhere but the draper's.

But Stephen could never admit that he relied so much on someone his family regarded as a jumped-up servant. He couldn't stand by himself; he hated having to lean on anyone; so he pouted and took his frustration out in little jabs at Tom.

"We need to get down to the hall and start planning the events of my reign," Stephen said. "You two have idled by the fire long enough."

"God's bones, Steenie," Tom said. "Haven't we earned one lazy day?"

They'd worked hard over the past week, building their case about the bastard and the heiress. Tom felt as if his wits had been taken out of his head, stretched in every direction, embroidered all over with extra bits, and then stuffed back inside his skull. He needed time to recuperate.

Stephen peered down the length of his pointed nose. "I think it's time you began to address me properly, Clarady."

Tom scoffed at him. "Can't I wait until I get my hose on, your most high and mighty lordliness?"

"Get them on, then."

Tom barked a short laugh. "I will not budge from this stool until the rain stops or I faint from starvation and fall off. *My lord.* If you want to go down, go. No one's stopping you."

They glared at each other. Tom felt an undercurrent of uncertainty. They had rarely fought, at least not openly. Their connection had been arranged by their fathers, but they'd rubbed along well enough until they separated last year at Cambridge. Tom's spirit led them into fun; Stephen's status got them out of trouble. That had always been their *modus operandi*, sharing Tom's father's money and Stephen's father's influence. A man needed both to succeed in the world. Could either manage without the other?

"If I go," Stephen said, his tone as icy as the sleet, "I'll have them throw you out. They only let you in to Gray's because of me." He wasn't talking about going down to the hall now. He meant moving out of the Inn altogether.

Tom's heart froze. Could he do it? Would he dare? Lord Dorchester would never allow Stephen to leave so soon. Would he? But whether or no: was the threat true? Would Gray's really expel him at the whim of an earl's son? Probably not, but what if Stephen told his father that Tom was leading him into sin, dicing and whoring? A vile slander, at least the part about the dicing. But if Lord Dorchester demanded his expulsion, could the benchers resist him? Why would they? He wasn't at all certain that Francis Bacon would stand up for him now that his debts had been settled.

He saw the satisfied smirk on Stephen's face and wanted to strike it off with the back of his hand. He pulled up his legs, ready to rise. Stephen backed up to the windows.

A knock sounded on the door, snapping the tension between them like a musket ball slicing through a bowline.

"Intro!" Ben called.

Trumpet slipped inside and shut the door quickly to keep in the warmth. He looked at the others with exaggerated shock. "Not dressed yet! It's nearly nine o'clock!"

Tom drew in a long breath. Crisis averted . . . for now. "I'm working on a song for Clara."

"Oh, *Clara.*" Trumpet rolled his eyes. "Let's hear it, then."

Tom played a bit of his new composition.

"Oh, limner fair, can you paint my heart,
Give color to my love for thee?
Enform my longings with your art,
And tell me how I must be?"

Trumpet winced. "Perhaps she'd like a nice fan?"

"Huh," Tom grunted. "What do you know about it?"

"More than you think."

Tom cocked an eyebrow, ready to pursue the topic of the Pygmy's putative knowledge of women. Ben interrupted to offer the boy a hunk of cheese-toast.

Trumpet shook his head. "I breakfasted in hall. My uncle wanted our new chambers to himself. He says he has work to do."

"It's vacation time!" Tom objected.

Trumpet shrugged.

"How are the new chambers?" Ben asked. He crunched into his overstuffed toast, dribbling crumbs onto the bricks.

"Warm. Blissfully warm. Our building shares a chimney with the kitchen, so we have heat day and night. *Gratis*, which Uncle Nat likes best."

Stephen said, "Trumpington, could you give me a hand with these laces? Those two haven't budged from the fire since they stumbled out of bed."

"That explains the soot on their faces." He half turned and mouthed *Trumpington?* at Tom, who moved his head in a barely visible shake.

"Were there many in hall?" Stephen asked, turning to give his new valet access to the laces that tied his doublet to his hose in back.

"Nearly a score." Trumpet's nimble fingers deftly threaded satin points and tied the ends in small bows. "Everyone wants to know what's toward. They're ready for fun and waiting for you to lead them into it."

Stephen shot a dark glance at Tom. "I have some ideas. We need music, obviously. *Real* music. And we must have some pranks." He plucked at his trunk hose to puff them out more fully as he sketched some of his thoughts on the matter.

Tom set his lute in a turned-up hat in the corner beyond the fireplace, stretched his legs forward and his arms straight over his head, yawning in a drawn-out roar.

Trumpet cowered behind Stephen, feigning terror. "A bear! Oh, horrible! Slay it, my lord!"

Stephen laughed. Good humor restored. Trumpet had a gift for managing the noble temperament. But he was far too bouncy. He was ruining Tom's lazy mood. And now that there were two fully dressed men in the room, he was beginning to feel a bit behindhand.

"I feel like a bear. I had the most appalling nightmare about escheats and torts, with old men in coifs and murrey gowns chasing me round and round the bencher's table."

Ben chuckled. "Wait until you actually have to argue a case in court. That'll tie your stomach in knots."

Tom flashed him a grateful grin. At least there was one person in the world who believed he had a future in the law. If only they could move Stephen out and Trumpet in. The boy would have to go to chapel — Ben was a stickler for the rules — but he'd get cheese and toast on Sunday mornings.

He rose and scratched his backside under the long tail of his shirt. Mumbling, "I'll dress, then," he shambled into the bedchamber.

Ben yawned too, but turned his yawn into a descending scale. Then he began to hum the tune that Tom had been plucking on his lute.

"Aha!" Tom shouted. "My tune *is* memorable!"

"Indeed it is," Ben said. "It's one of the most popular songs of our times."

"It's what?"

Stephen snickered.

Trumpet said, "It's 'Greensleeves,' you dolt. Didn't you know? I wondered why you chose a song about a prostitute as the tune for your ode *d'amour.*"

"It's not about a prostitute," Ben said. "That's a slander from the broadsides."

Tom groaned. "No wonder it was so easy to think of! Now I'll have to start from scratch."

Ben joined Tom in the bedchamber and began casting about for his clothes. Dressing was complicated with three men more or less of a size. They had endless trouble keeping their stockings sorted into matching pairs and sleeves had a life of their own.

Trumpet called from the outer chamber, "Best be quick about it. Mr. Bacon wants to speak with us."

Ben staggered around the half-open door, tying the points of a stocking to the laces on his shirt. "He does? When? Where?"

"Now. In the hall. Something about our investigations."

Tom cried with heartfelt exasperation, "Doesn't anyone understand the meaning of the word *vacation*?"

SEVENTEEN

"Let's have a beheading," Thomas Hughes suggested. "King Arthur can execute Sir Lancelot. Or Queen Guinevere."

"Absolutely not." Francis Bacon experienced a palpable shock of horror imagining the queen's reaction to such a scene. "Her Majesty would construe it as meddling in her prerogative. As a nudging toward the execution of the Queen of Scots. We must avoid that topic like a plague-bearing miasma."

He and a group of literary-minded barristers were spending the wintry morning in the hall devising a masque to amuse the court at Whitehall on Christmas Eve. Whether he was allowed to attend or not, she might divine his hand in the work and recognize it as an offering of his devotion.

"She needs a nudge," Hughes insisted. "A gentle one, of course. But the deed must be done, and soon. We can show her that her loyal subjects support the decision."

"No," Francis said. "Trust me. She'd be furious, and rightly so. The execution of a monarch is not a subject for foolery. We should stick to themes appropriate to the season and the setting. Themes celebrating our queen's beauty and wit."

"Same as last year, then," another barrister grumbled.

"Yes." Francis smiled. "Only different." He rummaged in his memory for scenes from Ovid, usually a rich source. He enjoyed the challenge of creating fresh amusements from stock materials. He especially enjoyed these collaborations with intelligent yet nonpolitical, colleagues. He could happily spend the whole day right here at this table.

A sudden draft made him shiver. He glanced toward the screens passage and saw his pupils filing in, shaking raindrops from their cloaks. They started to walk toward him, but he held up a hand and rose from his bench. Better to have this conversation in relative privacy. Since his quarry might well be a member of the Society, the fewer who were aware of his pursuit, the better.

"Surely you're not making those poor lads study during the mesne vacation, Bacon?" Hughes asked. "The Prince of Purpoole and his court?"

Francis smiled. "I am their Master of Revels, am I not? It's my job to advise them on our traditions and guide them toward sports that entertain without crossing the bounds."

He gestured his pupils closer to the fire in the center of the hall. They might as well be warm. "Were you able to speak with Lady Rich?"

"We were, Mr. Bacon," Whitt answered. "Lord Stephen posed our question to her."

The lads exchanged a round of shrugs and head shakes. Francis frowned at them. "And were you able to obtain an answer, my lord?"

Delabere looked at his feet and mumbled, "She was — she was —"

Francis relented. "I have met the Lady Rich. She has, shall we say, a forceful personality."

"Forceful," Delabere echoed, as if trying on the attribute. Francis had never met a peer for whom the word was less apt.

He waited in silence. The privateer's son cleared his throat and Delabere continued. "Her maidservant told us to tell you that she could also be indirect. The lady, that is. We didn't understand that part."

"Nor do you need to, my lord."

"Oh. Well, that's all right then. She also said — the maidservant, that is — that the limner is a Fleming by the name of Clara Goossens." Stephen expelled a breath, as if he had just completed a daring maneuver.

"Very good, my lord." Francis smiled approvingly. "And have you spoken with Limner Goossens?"

"Well, no." Delabere looked startled. "We don't know where she lives. Lady Rich didn't give us a direction. And yesterday was Sunday."

Francis sighed. "She can wait for the present. Your next task is to interview the two Wild Men that the sempstress saw in the lane. They must be retainers of the Earl of Essex."

"Today?" Delabere's countenance took on a mulish cast.

"I realize you have other demands upon your time, *Your Grace*." The honorific earned him a smile that transformed the young lord's sulky features. "However, we owe a debt to Mr. Smythson, do we not? To identify the villain who so untimely claimed his life?"

Delabere said, "I suppose we do."

"Your compassion inspires us," Francis said, ignoring the flash of disbelief in Clarady's eyes. "The next move may win the match. We can't know until it's played."

"Shall we call upon the earl?" Delabere asked.

Francis pretended to consider the question. Under no circumstances would he involve Essex until he knew what his servants had to say. "I rather think not, my lord. We don't know at this point if his men saw anything at all. I am informed that most of the earl's retainers are lodged at the White Lion on Fleet Street."

He expected them to leave at once, but Trumpington blurted out, "Mr. Bacon, if it please you."

Francis raised an eyebrow.

"Is it possible that the Wild Men murdered Mr. Smythson?"

Francis frowned. He hadn't considered that question, though he should have. He'd been so preoccupied with the tricky question of communicating with Lady Rich that he'd forgotten to fully examine the matter. If he left any avenue unexplored, however, he could be certain it would be the only one leading to a solution. He sighed. He longed to achieve that solution in time for Christmas Eve.

"Yes," he replied, sounding as vexed as he felt, "it is possible. Why were they chasing Smythson instead of attending on their lord?"

"Perhaps one of them had a grudge against lawyers," Whitt suggested. "Men have been known to lose everything in a badly fought suit."

"Or a badly brought suit," Francis said. "Too many forget that waging law is always a gamble. Yes, that's quite possible. Such a grudge, nurtured into hatred, ripened with strong drink, might well produce a frenzied attack. Either or both of them might have done the deed. Then, on recovering their right minds and seeing what they had done, they might have stolen the purses to cast the blame on a thief. And to keep the money, of course."

"That's even more horrible than a cutpurse," Clarady said. "Poor Mr. Smythson! First chivvied by drunkards in frightening costumes then killed for someone else's fault!"

His ready sympathy did him credit. The lad had qualities; if only he were better fathered. And did away with that absurd earring. Sir Walter Ralegh could get away with dangling gemstones from his head, but lesser men should content themselves with lesser displays.

Trumpington said, "What if Lady Rich paid the Wild Men to murder Mr. Smythson, to prevent him from, uh—"

"Writing a brief? Engrossing a bill?" Francis regarded the boy frostily. Doubtless this *idea clara* derived from

Welbeck's single-themed imagination. Trumpington's uncle was little better than a privateer, in some regards. "I hardly think a personage such as Lady Rich would stoop to such base instruments. Nor could she settle her disputes with Sir Amias Rolleston by dispatching his counselor. Sir Amias would simply do as he has done and engage another one."

"Won't it be dangerous to question these Wild Men?" Delabere asked. "They'll know at once that we suspect them."

Again, Francis pretended to consider the question. He doubted there would be any real danger. They were four active young men, not gouty old barristers, and they would be in a popular inn on a busy thoroughfare.

"It could be so, my lord, as you sagaciously suggest, and yet I see no alternative. As far as we know, those two were the last to see Smythson alive. The possibility that they are themselves the murderers is remote. Even if they did harbor some grudge, they would more likely content themselves with simply frightening the man."

"We should be wary, nevertheless." Delabere's chin jutted forward.

"Indeed you should, my lord," Francis agreed. "Always. Wary and respectful. Be discreet; be polite. Don't ruffle any feathers."

EIGHTEEN

The rain had stopped when the lads emerged from the hall after dinner. They repaired to their chambers briefly so Stephen and Tom could buckle on their rapiers. If they had to question murderous rogues, they'd best be prepared to defend themselves.

The White Lion Inn was a four-storied building near the Fleet Bridge. Tom told a footman that they were looking for Essex men. He pointed them toward the taproom. This was a low room paneled in smoke-darkened oak, with the choking, burnt smell of a chimney in need of cleaning. The tapster stood behind a counter, serving three men on tall stools. Four others sat around a table near the wide hearth playing Tarocchi with painted cards. They looked like they'd been whiling away the whole day in that fusty place.

The men's expressions were unwelcoming. The lads were at a disadvantage, in age and experience as well as in numbers. These men looked seasoned, battle hardened. They were dressed in red and white, the earl's colors. No doubt they'd fought beside their lord at Zutphen. They were at ease with one another, like men who had served together for many years.

They also looked bored. Tom smelled trouble, sharper than the smoke. Gathering his courage, he spoke first. "Good afternoon to you, Gentlemen."

"Good enough for some," growled one of the men at the counter. His face was heavily creased, as if a giant had stepped on him in his youth. Tom could imagine that foul-featured knave murdering someone in an alley out of pure meanness.

"Peace, Archer." One of the card players spoke with quiet authority. "I am Robert Thrush. We serve the Earl of Essex. What can we do for you boys today?"

Tom didn't much like that *boys*, but he let it pass. "We're looking for men who participated in His Lordship's pageant on Queen's Day."

"And what might you want with such men?"

"We merely wish to ask a few questions, good sirs," Ben said, holding his hands wide, palms up, to show his peaceful intentions. "About the events that occurred that afternoon in the streets below Whitehall. Perhaps you heard?"

"About the murder of that lawyer, you mean. We heard." Thrush shot a glance at his men that Tom thought held some private meaning. They knew something about that day, he'd wager good money on it.

"That's right," Ben said. "The lawyer who was killed was Tobias Smythson, our—" He abruptly changed course. "A member of our Society." Tom exhaled a breath of relief. No good would come of underscoring the fact that they were merely students. That's why they'd left their robes at home, in blatant violation of the rules.

"A member of your Society!" The rumple-faced man, Archer, jeered at them. "Don't tell me you stripling waste-goods are lawyers?"

All the men laughed, even Thrush. Tom saw Stephen's eyes narrow at the insult and his hand move toward the hilt of his rapier. Two of the card players followed the gesture with their eyes. One of them pushed his chair out from the table, feigning a need to stretch his legs. He was short and ginger-haired and younger than the others. He'd been regarding Trumpet with a mocking smirk.

Tom balanced his weight on both feet, keeping half an eye on Sir Ginger. The short ones, he knew from his association with Trumpet, were often the most volatile. He only hoped that they could get the information they needed before the brawl began.

"We are members of the legal profession, yes," Trumpet said, placing his fists on his hips.

"Even you?" Archer tilted his head, placing a finger against his chin. "Don't tell me: you work in the *lower* courts, where you argue *petty* cases and *misdemeanors* before a *puisne* judge." He shot a wink over his shoulder and his friends laughed on cue.

Trumpet bristled and stepped forward. Tom placed a hand on his shoulder and drew him back. They had a mission to complete before they gave these tickle-brained dewberries the thrashing they so plainly needed.

"We only want to ask a question or two, good sirs." Ben spoke in a mollifying tone. "A member of our Society was foully murdered. We have reason to believe that two members of your party were in the vicinity shortly before it happened. Perhaps they saw something relevant? Surely your Lord Essex, who is renowned for both his wisdom and his honor, would wish to see a killer brought to justice."

That set the man in his place. He grunted his assent.

Thrush smiled, displaying a crooked front tooth. "Naturally, we would be pleased to assist you."

Ben asked, "Were any of you among the Wild Men in the earl's pageant?"

"No," Thrush answered, too quickly. "We here were all shepherds."

"Are any of the Wild Men still in London?"

"No. Most of the pageant men have gone home."

Ben's shoulders sank. "And did they say nothing about that day before they left?"

Thrush turned on one elbow for a whispered consultation with his friends. Heads were shaken and then nodded; lips were pursed and then relaxed. Finally, a decision was reached.

One of the other men spoke up, still holding his cards flat against his chest. He was seated with his back to the fire and his plump cheeks were red as apples, even though his doublet was unhooked and gaping open over a wrinkled shirt. "The two you're thinking of are Gasper and Noke, from Crockleford near Colchester. They're not regulars; they came in to make up the numbers for the pageant." He made a sour face. "Nobody likes those Wild Man costumes, you see. They're itchy."

Ben nodded somberly, his eyes laden with sympathy for the rigors of pageantry. Tom couldn't muster sympathy for these louts at any price. Was this what all retainers did while their lord was at court? Idle the day away in stuffy taverns, hoping for some kind of trouble to rouse them out of their stupor? He would rather memorize *Bracton's Notebook* in Latin. Backwards.

"They saw something, though, didn't they?" Ben asked.

Apple-cheeks nodded. "They did; that's why they left. They feared to be involved and kept in London and then never get home for Christmas. One of them has a new baby coming, you see." He chuckled suddenly. "Didn't stop them making a tale of it before they left."

The fourth man grinned. He lowered his chin and shook his jowls, pretending to hold something up in his right hand. That was plainly a feature of the tale, because the retainers then chanted in unison, *"I've got a bone to pick with you, Counselor."*

They laughed, relishing the memory. "We all know it by heart," Thrush said. "From His Lordship on down."

Ben chuckled as though he too had enjoyed the story. "We understand there was some sort of chasing . . ."

Apple-cheeks answered, "That was Gaspar. Well, it was the both of them, but chiefly Gaspar." He shook his head and rolled his eyes. "'Twas his first pageant, you see. He hadn't thought to be kept standing for so long a time. And those Wild Man costumes are cursed uncomfortable. Horsehair sprouting all over your head and glued right onto your face; scratchy leaves and mossy bark and God knows what else tied to your chest. And all manner of whatnot draped about your neck: bones and twigs. Ugh. That's why us seasoned men would rather be shepherds; nice soft sheepskin, perhaps a garland or two . . ."

"Get on with it," Thrush said. "I'm sure these *men* of the law have other errands today."

Tom had to clamp his lips together to keep his mouth shut. He tightened his hand on Trumpet's shoulder as a precaution.

"All right," Apple-cheeks said. "Well, Gaspar and Nokes, being new and all, and nervous about the show, drank too much ale beforehand, and by the time the pageant was over, they were in a bit of a hurry. They went off in search of an office of easement but were taken short in the Privy Garden."

"In the queen's garden!" Trumpet objected.

"A shrub's a shrub, when you come down to it. The queen wasn't there, was she? So here's young Gaspar, taking a much-needed piss, and up pops this barrister from out of nowhere and starts scolding him. That's enough to nettle any man, especially one that's been standing about in an itchy costume all day. And young Gaspar has what you might call a misfortunate history with the legal profession."

Archer guffawed loudly. "Lost a third of his lands! You call that *misfortunate*? I call it criminal." The others murmured their agreement. Their expressions grew stonier.

Tom and Stephen exchanged a glance. A twitch of the eyebrow, the shadow of a nod: they were ready. They might have their differences, but they also had years of fencing practice together. They knew each other's moves better than these jolt-heads, Zutphen notwithstanding.

"So he chased the lawyer," Ben prompted.

"That he did," Apple-cheeks said. "He only meant to give the pompous fool a fright, you see, in return for the scolding. He capered about, shaking one of the bones from his costume and growling, *'I've got a bone to pick with you, Counselor.'* Getting a bit of his own back. It was meant as a joke, that's all. But the man squealed and jumped and gave such good sport that he couldn't help himself. He whistled up Nokes and they gave him a bit of a run. Harmless, they thought." He shrugged. "They were more than a little drunk."

"They must have chased him beyond the garden," Ben said. "Mr. Smythson's body was found in the alleyways to the south."

Thrush held up a hand. "That's not to their account. They didn't go back to see which one it was that died."

"Which one of who?" Ben asked.

"Which one of the lawyers." He grinned at their blank faces. "You didn't know? There were two barristers in those lanes that day."

Ben turned his head to frown at the others, who shrugged back at him. Tom was floored. He'd been expecting to hear about some hugger-mugger skulking through the precinct. Another barrister?

Things had suddenly turned much blacker.

Archer gave a coarse laugh. "Caught you with your breeches hanging, didn't we? You pettifoggers don't do much of a job keeping your own house, do you?"

"We're not petti—" Trumpet started forward, but Tom held him back. Excitement flashed across the face of Sir Ginger. He shifted in his seat to reveal a poniard.

"When did they see the second lawyer?" Ben asked.

137

The man shrugged again. "They weren't marking the minutes. Gaspar said he nearly ran into the other man, he was limping along so slowly. Something wrong with his foot, seemingly. Well, he knew at once it was a different fellow, but he cried 'Boo!' anyway. This one wasn't up for a game. He only smiled and said, 'Go along, then, my good fellow. Find someone with two sound legs to play with you.' So Gaspar left him alone. He says he saw the squealie one again and gave him a growl and a shake for good measure. Then he and Nokes went back to the tiltyard. It was only later that they heard what happened."

Tom said, "The limping one must have been Smythson. Then who was the other?"

Ben asked, "Did they mention anything, any detail, about the other lawyer?"

"Nothing special."

"Tall? Thin? Short? Fat?" Ben prompted, not hopefully.

Apple-cheeks shook his head. "Gaspar knew the two men were barristers by their gowns, that's all."

Ben nodded. "Well, it's more than we knew before. We thank you good gentlemen for your trouble." He bowed shortly. Tom followed suit, but Stephen and Trumpet stood fast with their hands on their weapons.

Apple-cheeks acknowledged the thanks with a tilt of his head. Thrush flicked a glance at Sir Ginger and the fourth man, who was quietly edging himself clear of the table. He smiled broadly at Ben. "Is there anything else we can do for you boys?"

"No, sir. I thank you. You have been most courteous." Ben said. He turned to the others. "Shall we be off, then, Gentlemen?" He slightly emphasized the honorific.

Sir Ginger drew in his legs so that his feet were squarely planted on the floor. He held up a beringed finger. "There is one small favor you lads might do for me."

Here it comes.

138

Ben, the ever courteous, felt obliged to respond. "We are at your service."

"You might give yon infant a good washing." He jerked his chin at Trumpet. "Something nasty seems to be sprouting above its wee lip."

His companions' laughter was interrupted by a scream of fury as Trumpet launched himself, full out, at Sir Ginger. Tom, who had been expecting some such move, caught the boy by the waist and hauled him bodily back.

Stephen took a step toward Sir Ginger. He made a sweeping gesture with his index finger over his upper lip. "We never mention the moustache, *Signor Buffone.*"

"Do you mock us, Minnow?" The fourth man slapped his cards on the table.

"Perhaps you'd like us to do the washing?" Sir Ginger man rose and faced Stephen, drawing his poniard from its sheath.

Steel sang as Stephen whipped his rapier from its hanger. Oaken chairs thudded to the floor as the Essex men leapt up, snatching their daggers into their hands. Tom thrust Trumpet toward the door, drew his sword, and took his position at Stephen's side. Stephen assumed the guarde of prime. Tom took the guarde of tierce. They grinned at one another. At last, an opportunity to prove their skills in the real world.

Ben tried to obstruct Trumpet, but the boy twisted away from him. He screamed, "I'll shave you bald-headed, you spur-galled gudgeon," and lunged again at the ginger man.

Men shouted. Steel clashed on steel. A shot exploded. Tom leapt aside as a ball of lead cracked through the floor at his feet.

The tapster held a smoking pistol in one hand and a cocked one ready in the other. "Not in my house! You'll take yourselves outside or the next bullet goes into a man's leg!"

Ben and the one called Thrush made pacifying gestures, mouthing words which went unheard. Tom pushed Trumpet toward Ben, who gripped the back of his jerkin and dragged him out the door. Stephen followed them slowly, walking backward, sword raised, eyes clapped on Archer's sneering face.

Tom was last. He watched his friends exit safely. Then he saw the fourth man struggling to rise from his bench behind the table and couldn't resist the temptation.

"Please, allow me to assist you." He grabbed the end of the bench and raised it high. The man sprawled into the rushes with a howl of rage.

"Ay me!" Tom clapped a hand to his cheek in mock dismay and dashed out the door. "Run!" he bellowed at his friends.

They dodged past a cart and a coach and a pair of donkeys loaded with sacks to the other side of Fleet Street.

Tom heard a shout from the tavern. "After them!"

Four of Essex's men dashed across the street, waving their weapons and shaking their fists.

The lads pelted down Water Lane. They'd be trapped at the river's edge, if they didn't look sharp. Tom shouted, "This way!" and led them into a maze of alleys.

He and Stephen sprinted ahead of Ben and Trumpet, trying to scout the route ahead. They rounded a curve, then another, and found themselves bump up behind the Essex men. They'd outrun the older, drunker retainers, coming around full circle.

"Ho, there!" Tom shouted. "You knotty-pated pumpions! You shaggy, mange-raddled curs!"

"If it's barbering you want, come get it!" Stephen cried. "We'll trim those shrubby excrescences from your poxy chins!"

Two of the Essex men roared and turned, drawing their swords. Steel clashed as the four men came together.

Tom felt power coursing through his veins. Fencing in the classroom was all very well, but this: this was glory.

He thrust with his rapier and parried with his dagger, giving as good as he got. He twisted to avoid his opponent's blade, bounded in to thwack him soundly on the leg, then leapt away again before the varlet could riposte. These men weren't mature: they were overripe. Youth was faster and sharper toothed.

He was laughing for sheer joy when he heard Stephen shout, "On your left!"

Tom shot a glance sideways and saw Ben and Trumpet racing toward them, still pursued by two Essex men. They were running at such speed that they tore right through and past the swordfighters. The Essex swordsmen cursed. "Catch that mouseling and the reeky rat beside him!" They ran after them.

Tom and Stephen were abandoned for a moment. They looked at each other and shrugged and then joined in the chase, waving their rapiers over their heads and whooping like savages.

Suddenly a figure appeared at the bottom of the lane. A large, square man wearing the thick chain of a city official barred the passage, flanked by two gigantic constables.

Trumpet and Ben skidded to a stop in the shit-soaked mud, barely managing to keep to their feet. The man closest behind them was not so agile. He stumbled and slid facedown in the muck. He goggled up at the looming figure, his besmottered face twisted in dismay. He scrabbled awkwardly as the rest struggled to push past one another in the narrow alley.

Tom sheathed his weapons and leapt over the prone man, barely breaking stride as he scooped Trumpet onto his shoulder. The lads easily outpaced the lumbering retainers, rounding the corner, racing out of reach of the long arm of the law.

NINETEEN

They ran all the way up Chancery to Holborn and the safety of the Antelope Inn. Tom stopped in the archway and dropped Trumpet from his shoulder. He was panting from running uphill with a nine-stone weight, but no longer in fear of being clapped in Bridewell gaol. He and Trumpet pushed through the door into the tavern. The room was too warm, but it was familiar ground. Safe.

"A tankard of dragon's milk, if you love me, Dolly," Tom called to the barmaid.

Dolly giggled at him and he gave her a wink.

Mrs. Sprye looked up from the table where she sat surrounded by writing implements, scraps of paper, and stacks of coins. She was wielding her peacock feather quill, which meant she was doing accounts. She always said that however badly the sums came out, she could derive a morsel of cheer from the pen.

Her first glance was one of absent-minded welcome. This was swiftly followed by a glare of outrage. "Trumpet, you naughty child! Have you been brawling?"

"Only a little," Trumpet bragged.

Tom looked at his friend for the first time since the affray. One stocking hung loose about his ankle, his shirttails billowed from his hose both fore and aft, and he had a muddy scrape running from his shoes right up the side of his torso and across his cheek. No blood was flowing, however, and nothing seemed to be broken.

Tom whacked Trumpet soundly on the back and grinned. "The lad's proved his mettle today, Mrs. Sprye! You should have seen him, straddling that foul-mouthed, ginger-haired hedge-pig, grinding his face into the mud. God's bones, it was a treat. Although," he added, speaking now to Trumpet, "we must work on your technique. Fisticuffs are quite a different matter from fighting with weapons. There are tricks you can use to compensate for your slighter weight."

Trumpet nodded eagerly. "I'm fast, though, aren't I? I got in under his guard. Did you see me? I was dancing circles around that weedy, dog-hearted—"

"Tom." Mrs. Sprye's tone was severe. "I expect you to look after this boy, not encourage him to go about brawling in the street. In broad daylight!"

Tom was stung. "It's nigh impossible to brawl in the dark, Mrs. Sprye. And look—" He put his hands on Trumpet's shoulders and turned him full circle. "Scarcely a scratch on him. A bit dirty, true, but I believe that Pygmies can be washed."

Trumpet and Dolly giggled. Mrs. Sprye growled deep in her throat to express her displeasure. She fixed a steely glare on the boy. "Washing is the least of what's in store for you."

Trumpet opened his mouth to protest, but she cut him off. "Go on with you! You'll find what you need behind the kitchen. Head to toe, mind!" She pointed an adamantine finger toward the rear door.

Mrs. Sprye took an aunt-like interest in the younger members of the Inns of Court, whether they lodged at the Antelope or not. She'd been known to patch up evidence of youthful stunts without informing the benchers of the particulars. But she drew a hard line against brawling, drunkenness, and harassment of wenches within the bounds of her own establishment.

Trumpet was a favorite because he was helping her with researches related to the book she was writing about women's legal entitlements, called *The Lawes Resolution of Women's Rights*. Trumpet was planning to specialize in widows and heiresses, which he claimed would be a lucrative practice. Tom considered the idea absolutely brilliant. When he'd learned enough law to hang up a sign, he could do worse than join forces with Trumpet.

Mrs. Sprye turned her attention to the two lidded tankards that Dolly was collecting into one hand. "Cups, not tankards, Dolly. If they want more ale, they can switch to small. Then go make sure that hobbledehoy gets put back in order."

Tom made a sad face at the smallish wooden cup that replaced his manly tankard but knew better than to argue with Mrs. Sprye. He sat down on the bench behind the table farthest from the door.

Stephen and Ben came limping in, arms linked across their shoulders. Ben seemed to have turned an ankle. "Ale, Dolly, and it please you," Stephen panted as he helped Ben to the bench at Tom's side.

"Make it dragon's milk, on me," Tom said. He pouted sadly at Dolly as she set the four small cups on the table and then leered with appreciation as she swung her hips saucily on her way out. She threw a wink over her shoulder, aimed more at Stephen than at Tom. It didn't matter which. She was so full of wenchly delights he was happy just to be in their vicinity.

Tom held his cup to his nose and inhaled the fumes rising from the double-strong brew. He felt its spirits infusing his own, restoring the balance of his humors. "I like this stuff," he said, smacking his lips. "It's peppery. It gets up the nose and right into the blood."

"Good," Stephen agreed. He swallowed, closed his eyes, and sighed deeply. "Very good."

Ben only nodded. The lads sat in silence for a while, letting the ale and the comforts of their favorite tavern work their cures.

Then Stephen clapped his cup on the table and stood up. "Jakes," he said and vanished through the back door.

Tom watched him go. He shot a sidelong glance at Ben, who was leaning against the wall with his legs stretched under the table, his eyes half-closed.

"What did you think of those Essex men?" Tom asked, trying for a casual tone.

Perceptive Ben caught the underlying note. He opened one eye and spoke with measured words. "They seemed much of a type, I thought. Lesser gentry, upper yeomen, in service to a great lord. Like you, I suppose, in some ways."

"Not like me," Tom said. Too fast: he'd betrayed himself. "For one thing, Stephen's not great. At least, not like Essex. For another, I'm not in his service, not anymore. I have plans of my own. Prospects. Like you. Don't I?"

"Well, my plans are no secret. A legal practice, perhaps a judgeship someday, if I'm lucky. I don't believe I know anything about yours, as yet." He smiled to draw any barbs that might be couched in that remark.

"I won't be like those Essex men," Tom said. "Devil take me, but I won't. Idle my days away in some stuffy tavern, waiting for Stephen or some other master to come tell me what to do? Feh. I'd rather follow my father to sea. Except that he won't let me."

Ben said, "Does he intend you to make a career in the law?"

Tom shrugged. "He wants me to become a gentleman. He's not clear how. And I'm willing, but not if I have to be like those Essex men. They stank of boredom. Couldn't you smell it? I'd go mad in a month's time."

Fingering the carvings around the rim of his cup, he shot a sidelong glance at Ben. "Do you think I'm capable? Of passing the bar, I mean?"

"Yes." Ben spoke without hesitation, looking him square in the face. Tom felt something complicated unknot in his chest. "You have the ability. You'll have to work hard, though."

"I can work hard. If I know what I'm working toward." He drummed his fingers on the tabletop, working up his courage for the most important question. "Will they throw me out?"

Ben sat straight up and looked around, startled. "The constables?"

"No, no. Relax, *camerade*. Will they throw me out of Gray's, I meant. If Stephen asked them to."

"Oh." Ben sighed and leaned back against the wall. He held his cup under his nose, inhaling the fumes while he thought for a few moments. "They rarely expel anyone, as far as I know, and then only for gross infractions of the rules. It has to be major, like fighting in hall, stealing, religious violations. You know, skipping chapel or singing mockingly in church. Or not paying your dues. Or having women in your rooms."

"We couldn't fit a woman in our rooms," Tom said, earning a chuckle from Ben. He felt vastly relieved. Those offenses were easily avoided.

"Although," Ben said, "they do have ways of nudging people out. They don't advance you. They don't call on you for bolts or case-putting. They just ignore you. A fair number of men give up and leave every year. Who knows exactly why?"

That was less reassuring. Tom had little to do with the benchers, but he did feel a certain coolness from them. From other members too.

"Would it help if I'd taken my degree? At Cambridge?"

"If you want to become a clergyman. That's a possibility for you. Many yeomen's sons take that path, through the university and into a living. It's perfectly respectable."

"A clergyman!" Tom was aghast. That dreadful prospect shook everything into place. If his choices were the church, a lord, or the law, he had no further doubts. "I want to be a barrister, like you and Trumpet. We could form a partnership."

Ben grinned. "That's not the worst idea I've heard." He stretched out his leg, giving his ankle a tentative turn. "If you want my opinion, Tom, I think you're better off staying at Gray's and refusing to be nudged out, if nudging is applied. Look at Humphries: they'd love for him to go, but he sticks like glue. Study hard, keep your nose clean. Curry favor with the benchers. Maybe a few—"

"Gifts." Tom nodded. That strategy he understood well. "I can do that." He drained his cup. He felt better than he had all day, apart from the sword fighting, which was pure fun.

"You can do what?" Stephen asked as he slid back onto his stool.

"Oh, nothing," Tom said. He had no intention of sharing his plans with Stephen. "I thought I'd try for another round."

Stephen shot a glance at Mrs. Sprye, who was scribbling away at her book. "She'll never let us. Will she?"

"We could try Dolly."

"No luck there either," Stephen said. "She's giving the Pygmy a whole bath, to judge by the kettles of water and brushes being lugged about. I don't envy the lad."

"You don't?" Tom raised his eyebrows. "Delectable Dolly? Hot water? Lots and lots of slippery soap?" He whistled softly.

Stephen popped his eyes open wide. "I'm next in line!"

They laughed together. Tom was glad for the lighthearted moment. Stephen's life would be easier but vastly less interesting. You could almost pity the wanwitted lordling. Almost.

The door to the archway banged open and the three lads startled. They looked at each other sheepishly; it was only Treasurer Fogg. "Gentlemen," Fogg nodded at the lads. "Mrs. Sprye, my light and joy," he said as he bent to kiss her upturned cheek.

"Foggy come a'courting, he did ride," Stephen sang, *sotto voce.*

Ben and Tom chuckled. Tom wondered why it was the highest poetry when youths and maids fell in love but basest comedy when persons of middle years did the same. Their lumpish figures, he supposed. And their appalling lack of shame.

He leaned back and closed his eyes. He had things to think about, plans to make. What sort of gift might Treasurer Fogg find influential?

"Look, my love," Mrs. Sprye said. "Mr. Humphries has paid his bill in full. After ten years of delays and excuses. It leaves his chambermate in a bit of a bind, but I can't blame him for preferring lodgings at Gray's."

Mr. Fogg rumbled his approval. "I've thrown a few of my lesser clients his way. Once I'm on the Queen's Bench, I'll not have time for any but the highest."

"Don't count your chickens before they hatch, my turtledove."

"Nor will I, my sweet chuck. I'm merely feathering the basket to keep them warm while I wait."

They twittered at one another. Tom smiled, eyes still closed. They reminded him of his parents.

Trumpet returned from his bath. Tom opened half an eye: the boy looked fresh enough to go a-courting. His clothes had been sponged and his cheeks scrubbed pink. He took a stool beside Stephen and picked up his cup of dragon's milk. He took small sips, making a sour face after each one. Tom wondered fleetingly if he should perhaps not have offered such potent liquor to one so young.

Ah, well. Maybe it would put hair on his chest. Or at least on his upper lip.

TWENTY

Francis Bacon paced the footpaths west of Gray's Inn, his thoughts whirling in a noxious cloud of irritation commingled with fumes of aggrievement. All he wanted in this world was peace enough and time, to read and think and write. These were his first, best labors, the means through which he was destined to make his contribution to the world. It seemed little enough to ask and yet proved to be as unattainable as the fabled Northwest Passage.

First, he had yesterday received another querulous missive from his Lady mother, seeking his advice on her vote at the next meeting of the Andromache Society. They were slated to decide whether to advance the career of Sir Avery Fogg. Lady Bacon insisted on peppering her letters with passages in Greek to conceal their meaning. From whom, Francis could not begin to guess. His assistant read Greek, Lord Burghley read Greek, the queen read Greek. Half the membership of Gray's had some Greek from their time at university. Perhaps she feared the messenger's mule might catch a glimpse and bray her secrets καθ'οδον — down the road — to London.

He might advise her to abstain, or better, to avoid the next Andromache dinner altogether. She had recently discovered a new Nonconformist preacher, more fiery than the last one. That should keep her well occupied in Gorhambury. Francis lived in constant terror lest she learn of his banishment from court. He shuddered to think of the hailstorm of importunate letters she would rain upon his uncle on his behalf. Her shrewish nagging did him more harm than good. She resented the way Lord Burghley exploited her sons for services, such as Anthony's intelligence-gathering in France and Francis's management of that encrypted correspondence. Francis also served as an interpreter for French emissaries and prisoners in the Tower. Necessary work, important work; he did it willingly. But it was work with neither thanks nor pay.

And now he had another letter from Anthony in Montaubon, where he was struggling to defend himself against a charge of sodomy without anyone in England finding out about it. Francis was sick with worry for him. What if the news leaked out before he was restored to good odor with the queen? He would be utterly unable to defend his brother. Helpless. Voiceless.

Anthony had good friends in France, but he needed money. This was scarcely news. He was chronically short of funds, owing to his extravagant tastes in clothing and generous gift-giving impulses. These were the faults of a courtier; Francis hoped he shared them. One could hardly stand before the queen in last year's shoes. All favors required tokens of gratitude. Keeping up a brave display was challenging since he'd been left with no estate by his father's untimely demise. His three hundred pounds per annum were barely enough to sustain a humble life at Gray's. Sir Walter Ralegh owned hats that cost more.

This was an old grievance, guaranteed to stir up choler and yellow bile, throwing his humors out of balance. Francis quickened his pace and stepped squarely into a puddle of mud. *Splendidus absolute.* Mud, he was welcome to, in abundance. Never mind that he could scarce afford to keep his feet decently shod.

Last, but hardly least, was the note delivered early this morning from Lord Burghley questioning his lack of progress in the Smythson matter. Did he think Francis had forgotten? He had known from the outset that the likelihood of success was slender under the most optimistic of prognostications, yet he demanded results as though he had merely commissioned a new pair of gloves.

Francis fumed, striding hard, oblivious to the golden leaves glowing in the morning light that slanted through the elms under which he walked. He was tired of striving to find his place in the world. Tired of expending his energies on mundane questions when he wanted to devise a method for revealing the innermost secrets of Nature herself. Tired of the endless cacophony of letters filled with conflicting demands.

Chatter, chatter, chatter, and nothing said of matter.

He laughed bitterly and decided that he would solve all these problems in a few bold strokes. Let them advance Avery Fogg to the Queen's Bench; let them make him Lord Chancellor. Why not? Let Shiveley, the new Reader, take his place as Treasurer of Gray's. Seat the whole benighted bench in Westminster; except for Francis, of course, who was too young and too arrogant for those lofty halls.

He would provide himself with a lesson in humility, going forthwith to Gorhambury to take the reins of his brother's estate into his own hands. Francis would marl the fields and clear the ditches and mend the hedges too.

As for the Smythson matter, why, he would confess to the crime himself. He'd be thrown into Newgate, where he could interrogate a representative selection of London cutpurses at his leisure. He'd winkle out the Catholics while he was about it. He had nothing better to do since he had not been called upon to prepare a Reading.

Francis made another full circuit of the fields, his thoughts writhing like eels caught in a weir. As his legs drove his feet along the path, his mind settled, returning to its accustomed order and tranquility — at least, in part.

He sighed. He would advise his mother to vote in Fogg's favor. The man had some distempers, but only minor ones, and might make a more compassionate judge because of them. He would try to urge some sense of economy on Anthony. Strategic gifts, not wholesale bribery.

The Smythson matter was more difficult. So far his only clues led dangerously close to prominent courtiers. He'd risked his uncle's censure — or worse — in sending that message to Lady Rich. He didn't know whether to hope his pupils would learn something useful from Lord Essex's men or return empty-handed. A negative report would spare him the need to find a way to communicate with the earl.

His anxiety mounted again at the thought. He shook his head. He needed a strong corrective for an excess of yellow bile. Something cold and moist: mushrooms, perhaps.

He turned back toward the Inn. He spied his four pupils coming through the postern passage. Good, they'd received the message he'd left with the under butler. He took a deep breath, willing himself to calm.

The four friends walked in order of height: Whitt, Delabere, Clarady, Trumpington. Did they do it on purpose? Perhaps the Lord Stephen liked to be flanked by tall men and little Trumpington was left to tag along as he might. He felt a stab of sympathy. He too had sometimes felt himself, as a boy, to have an insufficiency of brawn and a superfluity of brain. Time and maturity had obviated the need for the former and made the latter a distinct advantage.

Sometimes.

He stood where he was and waited for them to reach him. "Good morrow, Gentlemen."

"Good morrow, Mr. Bacon," they chorused.

"Did you learn anything useful from Essex's men?" He eyed them doubtfully. Judging by the colorful bruise around Trumpington's eye, they'd gotten themselves into an altercation.

"We did, Mr. Bacon," Whitt said. "The Wild Men in question have gone home, but their fellows told us they made quite a tale of chasing a barrister through the lanes that day."

Francis made a dismissive gesture. "We knew as much already."

"Yes, sir," Whitt said. "But we didn't know there were *two* men in barrister's gowns. One was limping and wouldn't play. The other ran, so they chased him. We surmise that the limping man was Smythson, since he suffered frequently from gout."

Francis nodded. He'd expected as much, from the evidence of the laundress. "Did they describe the second barrister?"

Whitt shook his head.

"Hm," Francis said. "Those men will have to be recalled to London for questioning." He sighed. Requesting favors from an earl demanded excruciating delicacy even when he wasn't under a ban. He'd have to get permission from his uncle first, which would mean betraying how little progress he had made.

They were watching him with disappointed faces. They probably thought they'd brought him information that would help him crack the case like a walnut. They couldn't know that they'd made his job harder. He dredged up a smile. "Well done. The next step is to speak with that limner."

Clarady said, "We don't know where to find her."

Francis raised his eyes briefly to heaven, his sole source of support in these trying times. "She's Flemish, I believe you said?"

"Yes, sir."

"Have you tried asking at the Dutch Church?"

They looked at him blankly.

"In Austin Friars? Broad Street Ward?" More blank looks. "Do you know *anything* about the City of London?"

Now they looked offended. No doubt they'd taken themselves on the standard tour of theaters, bear pits, and gaming dens and felt themselves sophisticated urbanites in full possession of their capital. He'd thought exploring the great City of London to be a customary diversion for Inns of Court men.

"Go to the Draper's Guild near Moorgate and ask for directions. Or simply listen for a man speaking Dutch and follow him." He'd meant that last as a joke, but they nodded gravely. Whitt drew out his commonplace book and pencil and made a note. Francis frowned. No one ever appreciated his little sallies.

"Mr. Bacon," Clarady said. "Is it possible that the second barrister could have been a man from Gray's? We've been worrying about it all morning."

Only for the morning? Why not yesterday afternoon?

Francis hesitated. He'd grown practiced in secrecy through managing Anthony's correspondence and was loath to impart information to those unprepared to wield it properly. On the other hand, the more they knew, the better they could assist him and the sooner this investigation might be concluded.

"Yes," he said. "I believe it must have been."

They gaped at him, dismayed.

"But how?" Whitt asked.

"And who?" Trumpington asked.

"And why?" Clarady asked, more pertinently.

Francis saw that he would have to explain the Catholic element to the puzzle. Trawling for witnesses was slow work and had thus far netted slender results. And if it came down to searching chambers, he would rather these energetic lads do the actual deed. But there were risks in telling them.

Young Trumpington might well be a crypto-Catholic. He was always skipping chapel and he lived with the somehow not entirely aboveboard Nathaniel Welbeck. His mother's family was in Derbyshire, home to many recusants. The other three lodged together. They would be hard-pressed to conceal a rosary, much less a priest or a barrel of pamphlets. It would have to be all or none. Whitt was clever enough and Clarady forward enough, but Lord Stephen was highly unlikely to be living any kind of double life. A single life was almost more than he could manage.

A greater concern was that the lads would babble about their mission in the tavern and the hall, sending their quarry deeper under cover, making him impossible to snare. All Francis could do was bind them to secrecy and hope for the best. A word to the wise was sufficient, but what of the less than wise?

The most serious risk was that the murderer must be in constant fear of discovery. He would be *vigilate*: always alert. If he became aware that the lads were tracking him, he might be moved to further violence. By drawing them deeper into this plot, Francis might be placing them in danger.

But a covert Catholic at Gray's was a risk to the whole society; indeed, such insidious conspirators were a risk for the kingdom and the very name of liberty. Catholics often allied themselves with Spain; the priests who wrote the inflammatory pamphlets were often paid by Spain. King Philip would like nothing better than to place his own pliant puppet on the throne of England. Lord Burghley and Sir Francis Walsingham had exposed plot after plot aimed at the assassination of Queen Elizabeth and the termination of her support for the Protestant Low Countries. The Inns of Court were prime targets for infiltration because here was where future administrators and men of affairs were trained.

The threat was real, of that there could be no doubt. The conspirator had proven his capacity for violence. He must be found and brought to justice. To do that, Francis needed help.

He regarded his pupils with a cool eye. They stood silently, if somewhat restively, awaiting his next question. He tilted his head slightly. "Do you know how to identify a Catholic?"

TWENTY-ONE

James Shiveley mounted the stairs to his chambers slowly, his shoulders hunched against the cold. He'd neglected to wear his cloak to supper. The light of his shielded candle preceded him. Its yellow glow drew the eye, making the shadows darker.

A man stepped out from the depths of the dark landing.

"Mercy!" Shiveley jumped. "You gave me a start. Were you waiting for me?"

"I wanted a word. I had a thought about the statute you've chosen for your Reading."

"Can't this wait until morning?"

"I might forget."

Shiveley frowned. What an odd remark!

His colleague moved closer and reached toward his candle as if to assist him while he unhooked his keys from his belt.

Shiveley took a step back. He suddenly felt boxed in. "I hardly think now is—"

"Allow me." The man grasped him firmly by the arm and swung him full about to face the steep descent into the black stairwell.

"What are you doing?" Shiveley's voice spiraled up. Fear had found him, too late to be of use.

Hard hands set flat upon his back and shoved. The candle flew from his hand. His keys tumbled, clanking. He struck the stairs on his shoulders. Pain lanced through his back. He rolled, helpless, down to the landing. There he lay, sprawled facedown, legs stravaging up the stairs behind him.

He groaned. "Help me."

Feet pattered down the stairs and stopped beside him. Hands cradled his face, their warmth reassuring. They lifted his head, testing the flex in the neck. And then twisted, hard.

Crack!

TWENTY-TWO

"I need a crown," Stephen whined.

The lads were breakfasting in hall. It was early — still dark outside and cold — but the bread was hot from the oven and the butter was fresh.

They'd made a point of arriving in good time for chapel that morning. Missing chapel had been first on the list of Bacon's tell-tales, which included crucifixes, rosaries, surreptitiously making the sign of the cross, and incense. Tom had sniffed under every door on his way down the stairs. He'd smelled sour oil lamps and unemptied chamber pots, but nothing sorcerous.

"This very instant?" Tom was tired of Stephen's constant bleating about clothing. There were better things for a man to think about. Beautiful women, for example, and how to court them. His mind turned again to Clara. His memory of her face had grown less certain over the weeks. Had he imagined the near-white goldness of her hair?

Bacon had instructed them to find her without delay, an order Tom was eager to obey. The prospect of finally meeting her fanned the flames of his desire.

He couldn't marry her, but she would understand that. He'd discussed the issue at length with Trumpet and Ben. They all agreed that whether he ranked as a new-feathered gentleman lawyer or a merchant-adventurer's son, a craftswoman was beneath him. If she were a maiden, naturally he would leave her in that condition. He could still go walking with her on a Sunday afternoon and revel in her beauty.

Stephen snapped his fingers at him. "Are you awake? I need a crown for our embassy to the Inner Temple. Today."

Tom hated that finger-snapping. Was he a dog?

"We need to find that limner." Ben echoed Tom's thoughts. "Mr. Bacon gave us explicit instructions."

Tom smiled at the way Ben said Mr. *Bacon*, as if mouthing the name of a reverend potentate. Not unlike the way Tom said *Clara*. To needle Stephen, he said, "Bringing Smythson's killer to justice is slightly more important than your tickle-brained embassy."

Stephen's chin jutted forward as he compressed his lips. Tom's own lip quivered as he fought the urge to mimic him. He was wrestling with his baser self when a cry rang out in the courtyard.

"Help! Help! Oh, horrible! Help!"

The lads leapt up and raced out, reaching Coney Court ahead of the pack. A man stood in the doorway to Colby's Building, his hands clapped to his face as if to hold his head together. "Horrible! Oh, help!" His lamentation filled the yard. More men spilled out from other staircases.

Tom and the lads sprinted toward him. "What is it, Mr. Fulton?" Ben asked, laying a hand on the man's shoulder.

Fulton's face twisted with anguish. "Horrible. Oh, horrible." He seemed bereft of other words.

Tom and Trumpet pushed open the door and entered the building. Their eyes were drawn to the figure sprawled across the landing.

"God save us," Tom breathed.

"Oh, no," Trumpet moaned. "Who is it?" He began to climb the stairs, slowly, fearfully. Tom joined him. Ben and Stephen stayed behind to guard the door.

The man lay chest down across the landing, arms splayed on either side. His long legs trailed up the stairs behind him. His head was twisted at an impossible angle, his face turned up at them. The narrow windows in the stairwell let in enough of the early light to see his features.

Tom shuddered. "It's Mr. Shiveley."

Trumpet turned away, breathing shallowly, hand gripping the railing hard enough to show white around the knuckles. Tom simply looked up, blinking, and let his mind go blank.

This was worse than seeing Mr. Smythson's bloodied body in the street. Then, they had been in the company of bold captains: larger than life and fully in charge. The scene had seemed almost part of the pageant, the last act of a dramatic tragedy. This was homely, private. Everyday life invaded by sudden death.

"He is dead, isn't he?" Tom said quietly, when his wits returned to him.

Trumpet made an odd mewling sound then replied in a fairly steady voice, "He must be."

"Who is it?" Ben called up. He and Stephen blocked the doorway, keeping the crowd outside from shoving into the entryway. They'd learned that much from Captain Ralegh.

"It's Mr. Shiveley," Tom answered. "It looks like he's fallen down the stairs and broken his neck."

Ben relayed the news to the men outside the door.

"What should we do?" Tom said. He felt awkward, absurd, standing on a tread in the middle of a stair. He couldn't persuade himself to go up or down. Neither felt right.

Trumpet looked up at Tom, his face pale. "We should wait." They faced the door, standing straight, shoulders back and heads up, like an honor guard.

They didn't have long to wait. They heard Fogg's resonant voice and then saw the man's stout figure fill the doorway as he moved Stephen and Ben aside with a wave of his hand. He took command, tapping Stephen and two others to shoo the crowd away and sending someone to bring the surgeon and the priest. He bade Tom and Trumpet to fetch a blanket from Shiveley's room to cover the body.

They tiptoed around it and ran the rest of the way up. The door on the left was wide open.

"This must be his," Tom said.

"Why is it open?" Trumpet said, stopping on the upper landing with a puzzled frown on his face. "Didn't you think he was coming up the stairs and somehow tripped and fell down?"

Tom nodded. "He must have unlocked it and then gone back."

"I suppose so."

They went in, walking softly. Tom felt like an intruder. Mr. Shiveley had enjoyed private chambers: the outer room held only one desk and the inner only one chest. The bed was covered with a fur-lined blanket.

"Let's hurry." Trumpet shivered suddenly.

Tom grabbed the end of the blanket and yanked it off the bed, dislodging the pillows at the head. Something fell to the floor with a clatter.

Trumpet picked it up. "Uh-oh." He held up what Tom thought was a necklace, until he saw the silver cross dangling at the end.

Mr. Shiveley had kept a rosary under his pillow.

* * *

Trumpet dashed off to fetch Bacon while Tom covered Shiveley with his blanket. Then he stood guard outside the chamber door. He pretended that he was just watching from a vantage point while Fogg managed the process of inspecting and removing the body. He and the surgeon agreed that Shiveley had tripped, fallen, and broken his neck.

They ushered the body out the door. The light in the staircase grew stronger as Tom stood and studied the scene. Something about it nagged at him.

He ran down to the ground floor and then climbed back up again, slowly, imagining himself to be a man of middle years as Mr. Shiveley had been. A weary man, trudging up to his well-earned rest. Tom held his left hand at shoulder height, as if carrying a candle to light his steps. He watched for obstacles in his path, but saw none: no stray rushes, no loose boards, no nails sticking out. When he neared the top, he pretended to trip on the riser. He fell forward, hands out — just a little, as an experiment — and then righted himself.

He mounted the last two steps and turned again to look down the stairs. He would have dropped the candle, but nearer the top than they had found it. And he would have fallen up — forward — not back.

He turned and pretended to unlock the door and push it open. Then he paused and cocked his head as if he'd heard a sound. He felt foolish, but wanted to play the scene out. He turned and walked to the edge of the stairs. Had he tripped from this height, he might very well have fallen all the way down to the landing. Then the candle might have ended up where it did.

Would he land facedown? Of a certainty, unless he somehow tucked himself into a ball and rolled part of the way, which seemed too athletic for Mr. Shiveley. Would he break his neck? Perhaps if he struck the landing head first, the weight of his body might snap the neck.

Tom stroked his moustache, thinking hard. Shiveley had probably tripped on the hem of his cloak. It was cold, he was old, he was juggling a key and a candle. Perhaps the outer door hadn't latched properly and he'd heard it creak and turned too hastily to go down and close it.

Tom startled as the door below did creak loudly and swing wide, admitting Bacon, followed by Trumpet,

Stephen, and Ben, who closed the door firmly behind him. Bacon wore a tight frown, lips pressed together, but his eyes were bright and his step was eager. They filed into Shiveley's outer chamber, where Bacon placed his hands on his hips and studied the room. He turned in a slow circle, taking note of the furnishings.

Tom admired his patience. He would have rushed straight to the largest chest and emptied it onto the floor. He inhaled slowly — quietly — through his nose. He smelled beeswax and ink and dry rushes, but no incense, unless that's what incense smelled like. He wasn't actually sure; he'd always imagined something cinnamony.

"You found the rosary under the pillow?" Bacon asked. "Did you find nothing else?"

Trumpet and Tom shrugged at each other. "We didn't look," Tom said. "We didn't think to. We thought that was enough. It is a rosary, isn't it? It has a cross on it, like you said."

Mr. Bacon smiled thinly in that way he had that made Tom feel like a numskull. "Yes, but anyone might have a rosary. It could have been his grandmother's, a sentimental keepsake. In itself, it is not solid evidence of seditious activities. We need something more compelling." He pursed his lips and strolled to the desk. He inspected a stack of books, opening each one and riffling the pages. A folded piece of paper fell onto the desk. He unfolded it and began to read.

"Aha." He turned toward Ben. "I knew there must be a letter somewhere. Still, it's curious . . ."

He trailed off, not sharing his thought. Tom supposed that they were too stupid to appreciate it. And how had he known there would be a letter?

Bacon said, "This must have been taken from Smythson's body. I believe these dark stains are blood." He showed it to them.

They all shuddered.

165

"This should serve as proof that James Shiveley murdered Tobias Smythson. It's as much as we're ever likely to find."

That was hard to swallow. Tom would never have pegged Mr. Shiveley as the conspirator. He was the sort of rule-minded stuffpot who tapped his finger on the table in front of you to make you pay attention while he patrolled the student tables during the after-dinner exercises. Smuggle forbidden religious pamphlets? Inconceivable.

"Yes," Bacon said, giving the letter a closer reading. "It's addressed to my uncle. I recognize Smythson's hand. It warns of a delivery of Catholic pamphlets from the Continent." He turned the sheet over and studied the back. "Blank. Hm. Odd that he would begin with a formal salutation and then terminate so abruptly, but . . ." He shrugged and folded the paper briskly, tucking it into his pocket. "No doubt he decided to present his findings in person and kept the letter merely as an *aide memoire*."

"Does he say how the delivery was to be made?" Trumpet asked. "Or when?"

"Not here. The pamphlets were produced in France and are to be paid for with English currency."

Bacon was definitely holding something back. *Not here*, he'd said. Then where? Well, they were only students. They couldn't expect the man to share his every thought. If Francis Bacon was satisfied, who was Tom to argue? He said, "The money must be here, then."

Bacon frowned. "So it must. Hm. It should be given to Treasurer Fogg for safekeeping. Open the chest and let's have a look."

"I'll help you," Trumpet said. He seemed to be relieved — happy, even — about the discovery of the letter. As if he'd had a grudge against Mr. Shiveley that was now paid in full.

They dragged the chest forward so they could fully open the lid. A small box lay right on top. Tom opened it.

"It isn't locked." He would never leave his cash box unlocked. He trusted his chambermates — well, he trusted Ben — but he wasn't so confident about the lock on the door.

"What of it?" Stephen said. "He lived alone."

"I fail to see the relevance," Bacon said. He poked a finger into the box, counting the coins. "They appear to be freshly minted. I wonder where he got them."

"It doesn't seem like much," Tom said.

"How much do you suppose there ought to be?" Now Bacon's tone was sharp. He was plainly keen to lay the Smythson affair to rest and not interested in any niggling oddities.

Tom resolved to keep his mouth shut. He had twice that amount in his cash box and he wasn't performing a Reading or paying for smuggled pamphlets in the near future. But if the rest of them saw nothing untoward, so be it. Tom could celebrate the end of strife as gaily as the next.

Bacon took the box from him, closed it, and tucked it under his arm. "I believe our work is done. We have our murderer, punished by God himself. We could have wished for man's justice as well, but we must be satisfied with what we receive. *Quod erat demonstratum.* I'll write a report for my uncle and then, with his permission, advise the benchers to be on the alert for the pamphlets. And you, Gentlemen, are free to pursue your revels. I heartily thank you for your efforts." He grinned at them — an actual grin. "Done in time for Christmas! Who could wish for more than that?"

Ben shook his head, bemused. "It seems too simple."

Bacon answered crisply, "Simplicity is often the sign of truth."

TWENTY-THREE

"Now, we find Clara." Tom and the lads stood in the courtyard the next morning, debating how to spend the day. Their first really free day, with full permission from their tutor. Fitful gusts of wind kicked leaves across the gravel and the sky was flat and gray. Tom didn't care if the father of all tempests was rising in the east. He was determined to find his angel at last.

"We don't need her anymore," Stephen said. He wanted to go shopping for princely accoutrements. "The Smythson matter is finished." His chin jutted forward, but with less conviction than formerly. He was beginning to notice that Tom was no longer catering to his moods, but he wasn't nimble enough to change course in a matter of days.

"All the better," Tom said. "Now we don't have to upset her with questions. I just want to tell her that I love her and lay my heart at her feet. Then we'll go get your cursed crown."

Ben and Trumpet stood to one side, chatting about which of the ancients would replace Shiveley as Reader. They'd grown visibly weary of the friction between Tom and Stephen. Tom couldn't blame them; he was tired of it himself. It wouldn't go on for much longer. Law studies were hard and dry as old bones. Stephen would get bored by mid-January and move on.

They strode down High Holborn, passing through the Newgate arch. As they passed an apothecary shop, they inhaled the invigorating aromas of pepper and cloves, breathing deeply to fill their noses and ward off the general stink of the streets.

Ben said, "I should pop in while we're here to buy a physic for Mr. Bacon. He likes poppy juice steeped in wine as a remedy for strain. He's been dreadfully overworked lately, what with the masque and the Smythson matter."

"Later," Tom said, not slowing his pace for a second. When had Ben become Bacon's personal physician?

They passed a coppersmith's with a display of brass jewelry on the shutter. "That's perfect!" Stephen cried, nearly tripping over a pig. "Tom, it will only take—"

"No!" Tom stopped and rounded on his friends. "No delays. No distractions. I've waited weeks, letting you put me off and pull me this way and that. Today we find Clara. Everything else can wait."

He turned on his heel, slipping on a slew of cabbage leaves but retaining his inner dignity. The lads followed him with a minimum of insulting retorts.

They passed the Draper's Guildhall. The Dutch Church could not be far. But here they picked up a tail of small apprentices with time on their hands and no minders. They followed Tom and the lads, lagging a few yards behind, kicking bits of garbage from the kennels in their general direction.

Tom was not best pleased to have an entourage of gleeking tots in blue livery. He turned and growled at them. They giggled and scattered but soon returned. Then Tom saw that Trumpet was trading scowls with them and showing them his fists.

He laid a hand on the boy's slender shoulder. "Cease and desist, Mr. Trumpington. No brawling today. We're going to find Clara and we're going to look tidy when we do."

They reached the old Austin Friars church. Tom felt his heart quicken in his breast and somewhere in the back of his mind an angelic choir sang *Clara, Clara, Clara, Clara.* He heard Ben say, as if from a great distance, "I believe this was once an Augustinian priory."

The church was small but beautiful, built of yellow brick, with a tall, narrow, stained-glass window. A potbellied man with a square blond beard leaned against a bulwark near the entrance, watching a boy polish the railings. As the lads came into view, his gaze shifted to them, taking in their students' robes. He flicked a sharp glare at the apprentices behind them, who disappeared down an alley.

He sighed in relief. One source of trouble dispersed. He truly needed to have a word with Trumpet about his belligerence. Fighting had its place; when necessary, a man did what he must. But the boy ought not to become one of those irksome short men who try to prove their manhood by an excess of aggression.

The churchman's expression brightened as the lads approached. "*Guten morgen,* young gentlemen. Vat may I do for you? Vud you care for a tour of our church?"

"Not today, Sexton," Tom said. The churchman's expression melted so dramatically that he hastened to add, "But it is a beautiful church and we would gladly see it on another day."

The churchman smiled broadly. He had large yellow teeth with large black holes between them.

"We're looking for someone who might be a member of your congregation."

"I am sexton here now fifteen years. I know everyone who lives in this parish. Their wives and their children and their aunts and uncles too."

Tom gave him his friendliest smile. "We knew the instant we saw you that you were the one man who could help us." His friends stood beside him and nodded.

The sexton puffed out his chest. "How may I serve you young gentlemen?"

Tom said, "We're looking for a Fleming named Clara Goossens. She's a limner."

The sexton nodded. "Limner Clara Goossens, yah. Very pretty, but och, that accent!" He made a sour face. "Still, Flemings are clean enough. She is regular in her Sunday attendance also. Quiet. She does not come around so much on any other day, but then she has her trade, *nicht wahr*? No sitting in church all week around doing nothing. Not like some." He shot a dark scowl at the door as if the church was crowded with noisy loiterers at that very moment.

Tom frowned at the church door too. "Clara *Goo-zenz*," he said, trying to imitate the sexton's pronunciation precisely. The name felt round and rich in his mouth, like honeyed cream.

"Ja, that's good," the sexton said. "The Widow Goossens, I call her. But now it seems she might be or she might not be."

Tom cocked his head. "How is that, Sexton?"

The sexton cast a quick glance at his boy, who had stopped polishing to listen. He wagged his finger at him and the boy moved on to another stretch of railings with his rag. The sexton licked his lips, as if ready for a juicy snack, and leaned toward Tom.

"Only this morning! Here I am, same as always, after the morning service. Well, the porch needs sweeping, *nicht wahr*? The boy does nothing without me to watch him. And so here I am, same as always, and along comes a big square *kerl*, like a block of limestone on two legs. Well, up he comes to me and he says, 'This is the Dutch Church, is that not so?' Of course I knew at once he was a Fleming by the way he talked. And I say, 'Yes, it is, but you are late; the service is over.' I would tell him when to come back, but he cuts me off, so rude, and says, 'I do not come for preaching. I search a limner named Clara. I know not what surname she might be using.'" The sexton poked Tom in the chest and said, "Haw! What do you think of that?"

Tom was not amused. "Who was he?"

"Och, that is the most funny part!" The sexton threw his head back and laughed in loud caws: "Haw! Haw! Haw!"

Tom wanted to grab the gabbling old goat by the shoulders and shake him.

The sexton went on with his tale. "I say, 'What are you wanting with our Clara?' So then this great block of a man, he says to me, 'I am her husband, me.' Well, a man ought to know his own wife's name, *nicht wahr*? Haw! Haw! Haw!"

A husband! That meant that Clara was a wife, not a widow. Tom's heart sank. Widows were the best: experienced, mature, wise in the arts of love. They didn't require cajolery and flattery and tickles under the ear just to show a bit of ankle. Wives, on the other hand, were bad news. He'd never heard any good endings to amorous adventures involving wives. Then his thoughts caught up with the sexton's words. Why *wouldn't* the man know his wife's surname?

The sexton was watching him with a glint in his eye. He knew full well what effect his news was having.

"What did you say to him?" Tom asked, resigned to playing the old man's game. He'd come to find Clara. He'd take whatever he learned and bear it like a man.

"I said, 'Her late husband, you mean.' Haw! Haw! Because she told us she was a widow."

"Well, is she a widow or isn't she?" Tom stretched a smile across his lips in an effort to keep his temper.

The sexton grinned and nodded as if Tom had finally gotten the joke. Then something caught his eye behind the lads. "Maybe you should ask him!" He pointed across the street.

Tom turned and saw a big man coming out of a shop carrying a small cask on one shoulder and a large, square-bottomed sack slung over the other. He strode down the center of the street, forcing people to jump out of his way.

"No, she will never like so much wine," the sexton said, shaking his head. "The Widow Goossens never takes more than a thimbleful of the very smallest ale. A nice piece of mutton or a fat fish, that is a better present for her."

"Is he going to her house now?" Tom asked.

"Why not, if he is her husband?"

"So you told him where she lives," Tom persisted.

The sexton shrugged. "Why not? Is it a secret?"

Tom clenched his fists and then forced himself to unclench them.

"Won't you please tell us also, Uncle?" Ben asked.

"Why not?" The sexton eyed Tom's twitchy hands and cackled. "She lodges with the surgeon, Elizabeth Moulthorne. All women in that house. All Flemings!" He pointed down the street with his chin. "On Oat Lane. Down Austin Friars, on around past the Guildhall. Then on a bit more, turn right before St. Anne's. You'll see the surgeon's sign."

"Let's just follow that knave," Trumpet said.

The lads set off at a brisk pace. Or as brisk as they could manage in the crowded district. At this time of day, the city was clogged with traffic. People on horses, donkeys with wagons, men wheeling carts. All manner of folk carrying all manner of baskets and sacks, on their hips and shoulders and backs and heads. Dogs and pigs and small children ran through the crowds at knee level.

"A widow," Trumpet said, ducking under a sheaf of poles being carried by two men in stained tunics. He bounded up to Tom's side.

"A wife," Stephen said. "You're wasting your time. *And* ours."

Tom shot him a quelling glance. Stephen shrugged, not caring.

"Maybe the blocky man was lying about being her husband," Trumpet said.

"Seems an odd thing to lie about," Ben said. He twisted to walk sideways for a few steps, slipping between a pair of unbudgeable gossips.

"I'd like a better look at him, at least," Tom said. He jumped up to see over the tops of people's heads. "He's just ahead of us! Look there!"

He pointed, picking up his pace. He dodged around a donkey whose panniers were being unloaded through the front window of a grocer's. He closed the gap between him and the blocky man, who was easy enough to follow: slightly shorter than Ben and nearly twice as wide. One arm supported the cask of wine on his broad shoulder, displaying a beefy bicep.

Tom longed to challenge him, but this was no squirrely apprentice. This was a grown man, hardened by labor. He wished he'd worn his rapier, but it was liable to attract a constable. Students at the Inns of Court were forbidden to wear swords with their robes and all the authorities knew it. Still, he had his friends. Trumpet could thrash the man about the knees while he and Ben took turns avoiding his fists. Stephen, presumably, would not trouble himself to help.

The thought made him angry and that gave him courage. He jogged closer, shouting, "Hoi! You there! Goossens!"

The name made the man stop and turn around. He met Tom's smile with a hostile glare. Tom held up a hand. "A word, and it please you."

The man's gaze flicked up and down, taking in Tom's rich clothing and sleeveless black robes. He hesitated for a moment and then snarled, baring his teeth and thrusting his square head forward. Tom quailed, stepping backward onto Ben's foot. The man's eyes zipped to Ben then back to Tom. He grunted, turned, and dashed down a side street.

Tom ran after him. A cart trundled out of an archway and spanned the whole street. By the time it had passed, the man had disappeared.

Tom trotted back to his friends. "I lost him."

"Never mind," Ben said. "He didn't look like the talkative sort."

Trumpet nodded. "He looked like the pounding-you-into-dust sort."

"It's Clara we want," Ben said. "She's the only one who can answer your questions."

Tom couldn't argue with that. Although, the joyous anticipation of the day's beginning had evaporated like wine spilt on a hot stone, leaving only a wish and a pungent scent.

* * *

Oat Lane was so short it barely qualified as a street. The hall of the Worshipful Company of Pewterers occupied most of one side. The other was lined with a row of houses. A sign with a bowl full of blood painted on it hung over one door. The bowl was bright copper; the blood vivid red. Tom wondered if Clara had painted it. The house it marked was tall and narrow: four stories high and one room wide. Its unsteady shape was supported on either side by squatter buildings. Each floor had windows in diminishing sizes, all the way up to the top.

Tom thought he saw a flash of bright hair inside the topmost window. He called up to it, "*Angela luminosa!*"

Trumpet laughed. "She can't hear you from this distance, fool. You'll have to knock on the door."

Ben simply walked up and opened it. "It's a surgery." He pointed up at the sign. "No need to knock." The others followed him in.

They found themselves in a square room crowded with cupboards and narrow worktables bearing bottles of colored liquids, bowls of herbal stuffs, and instruments of unknown function. More herbs hung in sheaves from the roof beams. It smelled like an apothecary — pungent and woodsy — with the addition of the metallic scent of blood. A sturdy woman of some thirty years bent over a man lying in a wide chair with his feet raised on a cushion. She held a copper bowl to catch the steady trickle of blood running from a neat cut on his arm. The man's eyes were half-closed and his expression was dreamy.

The woman's head snapped toward them and then back to her patient. "I am busy, do you see? Come back in half an hour."

Tom took a step closer and cleared his throat.

She glanced at them again, this time registering the quality of their clothing. "*Vas ist?* Your tooth?"

"No, Surgeon." Tom bowed slightly. "We wish to speak with your lodger, Clara Goossens."

She shrieked incomprehensibly, "*Lijskin!*" causing her patient to jerk. "Sshh." She patted his leg. She wrapped a strip of white linen around the wound and tied it in a neat bow. "That is *gut*," she murmured. "Eyes close, please. Now you rest."

A girl of about twelve came in from the back of the house. She stared at the lads as she dropped a shallow curtsy. "Madam?"

"Fetch Clara. Quick, quick, quick! Gentlemen do not like to be kept waiting."

The girl scooted past Tom and pattered up a steep flight of stairs.

The surgeon rolled the remainder of her bandages into a ball and tucked them into a box on the table. She stood and faced the lads, folding her arms under her bosom. "You want portraits, yes?"

"No," Tom said. "Or rather, yes." He would love to sit day after day, watching Clara paint him. Unless they would have to sit here in front of this formidable individual. She

176

couldn't very well come to Gray's; women under forty were not allowed in any capacity.

"Yes or no?" The surgeon was plainly a woman with no tolerance for ambiguity. She frowned, drawing her eyebrows into a sharp V. "Do you play with me?"

"Never, Surgeon Moulthorne," Tom vowed. He had seldom met a less enticing playmate.

A clatter on the stairs spared him further explanations. The maid skipped back to where she'd been. Behind her, Clara descended slowly in a plain woolen gown. Its simple lines displayed her lithe yet womanly figure to advantage. The dove-gray color seemed demure until she lifted her face to reveal the brilliant depths of her sapphire eyes. A linen coif set off the perfect pallor of her cheeks and the gleam of her golden hair. She moved with the unconscious grace of a doe.

Ben said, "Unh." Stephen gave a low whistle. Trumpet whispered, "Limner, limn thyself."

Tom ignored them, looking up at Clara. Their eyes met and held in an unbroken gaze of mutual wonderment. Tom let himself be absorbed by her gaze, explored by it. He felt that she was seeking something inside his very soul. He hoped she found whatever it was that she wanted.

She reached the bottom of the stair and stood with one hand on the newel post. "You're Tom."

He nearly suffered a rapture watching her pillowy lips wrap themselves around the single syllable of his name. He stood dumbstruck.

Trumpet cleared his throat, breaking the spell. He bowed shortly. "Allow me. I am Allen Trumpington. My companions are Lord Stephen Delabere and Mr. Benjamin Whitt."

At the mention of Stephen's title, the surgeon grabbed a cloth and started polishing everything within reach.

"At your service, Goodwife." Ben offered her a quarter-bow. Stephen merely smiled and tilted his head in a condescending way.

Half of anything was never enough for Tom. "I am Thomas Clarady, son of Captain Valentine Clarady and a member of the Society of Gray's Inn. I place my life and my service at your command." He swept off his hat and made a full bow, forehead to knee, toe pointed.

He heard a gentle laugh and glanced up. Clara's eyes shone with delight. He had pleased her with his extravagant gesture.

He rose and took one bold step toward her. Her eyes grew rounder. He looked down at her, thrilling to the sense of her size and shape, so near he could almost feel the warmth of her body. She was almost as tall as he was, almost up to his nose. Perfect for kissing her on the forehead. But he wanted to gaze forever into her lushly lidded eyes. He could see old sorrows in the slight shadow about their edges. Yet her sensuous lips promised a deep capacity for joy.

"Clara," he whispered.

She smiled hesitantly. She glanced toward the surgeon then back at Tom. She pursed her lips and he felt himself pulled helplessly toward them.

Ben chuckled softly. He used his long arm to turn Trumpet, who had been standing blatantly gawking, toward the surgery. He cleared his throat meaningfully at Stephen, who quirked a lip and turned as well. Ben said, "Might I inquire as to the services that you offer here, Surgeon Moulthorne?"

Tom let the others fade into the background, focusing his full attention on his lady love. "Clara. May I call you *Clara?*"

"No." Her answer came with a coquettish grin that poured hot oil on Tom's ardor. Then her expression darkened. "You've come about that man. The one who was killed that day."

Tom reached for her hand and stroked it comfortingly. "No, my angel. That's all over. The murderer has been caught. Or, rather, discovered. He's dead."

"The murderer is dead?"

"Yes. Yes. It's all right. It's all over."

"How came he dead?"

"God punished him," Tom said. "He fell down the stairs and broke his neck."

She raised her eyes. "Merciful heaven." Tom could barely catch the whispered words.

"I've been searching for you." He kissed her hand lightly. She had calluses on her fingers, from her brushes, he supposed. He planted a kiss on each one, savoring her indrawn gasp. He raised his eyes to meet hers. "I've thought of nothing but you for weeks. I wrote a song for you."

"I would like to hear your song."

"I'd like to play it for you. I'll call again, if you'll allow it." She nodded, but Tom saw something wary in the back of her azure eyes. "We could go for a walk. Have you seen the bears in Southwark? Or, or — perhaps a cockfight?" She didn't seem tempted by blood sports. He racked his brains for some gentler diversion. "The theater? Or we could go watch the madmen in Bedlam?"

She laughed. Angelic trills that chased the reserve from her eyes. "A walk would be nice."

He dared to ask, "May I kiss you?"

Her eyes flashed. He knew she wanted him to, but she withdrew her hand, glancing toward the surgery. Tom heard the rumble of Ben's voice. His friends were still covering for him. He captured her hand again, drawing it to his breast. He bent his head, slowly, and kissed her once, lightly, on the lips.

She sighed and closed her eyes. He kissed her cheek and was about to return to her lips for a deeper touch when he heard a throat clearing sharply behind him.

Stephen stood two feet away, an expression of mock concern on his angular features.

"Go away, Steenie."

"The surgeon's coming. We can't distract her forever, you know."

Clara withdrew her hand, her cheek, her whole shimmering person to a spot beyond Tom's reach at the foot of the stairs. He sighed dramatically and she favored him with a smile.

"May I come again?"

"In one week," she said. "Let us see if you can remember me for that long."

"Oh, he'll remember," Trumpet said, joining them in the entryway. "He's talked of nothing else for weeks. We're glad to know he didn't imagine you."

Tom watched Ben separate himself from the surgeon with a short bow. She then ostentatiously took up a position at a table from which she could keep an eye on both her patient and her lodger and began to measure ingredients into a stone bowl.

Stephen winked at Tom and then treated Clara to his best lordly smile. "We did have one small question, Goodwife Goossens. Or is it Widow Goossens?"

Clara's face turned to marble.

Tom glared at him. "Not now, Stephen." He reached toward Clara, but she took a step away from him. "It's not important, *Angela*. We can talk about it later. But only if you want to."

Stephen clucked his tongue. "I know you're too delicate to ask, Tom, old chum. Or perhaps you're not quite at that stage of your, em, negotiations, shall we say?"

"Ignore him," Tom said to Clara, but the wariness had returned to her eyes.

"We met this fellow outside, you see." Stephen was having all kinds of fun, kicking holes in Tom's romantic moment. "Or nearly met. Big blocky churl? We followed him here, but he ran away from us. We couldn't imagine why. Except that garrulous old sexton at your church told us the knave actually claimed to be your husband."

Clara blanched and took a step backward up the stairs, laying a trembling hand upon the rail.

Ben had gone back to ask the surgeon about the simple she was preparing. Now he returned, oblivious to the tension of the moment, and spoke directly to Clara. "Forgive me, Goodwife, but I find myself still a little curious. Did you, or did you not, see the second barrister in the lane on Queen's Day? I'd like to set the record straight."

"Ben." Tom shook his head. "Not now."

Clara looked doubtfully from one to the other. "Barrister. They are those that wear the velvet welts on the sleeves?"

She pronounced it "welwet welts." Her accent softened all the hard corners of the English language. Tom could watch her plush lips roundly pronouncing the phrase "welwet welts" for all eternity and know himself to be in paradise.

Trumpet plucked at his sleeve. "Tom, you do need to know: is she a widow or a wife?"

He smiled at Clara over Trumpet's head to show that he was on her side. Although, if he was honest, he did want to know and didn't mind being spared the asking.

Clara looked down at Trumpet and a half smile curved upon her lips.

Stephen sauntered forward. "You see, *Clara*, we're finding this all a bit odd because your patron, Lady Penelope Rich, with whom I spoke only a few days ago — so gracious, really, a true lady — is under the impression that you are a widow. It was she who gave me your name.

I hardly think Her Ladyship would appreciate being deceived."

Clara's eyes went wide. Her hand flew to her mouth. She took another trembling step backward up the stairs.

Trumpet reached toward her. "We would never —" But Clara shook her head, holding out a hand to forestall him.

Tom growled, "Stephen, if you don't march straight out that door, I will thrash your lordly arse from hell to Holborn."

"Stephen doesn't mean it," Trumpet said, giving Clara a wink. "Lady Rich terrified him. She terrified us all! We wouldn't speak to her again if our lives depended on it."

Stephen sneered at Tom; his job was done. He strolled to the door and pulled it open. Trumpet followed him, scolding, "That was completely unnecessary."

Tom reached again for Clara, but she shook her head, eyeing him as if he had turned into a menacing stranger. He'd meant to defend her. How had things gone wrong so fast? He clasped his hands to his breast in supplication, but again she shook her head. She said, "Go. Please."

He placed a kiss on his palm and blew it to her. Then he turned full around and bared his teeth at Lord BeetleBrain. Stephen cackled and skipped out into the street. Trumpet pressed his hand against Tom's chest. "No, Tom, it isn't worth it."

"Out of my way, Pygmy." Tom pressed forward. "I'm going to pound him so deep into the kennels he'll be washing shit out of his hair for a month."

Trumpet gamely kept himself one step ahead.

As he approached the door, Tom heard Ben say, "Don't fret about Stephen, Goodwife Goossens, I pray you. He'll say nothing to your patroness. But about Queen's Day. The murderer was another barrister. Did you see him? A tall, redheaded man."

"But, no," Clara said, sounding puzzled. "He was neither."

The door swung shut.

TWENTY-FOUR

Clara lifted her skirts and raced up the stairs, all four flights, to her own room. She clambered up onto her worktable, bare knees against the worn wood, and peered out the window at the street below. There he was: his golden curls spilling out from under his hat, his shapely legs bright in their green stockings. He shook his fist at the young lord, but his other friends clutched his jerkin, pulling him back. The lord skipped backward, laughing tauntingly, until he stumbled over a rooting piglet and fell smack on his bottom in the filth.

Clara plopped wide-legged on her table, heedless of the drawing paper crumpling under her rucked-up skirts. She curled a fist to her mouth to smother a scream. She kicked her heels and laughed until tears spurted into her eyes.

In less than one incredible hour her world had been torn to shreds, as if a cannonball had blown through her chamber window. First comes the golden youth, the beautiful young man who had called to her beneath her window. She'd dreamt of him, she'd sketched him, but she had never expected to see him again. And yet here he came to Mrs. Moulthorne's door. He'd remembered her. He'd searched for her. He loved her.

He'd kissed her.

She touched her lips with a wondering finger. Such tenderness. She'd never felt anything like it. For a moment — a brief moment — he had given her courage. It flowed from him like wine from a barrel. He was bold and kind and foolish and frank and far more handsome than any man she had ever imagined would hold her hand in Mrs. Moulthorne's surgery.

But the moment had vanished, ripped apart by the thin-lipped lord. He was angry with Tom, that much was clear. Then why not fight with him? Why threaten her?

She cried aloud then smothered the cry with her hand. She'd be ruined if he went to Lady Rich and accused her of lying. It mattered not if she were married or widowed; what mattered was that she had not told the truth from the outset. The faintest breath of scandal and her days of painting wealthy women in clean chambers would be over. She'd be forced to go back to scrounging odd jobs from printers or painting cloths for merchants' wives to hang upon their walls.

"Clara!" A deep voice thundered far below stairs.

Clara clutched both hands tightly to her chest as if to keep her heart from pounding out of her body. She slid from the worktable to her feet.

Caspar!

She'd forgotten about him. Fool! She should have run.

When her father died, Clara had been left with no dowry other than her beauty and her talent. So she had accepted the proposal of Caspar Von Ruppa, a sculptor who pretended to admire her painting. For a while, the marriage worked. Until Caspar hit a dry patch with no work and was forced to ask Clara for drinking money. Or when he had a job, but things went badly and the patron chided him for some fault. Any insult, any grievance, called down a storm upon Clara's head. And her face and her body. Once he had beaten her so badly she hadn't been able to show herself in the village for three weeks. She'd lost a client because of it.

She'd fled to Antwerp to live with an aunt. Too near. She'd crossed the German Sea and made a life for herself in London, calling herself *Goossens*, her mother's maiden name. Gradually, her reputation as a limner had grown until she was painting some of the most famous faces in the realm. Now all of that would be destroyed.

Heavy footsteps pounded closer, shaking the whole house. The door burst open and her hated husband filled the frame. No escape: not even a window large enough to fling herself from, four stories down to the street.

She was trapped.

She cowered against the farthest wall, hating herself for cowering but too fearful to stand and take what was coming.

Caspar stood inside the door holding a cask on his massive shoulder and a sack in the other hand. He looked her up and down, then his eyes roved around the room, taking in the stoic furnishings. "Clara," he sang, in a mocking tone. "Mine *lieveling*. Your loving husband has found you."

She willed her hands to her sides and forced composure onto her face. She could feel her lower lip trembling. *Grant me rage, my blessed Savior. Not fear.* Rage gave her strength.

That, and the sound of excited voices rising from the floors below. She was not alone in this house of sturdy craftswomen.

"No sweet kisses?" Caspar smacked his puckered lips at her. Dropping the sack, he lowered the cask to the floor and gestured at it with hands spread wide. "Look! I have brought a present for you!"

"I do not drink wine by the caskful." Clara struggled to speak in a steady voice. "What is in the sack?"

He grinned. "Not for you. A special delivery. You know the Jesuits and their politics. The money they spend! Work in England pays me double."

Smuggling. Caspar always carried a little something extra when he traveled abroad for a job. That sack looked too heavy for lace. Probably banned books or religious pamphlets. Nothing that concerned her. Why couldn't they be content with the books they had here already?

She studied his face, noting the grayness of his skin and the hardness of his features. *He's becoming like the stone he works.*

"You can't escape me," he said. "I always find you. I found you here. It was easy."

That gossiping sexton! But she couldn't blame him. How could he forestall an act of God?

"Come, *lieveling*," Caspar said, beckoning with a meaty hand. "Come give your man some loving. I have been so lonely."

He puckered his lips again. The gesture turned Clara's stomach. "If you touch me, Caspar Von Ruppa, I will kill you where you stand."

"What?" He tucked his chin in surprise at her ferocity. He pretended to be afraid. "Will you strike me with your little fist?" He leered at her. "Will you spank me?"

Fury boiled through Clara's veins. "Out! Out of my room! Out of my life!" She thrust her hand out to push him back.

Her fury was hot enough to scorch him — at first. He did step back. For a moment. She smiled. A mistake. His eyes narrowed and she saw his powerful hands curl into fists.

Then she saw her landlady — no small woman — and all of the other lodgers, streaming up the stairs armed with pans and brooms and pokers. They stormed into the room, flowing around Caspar like an angry river roiling around a great gray rock, and ranged themselves in front of Clara.

"You will leave my house," Surgeon Moulthorne said. "You are not welcome here."

"She is my wife." Caspar glowered down at them.

"Leave!" Clara, emboldened by her defenders, reached past them to push Caspar with her open hand against his chest. He gaped down at it in amazement.

"Out!" she cried.

He grabbed her wrist. She wrenched it from his grasp and pushed him again. This time the other women stepped forward also, brandishing their implements.

Caspar looked from one to the other, shaking his head like a bear baited by snapping dogs. Clara pushed him back another step. Two of her neighbors got behind him and began to pull. He growled at them; one whacked him on the shoulder with her broomstick. Caspar flinched and flailed a fist at her. Another woman cracked her poker down on his wrist.

They surrounded him and forced him down the stairs. Clara stood on the top step, vibrating with anger. She raised a fist in the air and screamed at the top of her lungs, "I'll kill you before I let you strike me again!"

TWENTY-FIVE

Francis Bacon struggled to focus his attention. He was writing an essay about knowledge — how to identify sham philosophers who substitute false coinage for the true — but his mind kept wandering back to the previous week when he'd stood in James Shiveley's chambers with his pupils. He could not repress the nagging feeling that he'd overlooked something important, dismissed some vital fact in his eagerness to relieve himself of an onerous task.

A vision of a paltry number of shiny silver coins in a flat oak box kept pushing itself into his thoughts. The coins in his own cash box were of varied hues and shapes: some worn, some bent, some chipped about the edges. When had the last official coinage been produced? Not recently, he was certain. Then how had Shiveley managed to find a matched set of new coins?

Francis shook his head to dispel the nagging vision. He had sent his final report to his uncle; the matter was closed. He must discipline himself to banish it from his mind.

A knock sounded on his chamber door. His assistant, William Philippes, rose from his desk in the corner to answer it. He spoke to someone briefly, closed the door, and returned.

Francis's heart leapt. Could it be a letter from Lord Burghley, lifting his ban and inviting him back to court? "Who was it?" He tried to keep the sound of hope from his voice.

Philippes wasn't fooled. He was hopeful too since his father's suit was in abeyance while Francis, his chiefest friend at court, was in disgrace. Patronage had been his to give, in better times, as well as to seek.

"Only the under butler. The benchers request the favor of your presence in the hall. They are ready to announce the name of the new Reader."

"So soon?" A mere week: it must be a record. But the honor of Gray's Inn was at stake as well. A shabby Reading would shame the whole Society and Lent was fast approaching.

* * *

One look at the stormy expression on Treasurer Fogg's face told Francis that his biggest competitor had not been chosen. He kept his eyes on the floor as he walked to his seat to hide the gleam of victory. He was now the only logical choice.

When Fogg pronounced his name, George Humphries cried, "Impossible! Impossible! By all rights, I should be next!" Welbeck drowned him out with a torrent of invective.

Francis allowed himself a small grin. With heroic effort, he would rise to this occasion and deliver a Reading that would cast the other Inns of Court into the shade. He ignored the protests raging about him and turned his thoughts to the enjoyable problem of choosing a statute that raised questions with both crowd-pleasing drama and intellectual interest. He should have little trouble outdoing whatever poor James Shiveley might have planned.

The vision of shiny coins in a flat box rose again in his mind. He wouldn't have credited Shiveley with sufficient imagination for conspiracies. Nor with the courage to engage in clandestine deliveries, for that matter. But if

Shiveley had not been the conspirator, how had Smythson's letter found its way onto his desk?

TWENTY-SIX

Tom Clarady tried to see Clara twice during the following week. Both times he was rebuffed by the uncharmable surgeon and told to return on the date appointed. No sooner. So he contented himself with sending daily gifts of sonnets and trinkets: a blue satin ribbon, an Italian glass bead, a lock of his own hair.

His friends urged him to distract himself from his lovelorn state by joining in the revels at the Inn. At first, he refused to play any game of which Stephen was the captain. Then Ben convinced him that the season of Misrule was a hallowed tradition at the Inns of Court in which all gentlemen participated as a matter of honor.

Stephen was in his element. That his princedom was a mere figment deflated his puffed-up self-importance not one jot. He attracted a new circle of toadies and began to prattle about taking up some role at court. Tom wished he would pack up and leave, although he felt a cold clench of dread about his possible parting shot. Would the benchers throw him out on his arse? His only plan was to lash himself to the mast and hang on. Something would turn up. Something always did.

Tom gave himself over to a week of unfettered revelry and swiftly earned the respect of his fellow Graysians for his willingness to risk life and limb in pursuit of mischief. He stole a flag from the court of the Middle Temple in broad daylight, racing up Chancery Lane with a pack of furious lawyers at his heels. He bodily ejected no fewer than five spies from Lincoln's Inn who were laboring under the delusion that Gray's kept its official secrets stored in the wine cellar.

Trumpet was the chief onsetter of their more perilous forays. The boy was fearless and had a gift for strategy that Tacitus would have admired. He and Tom were well matched in spirit and found themselves having twice as much fun without Ben and Stephen slowing them down. No debate, no quibbling— just dive in and start punching!

The only low point in the week came when Tom's *Lay of the Limner* was laughed off the dais, handing the prize for best ballad to newcomer Thomas Campion. He could only hope that Clara liked it better than the finicky lackwits at Gray's.

* * *

Later that week, Stephen commandeered the benchers' dais after supper to conduct a review of the men he had chosen for his embassy to the Inner Temple. He sat in the center seat, with his privy council on his left and his new toadies on his right. Each would-be retainer was obliged to array himself in the costume he proposed to wear and present himself for the Prince's approval.

"*Cross garters?* In 1586?" Stephen scoffed. "What's next, a codpiece? Are you perchance on your way to the annual dinner of the Fishmonger's Guild? Away with you! Your *ensemble* pains my eyes even by candlelight."

The hall was lively that evening. Half of the room had been cleared for dancing. Flutes and tambors wove a musical thread through the general tapestry of noise. The other half of the hall was devoted to gaming: dice, tables, and primero. Tom preferred to spend his money on things that he could keep, like gloves and buttons, but the house took a percentage of every bet. Another cut went into the pockets of the butler and under butler. The rest was used to fund the revelries; so, in a sense, all losses were gains.

Stephen judged costumes with the zeal other men gave to Parliamentarian debate. He ought to have been born a tailor. He had an impeccable eye for line and color and an intuitive sense of when a man had gone too far with his embellishments. "A ruff should frame the face, not block the doorway," he pronounced. Tom quite agreed.

Many men were eager to receive his advice. The season of Misrule was a welcome opportunity to shed the gloomy hues legislated by the benchers. A man could scarcely cover his naked frame without perforce dropping a shilling in the box. Were they monks? They were not. They were men of the world. Tom was grateful for Stephen's tutelage in this area. Knowing how to dress for every occasion was likely to be more useful to him in the long run than the forms of action or Aristotle's rhetoric.

Tom, Trumpet, and Ben contributed to the judging by tossing dried peas at the worst sartorial offenders and whistling and stamping their feet for costumes of exceptional artistry.

Bacon and a group of barristers sat at the ancients' table working on the Christmas Eve masque. Trumpet's uncle, Nathaniel Welbeck, kept waddling over and quacking insults. Humphries pattered behind him as usual, bleating short laughs. He'd gotten bolder lately; he even dared a few jibes of his own. Bacon treated them both with supercilious disdain, but Tom detected a tremor of effort in the display.

"He doesn't seem to be having much fun," Tom said. "I thought he wanted to be Reader. You said it was a huge honor."

"It is," Ben said, "but it's also a huge amount of work. And it's stirring up all the old resentments with the other ancients. I'm honestly worried about his health. But he insists on driving himself to write this masque on top of everything else."

"He should have turned down the Readership," Trumpet said. "My uncle says —"

"Your uncle is the chief offender," Ben retorted. "He and Humphries will drive poor Mr. Bacon into an early grave."

Tom tuned them out. He didn't care a fig about politics at Gray's. He wanted to think about Clara, to invoke her beauty in his mind's eye and remember the shivery thrill of her muted consonants and voluptuous vowels. He felt full of thrumming energies, straining to be unleashed.

"Her lips are too big." Trumpet broke into his reverie. He sounded like he'd been pondering the topic for some time and had reached a final ruling. "They seem unwholesome, like overripe fruit."

"Her lips are magnificent," Tom said.

"Her eyes are too deeply set," Trumpet said. "They look secretive, ill-tempered. That type doesn't age well. Trust me, in a few years, she'll look like a hag."

"Angels never age." Tom's love was imperturbable.

"The thing that bothered me," Ben said, leaning across Trumpet, "was that she never answered the question about her marital status."

Tom shrugged. "Stephen frightened her. And you confused her, barging in with your questions. English is not her native tongue, may I remind you. If it were, she couldn't say *Tom* in that delightful way." He pronounced it again, softening his voice and rounding his lips: *"Tom."*

Trumpet groaned. "I need more wine." He waved at the under butler who was monitoring a boisterous game of dice. The man raised a questioning hand and Trumpet mimed filling a cup from a pitcher. The under butler nodded and drifted off toward the buttery.

"She was evasive," Ben said, unconvinced. "Something isn't right. And what of that last?" He looked at Trumpet.

"I wondered about that too." Trumpet met his gaze. "I thought she said, 'But he was neither.'"

"That's what I heard," Ben said. "Meaning that the second barrister was neither tall nor redheaded. Meaning it couldn't have been Mr. Shiveley. Didn't you hear it that way, Tom?"

"No. And if I did, why would I care? It's over. Case closed."

Trumpet and Ben traded dour looks. "It isn't over," Ben said. "Shiveley may have been the Catholic conspirator, but I don't think he was the murderer."

"I don't think so either," Trumpet said. "Not the murderer, I mean. He was probably the conspirator."

"Mr. Bacon said the matter was closed and we were free to enjoy the revels." Tom shot a sly grin at Ben. "Are you disputing the foremost legal mind of his generation?"

Ben frowned. "No, of course not. But —"

"Cheer up," Tom said. "Maybe someone else will die mysteriously and we'll get to investigate again. I'll be the first to volunteer. However —" He held up his index finger. "Dead men do not love."

"Oh, spare us!" Trumpet pretended to be choking on Tom's rhetoric. The pretense turned into a real cough. Luckily, the under butler arrived with a fresh pitcher of wine. Trumpet opened his purse and drew out a few coins to pay for it.

"Those are nice and shiny." Tom plucked one out of Trumpet's hand to examine it. "Like the ones in Shiveley's box. Where'd you get them?"

"From my uncle."

Tom turned to Stephen. "Look, Your Grace, what do think of these? Nice, no?"

"Very nice." Stephen took the coin and turned it over and over, admiring its silvery sheen. He said to the under butler, "Let's hold back a supply of these, as you find them. I'll use them for special tips."

"Very good, my lord." The under butler held his palm out to receive the coin. Stephen made him wait; he loved to make people wait these days.

Tom snatched it from him and dropped it in the servant's hand. "Let the man get back to the tables, Your Grand Purpoolishness. You need the revenues."

Stephen treated him to a display of earlish disdain. Tom marveled at how little it impressed him. Once upon a time, it would have had him scrambling to make up.

Now all he wanted was to gaze endlessly into a pair of sapphire eyes. He murmured to himself, rounding his lips in a kissable pucker, "Welwet welts."

Ben chuckled. Trumpet groaned. "Here we go again."

"He can't understand anything but poetry," Ben said. "We'll have to speak his own language. Let's see . . ." He thought a moment and began a verse. "*Not Cupid's arrows cause my heart to melt, nor—* uh—" He waved his hand in a circle as if summoning a line. "*Nor Cupid's footsies tread my wool to felt?*"

Trumpet, giggling in short spurts, added, "*Nor Cupid's farts which here we've surely smelt.*"

Stephen laughed in genuine mirth for the first time that evening. He intoned the final line: "*Nought sears my soul like Clara's welwet welt.*"

Tom sat in silence for a full half minute, staring into his cup of wine, nodding his head with a half smile playing about his lips. Then he said, in a mock Italian accent, "I will draw and quarter each and every one of you and stake your heads over the Temple Bar."

TWENTY-SEVEN

The next day was fine; at least, it wasn't raining. Tom penned a short love note to send with his daily offering to Clara. Today, it was a ruff his mother had embroidered that was too small for him but very nice. Then he joined the other lads in the fields behind Gray's to practice shooting and archery. According to Ben's father, it was incumbent upon all gentlemen to maintain the skill. Longbows were well enough for traditionalists, but Tom was a modern man. He preferred his pistols. He liked the bang and the flash and the sharp stink of the smoke.

After dinner, Stephen summoned his court for a short conference. Tom, Trumpet, and Ben were directed to meet with their counterparts at the Inner Temple to plan the procession for the upcoming embassy. Ben grumbled about stealing time from Mr. Bacon, but the others persuaded him.

"The fresh air will revive your mind," Tom argued. "You're no use to him if you're all stale and fusty."

The meeting was entirely successful. They quickly agreed that the Inner Temple embassy would await the delegation from Gray's at the Temple Bar, the traditional point of entry for monarchs into the City of London. This quadrupled the length of the journey from Gray's since in order to arrive on the western side of Temple Bar, they would have to ride up Holborn all the way to Broad St. Giles, then down Drury Lane to the Strand.

Stephen would be immensely pleased. Where is the grandeur in a procession that processes directly from point A to point B? And the open fields along their route would allow ample space for spectators.

Trumpet made a note: round up an impressive number of spectators.

Their labors done, they were able to devote their attention to the drinking of a goodish quantity of a quite superior ale. Tom found the Inner Temple men to be most hospitable. He felt himself truly in his element amongst these sophisticated wits, especially after the fourth pitcher.

"S'wunnerful gennelmun," he declared, as the lads staggered outside. A cool riverine breeze danced out of the Temple gardens and slapped him on both cheeks, dashing off some of the stupor laid upon him by the drink and the overheated chamber.

"Treated me like a gennelmun," he added.

"Why wouldn't they?" Ben asked. He'd had to turn himself around twice to get aimed toward home.

Tom shrugged. "When'm with Stephen, it's always 'Lord this, Lord that, oh, no trouble, Clarady here will pay.' M'a purse wi' legs."

"Stephen's not here," Ben astutely observed.

"People take their people's faces at face value," Trumpet said, almost comprehensibly. He stopped and burped voluptuously. He smoothed his moustache. "Better. Tom. You dress like a gentleman. You talk like a gentleman. Ergo, you are a gentleman."

"It's that simple?"

"Simplicity is often the sign of truth," Ben quoted, raising his right arm for emphasis. The gesture sent him reeling sideways. Tom steered him forward again.

They reached the arch that broached onto Fleet Street and paused to collect their wits before diving into the traffic. Sunset was nearly upon them. Shopkeepers were taking in their wares and pulling up their shutters while shoppers pleaded for one last purchase. Coaches rattled down the center of the thoroughfare, splashing muck with scant regard for people on foot.

"Look there!" Ben cried. "It's Clara's husband!" He pointed across the street at a blocky man with a heavy sack slung over his shoulder.

"He's still got that sack," Trumpet said. "Perhaps he's some sort of porter."

"Whatever he is," Tom said, "by my mother's virtue, I'll speak to him. I want to know what he means, spreading lies about my angel."

Ben grabbed his arm. "Don't even think of it, Tom. You're too drunk."

Tom grinned. "F'weren't drunk, I wouldn't have the stomach to try him."

He dashed across the street, squeaking past an oncoming coach. The driver cracked his whip after him, cursing fluently. Tom twisted in midstep, gave the driver a half bow, then stuck up a finger and jogged on.

"Hoi! You, there! Fleming!"

The man turned and growled at him. "You again! What do you want with me?"

Tom slowed to a stop, barely panting. "I want a word with you. About Clara."

"My wife?" The man squared his jaw, emphasizing the cragginess of that feature.

"She says otherwise."

"Then she lies."

Tom's nostrils flared. He wanted to pulverize the man, but he wasn't cup-shot enough to throw the first punch. Then he spotted something that might change the balance.

Trumpet had sped around the other side of the street and was now creeping up behind the Fleming on tiptoe, grinning so broadly his pixie eyes were nearly closed.

Tom fixed his own eyes on the Fleming's face to hold his attention. He tried to ignore the trio of apprentices who, attracted to law student robes like bluebottle flies to a dung heap, were stalking Trumpet in a scathing imitation of his drunken skulk.

Out of a corner of his eye, Tom saw Ben sauntering toward them, hands behind his back, whistling "Fair Phyllis I Saw Sitting All Alone." The Fleming cast him a distracted glance.

The good citizens of Westminster, smelling trouble, scattered to give them a wide berth.

Tom smiled at the Fleming — a bright, friendly smile — and bobbed his head courteously. That confused the jolt-head. Then, by way of making conversation while his confederates gained their positions, he said, "I suppose someone must have told you — your mother, perhaps, or your father, though I doubt you ever knew him — that you're an idle-headed canker. A rank pustule? No? Not even an irksome, crook-pated, pathetical nit?"

The Fleming, his face as red as hot steel, roared and swung a fist like a blacksmith's hammer.

Tom ducked, bounced back up, and popped him on the chin. "God's bollocks!" he wailed as he cradled his injured hand. "What're you made of?"

"Little English," the Fleming sneered. "Perhaps I'll crush you." He set his sack on the ground by his feet and rubbed his hands together. He reared back to give himself plenty of room to swing.

Ben glided in at the critical moment and extended a long leg, causing the Fleming to miss a step, overbalance, and trip over Trumpet, who was crouched behind him with his hands on his knees. He fell flat on his back, where he was pounced upon by three gleeful apprentices and one small gentleman of Gray's.

"Oh, you've dropped your sack." Ben picked it up and hefted it as if trying to guess its weight. He muttered, "Something about this shape . . ."

"Give me that," the Fleming shouted. He reached out a massive arm, plucked one of his diminutive tormentors from his chest, and tossed him aside.

Tom danced around his apprentice-infested adversary, seeking a way to inflict damage on his target without harming any of his allies.

Ben opened the sack and let out a sharp whistle. "Now here's an interesting turn of events." He reached in and pulled out a few sheets of paper.

The Fleming bucked and rolled, scattering boys onto the ground. He surged to his feet and aimed himself toward Ben.

Tom shouted, "Look out!" and leapt in front of his friend. To do what, he had no idea. But this was his fight.

The Fleming thrust him aside with one granite fist to the shoulder. Ben jumped out of reach, dropping the sack. The Fleming scooped it up and plowed past them, nearly trampling Trumpet, who rolled out of his path in the nick of time.

"After him!" Tom yanked Trumpet up and then winced at the pain in his shoulder. He was lucky the man had been off balance.

They pelted after him. "Move!" Tom roared at one of the apprentices, who hopped into a doorway.

The Fleming ran up Chancery Lane. Tom swerved after him, slipped on a heap of horseshit, and caromed into a pieman who was coming the other way. He and the man grabbed each other to keep from going down, but the tray and the pies went flying. Trumpet skidded on his heels behind them, clutching at a signpost and swinging halfway around.

"I'm sorry," Tom said, desperately trying to keep an eye on the Fleming while freeing himself from the pieman's panicky grasp.

The man stared down at his pies, broken and begrimed in the filthy street, and burst into tears. "I'm ruint!"

"Oh, no. Don't cry." Tom glanced up the street. His quarry was gone. He sighed, recognizing defeat. "Please," he said to the pieman. "Let me pay for what I've damaged." He pulled out his purse.

Trumpet delicately plucked the pie tray from the mire and handed it to the pieman with a small bow. The man took it, but kept his eyes on Tom's purse.

"Can't any of these be saved?" Ben studied the mess on the ground. But then they were jostled from behind by a trio of women so absorbed in their chatter that they failed to notice they were mashing good pork pies beneath their feet.

Tom sighed again and fished out a larger coin.

TWENTY-EIGHT

Now I'm sober again," Tom said. "All that lovely ale, wasted. Let's get a drink on the way home."

"Anywhere but the Antelope," Trumpet said. "Mrs. Sprye will banish me forever if she sees I've been brawling again."

"Worse," Tom said. "She'll banish us along with you."

They stopped at an alehouse off Chancery Lane for a quick draft. Ben and Tom availed themselves of the jakes in back, dabbling their hands in the water barrel after. Tom tucked in his shirt, restored one fallen stocking, and was more or less as good as new. Trumpet, too fastidious to use the stinking privy, was once again bedraggled from head to toe. He went on inside and ordered three large mugs of small ale.

"I'm not through with that clay-brained Fleming," Tom said, lifting his mug. "Why does he run from me? Why can't he answer one simple question?"

Ben and Trumpet exchanged weary looks. "I believe he did," Ben said. "Didn't I hear him say, 'My wife' when you asked him about Clara?"

"She's a married woman, Tom." Trumpet slapped him on the shoulder. "Accept it. But she doesn't live with the brute and I'd say she hates him."

"Who doesn't?" Tom grumbled. "Whether she lives with him or not, he's still popping up everywhere I go, getting up my nose. I'd like to have it out with him once and for all, but—" He rubbed his sore hand ruefully. "And it's uncourteous to draw a blade against an unarmed foe. So I'm stuck with the block-headed whoreson."

"Not for long," Ben said. He'd been reading one of the sheets of paper he'd taken from the Fleming's sack, tilting backward to catch the light from the one miniscule window the alehouse boasted. "He'll soon be lodging in the Tower with his movements well restricted." He waved the page at his friends, his dark eyes gleaming. "This is one of the pamphlets Smythson's letter was warning about. Drink up, *camerades!* We've got to get these to Mr. Bacon without delay."

Tom gulped the rest of his ale.

"Let me see that." Trumpet took the sheet from Ben, reading it as they walked outside.

Tom slid tuppence to the alewife. "A purse with legs," he muttered, hurrying after them. "What's it say?"

Trumpet handed him the page. He tugged at Ben's sleeve. "We can't go that way."

"It's the straightest path." Ben was facing up Chancery.

Trumpet shook his head. "We have to go around. Mrs. Sprye will see us anywhere on High Holborn. Or her servants will, which is the same thing."

Ben growled but gave in. Banishment from the Antelope was a dire fate for any student at the Inns of Court.

"Wait one moment." Tom held up a finger while he stopped to read the pamphlet. Titled *Admonition to the Nobility and People of England and Ireland*, it seemed to be about crusades and chivalry. Then he realized that was merely a thin veil over a call to support a Spanish invasion to murder Queen Elizabeth and place a Catholic on the throne of England.

Tom was shocked. He was outraged. He shook the page at his friends. "Who would read such villainous tripe!"

Ben shook his head. "Deluded people, people with romantic fantasies about the past."

205

"People who have been set down or prevented from rising," Trumpet said. "Not everyone is happy with the way things have changed here. My uncle says—"

"Our queen is the greatest monarch in all Christendom." Tom stabbed a finger at Trumpet for emphasis. "The. Greatest. If Mr. Welbeck says different, he's wrong. My father would have him flogged for even thinking otherwise. God's whiskers, I'll flog him myself!"

"Can we at least walk faster if we have to take the long way round?" Ben pleaded. "The Fleming must have been on his way to deliver those pamphlets. If we hurry, we might catch the receiver."

They took the back roads, angling up to pass the western edge of Holborn. The sun sat on the horizon, casting long shadows across the empty farmland. They left the path when it veered north toward the duck pond, cutting straight across the fields. As they passed into the shadow of a large holly, Tom tripped over something thick and soft.

"What the devil?" He stooped to peer beneath the shrub. "Oh, no! Not another one!"

A man lay sprawled full-length under the holly with his arms outstretched as if he had been dragged.

"I don't believe it," Trumpet said. "Why us?"

"It's the Fleming," Ben said. "Look at those shoulders." He bent, took hold of the man's torso, and tugged him over, rolling him out of the shadows so they could see his face. "It's him, all right."

"Oh, horrible!" Trumpet clapped his hands to his face. "Look at his belly. He's been stabbed."

The Fleming's midsection was dark and wet.

Ben smiled grimly. "Well, Tom, it looks as if your angel is a widow after all."

TWENTY-NINE

Francis Bacon sat at his desk, writing faster as the evening descended, loath to suffer the break in concentration that rising to light the candles would entail. Pinnock was visiting his family in Hackney and his assistant, Philippes, had been sent to Dover with a packet of letters, so Francis was obliged to fend for himself.

Someone pounded on his chamber door.

"*Intro*," he called, without pausing.

"Mr. Bacon?"

"One moment." Francis held up his left index finger, dipped his pen in the inkpot, and dashed off the rest of his sentence. Then he set his quill in its holder and looked up.

Benjamin Whitt stood in the doorway, a troubled expression marring his plain but pleasant features.

"Mr. Whitt? What's amiss?"

"Another body, sir. Another murder."

Francis frowned at him. "Have I been appointed coroner for Gray's Inn?"

"No, sir. Forgive me. But—" Whitt faltered.

Francis relented. He had been appointed, if *sub rosa* and *ad tempus*, investigator of suspicious deaths. "Stairs?"

"Stabbed."

"Hm." Francis frowned again. "Like Smythson?"

"No. Less blood. Probably only one or two strikes. It's hard to be certain in the twilight."

"Where?"

"In the fields." Whitt tilted his head toward the west.

"A Gray's man?"

"No, sir. A Fleming."

That was a surprise. Francis blinked, twice. He smiled suddenly. "One so seldom encounters Flemings in the ordinary run of things, yet here they are, thickly populating our recent events." He knew his levity was inappropriate, but he felt a little giddy, as he often did after a period of intense concentration.

"It is odd, sir," Whitt ventured.

Francis composed himself. "Any relation to our limner?"

"Supposedly, he was her husband."

"Supposedly?"

"She said nay, he said yea. Tom quarreled with him on that score scarce half an hour ago, across from the Temple Bar."

"He didn't stab him, I suppose."

"No, sir!" Ben looked chagrined. "We all got a bit involved in the affray. But the Fleming ran away unharmed."

"Hm." Clarady's *affaires de coeur* were unlikely to be relevant. Francis ran a hand over his head and glanced out the window. It would soon be fully dark. "I suppose you want me to come look at him?"

"Yes, sir. I wouldn't bother you, but for this." Whitt stepped forward to hand him a printed sheet of paper.

Francis unfolded it and leaned back toward the window. A single glance told him everything. "Oh, dear." He caught Ben's eyes. "The pamphlets from Smythson's letter."

"Yes, sir. And today is the seventeenth. The half moon?"

Francis clucked his tongue. "I'd forgotten all about the date." He skimmed the page while Whitt explained how he had obtained the sample. The prose was elegant in places. He smelled the involvement of the English Jesuit College in Rheims. Catholic missionizing aimed at England was the principal export of that community.

He should have known better. Shiveley's death had been too convenient, too timely, too well aligned with what he had wanted to find. He cast his mind back to the scene in Shiveley's chambers. In his eagerness to be done with the matter, he'd overlooked a number of details that ought to have been pursued. He gazed bleakly at his quill and inkpot. He'd have to write to his uncle again to retract his earlier pronouncement of success. His hopes of a swift end to exile were snuffed out. And he still had a murderer and conspirator to catch.

"Well, let's go have a look at him." Francis rose from his desk and glanced down into the yard. Three men were jogging past the hall toward the gap between buildings that gave access to the fields. "You couldn't have chosen a worse time to find another body: right before supper during a mesne vacation. No one has anything better to do than gawk."

Except me. He fetched his rabbit-lined cloak from the inner chamber and followed Whitt outside. One might almost believe that these murders were deliberately intended to prevent him from producing an historic Reading.

* * *

They rounded his building and passed through the gap. A man ran past them, returning to the hall, shouting, "Your Grace! Your Grace!"

Francis's head whipped around. There had been no dukes in England since Catholic Norfolk lost his head for conspiring with the Scottish queen. Then he remembered: the Prince of Purpoole and his court of Misrule.

He quickened his pace. "We must hurry. We'll have a crowd in a minute."

No need to wonder how the news had spread. The privateer's son was stomping about the landscape, gesticulating wildly, shaking a piece of paper at the Trumpington boy. A few heated words carried toward them on the wind: "— a perfidious popish plot that my father —"

It would seem that the vaunted loyalty of privateers was not altogether feigned. Still, there were appropriate times for expressions of patriotic fervor. This was not one of them.

Glancing over his shoulder, Francis saw clusters of men standing at the windows of Colby's Building, watching the scene in the fields. He spoke urgently to Ben. "He must stop that shouting."

Whitt called, "Tom!" He made a throat-slicing motion with his index finger.

Clarady responded with a wide-armed questioning gesture. At least he stifled his ranting.

They covered the few remaining yards and joined the other two. Clarady awaited them with his hands on his hips. Trumpington was pacing around the holly bush, peering at the ground as if searching for something. He straightened now to face the newcomers.

"We only have a minute." Francis pitched his voice low. "I strongly advise that we keep the elements of our prior investigations to ourselves."

Clarady winced, shamefaced. But perhaps his shouts had not been clearly heard. The wind was blowing from the east.

"We mustn't alert the conspirator to our special interest in this matter." Francis turned now to look at the source of the trouble. The light was rapidly fading, their shadows stretching back toward the Inn. Even thus dimly revealed, the sight was repellent. The man had been enormous, barrel-chested with massive limbs. Yet now he lay slack and wasted on the ground. Francis's eyes skittered across the darkened midsection, glistening thickly in the twilight glow. He recoiled, tasting a bitter gorge, as if someone had forced a noxious potion down his throat. He shuddered and turned his back.

He spoke to Trumpington. "Did you find anything?"

"Me?"

"Weren't you looking? Just now?"

The boy shrugged. "Not really. Well, a little. It's too dark to see. There isn't anything, anyway. Sir."

He seemed distracted. Francis could see no special reason for it in the situation at hand. Granted, the sight of this body was disturbing, more so than he would have expected. After all, the fellow had been a stranger. Why should the mere sight of a corpse elicit such a reaction? Or perhaps it was the sharp smell of fresh blood? The ominous effect of the lowering light? It was curious — and frustrating — how little control one's intellect had over one's visceral responses.

He shook his head. This was no time for introspection. He turned to Whitt. "You mentioned a sack."

Whitt said, "Yes, sir." Then to the others: "Isn't it here?"

"No sack." Clarady sounded thoroughly disgusted. "The poxy traitor must have taken it."

"It might still be out here somewhere." Trumpington frowned at Clarady. "We can make a thorough search in the morning."

"Morning will be too late," Francis said. "The sack must have been received by the conspirator. Otherwise it would surely still be in the Fleming's possession."

"He might have hidden it nearby," Trumpington said. "He might have wanted to hold it back until he got his money."

"Did you find a purse?" Francis asked.

The boy blanched. "I didn't look. I didn't want to put my hands . . ."

Francis shuddered. "No, of course not. Hm. Well, I see no sensible reason to hide the goods before meeting with their receiver. We'll assume the sack is now in possession of our conspirator." He paused. "Do we know the Fleming's name?"

The lads shook their heads.

"No matter." He tried to think of other useful observations that could be made at this point. That the man had been stabbed, like Smythson, was probably relevant. The lack of frenzy could be the result of prior experience. If this were indeed the killer of Smythson and, he must now suppose, Shiveley, he was growing accustomed to violence. Which consideration leant greater urgency to the need to apprehend him.

His thoughts were interrupted by Treasurer Fogg's voice booming across the field. "Hold the rest back! Let no more into the field until further notice."

Francis spoke rapidly to his pupils. "We'll discuss this later. No one else knows yet of the probable connection between this death and the earlier ones. We must keep that to ourselves as long as possible to avoid alerting the killer. Don't volunteer any more than is necessary. Don't say anything about our previous investigations, Lord Essex's men, or the limner. Do not utter the word *Catholic*. And don't mention the sack."

Fogg strode up, followed by half a dozen benchers and ancients, including Nathaniel Welbeck and George Humphries. "Bacon? What's the matter here?"

Bacon said, "My pupils found this man as they were returning from — er, to the Inn."

"Is that so?" Fogg turned his heavy glare toward the boys.

"Yes, sir," Clarady responded. "I stumbled upon him, literally. He's dead. Stabbed."

Whitt added, "We naturally called upon our tutor first. To advise us."

Francis caught Whitt's eye and shook his head minutely. Too much information. Whitt grimaced; Fogg noticed. Francis's heart began to sink.

"Why would you need advice?" Fogg asked. "You should have come directly to me." He moved in to inspect the body on the ground, the others close behind him. They recoiled as one from the terrible sight. "Ugh." He blew out a noisy breath. "Any idea who he is?"

"None whatsoever," Trumpington replied, too quickly.

The boy was studying his uncle's costume as if he himself had tailored it and feared to have erred in some essential detail. He seemed especially concerned about the cuffs and sleeves.

Welbeck noticed the scrutiny. He preened himself, turning slightly this way and that. "I see you admire my new doublet."

"It's very clean," Trumpington said.

Francis thought that an odd comment, but it apparently held meaning for Welbeck. He replied, "Yes, indeed. Nary a blemish. You needn't concern yourself on that account."

A domestic matter. Francis dismissed it from his attention.

Humphries spoke. "I think it's odd that these two —" He tilted his scraggly beard toward Clarady and Trumpington "— are always on the spot whenever a Gray's man is found dead. Or a man found dead at Gray's."

"What's odd about it?" Fogg asked.

Humphries pulled in his chin. "Nothing. Nothing. It's just —" He cast his eyes about as if seeking support. No one offered any. "Here we have a man who has died suddenly, by violent means, and here again is Bacon with his . . . with his . . . with his piglets."

"Ha!" Welbeck barked his approval of the insulting yet inane remark. "Good one, Humphries!"

"I prefer 'Francis and his franklins,'" Francis said, unable to resist a challenge of verbal skill. Really, a man's facile tongue was as much a traitor to his better judgment as Gray's hidden conspirator was to the queen's peace.

He earned a smirk from Welbeck and a small frown from Whitt, who perhaps did not appreciate the downgrading of his social status. No one else seemed to grasp the outmoded reference.

"Have you any idea how this man came to die here, just outside our Inn?" Fogg asked.

Francis drew a breath to answer but was forestalled by Welbeck. "Looks to me like a falling out among thieves."

"Me too," Humphries said. "A falling out. An argument. Some sort of dis —"

Fogg's brows beetled at him. "We know what *falling out* means, thank you, Humphries. Why here? There's nothing out here but Gray's."

"Perhaps they were traveling north," Welbeck said. "On their way to Oxford."

"Could have been Oxford," Humphries said.

"Except that they weren't on the road," Fogg said.

"They may have been avoiding the road," Welbeck said. "Avoiding notice. Thieves would think in such terms."

"They would." Humphries nodded. "Certainly they would."

Francis was not unhappy about the trend of their discussion. A hypothesis based on the behavior of thieves nicely covered the scanty facts and led to no undesirable further speculations. Like so much academical philosophizing, it was superficially plausible yet wholly divorced from reality.

Fogg frowned, pushing his lower lip in and out. "I suppose that could be the case. Or these thieves may have been conspiring to commit acts of caption and apportation — larceny — at Gray's."

"Security has grown lax," one of the benchers said, inaugurating a widespread grumble about nonspecific lapses of responsibility.

Francis was about to interrupt them to suggest that the body be removed before the light failed, when he saw a band of men with torches passing through the gap. They marched across the field in formation, led by Lord Stephen. The torches drove the dregs of the day before them, replacing the omniluminescent gray of twilight with bronzy flares. They arrayed themselves around the group.

"Mr. Fogg. Gentlemen," Lord Stephen said. He flashed a supercilious smile at his messmates then returned his attention to the Treasurer. "I assumed you would need assistance."

"Very thoughtful, Your Grace." Fogg smiled. "The light is indeed most welcome."

Lord Stephen beckoned one of his torch men to follow as he stepped toward the holly bush. He took a quick look at the body and cried, "Why, it's the Fleming! How came he here?" He cocked his head at Francis as if expecting an answer. Then he gasped and pointed at the eastern sky. "Don't tell me: tonight is the half moon. Am I right?"

"My lord," Francis said, "if you —"

"Do you know this man?" Fogg demanded.

"Stephen," Clarady said, his voice low and tense with warning. "Say no more."

Delabere frowned at him. He answered Fogg, "Of course not. How would I know him? He's a man of mean estate. Some sort of laborer, we assumed. Ugly, isn't he? But you should see his wife!"

He grinned at Fogg and Francis felt his heart clench in his breast. Heaven help them, the fool was being charming. He'd found himself in the center of attention, before a group of senior men, and meant to impress them. He could never do so with his legal knowledge — for that he have none — so now he meant to display one of his few talents: gossip.

"My lord," Francis said, "I must beg you to —"

Delabere cut him off with a little wave, as if to say, *Don't trouble yourself, I'll explain everything.* "We went to interview the said wife for Mr. Bacon. You know, about the Smythson matter. And, of course, because Tom had fallen madly in love with her. As per usual." He rolled his eyes.

"What Smythson matter?" Fogg looked sharply at Francis.

"Stephen," Clarady said, "kindly shut your lordly trap."

One of the prince's retainers stepped toward him, squaring his shoulders. "Mend your words when you address the prince, sirrah."

Clarady flushed darkly at the insult.

Delabere grinned nastily at him. "Well, she truly is a beauty. I might be inclined to have a go at her myself. But a limner? Really, Tom. Tradeswomen are more trouble than they're worth, I've told you time and again."

Clarady muttered through his teeth, "One more word, Steenie, and I'll lay you flat."

Delabere scoffed at him and cast a glance over his shoulder to indicate his coterie of devoted followers. Clarady's ability to influence the young lord had apparently come to an end.

"What about this so-called Smythson matter?" Fogg demanded.

"Yes, it's quite remarkable, really," Stephen babbled on. "This extraordinarily beautiful woman was standing in a window overlooking the lane where poor old Mr. Smythson was murdered. Can you imagine the luck? We're fairly certain she saw the whole thing."

"She's a limner?" Welbeck said.

"There was a witness?" Humphries said.

"Well, we never actually asked her," Stephen said. "When it turned out that old Mr. Shiveley had done the deed — which was a surprise to me, I can tell you, I never would have thought it — we never bothered to ask Clara whether she'd seen him there that day or no."

"Clara who?" Humphries said. "Where does she live?"

"Clara Goossens, of Oat Lane." Stephen pronounced the O's with an exaggerated foreign accent.

Clarady roared, "You weasel!" and lunged at him. He was pushed back by three of the prince's retainers.

"What's wrong, Tom? Afraid of poachers? You'll never get near her, you know. She's guarded by an absolute *dragon* of a female surgeon, if you can imagine such a creature. Truly frightening." Stephen shuddered dramatically. He was enjoying himself to the hilt. "But it's simply too astonishing, really, just too amazing, that along should come her *alleged* husband — the Fleming, as we called him for want of a name, as if we cared to know it — to get himself killed in our fields, right here, on the day of the half moon, just as old Smythson predicted in his letter."

"What letter?" Fogg turned his scowl on Francis. "What Smythson matter? What limner? Bacon, I demand an explanation."

Francis leaned toward him, making a futile attempt to direct his words to Fogg alone. "Treasurer Fogg, I crave your patience, this is hardly the place —"

"What had James Shiveley to do with all this?" one of the other benchers asked.

A general clamor arose. Francis was pelted with questions from all sides. At the edge of the group on his left, he saw Clarady arguing furiously with Lord Stephen, bodily restrained by three of the lord's retainers. On his right, Whitt and Trumpington stood back-to-back, stammering non-answers to a spate of queries. The Fleming lay forgotten under his shrub.

Francis closed his eyes and pinched the bridge of his nose.

THIRTY

Perhaps it's not a complete disaster," Whitt said.

No one answered him. Francis and his franklins were walking slowly back toward Chapel Court. He had finally managed to pull Fogg aside, promising that he would explain everything, but not there, not then, and not to everyone. First the body must be carried into shelter and the authorities must be notified.

The other men, led by the prating Lord Stephen and his honor guard of idiots, accompanied the litter bearing the Fleming's remains to the sacristy. The lawyers bickered about whether the Sheriff of Middlesex or the Queen's Coroner should be notified first.

Of course, they both should be notified, as nearly simultaneously as could be achieved. The protocols in this area were unclear and tended to revolve around the relative importance of the matter to the queen. Knowing what he knew, Francis intended to dispatch a note to his uncle that very evening.

They reached his stair. The servants were lighting the lanterns that hung before the doors. The sky was fully black in the east but for twinkling stars. Men were queuing for supper outside the hall, talking animatedly about the body in the field. Many faces turned toward Francis with expectant curiosity.

He ignored them. All he wanted was to return to the peace of his own chambers and a simple meal beside his own fire.

But not quite yet.

"A word, Gentlemen, if you will." He beckoned his pupils to follow him into the relative privacy of his staircase. He pulled open the door and encountered pitch-darkness. He'd forgotten to bring a candle in his earlier haste.

He felt a long arm reach over his shoulder and turned his head to face directly into the broad shoulders of the privateer's son. For a brief moment, he felt sheltered by a strong body and the warm smell of an active man. He inhaled slowly, savoring the sensation. A man who valued his privacy learned to appreciate rather than pursue.

Clarady lifted the lantern from its holder and grinned down at him. "We'll light you to your door." He stepped backward, breaking the spell.

"Thank you." Francis preceded them into the staircase. "You needn't come up; we'll only be a moment."

Clarady balanced the lantern on the newel post. The slots in the metal wind guard cast shadows in contorted shapes up the stairwell. Francis sat himself on a step about midway up. His pupils stood beneath him in postures of attention. He appreciated the leveling of heights.

"I fear I was overhasty in concluding our investigations," he said. "I confess, I was too eager to dispose of the matter."

Whitt said, "We were all glad to reach a conclusion."

Francis smiled at him, grateful for his willingness to share the blame. "Nevertheless, the decision and the responsibility were mine. Now we must begin afresh. The Fleming's murder cannot be unconnected to those of Tobias Smythson and James Shiveley. Occam's Razor won't allow it."

"Who's Occam?" Trumpington asked.

Francis blinked at him then remembered that the boy had not attended university. "Occam's Razor, also known as the *lex parsimoniae*, states that 'entities must not be multiplied beyond necessity.' That is to say, we ought to choose the simplest solution, the one requiring the fewest additional causes or stipulations. In the present matter, it is simpler to assume that one murderer is responsible for all three of the deaths related to Gray's than it is to propose a separate killer for each victim, thereby multiplying the causes or motives."

Trumpington frowned. "You're saying that if we find three murdered men, we should assume one single murderer. But if we find three horses standing in the yard, we don't assume they were all ridden in by a single rider."

Whitt clucked his tongue. "That's different."

"How?" Clarady asked.

Francis pursed his lips. "No, it's a sound analogy. It shows us that our information is as yet insufficient. If we were able to observe, for example, that two of the horses bore packs instead of saddles, we could comfortably conclude that a single man had brought all three horses into the yard."

"But if all bore saddles," Trumpington said, "it would be simpler to assume three riders than to concoct a tale whereby one man somehow came into possession of two riderless mounts."

"True enough," Francis said. "Unfortunately, we have no signs here as easily read as packs and saddles."

"Are we sure that James Shiveley was murdered?" Whitt asked.

"I am." Clarady seemed to surprise himself by the assertion. "Begging your pardon, Mr. Bacon, sir. But I think I thought it at the time. Things weren't right. Things were odd."

Francis wished that someone would teach the man to organize his thoughts before opening his mouth. Then he remembered that was his job now and restrained his impatience. "Elaborate, please, Clarady. What did you notice?"

"It wasn't anything that was there. It was the things that weren't there."

"You're talking riddles," Whitt said. "How could you see what wasn't there?"

"Easily," Trumpington snapped. "Let him talk."

Clarady gave one short nod. "First, the money. There wasn't enough of it."

Francis said, "You mentioned that at the time. I see now that I was overhasty in dismissing that fact. It was a clue."

Clarady shrugged and offered him a tight smile. Francis took the gesture as an acceptance of his oblique apology.

Francis said, "Shiveley would have laid in sufficient coins to pay the deliverer. Our killer could not resist so tempting a prize. Why waste a good murder?"

Clarady said, "Then there was the cloak. I remember wondering how Mr. Shiveley managed to trip himself on his own stair. Yes, it was dark, but still, he lived there. He went up and down those steps many times a day. We all thought, well, he must have heard a sound and turned too quickly and tripped on the end of his cloak. And that's what I remembered later: he wasn't wearing one. So he couldn't have tripped on it."

Trumpington snapped his fingers. "That's right, he wasn't! I remember thinking the same thing and forgetting it in the same moment."

"I've tripped on my own stairs more often than I care to admit," Francis said.

"Your mind is occupied with important matters," Whitt said.

Francis smiled at him. It was comforting to have so understanding an ally. Whitt was too tall and could hardly be described as comely, but his other attributes made up for those superficial failings. "I've never actually fallen to the bottom of the landing."

"I have." Clarady grinned ruefully. "Granted, I was drunk at the time. But I've never broken my neck nor even come close. I don't think it's that easy. I think maybe —"

"The killer did it for him." Trumpet twisted his hands and made a cracking sound.

"Ugly." Francis shuddered. "Also the act of a cold mind. Unlike Smythson's frenzied murderer." He thought for a moment. "It's possible. But your evidence is inconclusive."

Clarady frowned. He smoothed his moustache, a habit when he was thinking.

They all fell silent. The cheap tallow candle in the lantern hissed and spat out a gust of muttony smoke. The light in the stairwell flared up and then retreated as the wick sank into the melted fat. Only the slits on Francis's side of the lantern still glowed. The other men were cast into shifting shadows.

"The keys!" Clarady's outburst echoed up the stairwell. "I keep forgetting the cursed keys."

"Shiveley's keys, I presume? Were no keys —"

"They weren't there." Clarady caught himself. "I beg your pardon, Mr. Bacon. But I walked up and down those stairs, searching for something that might have made him trip. I remember the candle and the spill of dried tallow. I would have noticed a bunch of keys. And the chest was unlocked and so was his money box. Nobody leaves their money box unlocked."

"I was present when the chaplain reported to the bench." Francis reviewed the meeting in his memory. "He listed the items removed from the body, as a matter of course. No keys were mentioned."

"The killer took the keys." Clarady grinned triumphantly.

Francis smiled his concession. "Gentlemen, I believe we have sufficient grounds to conclude that James Shiveley was murdered."

Trumpington said, "It could have been a thief. The thieves that the Fleming fell out with, as my uncle suggested."

"I believe we can now dispense with that facile supposition."

"It wasn't thieves, is what he means," Clarady said.

"I speak English, thank you," Trumpington retorted. The boy was in an ill humor tonight, indeed. "My point is that we have no reason to assume the Fleming was killed by the same man that killed Shiveley."

"We do, though," Whitt said. "The letter, remember? In Smythson's handwriting, which we all recognized, warning of the delivery of the pamphlets, which the Fleming was carrying just before he was killed. The letter in the book on Shiveley's desk."

"A letter we were meant to find without delay," Francis added. "Like the rosary. I now believe both of them were planted to lead us to the desired conclusions without looking too closely at anything else." He shook his head at the stubborn boy. "I'm afraid there's no question that these deaths are related. The letter links them explicitly."

"It's probably a Spaniard." Clarady practically spat the word. "Or the French papist who wrote that villainous tripe."

Francis was startled by the abrupt tangent. "I assure you, there are neither Spaniards nor Frenchmen at Gray's Inn. Since we are societies wholly devoted to the study and practice of the English common law, the Inns of Court hold little attraction for the citizens of other nations."

"It could still be an outsider," Trumpington said. "A Jesuit priest, hiding in someone's chambers."

Francis clucked his tongue. "Unlikely. Think, Gentlemen! This man knows us. He knew that Smythson was attending the Queen's Day pageant. He saw him leave early. He followed him and killed him in the alley. He knew where Shiveley lived and at what time he went up to bed.

He walked with him or waited on the dark stair. He also knew the moment at which the Fleming would arrive in the fields west of the Inn to deliver his sack."

Whitt nodded. "The killer must have been someone that Shiveley knew. If a stranger had accosted him on the stair, he would have struggled, drawn his knife. Things would have looked very different."

"Was he out there, do you think?" Clarady asked. "Just now, in the field?"

That was a cautionary thought. That meant that the murderer-*cum*-conspirator was now privy to both the fact of Francis's interest in the matter and to the best remaining avenue for investigation.

"If he was, then he knows we're looking for him." Whitt echoed his thoughts. "He'll get rid of any evidence that could betray him."

"Then we'll never catch him," Trumpington said.

"I think we will," Francis said, although he had no grounds for such confidence.

No, that was wrong; he did have grounds. Excellent grounds. He'd pit his wits against any man in this Society and be certain of the outcome.

"What can we do now?" Clarady asked.

"I have to tell the benchers something," Francis said. "Too much was said out there." He considered his strategy while his pupils stood silently, waiting. They'd learned not to interrupt him when he was thinking, which touched him more than he would ever reveal. "Even if one of them is the killer, it is best to address them as a body. There is one benefit: they can order a comprehensive search of chambers."

"They can't search every room at once," Trumpington said.

"But they can order everyone into the hall while the search is conducted. It's been done." Francis rolled his eyes at the memory of that chaotic day. "All manner of distracting nonsense will be turned up, but something of use may emerge. More urgently, we must speak with that limner of yours. We must know what, if anything, she saw."

The lads exchanged a round of glances. They already knew something on this score. Francis felt a prickle of irritation. Why hadn't Whitt kept him apprised?

Whitt lowered his head and spoke to Clarady, "We have to tell him."

Clarady pulled Whitt by the sleeve, drawing him deeper into the shadows. "I don't want her involved," he whispered. "Look what happened to the Fleming."

Whitt whispered back, "She's already involved. Stephen blabbed her name to everyone out there."

Clarady hissed, "That's why! She's in danger."

Trumpington moved in behind them. His whisper buzzed with high-pitched sibilants. "She must speak. Her testimony is crucial."

Their hissing was an affront to the ears. "I can hear you, you know," Francis said. "Darkness is no impediment to sound."

Clarady drew in a deep breath, exhaled noisily, and nodded at his friends. They grouped themselves again at the foot of the stairs. Francis folded his hands upon his knees, preparatory to the receipt of the disputed information.

"We went to see her," Whitt said. "Saturday last. Not to ask about Smythson, but because Tom —"

"I understand that part," Francis said.

Whitt nodded. "We asked after her at the Dutch Church, as you suggested. That's where we saw the Fleming. Her husband, we were told. We followed him, but he ran and we lost him. So then we went on to the limner's house and spoke with her. She assumed right away that we had come about Smythson. That alone is evidence that she saw something pertinent."

"It was the day I first saw her," Tom said. "Smythson's murder is *why* I saw her. Of course she would assume we were there for that. It doesn't signify anything."

Trumpington said, "She knows something, though."

Would they never deliver the main thrust? "What, exactly, does she know?"

Whitt said, "We don't know, exactly. Tom reassured her that Smythson's killer had been identified and that it was all over. No one wanted to upset her." He grinned apologetically. "She really is extraordinarily beautiful. But I was curious if she had seen anything after all. You know, just curious."

"It remained an open question," Francis suggested.

"Yes. I wanted to close it. I asked her if she had seen a barrister and she said, 'Are they the ones that wear the velvet welts?' That made me think that yes, she had seen a barrister in that lane. She's an artist. She notices details. Then, as we were leaving, I asked if she had seen a tall, redheaded man. And she replied, 'But he was neither.'"

Francis smiled. "She saw him."

"She never said that," Clarady said.

"She did," Trumpington said. "I was looking right at her, past your shoulder. And she looked perplexed — uncertain — when she said it."

"I would like to speak with her myself," Francis said. "Bring her to the Antelope Inn tomorrow, if you please. Before dinner. Shall we say ten o'clock?"

"I'll go now," Clarady said. "She needs protection."

"You can't go now," Francis said. "It's dark. The city gates will be closed and you have no plausible excuse to offer the guards. I'm sure she's safe enough in her own home." Francis stood and shook his cloak to clear the folds from around his feet. "And she'll be safer still once she's told us what she knows."

THIRTY-ONE

Francis undid his cloak and tossed it onto a chest. With scarcely a pause, he picked it up and put it on again. He'd forgotten to ask Whitt to order his supper. If he wanted food, he would have to sup in commons.

The hall was alive with speculation about the body in the south field. Several men turned toward him as he made his way to the ancients' table, hoping he would have the full story. He offered only bland comments, striving to seem as if he knew no more than they. His messmates glared at him in an unwelcoming manner as he took his place. "No more *investigating* today?" Welbeck sneered. "Stairs quite free of unwanted corpses?" Francis saw no value in responding to his feeble sallies.

"I should have thought you'd be busy writing letters to your uncle," Humphries said. "Maybe he'll make you Treasurer."

"I fail to follow your logic," Francis said.

"A man dies, and you move up," Humphries said. "Another man dies, and up you go again."

"You can't deny it," Welbeck said.

"Of course I can," Francis said. "I passed the bar years before Tobias Smythson was killed. And my election as the Lent Reader has nothing to do with my uncle. In point of fact, he's not well pleased with me at present, owing precisely to unresolved questions surrounding the deaths you propose as my stairway to success."

"You see," Humphries said, his goatish beard bobbing as he nodded, "he instantly thinks of stairs when he thinks of the Readership. That's a guilty conscience speaking." He and Welbeck exchanged dark looks.

Francis sighed. Did they genuinely believe any of their own nonsense? He was spared the need to respond by the arrival of a savory pottage rich with mutton and redolent of winter herbs. A simple dish but as good as a feast when well prepared.

He ignored his messmates while he ate, although they continued their jibes and snickers for a while, entertaining each other with their paltry attempts at wit. Fortunately, he had excellent control over his attention, which enabled him to ignore background noises almost completely.

He set his mind to review the problem at hand. His pupils would bring the limner in the morning to be interviewed. That might prove conclusive; however, it was equally likely to be of little practical use. She might have seen a barrister's gown, but not a barrister's face. Not tall and not redheaded. That didn't narrow the field much. Francis let his gaze wander through the hall. He saw fewer than a dozen men with hair as red as Shiveley's. 'Tall' was a relative term. Tall compared to Tobias Smythson, a man of average height? She would have been looking downward. Surely that would have an effect on her perception.

He tore a piece from his loaf of manchet and chewed it thoughtfully. The flour had been less well sifted than could be desired; the crumb had tiny bits of grit.

He wished there were more that he could do. He needed a way to flush the killer into the open where he could be caught and get this filthy business over with. Not only because he longed to spend Christmas Eve Day in the queen's presence, but because these terrible murders had to be stopped.

He decided to write to his lord uncle in the morning. That was a ticklish task and he was too tired tonight. Tonight, he wanted nothing more than a few pages from the volume of *Essaies* by Michel de Montaigne that his brother had sent him from France. Something light yet pithy; then early to bed.

Those Wild Men, the Earl of Essex's retainers, should be recalled to London as soon as possible for questioning. Perhaps they could be brought to Gray's for dinner under some pretext, to look about the hall and try to spot the man they'd chased. But how to summon them? Courtesy demanded that he ask permission of Essex before writing to his retainers. He'd have to ask his uncle to do it. More delay and frustration. Sending messages through his uncle made him feel like a schoolboy on probation, which was more or less his position.

He glanced toward the benchers' table. Treasurer Fogg sat with a fixed smile pasted on his face, pretending to listen to the talkative man beside him. Francis was not the only one preoccupied with cares this evening. He remembered his suspicions concerning Fogg, Smythson, and the widow Sprye. What if the Catholic business were a separate matter? He'd neglected the other possibilities. Courtship and court appointments. Ambition and desire. Adding conspiracies to Fogg's slate of activities seemed excessive, but then, he was a man of parts.

* * *

Bacon finished his meal and prepared to leave. The hall was being transformed into a pleasure palace for the evening revels. Minstrels tuned their instruments in the gallery above the screen. Servants dismantled each trestle table as soon as its occupants rose, rearranging them around the walls for dicing and cards. The hanging candelabras were filled with rosemary-scented oil that gave the room a holiday flavor. A few men had already started dancing around the central hearth. The butler hovered near the door, ready to greet arriving guests. Women would grace the hall this night as well, adding the color and sheen of their wide skirts to the festive spectacle.

Christmastide at Gray's Inn. Francis normally enjoyed the convivial season, supping in commons two or three times a week and often staying for the music. This year, however, with little prospect of being allowed to spend Christmas with the court and these foul murders still laid upon his shoulders, he was simply exhausted.

Bed for him, and a good book.

George Humphries appeared beside him. "Leaving so early? You'll miss the fun."

"I've had enough excitement for one day."

"I'll walk with you," Humphries said. "I left some papers in the library that Welbeck has been asking me for."

They wormed through the press of gaily dressed revelers at the door. The night air felt cold and fresh on Francis's face. Lanterns were lit beside each door. Large torches marked the gate to Gray's Inn Road, where a pair of horses nosed through the arch. Yellow candlelight glowed behind a few panes around the yard, but only a few. Most men would be in the hall tonight.

They crunched across the gravel in silence. They had almost reached Francis's stair when the matched black horses clattered into the center of the yard, drawing a black coach as lustrous as a jewel box. The liveried footman jumped down and opened the door, from which debouched a riot of brilliant silks and velvets.

The Earl of Essex and his sister Lady Penelope Rich had come to Gray's to gamble. Francis couldn't be faulted if courtiers came to him. This was an opportunity not to be missed.

He took two steps toward the coach then turned back to his nearly forgotten colleague. "You'll excuse me, I trust." He walked on. Behind him he heard Humphries mutter, "No less than I would expect."

Francis skipped a little to catch up with the young nobles. He hastily smoothed his hair with the palm of his hand and checked the front of his doublet for smears. He circled around to approach them from the direction of the hall. They might assume he had come out to welcome them. He bowed from the waist. "My Lord Essex. How kind of you to grace our humble Society." He turned two degrees and bowed again. "Lady Rich." He quoted from one of the sonnets dedicated to her:

"Stella sovereign of my joy,
Fair triumpher of annoy,
Stella star of heavenly fire,
Stella loadstone of desire."

The charmed couple favored him with a friendly laugh. Lady Rich said, "I'd rather a poem from your own fertile mind, Mr. Bacon. They say that angels lend you feathers from their wings to make your quills."

"I am profoundly flattered, my lady." He bowed again.

"I understand congratulations are in order," Lord Essex said. "I'm greatly looking forward to your Reading. Might one inquire as to the topic?"

Francis was elated. He'd had no idea the earl took an interest in the law. They chatted about advowsons as they entered the hall and found their way to a dicing table. The earl fully appreciated the intriguing ramifications latent in the whole notion of incorporeal hereditaments. Even in so brief an exchange, Francis felt that a genuine bond had been established. Did he dare suggest — or rather enjoin, or plead — that the earl might utter a syllable or two in his favor to the queen? He shuddered. Better not; his uncle would hear of it. He heard everything.

231

Francis made a show of establishing Lord Essex in the best spot at the table. He turned to assist Lady Rich and found her staring across the room, eyes narrowed with hostility. He followed her gaze to Treasurer Fogg, who was playing primero with some judges from the Queen's Bench. Sir Avery shot anxious glances at her whilst pretending to be absorbed in the game.

The Rolleston case, Francis understood at once. He'd heard that Sir Amias had asked Fogg to step in after Smythson's death. Or was it after Shiveley's? The litigious merchant was no respecter of station. Rumor had it that he was threatening to bring Lady Rich herself before the bench. Impossible, of course. Why even suggest it? And yet, apparently, he had. The unwanted message would perforce have been conveyed by his counselor at law.

He felt a tug at his sleeve and turned toward the lady with a smile on his lips. "How may I serve you, Madam?"

"Mr. Bacon," she said, eyes glinting, "I've got a bone to pick with you."

* * *

Later — much later — Francis stumbled across the yard to his chambers. His head buzzed as if colonized by a swarm of angry bees. Too much wine, too much talk, too much noise. Too many people.

He knew that buzzing. He would be sick in the morning. In fact, he would probably be in bed for the better part of the week. Whitt would have to attend him in Pinnock's absence. How would he manage to summon him?

As he reached a weary hand for the door, a flash of movement caught his eye. He turned his head and saw Thomas Clarady bounding out of a door to the Gallery, a lute strung across his back. He sprang across the yard and into a waiting coach.

Ah, the energy of youth! Francis was too exhausted to envy him. He trudged up the stairs to the blessed silence of his solitary room.

THIRTY-TWO

A plaintive melody carried by a clear voice woke Clara from a dreamless sleep. At first, she did not know if the sweet music rose from the street or fell down from Heaven. Had she died during the night and woken in her Maker's golden hall?

Then her mind roused enough to attend to the lyrics. She grinned into the darkness and smothered a laugh in her pillow. None but her Tom could write a song so dreadful and then stand singing it in the public street!

He'd wake everyone. The mad boy, she must stop him. She flung off her covers and fumbled for her shift. Her cloak hung from a hook by the door. She wrapped it tightly around her body and padded down the dark stairs, bare toes cold on the smooth oak boards. She gave no thought to her intentions. She made no plan. Tonight, her heart knew what it wanted.

She lifted the heavy latch and swung the front door wide, letting in a rush of cold air. Tom stood clear of the overhanging upper story bathed in the white light of the half moon shining directly overhead.

"*Amore mia!*" He riffled the strings of his lute in a dramatic flourish.

"What do you mean, good sir, by standing in my street and disturbing my neighbors?" Her scolding words were contradicted by the giggle in her voice.

He swung the lute behind his back and stepped toward her. He took her hand and caressed it, his face serious. "My beloved, I've come to tell you. Your husband is dead."

She gasped. "Oh, Tom, you shouldn't have!"

"I didn't."

"Then who? How?"

He drew her closer, stroking her hair, gazing down at her with ardor such as she had never felt before. "Does it matter?"

Did it? How could it not? A man was dead, a man who had once shared her bed. A man from whom she'd fled in terror. Her mind whirled. Caspar was gone. She was free.

"You mad fool!" Clara flung her arms around him, laughing. "Come up with me."

"Are you sure?"

She laughed again, suddenly drunk with joy, with freedom. Of course she wasn't sure. She was certain that inviting this beautiful youth up to her room was utter, shameful, unspeakable lunacy. He was a gentleman of the Inns of Court. He could do as he pleased. She was a tradeswoman whose livelihood depended on her reputation. She'd be ruined if anyone saw her. She didn't care. She would blame the moonlight.

This night, this one night in all her sad life, she, Clara Goossens, would know love.

She took his hands, drawing him silently up the long stair to her narrow room. She lifted the lute from his shoulders and laid it on her worktable. She undressed him, untying every lace with care. He stood and let her take her time, a glittering fire in his eyes.

At last he was naked, as tall and well formed as a Roman statue. She pulled off her shift in one smooth motion and took him to her bed. There she reveled in him, loving him in every way she knew, with her clever hands, her wise heart, and her eager body.

* * *

Clara woke to see daylight streaming through her window. She sighed and stretched, deliberately rubbing the length of her body against Tom's. That woke him, barely. He murmured something in her ear, tickling her with his warm breath and short beard, sending shivers of pleasure racing across her skin. She giggled and he wrapped his arms around her, loving her with strength and tenderness. And then again.

He's too young for me. He feathered kisses lightly across her face, her neck, her breasts, and her belly. *He's too high above me.* He captured her lips and warmed her to the core with a deep kiss. She stopped worrying about the future for a few delicious minutes more.

* * *

Tom awoke with a start. Church bells were tolling eight of the clock, and someone was pounding on a door somewhere far away, loud, echoing. Three blows and a pause. Three blows and a pause, like a sledge hammering a nail.

Where was he?

Then he felt her in his arms, warm and soft and smelling of woman and roses and faintly of paint. Clara, his *angela luminosa*, truly his at last. He smiled to himself as he nuzzled Clara's shoulder, inhaling her rich fragrance, storing it up in his memory like hay stacked in a deep barn.

He'd had sex before, naturally; he was no stripling boy. He and Stephen had sampled most of the brothels in Smithfield. He'd had his share of tavern wenches in empty chambers and dairy maids in haystacks and even once a restless wife in the musty storeroom behind her shop.

Women wanted him, and he was generous by nature.

This was different. He loved Clara and she loved him. Love made the act transcendental. *"Angela mia,"* he whispered into her downy neck. *"Ti adoro."*

Ah, he'd woken her. No, she had been awake and savoring this moment too. She stirred and started to sit up. He snuggled her closer to his chest. "It's someone with a tooth that needs pulling. Naught to do with us."

"I do not believe so." Clara wriggled against him for a blissful moment then slapped him on the arm. He released her. She sat up, clutching a corner of the blanket to cover her breasts, for the warmth.

Which Tom knew because they had left modesty far behind last night.

He propped himself up on one elbow. "What else could it be on a Sunday morning?"

She hissed at him to be silent and listened intently to the sounds of the house. A murmur of voices below, some of them men's by their pitch, but what of it? A surgeon's hours were not fixed like a goldsmith's.

A patter of slippers on the wooden stairs stopped outside Clara's door, followed by a series of sharp raps.

Clara didn't call out to ask who it was. She slid from the bed and wrapped her cloak around her naked body and opened the door the barest sliver. *"Wat is het?"*

Tom hoped it was something easily managed. He wanted to explore her all over again, from her nose to her toes, in full daylight, using his eyes this time as well as his hands and his lips. He had also been hoping for a chance to leave her room unnoticed. He'd meant to slip out at dawn, but it was too late for that. Perhaps everyone would go to church. He grinned. Perhaps he'd be forced to spend the whole day in Clara's bed.

Alas, no. Clara and the woman on the other side of the door spoke in Flemish, but their mounting alarm needed no translation. Tom knew the sound of trouble when he heard it.

The whispers ended. Clara shut the door and leaned against it, staring at Tom with terror in her eyes. Her palpable fear sent a jolt right through him.

He leapt from the bed and wrapped his arms around her, gathering her into the shelter of his body. "What is it, my darling?"

"They are here for me." She tilted her face to him.

"Who? What? Why? I won't let them."

She shook her head. "Nay, you cannot help me."

"It's about him, isn't it? That pusillanimous varlet. Your late and unlamented husband." Tom had told her, in the whispers of the night, about the Fleming's murder.

"They want to question me, she says. They will take me to Newgate."

"Newgate!" The prison was notorious. He took her face in both his hands and held her gaze, willing his strength into her heart. "I will protect you, my angel."

She smiled wanly, but shook her head. "You cannot. The undersheriff is here himself with a letter."

"A pox on the undersheriff and his letters!"

They helped each other into their clothes. They combed their hair and splashed water on their faces from the bowl on Clara's nightstand. They stood face-to-face in the center of the small room and gave each other a final inspection. However tidy their appearance, Tom's mere presence on the scene at such an hour guaranteed what conclusions would be drawn by those below.

The bottom of the stair was blocked by a group of women who stood with linked arms, glaring at a pair of burly constables. They parted to allow Clara and Tom to descend, gaping at Tom and whispering in Flemish after they had passed. The constables leered and snickered, making Clara blush.

Tom's own cheeks burned. He glanced at her, but she kept her eyes riveted on the rush-strewn floor. He'd made her a whore by emerging from her bedchamber so early on a Sunday morning. He hoped he could make up for it by sending this undersheriff packing. He was a gentleman of the Inns of Court after all. At least, he was dressed like one.

Elizabeth Moulthorne stood in her surgery, clutching a blue woolen cloak about her neck. She glowered furiously at a man wearing a large pewter badge.

"Are you one Clara Goossens?" The undersheriff read the name from the letter he held in his flabby hand, mangling the pronunciation and making Clara sound like a backward goose girl.

The man had a sunken chest, a vast, round arse, and pinstick legs. Worse, he had dressed himself in a putrid mustard color that emphasized his florid complexion. Tom wished Stephen was here to share his contempt for this sartorial disaster. And to play the lord, summoning centuries of inherited hauteur to send this minion packing.

Tom was suddenly keenly aware of his own powerlessness. Absurd as this paunchy man might look, he had authority in the badge on his chest and the document in his hand. Not to mention the burly constables, either one of whom was a match for Tom. A sinking feeling in the pit of his stomach told him the cause was lost.

He wrapped a protective arm around Clara. "What is the meaning of this intrusion? Don't you know today is the Sabbath?"

The undersheriff attempted to look down his nose at Tom but failed since he was the shorter by several inches. "I have a warrant for the arrest of one Clara Goossens, Fleming, resident of this house."

"On what charge?"

"She's wanted for questioning in the death of her husband." The pewling official consulted his letter. "One Caspar Von Ruppa, also a Fleming. Murdered by stabbing to death with a knife."

Gasps arose from the women on the stairs. "Oh, Clara!" one said. "You shouldn't have!"

"I never did!" Clara cried.

"Of course she didn't kill him," Tom said. "She couldn't have. I am he who discovered the corpus. We came upon it only moments after the deed was done. The Widow Goossens was nowhere in the vicinity during the critical interval." He struggled for legal terms, formal terms, anything that would make him sound more important than the youthful lover he was.

"No one claims that she herself held the knife that killed him." The undersheriff clearly meant to imply that she had arranged for that knife, however. "She is merely wanted for questioning."

"She can be questioned here, then, in the company of her landlady and of myself."

"No. She is to be taken to Newgate Prison and held there at the pleasure of the queen until this matter has been resolved."

"By whose order?" Tom reached his hand toward the official. "Let me see that letter."

"The warrant is signed by one Sir Avery Fogg, Treasurer of Gray's Inn."

"What!" Tom released Clara and stepped forward to snatch the letter from the man's hand. He read it through rapidly. Sure enough, there was Fogg's signature at the bottom.

Why hadn't he paid more attention when they'd gone to observe the courts in Westminster? He'd spent most of the term whispering jokes, mocking costumes and mannerisms, instead of learning the law. Now he needed it. If only Ben were here, or even Trumpet. He wanted to howl his rage to the rafters and lift this tottering undershit by the ears and shake him into pieces.

But he couldn't. He could do nothing but stand with clenched fists and flaming cheeks, impotent, while the undersheriff tilted his chin at the constables. They laid their sweaty hands upon Clara's slender frame and bore her, weeping, out the door and into a waiting cart.

"Tom!" she wailed, the hopelessness in her voice shredding his heartstrings.

He followed the cart down the lane, stumbling on lumps of garbage, heedless of his velvet slippers. "I'll get you out. I promise you, sweetling."

THIRTY-THREE

The stench of Newgate Prison was overwhelming. Clara's eyes burned and watered, adding the shame of tears to her misery. She wanted to appear confident that her powerful friends would soon secure her release. She wanted to hold tight to what shreds of dignity she could because she feared that if she wailed and whimpered, the guards would think her friendless and treat her with cruelty as well as contempt.

She felt screams rising from her belly, tasted bile in the back of her throat, and swallowed both down.

She feared to weep, but she was helpless to stem the water streaming from her eyes. The stink was like a force, a gale, a *hurricano* of foulness. Countless years of human waste and sweat and sickness lay heaped in rotting piles of straw. The stench made the privy shared by the members of Clara's household and the other houses around their yard seem like a garden in June.

One night of abandon in all her careful, cautious years — one single night of love — and down came her punishment, swift and absolute. From paradise to perdition in a stroke. This was Caspar's doing. Even in death, he found a way to reach out and torment her.

The guards were not kind, not in any tiny way, but they did not molest her. They barely spoke to her. They took her mother's ring for their entrance fee. Clara did not understand how they could charge her a fee for putting her in prison, but they could do as they liked with her now. Her ring was by far the least terrible price she could imagine paying.

They led her into a cell no larger than her room at home, but this place held no bed, no chest, no sunlit worktable. One small barred window kept the cell from utter darkness. Layers of filthy straw covered the floor, heaped up in places to form beds. One sodden corner apparently served as the privy. Two women sat in the straw, blinking at the sudden light from the open door. Clara could not begin to guess their ages. Their faces were ravaged by pox and poverty, but their limbs seemed sound, and they were agile enough as they rose to their feet. They leered at Clara with gap-toothed grins.

"Oooo, what's this, then?"

"What 'ave ye brought us, Jarman, me love?"

Clara shrank back, unwilling to step across the threshold. The guard pushed her forward, hard enough to send her stumbling into the arms of her new cellmates.

"Don't muss 'er up too much, dearies," the gaoler said with a chuckle. "I'll wager she's worth a shilling or two."

"What'll be our share, eh?" the darker one asked. She got no answer. Whether she was swarthy from birth or from layers of dirt, Clara did not care to guess.

The door swung shut, leaving her in a gray gloom.

"'Er looks a lady, Millicent, don't 'er?"

"Nar, Gracie, 'er's no lady. 'Er's a shopkeeper or a smith's wife or the like."

"Clean," Millicent said. Clara felt thick fingers crawling through her hair, plucking out the pins that Tom had helped her place that morning.

"Nice shoes," Grace said. Clara felt her shoes being tugged from her feet. She tried to pull her legs back and got a sharp pinch on the thigh. "Be still, or pinches ain't all ye'll get."

"This hair's worth a penny or two," Millicent said. A ragged fingernail scraped Clara's ear as her hair was pulled back. "Reckon Jarman'd lend us a scissor if we split the take?"

"Shoes're mine," Grace said. "Warm, they are. An' look: they fit me perfect."

Clara closed her eyes and willed herself into the nowhere that had been her refuge when Caspar beat her.

THIRTY-FOUR

Tom spent the better part of an hour alternately pleading, bribing, and threatening the officials at Newgate to let him at least visit Clara to see how she was housed. No one would listen to him. He went outside and prowled the perimeter, hopping up to peer through barred windows, craning his neck. Hands were thrust out at him, waving and grasping. Inmates pressed their grimy faces against the bars to jeer at him or whisper coarse promises. He had to leap aside to avoid a stream of piss that one brainsick prisoner launched at him.

"Tom!" He whirled around. Ben and Trumpet jogged across the street.

"We're going to St. Paul's to hear the sermon." Trumpet looked him up and down. "Your shoes are a disgrace."

Tom gaped at him like a man bereft of human speech.

"What's wrong?" Ben asked.

He told them everything from the moment he'd left Gray's the night before, leaving out the private bits. He handed Ben the letter, which he had carefully stowed in his purse.

Ben clasped his arm. "Tom, hear me. Newgate is filthy and verminous and the other inmates may be fairly nasty, but they'll not harm her. Neither the prisoners nor the guards. Not seriously. There's time to negotiate."

"Are you sure?" Tom eagerly grasped at the straw.

"Nearly sure." Ben rubbed his dark beard. "Let's go talk to Mr. Bacon."

"No. Mrs. Sprye," Trumpet said. "She'll want to know what her dear Sir Avery has been up to."

"Mrs. Sprye." Tom allowed himself to breathe again. "She'll know what to do, and she'll make Fogg do it."

"This is all wrong," Ben said.

"No, it's exactly right." Tom felt strength returning to his sinews. "We need to talk to Mrs. Sprye at once. And then Mr. Bacon. Between the two of them —"

"No, this letter is all wrong," Ben said. "It's not Fogg's hand, for one thing. You've seen it yourself on those endless notices the benchers post about not wearing velvet shoes and getting a shave every three weeks."

"I knew there was something wrong with it!" Tom crowed.

"And the language is too simple." Ben handed the letter to Trumpet, who had been tugging on his sleeve. "Fogg uses more Latin. I tell you, Tom, Treasurer Fogg did not write this letter."

"Then who did?"

THIRTY-FIVE

Clara sat, head bowed, on the dank floor, wearing only her shift and underskirt. The rest of her clothes had been stripped off by her fellow inmates.

The cell door groaned open and the guard stood in the sudden frame of light. "Hoi! I told you to leave 'er be."

"'Tis only 'er clothes," Millicent whined.

"She's got friends, I tell you. Look — they sent'er a basket already."

Clara's eyes snapped open. Tom! He hadn't forgotten her.

"Mine!" Millicent and Grace scuffled forward, hands outstretched and fingers grasping.

"No, no, no! It's'er present. She orter get first dibs." The guard shoved the whores aside and set the basket in Clara's lap. Her hands curled around it protectively, though she knew it would be snatched away from her the minute the door closed.

"What'd they tip you, then, eh Jarman? Somethin' 'andsome?"

"Wouldn't you like to know?" Jarman chuckled as he left.

"Gracie," Millicent breathed. Clara recoiled from the black stink that flowed from her rotten mouth. Even as she turned her head, she registered surprise that she was becoming able to distinguish degrees of foulness. God help her when this hellhole no longer stank!

"A bottle o' tinto, by all me dead 'usbands' sufferin' souls!"

Millicent's arm plunged into Clara's basket and withdrew a bottle with a long cork. "Ahhhh," she sighed. "'Ere's me lovely."

She took her prize over to the largest heap of straw and pulled the cork with a resounding pop. She sat back against the oozing wall, stretched her legs before her, and took a long draught.

"A cheese! A 'ole cheese! An' bread, Millie, by your 'usbands'!" Grace snatched the largest lump in the basket and retired to her own tuft of straw.

Clara was left alone, mercifully, in the middle of the cell with the basket in her lap. She didn't mind the thefts; on the contrary, she was grateful for the distraction. Her undressers had not been gentle. Her body was bruised and scraped from their pinches and rough hands. She had feared they would strip her stark naked, leaving her to freeze in the night.

She turned her eyes to the basket, letting her vision adjust to the sparse light. She ran her hands over the contents: hard rolls, a sausage, apples, even a napkin. A hearty meal under other circumstances. She couldn't imagine being able to eat in this place. She hoped she wouldn't be here long enough to learn otherwise. She was surprised to find no note. It wasn't like Tom to send her a gift without one of his foolish sonnets to go with it. She smiled bitterly. The sight of his writing, even in light too dim for reading, would have given her some sense of him, some comfort.

She lifted an apple and turned it in her palms. It felt so ordinary, so simple and sane. It didn't belong in this nightmare. She felt a twitch under her thumb and held the apple up to catch the meager light. A worm poked its head out of the wholesome fruit.

That is wrong.

Her Tom would never send her a piece of wormy fruit. He would have examined every apple in the fruiterer's stall, selecting only the most perfect ones for her. And he would have written her a poem comparing her cheeks to apples or, knowing Tom, to leeks, because *cheeks* rhymes with *leeks* and he would find no rhyme for *apples*.

This basket was not from Tom. She knew it in her very soul. Then who had sent it?

She heard a coarse retching from Millicent's corner and saw the bottle fall from the woman's palsied hand as she clutched her throat, writhing in agony. Grace lay sprawled on her back, tongue lolling, the half-eaten cheese on the floor beneath her limp hand.

Poison!

Clara sprang to her feet and began pounding on the door with both clenched fists.

THIRTY-SIX

The chapel bell tolled nine. Francis Bacon groaned. Why did that accursed bell have to be so infernally loud? He rolled over and covered his ears with a pillow. He felt as though his brains had been baked in a kiln. His head was too hot and his feet were too cold, and he was ferociously thirsty.

Why did his wretched boy have to choose this week to visit his family? What great need could his parents have of him when Francis was lying here sick and unattended? And where was Whitt? Why was there no one to care for him? His father's house had employed more than seventy servants. Now he had not so much as a pot boy to fetch him a cup of beer. He felt utterly abandoned.

He struggled out of bed and managed to dress himself sufficiently for a brief foray across the courtyard to advise the butler of his needs. He pulled his door shut and stood on the landing for a moment, pressing his palm to his forehead. He was quite certain he had a fever. He'd need a sudorific tonic, laced with poppy juice, administered hourly. A noise opposite assaulted his ears. He glanced toward the library.

"Oh, it's you. A bit early for research, isn't it?"

"It's nearly nine of the clock. Not everyone spends the whole morning in bed."

Francis huffed. "I'm ill. Besides, it's Sunday." He hesitated. "Isn't it?"

A laugh. A rather unfriendly one. Francis felt a shiver run up his spine. He did have a fever. He must get back into bed immediately.

"Yes, it is Sunday, Your Readership."

Francis waved a limp hand to deflect the sarcasm.

"Actually, I wanted a word with you."

"It will have to wait," Francis said. "Tomorrow. Or the next day. I'm quite ill. Can't you see that I'm suffering?"

"That will soon be over."

How would he know? Francis took a step down the stairs. Then he felt hard hands pressing against his back, driving him forward. His feet lifted from the floor. He fell, tumbling, limbs banging against the age-hardened oak of the balusters.

Merciful God, he thought. *I understand it all.*

And the rest was silence.

THIRTY-SEVEN

Tom marched up Holborn Street, setting a punishing pace with his long legs. A church bell had just tolled nine of the clock. Clara had been arrested one whole hour ago. Time was of the essence.

"First we talk to Mrs. Sprye, and then we pound Treasurer Fogg to a bloody pulp." He threw a glance over his shoulder and saw Trumpet jogging along behind. Even Ben was panting slightly. He slowed his pace.

Ben said, "Mr. Bacon first. He'll know for certain if this is Fogg's hand. He'll also know how to post bail."

"Yes, yes, Mr. Bacon knows everything." Tom was in no mood to humor Ben's hero worship.

"Well, he does," Ben said, unfazed. "Besides, I want to check on him to see if he needs anything. He was up too late last night. It doesn't agree with him."

"Doesn't agree with him," Tom muttered. Then he shouted, "The love of my life has been thrown into the foulest, most dangerous prison in Christendom and you're worried that your tutor might have a little hangover?"

Ben looked abashed, which made Tom feel even worse.

"We'll get her out, Tom," Trumpet soothed. "Maybe not today since it's Sunday, but tomorrow. You'll see. Mrs. Sprye knows every judge in Westminster and the gaol delivery justices too. Half of them owe her their positions."

"Don't forget that Mr. Bacon wants to talk to Clara too," Ben said. "He'll help us, I promise you."

"Fine. Mr. Bacon first, then." Tom cut recklessly across Holborn and stormed up Gray's Inn Road and through the gateway, waving impatiently at the porter as he passed. "He'd better be awake."

They marched across the yard. Tom flung open the door. He nearly stepped on him, the frail figure splayed on the floor at the foot of the stairs.

"Francis!" Ben cried. He knelt beside him, his face white.

"Is he dead?" Tom's heart clenched with dread.

Trumpet knelt on the other side and placed trembling fingers on his neck. "He's alive." He moved a hand under the man's nostrils. "He's breathing." His voice quavered with tears of relief.

Tom breathed in then out. Tears stung his own eyes. "Thanks be to God in his heaven."

"We must get him upstairs," Ben whispered.

Tom nudged Trumpet aside and bent to gather the slender form into his arms. He took the stairs as quickly as he could without jarring. Ben kept pace beside him, his hand on Bacon's forehead as if that would somehow help. Trumpet ran ahead to open doors.

They passed straight through the outer chamber. Tom barely noticed the opulence of the furnishings as he hurried in to lay his burden gently on the wide bed. Ben removed Bacon's ruff, cuffs, and doublet. Tom slipped off his shoes and unfolded the lambskin coverlet that lay across the foot of the bed, drawing it up over the still figure. Trumpet arranged pillows, taking the opportunity to run light hands over his head.

"A bump — a big one — but no blood. Not too bad." He smiled at Ben, who was weeping openly with fear.

Tom heard a soft boom from the stairwell. He nipped into the outer chamber and peered out the window. He went back into the bedchamber. "Someone went out, I think, but I missed him. The court is full of men, walking here and there. It could have been any of them."

Mr. Bacon groaned softly. His eyes fluttered open. Ben took his limp hand and patted it. "My bed," Bacon said. "How?"

"We found you at the foot of the stairs," Ben said.

The lads exchanged worried looks. Tom knew they were all thinking the same thing: Bacon had been pushed, like Shiveley. Thanks be to God they had come straight to Gray's instead of stopping first at the Antelope. If they had arrived even a few minutes later, he was certain they would have found Bacon's neck snapped.

The murderer that was loose at Gray's was growing bolder. "Thank you, Gentlemen." Bacon's eyes closed. His lashes lay black against his too-white cheeks. He lay still, breathing soft, regular breaths. A minute passed; another.

"Should we go?" Trumpet whispered. "Let him sleep?"

"Not sleeping. Thinking." Bacon opened his eyes and looked sideways at Ben. "Mr. Whitt, would you be so kind as to fetch my desk and take dictation? I may never have another opportunity to describe the effects of a blow on the head from the perspective of the victim."

Tom was nonplussed, but Ben rose without comment and went into the study. He returned with a portable writing desk decorated with the Bacon coat of arms. He drew a stool to the side of the bed and sat, placing the desk at his feet.

"Mr. Bacon," Tom asked, "shouldn't we send for a physician?"

"Yes, please do. But not yet." Again his eyes closed, but briefly this time. "I can't remember." He sounded nettled. "I went out on my landing, meaning to go down to the buttery. I spoke with someone. I can almost see his face and hear his voice, but I cannot form a name in my mind."

"You must rest," Ben said. "Don't strain yourself."

Bacon looked at Tom. "Have you brought the limner? Does she have the tools of her trade? Perhaps she can help me remember."

Tom shook his head. "I'm afraid I have bad news." He told him about Clara's arrest, glossing over his reasons for being on the scene first thing on a Sunday morning.

"If Fogg sent that letter, then he is our killer," Bacon said. "Conversely, if he is not the killer, he did not send the letter. There is no reason for the limner to be questioned in the matter of the Fleming's death."

Tom pulled the letter from his pocket and unfolded it. He started to hand it to the prostrate man, hesitated, and gave it to Ben instead. Ben held it so that Bacon could see it without moving his head.

"Well," he said, after a brief perusal, "that is not Fogg's hand. His clerk might have written it, but it doesn't seem his style either. I would expect more verbosity. Perhaps with some thought . . ."

"You must rest," Ben insisted. He folded up the letter and tucked it into the desk. "You've had a very narrow escape."

Bacon turned his hazel eyes toward Ben. He suddenly looked very young and very vulnerable, lying injured and helpless in his vast bed. "Will you stay with me?"

"Every minute." Ben took his hand and clasped it firmly in both of his own.

THIRTY-EIGHT

Dinner that day was a tense affair. Stephen, unable to pry any details about Bacon's accident out of either Tom or Trumpet, resorted to loud ramblings about his reign of misrule. Tom pretended to listen while he constructed an elaborate masque in which he rescued Clara from Newgate by stealth, substituting Stephen, unconscious and dressed as a harlot, in her place.

After dinner, Tom and Trumpet spent a good hour running errands for Ben on Bacon's behalf. They sent a boy to fetch the one physician Bacon trusted; they instructed the staff of Gray's to deliver hot water and light meals on a schedule, but quietly, quietly; and they bundled up a supply of fresh linens, a favorite pillow, and other necessities for Ben, who refused to stir from Bacon's bedchamber until his servant returned.

Ben couldn't even hear words not related to Bacon's comfort. When Tom tried to tell him about Clara's predicament, he'd looked at him as if he were speaking gibberish. He guarded Bacon like a dragon guards a chest of gold, barely allowing Tom to peek at him through the doorway. There would be no help from that direction.

Tom racked his brains for another source of trustworthy advice. Luckily for his overstrained wits, the answer sprang quickly forth: Mrs. Anabel Sprye at the Antelope Inn. She knew every judge in Westminster and would understand Tom's involvement in the case without insisting on any uncomfortable details.

Trumpet came with him. They were silent as they walked down to Holborn, each occupied with heavy thoughts. Tom felt that he was trapped in a shrinking chamber, walls closing in and squeezing out the very air he needed to live. Smythson's death had been horrible, of course, but unreal; painted, as it were, with the colors of the Queen's Day pageantry. Shiveley's death had been shocking and sad, but Tom had hardly known the man. If his death had truly been an accident, he would almost have forgotten it by now.

The Fleming, though: he'd had a conflict with the Fleming. A powerful connection, in fact. Tom had hated him. He'd wanted to slice him through with his rapier, to cow him with his superior status. He'd wanted him defeated, brought to his knees, banished from Clara's life.

But not dead. His death had left Tom with the frustration of deeds undone.

Now Clara was falsely imprisoned in a perilous gaol. His fear for her ran hot and constant, driving him through every new-demanded chore in a feverish agony. Never in all his life had he felt so useless. And now Bacon, who on a normal day made Tom feel like an upstart pantry boy grasping at honors he couldn't understand, lay on his bed all pale and fragile, snatched from death's snapping jaws by the sheerest accident of choosing one errand over another. More than anything, Tom wanted to prove to his brilliant tutor that he, the privateer's son, was worthy of inclusion in the Society of Gray's Inn.

He couldn't do that if the man were dead.

This murdering traitor must be stopped. Tom had to stop him. When this had begun, it had seemed a new sort of game. Tom had been one of four friends guided by a clever tutor. Now Stephen, bosom companion for many years, had turned into a prattling, make-believe prince who had betrayed a crucial secret. Not to mention making a perfect jackanapes of himself. He was worse than useless.

And Ben, the man he'd come to admire and rely on for guidance, chose to sit by Bacon's bed night and day, oblivious to the world outside the chamber.

Not that Tom blamed him. A guard was definitely required, and at this point, they didn't know who they could trust.

That left Tom with only Trumpet to help him rescue Clara, solve the murders, and put the world right again. After which, he decided, he would bundle up Clara and Ben and Trumpet and Francis Bacon too, if necessary, and carry them back to his mother's house in Dorset, where everyone would be safe, and he could lie on a soft bed in a warm room and let his sisters and aunties and Uncle Luke pamper him and feed him sweets until this whole miserable season of misrule had faded into a humorous anecdote.

* * *

Mrs. Sprye was shocked to hear of Clara's treatment at the hands of City officials.

"That pompous, potbellied porker." She added a string of ungentle epithets concerning the undersheriff's relatives then launched into a diatribe about the audacity of men who dared to abuse respectable craftswomen, ending with a pessimistic assessment of the undersheriff's chances of reaching higher office or ever again having satisfactory relations with his wife.

"We'll have her out in two shakes of a puppy dog's tail," she promised. Tom felt the pressure of his dread for Clara abate for the first time since she'd been lifted onto that cart.

Mrs. Sprye outlined their plan with the snap of a seasoned general. Tom could do no more today since it was Sunday. First thing on the morrow, however, he and Trumpet were to assemble a list of necessaries that she ticked off on her fingers: bed linens, underclothes, a thick blanket, food that would keep for several days, candles, a tinderbox, and other oddments. Tom repeated each item under his breath, committing the list to memory.

Mrs. Sprye smiled at him, crinkles softening her sharp eyes. "Don't go buying rich stuff now, my boy. They'll only steal it from her. Plain but serviceable, that's what you want."

She herself would sit down at once and write letters to half a dozen judges, including the one responsible for gaol delivery at Newgate. Sir Avery Fogg was due at the Antelope within the hour and would be gifted with a piece of her mind. She was sure — nearly sure — that he'd had nothing to do with the writing of that warrant. If he had, by her late husband's hopes of everlasting bliss, she'd roast his feet in the fire right there in her tavern.

Tom smiled for the first time in hours. "I love you," he told her, knowing she wouldn't take it the wrong way.

* * *

Tom and Trumpet took the shortcut back to Gray's. By mutual unspoken consent, they turned west to detour around the spot where the Fleming had died. They would walk up past the duck pond and enter Gray's from the north.

They rounded a dense thicket of hazel and were surprised by a lad about Tom's size, who planted himself in the middle of their path and confronted them with his hands on his hips.

"What have we here? Purpoole's Captain of the Guard and Master Intelligencer strolling along, all by their lonesomes, without any retinue? What d'ye say, lads? Shall we take 'em?"

Three other men emerged from the thicket. "They'll fetch a pretty ransom," one said.

"Lincoln's men," Trumpet snarled. Lincoln's Inn stood south of Gray's on the other side of Holborn. The rivalry between the two Inns of Court was centuries old and fiercely maintained. Its members rarely ventured this far into enemy territory. "A flock of prancing coxcombs. We don't have time for this."

Tom wasn't so sure. He found the prospect of a good brawl agreeable in the extreme. He'd thrash these beef-witted dewberries inside out. He'd stand them on their heads and then he'd kick their bilious backsides black and blue and send them yelping back to their own hall.

He grinned at them, rubbing his hands together in anticipation.

"I'll take the knave in the middle," Trumpet muttered out of one side of his mouth.

"Good," Tom said. "I'll take the rest of them."

He waded into the fray with gusto, laying about him with his long arms and his heavy fists. All of the fear and lust and frustration of the past few days boiled into his veins, filling him with a scalding exaltation of battle glory. He soon sent his would-be assailants scurrying for the safety of their own Inn.

Only one left. He grabbed the knave from behind and lifted him right up over his head. Someone was shouting, "Tom! Stop!" but he ignored the quibbling naysayer. He twirled twice around with his enemy wriggling helplessly in his mighty hands and threw the dastard full length into the duck pond.

He laughed as he watched the puny minnow floundering through the lily pads. He laughed louder as the measle slipped and fell back into the mud on his little round rump. Then his eye was caught by something furry floating toward the bank.

Not a rat. Certainly not a duck. It looked like a serjeant's coif made of hair. Curious, he stepped gingerly to the edge of the pond and fished it out.

"What ho! It's a wig! And a funny sort of a moustachio too." He held them up. "Trumpet, look what I found!"

He looked behind him. No Trumpet. He looked at the wig in his hand. Trumpet-colored hair.

A disturbing thought crept into his mind. He turned slowly back to watch the varlet floundering in the pond. His eyes were open, he knew he was awake, and yet he could not be seeing what he saw. He took a few steps closer, his feet moving unbidden into the water.

There, kneeling among the lily pads, draped in long green strands of pond scum, was a beautiful, soaking wet, raven-haired girl with fury flashing in her emerald eyes.

Tom was gobsmacked. His legs turned to jelly and he sank backward onto his rump in the mud.

"God's light, Trumpet." His voice sounded hollow in his ears. "You're a girl."

THIRTY-NINE

Tom covered Trumpet's head with his jerkin as they
scurried on to Gray's. They slipped into Trumpet's
staircase without being seen. Luckily, Mr. Welbeck was out.
Trumpet locked the door behind them. Tom grabbed him,
or her, by the shoulders and turned her, or him, around.
He studied his erstwhile boon companion's features as if
he had never seen a human face before.

"You're very pretty," he said at last.

Trumpet grinned up at him, eyes dancing.

"That moustache was pathetic. I felt sorry for you."

Trumpet laughed. The laugh sounded musical. Had it
been musical before?

"How long have you been a girl?" Tom realized the
minute the words left his lips how absurd they were.

Trumpet's giggles were contagious. Soon they were
both howling with laughter, leaning against each other for
support.

Tom felt weak, as if his bones had turned to soggy
strips of pastry. "I think I'm going to fall down."

"Here, sit." Trumpet helped him to a stool. He only
landed half his arse on the first try and had to stomp a leg
out to keep from capsizing. He balanced his elbows on his
thighs and carefully lowered his head into his hands.

Trumpet stood beside him, patting him on the back.
"You've had a difficult day." His voice trembled with
laughter.

Tom groaned his agreement. "Is everyone a girl?"

Trumpet giggled again. Had he always been such a giggler?

"Is Ben a girl?"

More giggling. Well, that one deserved it. No one could be less girlish than Benjamin Whitt. The man had hair on his back and his voice was an octave lower than God's.

A hideous thought flashed into Tom's mind and he sat up straight. "I took you to a brothel!"

Trumpet nodded happily. "That was one of the most interesting experiences I have ever had. That whore was most informative. I can't thank you enough for taking me."

Tom watched her with amazement. It was like watching a pony discourse on the art of embroidery. He blinked several times and shook his head. It didn't help. "That's why you insisted on a private room."

"I'm fairly certain you would have seen through my disguise if I'd stayed with you."

"You were in there for an hour!" Tom knew there were more pressing questions, but he couldn't get past this one. "What in the names of all the Seven Seas were you doing?"

"Talking," Trumpet said. "Mostly."

Tom knew that *mostly* would haunt him for many sleepless nights to come.

She, or he — no, definitely she — giggled again. Her giggles were cute. Charming, even.

"You're adorable," Tom said, not realizing that his mouth had opened.

Trumpet's eyes flashed and Tom was rocked back in his chair as a very wet, very sturdy girl landed in his lap. She threw her arms around his neck and kissed him. Next thing he knew, he was kissing her back with considerable pleasure.

"Wait, wait, wait." He managed to free his lips and disengage her arms from his neck, budging her off his lap with a shake of his knees. He shot a brief prayer of thanks for last night's vigorous love-making and its calming effect on the said lap. Which thought brought a twinge of guilt about Clara; not that he needed another reason for not kissing his old comrade.

Which thought overloaded his feeble wits altogether.

Trumpet sighed. "You have no idea how long I've wanted to do that."

"Don't tell me, I beg you." He scratched his beard and gazed at the floor for several long moments. Was it in truth a floor? Or was it painted paper, like the scenery in a masque? He tapped on the floor with the toe of his soggy boot. It felt solid enough.

He remembered the other question. "Who are you?"

"I am Lady Alice Trumpington, only child and heiress of Lord William Trumpington, the third Earl of Orford." She sank into a full court curtsy with an agile grace that would have left the average noblewoman gnawing her lips in envy.

Tom wasn't surprised by the grace. He had coached the lad at fencing and found him an able opponent.

"Why?"

"Why? To learn the law, of course." Trumpet seemed to think the reason was self-evident. "Books are not enough. You need the moots and the bolts, the case-putting after supper. Full immersion in the subject and the language. You need a man like Ben to help you through the hard parts. Would Francis Bacon tutor a girl in Law French?"

"But women aren't supposed to learn the law. It's too strenuous for them. They aren't allowed in universities either."

"And why shouldn't we be? We have brains, have we not? Should we not exercise them as we exercise our bodies? Do you want untutored idiots rearing your children and managing your estates?"

Tom shrugged. "My mother isn't an idiot, and she manages our estates expertly. With the help of a competent steward, of course." He wasn't much interested in this dispute, having heard it time and again from Mrs. Sprye. But he enjoyed the way Trumpet tossed her raven hair and stamped her little foot. How had he never noticed the lushness of her lashes? He shook his head. He was in love with Clara, and one woman was more than enough at present.

Trumpet blew out her impatience with his lack of interest in her lecture, forming a neat pout with her cupid-bow lips.

Tom shook his head again, harder. Thinking about Trumpet as a girl was equal parts stimulating and disturbing. No, at least three-quarters disturbing.

She watched him, her expression a mixture of amusement and disappointment. "I'm going to change." She turned on her heel and stalked into the inner chamber.

"Into what?" Tom called after her. "A unicorn?"

"Ha-ha," came the witty retort.

Tom got up and started poking around the room. These chambers boasted an exceptionally large hearth lined with soot-blackened bricks. No fire was lit and yet the room was quite comfortable. "Why is it so warm in here?"

"We share a chimney with the kitchen."

"Ah. I forgot. You're lucky."

"I love it. I hate to be cold."

"Like a girl," Tom said softly. He thought back over the past three months, lingering over scenes in which he perhaps ought to have recognized that Trumpet was a girl. She'd always refused to use the privy in company, but her excuses were plausible enough. Some boys — and men — were like that, even on board ship. They couldn't piss if anyone was watching. Then at dancing and fencing lessons, where they stripped off their doublets for the freedom of movement, she'd always kept her shirt buttoned up right to her ruff. He dug into that memory. No, there'd been nothing to see beneath that shirt. No wobble, no bobble.

No nipple. She must have bound her breasts with white linen. Unless she was flat-chested. Otherwise, everyone dressed and undressed in their own chambers. Why wouldn't they?

He had to give her credit at the skillfulness of her deception. "You're a very good boy." That didn't come out quite right.

She laughed, understanding his meaning. She always did. "Why, thank you, kind sir. My uncle helped. He enjoys the deception as much as I do. He likes putting one over on the other barristers. He's the one that came up with the wispy moustache. He said men would feel sorry for me and not want to look at me directly, for fear of shaming me."

"Your uncle is too clever for his own good." Tom ruffled through the papers on the desk he guessed was Trumpet's. Her commonplace books were as tidy as Ben's, inscribed in her neat, round hand and cross-indexed, with a table of contents inside the cover. "Why do you want to study the law? You're good at it, mind you. You're ten times the scholar I am. But why bother? It's excruciating."

"It's fascinating."

"But you're an earl's daughter. You should be at court. You could be a lady-in-waiting to the queen, like those girls we saw the other week."

She squealed in disgust. "Can you imagine how boring that is? Waiting: that's what ladies-in-waiting do. You live in a common bedchamber, constantly chaperoned by the queen's old cronies. You can flirt with men who only want your father's title and your dowry, you can do needlepoint, you can play with clothes, and that's all. No fencing, no brawling, no moots, no brothels. No challenges. Nothing! I'd rather be like Clara and earn my own living."

"I sincerely doubt that Clara has ever visited a brothel."

"You know what I mean."

He did. Her complaints reminded him of his scorn for the life of those Essex men. "I do. I think I do. Those people at court did look peevish, didn't they? Bored and bitter and struggling to hide it. I care about clothes as much as the next man, but I'd hate for that to be the center of my existence. A man needs a purpose in life."

"So does a woman," Trumpet said.

"If you say so." He began to browse the books on the shelf. Some of them were probably Trumpet's. He wondered what she would do with her law books when she went back to being an heiress. "You don't have to go to court," he called over his shoulder. "You could stay home and do whatever earls' daughters do."

"They do nothing." Trumpet's head appeared around the edge of the door.

"They must do something."

"No, they don't." Her eyes flashed. "An earl's daughter is expected to be as idle as a midwife in a nunnery. Decorous and passive. She can read devotions. She can study certain kinds of literature, chiefly religious. Certainly not Ovid or Horace. Nothing too exciting: no battles or seductions. At least, not when anyone's looking. She can practice dancing, but no leaping. She can play the virginals, but not too well. She can ride; that's the only good thing."

"I can't imagine you sitting in a window reading devotionals all day," Tom said. "You'd be out brawling with the stable boys or dismantling the east wing or some such."

She gazed at him with an inscrutable expression. "You'd let me, wouldn't you? If you were my husband."

Tom frowned and shook his finger at her. "The brawling has to stop. Not only because it's obnoxious but because sooner or later you're going to get hurt and need a surgeon and then your secret will be out." He stopped short. He'd just given his approval for the whole scheme. Ah, well. He liked Trumpet; he had from the first. He couldn't stop now merely because the lad was a lass. He shrugged. "Ovid? Fencing? I have no objection. The east wing would be entirely your concern."

She sighed. She didn't seem to have made much progress on the dressing front, but then Tom couldn't see much. He tilted his head to get a better look.

She drew in a sharp breath and flung open the door, revealing herself clad in nothing but a long shirt and her raven tresses. The shirt was not opaque and she was definitely not flat-chested. Her figure was womanly in every way except that her limbs showed the sleek lines of muscles that could lift more than a feather fan.

Tom's jaw dropped. "God's light, Trumpet," he whispered. "You're a woman!"

She put one hand on a curvy hip and flaunted her figure. The lad had never been shy. Tom acknowledged the effect with an appreciative grin.

"How old are you?" he demanded.

"I'll be eighteen in April." The woman whose sometime name was Trumpet padded toward him on her well-arched and finely boned feet. Tom suddenly felt very much like a pig being stalked by a panther.

"Wait one minute." He took a step backward.

"I could help you forget about Clara," she murmured in a throaty voice.

"Oh, no," he said. "I mean — I mean: no, no, please no. You're an earl's daughter." He held out both hands to stop her. "I am absolutely, positively certain that Trumpet was a virgin when we took him to that brothel. You rather obviously didn't know, er, how things worked. And since all you did in that place was talk, I am equally certain that you remain a virgin still."

"I don't have to be," Trumpet-Alice purred. She walked her long fingers up Tom's arm and curved her hand around his neck. The gesture arched her back, lifting her ripe breasts fully into his line of sight.

Tom's body hummed with a more than willing response. His heart turned somersaults of confusion in his chest. His brain — last out of the gate — told his lesser parts to behave themselves and answered, in a strangled voice, "I am absolutely, positively certain that you do." He grasped her hand and returned it to her. "I beg you, my dearest friend Trumpet, turn yourself back into a boy. At least until the present crisis is over."

She regarded him through her lush lashes for a moment, lips curved in an inscrutable smile. "I knew you'd say no." She raised herself up on her tiptoes and kissed him lightly on the cheek. Then she flounced in a manner most feminine back to her bedchamber. The which environment Tom steadfastly refused to contemplate.

He blew out a breath, rubbing his hands over his head and pulling on his hair. Law school was infinitely more perilous than he had imagined it would be. "You still haven't told me why you want to be a lawyer," he called once the panther was safely back in its lair.

"I don't want to *be* a lawyer. I only want to learn enough law to hold on to my own property when I marry."

"Is that hard to do?"

"Yes." Her voice dripped with scorn. "If the men who are supposed to love and protect you turn out to be villainous, onion-eyed varlets whose only thought is piling up riches so they can gamble them away, it is."

"Ah," Tom said. "And this oniony puttock would be — let me guess — His Lordship, the earl? Your father?"

"In a nutshell. He's a greedy tyrant, a money-grubbing brute, and a foul pustule."

Tom chuckled. The lad had a gift for cursing.

She wasn't finished. "He married my mother for her money and stole it all away from her. As much as he could get his hands on, anyway. Her first husband did a good job of tying up the bulk of it in uses and trusts. But my father gave her nothing, no allowance, barely clothes enough to keep her warm. He squandered what should have been her allowance on mistresses and harebrained schemes. And he was cruel to her. He never laid a hand on her, not that I ever saw, but he belittled her at every turn. He broke her heart. I know that's why she died."

"I'm so sorry." Tom couldn't imagine it. His father was away at sea for months on end, but he and his mother loved each other deeply. They delighted in each other, more even than in their children, on whom they doted full well. His home life had been sometimes chaotic, what with his father's hazardous adventuring and the peculiar folk drifting in from ships for periods ranging from days to years. Their fortunes had risen and fallen like a ship in a heavy sea. But he had always been safe and loved.

"Thanks," Trumpet said. "I know you don't understand. Be glad you don't. Then my father did the same thing again to his own sister. When her husband died, he sent in a phalanx of lawyers and stole her estate right out from under her feet. She lives with us now in a corner of the old wing, creeping about like a mouse, grateful for crumbs."

"That's awful." Tom's aunties' chambers were every bit as gracious as his mother's. They were authoritative persons, to be respected and obeyed. Or charmed and wheedled, depending on the occasion. Together with his Uncle Luke, the one-legged boatswain who had saved his father's life back when Tom was a baby and lived with them thenceforward, they formed a sort of household Privy Council.

He spied a fat almanac on a high shelf and took it down, thinking to consult his horoscope. He could use all the advice he could get at this juncture. He called out, "But what can you do? He is your father after all." He wanted to keep her talking. Talk was safe. Talking was far, far better than coping with scantily clad virgins who used to be boys.

"I can learn the law, so I can defend myself. With knowledge and a trustworthy lawyer, I can lock up my mother's hidden assets in unbreakable trusts. I won't be cheated by my father or my husbands."

"How many husbands are you planning to have?"

She didn't answer.

Tom laid the almanac on Trumpet's desk and lifted the cover. The book fell open in two halves, the pages glued together with a square cut out of the center of each side. One half held a set of six disks made of hard clay. He was only mildly surprised. The season of Misrule had infected the whole Chain of Being. Naturally, a book would not be a book.

Curious, he picked up one of the disks and examined it. It was shaped like a thin, flat cup, with a design etched into the bowl. A design exactly like that on an English shilling.

"Trumpet?"

"It's a mold for counterfeiting." Her voice came from right behind him. He spun around, ready to defend his — or her — virtue.

But she had reverted to boyhood, complete with moustache. The transformation was remarkable. Tom breathed a sigh of relief. "Much better."

"I know." Even her voice sounded different. He detected no trace of musicality. At least he wasn't that much of a fool.

"So, your uncle is a coiner?" He was grateful to have a fresh topic ready to hand. "How long have you known?"

"About the coins? Not long. That he's a crypto-Catholic and has been working with the Jesuits to distribute pamphlets and smuggle priests into England?"

Tom gawped at her.

She nodded. "Since last summer. I came across a stack of pamphlets in his house when I stopped on my way to court to become a lady-in-waiting. We reached an agreement and my plans changed."

"You've been blackmailing him."

She shrugged. "Blackmail is such a strong word. Some might say an ugly word. But not, in this case, an incorrect word."

"How could you keep this to yourself? Especially since Smythson was murdered. Did you never think to tell someone, like the queen, perhaps? Or at least Mr. Bacon."

Trumpet clucked her tongue. "Tom, Tom, Tom. You do not understand how blackmail works. I keep your secret —" she tapped him on the chest, once for each word. "— And you give me what I want. If I told anyone, I would have to go home."

"But these pamphlets are dangerous! Even Ben thinks so."

"Fie! You read one of them. They're the most pathetical piffle. Besides, they were meant to go straight to Derbyshire, where, I assure you, everyone is already a Catholic. They won't convert a single soul."

"What about the coins? You saw them the other night at the gaming tables. Those people have been cheated."

She shrugged. "A few gamblers won less than they thought. The losers lost less, so it evens out."

"That actually sounds almost logical."

"Thank you, sir." Trumpet executed a tidy half bow. When she straightened, her face was sober. "There's worse, though, Tom. I'm afraid my uncle killed the Fleming. I found a shirt with bloody cuffs wadded up behind the cupboard."

"How did you —"

"I looked because he's gone. His saddlebags and most of his clothes are missing."

"Since when?"

"Last night sometime. We were up so late, remember? With all the gaming and dancing in the hall. He wasn't here when I dragged myself in. When I woke up, I realized that he hadn't slept in the bed."

Tom bristled. "You share a bed with your uncle?"

"No, I have a trundle bed. He goes out before I get up. My clothes are tailored so I can dress myself and my laundry goes to the Antelope."

"Mrs. Sprye knows about this?"

Trumpet tilted her pretty head and laughed. "It was her idea in the first place. Well, we thought of it together, all three of us. That's irrelevant. The point is that Uncle Nat killed the Fleming. And now he's flown."

"Why didn't you tell me about this before? It's slightly important, don't you think?"

Now Trumpet folded her arms, tapped her foot, and glowered. "When precisely was there time? It's been *Clara, Clara, Clara* since we met you outside the gaol this morning."

Tom chose to ignore the unmistakable whine of jealousy in her voice. He swiftly vowed to ignore that particular bramble patch for as long as possible. "Do you think your uncle killed Mr. Smythson? And Shiveley?"

"No, I don't believe he did. He seemed genuinely grieved by their deaths. One evening, he went on and on about how nothing was being done to bring Smythson's killer to justice. I was the only one here, his only audience. Why would he bother to put on a show?"

"We have to tell Mr. Bacon."

"I know." Trumpet sighed. "It's all ruined. I'll have to leave Gray's and go home or to court. No more wandering the streets of London with you and Ben, going where we please and doing what we like. Eating pies outside a stall. No more going to the theater without a guardian. No more taverns, no more moots. Nothing fun."

He felt a surge of sympathy. Trumpet was a born lawyer, every bit as good as Ben. If she'd wanted to be a soldier or a sailor or something requiring manly strength, that would be a different matter. But the law was a sedentary profession. The Westminster courts were full of women, pressing suits and answering warrants. By the winds that filled his father's sails, the queen herself was a woman. Why shouldn't Trumpet argue cases if she wanted to so badly?

Tom didn't like to see his friends cast down. He'd have to think of a way to help her, after he freed Clara from Newgate, got Mr. Bacon well again, and sent the Gray's Inn murderer to the gallows.

* * *

By the time Tom had finished changing into dry clothes in his own chambers, the horn was sounding for supper. As they sat in their usual places, Trumpet's eyes drilled into him, willing a message into his mind. No need. He nodded to show he understood: Stephen must not know about her deception.

They ate in silence. Stephen seemed to assume their glum mood was the result of Bacon's accident and left them to it, chatting gaily with the men on his other side.

Which suited Tom perfectly. He couldn't cope with conversation tonight. Trumpet kept his eyes riveted on his bowl as he picked through his pottage with his spoon. Tom found his brain unable to form thoughts of any kind. He ate four bowls of pottage and three loaves of bread, chewing his food with as little heed as a weary mule turned onto a grassy sward.

The meal ended and everyone rose to begin the evening's entertainments. Tom wanted nothing more than the peace of his own chambers. He murmured to Trumpet under cover of the general hubbub, "Will you be all right alone tonight?"

"Of course."

Tom went to bed at the unheard-of hour of seven o'clock and slept the dreamless sleep of an exhausted man.

FORTY

Clara sat in a huddle in the straw, shivering in her thin smock, her bare arms wrapped around her bare knees. She'd slept for a while curled up on her side but had been woken by a clanging somewhere deep within the gaol. One whole day and one whole night in hell: whatever sins she had committed in her life, she had surely paid for some portion of them here.

She shut her eyes. They were useless anyway; the cell was so gloomy and so vile to look upon. Would she ever see beauty again or raise a brush to paint it? She remembered the first time she had taken her father's easel outside to paint the bridge over the Groenerei canal. It had been a glorious day, fine and clear with a lovely light. That was when she knew with perfect clarity that this would be her work. Then the sky had darkened. A clap of thunder stood her hair on end. Rain poured from the sky, drenching her clothes and ruining her painting. She ran all the way home, where her father had rubbed her wet hair with a towel, chuckling at her dismay.

"*Oh, mijn lieveling*, sometimes it rains. We get wet and run home. We dry ourselves by the fire and go out again the next day when the sun is shining again."

Her father remembered the sunshine. She remembered the rain. Tom was like her father in that way. Would he remember her? Would he help her? He was her only hope of rescue. She bade her mind's eye to visit his open face, his golden curls, and his sun-kissed skin. She sighed at the memory of his warm caresses and shivered again. So cold; too cold.

The heavy door groaned as it swung open, a band of golden lamplight widening in its wake. In the beam of light stood Tom, her golden lover, his arms heaped with parcels. Clara pinched at her cheeks with both hands, whimpering anxiously. Was she dreaming with her eyes open now? Had her mind broken?

But then she noticed one of the objects the vision of Tom held around one arm: a wreath of green holly sprinkled with bright red berries. She could never have imagined that; no one could. Only Tom would bring a Christmas wreath into Newgate Prison. The vision was real. He had come for her.

He stood blinking at the gloom for a moment then dropped his burdens on the floor and whipped off his cloak, reaching her in two short strides. He wrapped the thick wool around her, tucking one end firmly under her arm as if she were a child. Then he wrapped his strong arms around the bundle he'd made of her, sheltering her head under his chin. He rocked her gently where they stood, murmuring shushes and sweet words.

Tears rolled down her cheeks. Not since she had grown too large for her father's lap had she felt so warm and safe. It wouldn't last — nothing good ever did — but she would store the feeling up against future troubles.

As her tears subsided, she told him about the poisoned wine and cheese and the deaths of her tormentors. Tom hugged her tighter and spoke to someone over her shoulder. "Our villain is cleverer than we thought." For the first time, Clara realized he hadn't come alone.

She buried her face in his chest again for one last breath of pure comfort then raised her head. Looking over his shoulder, she saw the short, dark boy who had been with him on the day he'd found her in the surgeon's house. The boy stood on the threshold. He had a handkerchief tied under his nose as a defense against the stink.

The boy nodded and turned toward the jailer, who stood just outside the door. He snapped his fingers and spoke sharply, in tones that reminded Clara of the way Lady Rich spoke to her servants. Soon a bustle enveloped her and Tom as servants scuttled in and out, sweeping away the foul messes, scrubbing the floor and walls with buckets of sudsy water, and building a new bed of clean straw. Tom released her to rescue his gifts and soon her arms were filled with soft linens, blankets, and pillows. His arms were strung with baskets of hard rolls, sausages and cheese, a cask of beer and a wooden cup, candles and a tinder box. She even saw a sheaf of rolled papers — more poems, no doubt, to beguile the lonely hours.

The smell of tansy and lavender rose through the little room. Clara felt a fresh alarm rising with it. She met Tom's eyes. "How long do you intend for me to stay in here? I could live for a month on all this bounty."

"I'll free you as soon as I can, my darling. A day or two, I promise. No more than a week. They'll deliver the gaol before Christmas. I'll pay anything to get you out. It's my fault you're here at all."

"No, it isn't," his friend said. He'd had a disagreeable expression on his pretty face since they'd arrived. It looked more like jealousy than distaste for the gaol. Now he pulled the handkerchief from his face, ruffling his moustache. "It's Stephen's fault."

"I should have known he would spill the beans," Tom answered him. "I should have shut his mouth up faster."

Clara frowned. "What beans are these?"

Tom explained what had happened at the scene of Caspar's death. He had told her none of this on Saturday night. Why not? When he finished, she said, "Now many people know that you think me a witness to that terrible murder on Queen's Day."

"Were you one?" The boy faced her with his hands on his hips. "Did you see anything at all?"

Clara studied the little figure, noting the fineness of the facial bones and the balanced proportions of the lithe body. The wispy moustache was no longer quite straight. This person was not a boy, waiting for time to thicken his jaw and broaden his shoulders. This was a woman: young but fully grown. Did Tom know? Men could be very stupid.

But his eyes were fixed on her. "I am abased with sorrow that you must endure this nightmare, my dearest darling. I beg you, by my love for you, tell us what you saw that day. The slightest detail could help."

"And then what happens?"

"Then we catch the murderer and bring him to justice so he can't murder anyone else."

"I mean, what happens to me?"

"Why, nothing. Or anything." Tom looked confused. Hadn't he thought about this part? "You can go on about your life." He favored her with a dimpled smile. "Only now with me in it."

The smile was not so persuasive here in this cell, which was still dark, if not as wretched. Tom would leave soon, taking his smile, and then all these nice gifts would be taken away from her. "I cannot go on about my life while I am in this horrible dungeon."

"Well, no, of course not. Of course you'll be released."

"But only if I tell you what I saw. If I saw anything, that is."

"No, no," Tom said. "You'll be released no matter what. They're holding you for questioning in the matter of the death of the Fleming — your husband. But we think we know who killed him."

She blinked at him. "You know who killed Caspar and still you leave me in this dark hole?"

"No! I mean, yes, we think we know, but we can't be sure. We have no proof." He shot a desperate glance at his friend for support and got nothing but half a shrug. The friend did not care if she were released or not. Clara couldn't imagine why this woman would go about dressed as a young lord, but she was obviously very self-willed and equally obviously possessive about Tom. She was no ally for Clara.

Tom gave it one last try. "It's not that simple, sweetling. Nobody will believe us, anymore than they believe you. The man we suspect has disappeared. We'll have to put the whole story together, all the murders, with evidence and testimony from witnesses, like you. Then we can make a case to set before the judges. That's why you must tell us what you know."

Clara shook her head. "I cannot think in this horrible place. First you must get me out. When I am home in my room, safe and clean, then I will try to remember for you."

FORTY-ONE

B en ushered Tom and Trumpet into Bacon's chambers. Not being burdened by an unconscious man this time, Tom was able to appreciate the furnishings. *Appreciate* was too small a word: he goggled at the luxury. Francis Bacon lived like a young prince in the privacy of his rooms. His father had denied himself nothing when he built and furnished this house. Let others live in plain chambers; the sons of the late Lord Keeper merited more.

The study chamber was well supplied with natural light, having windows on both the east and the south. Silver candlesticks held expensive beeswax candles. Tall shelves bore stack after stack of books in oiled leather or velvet bindings, more books than Tom had ever seen in one place. Between the shelves hung silken tapestries illustrating Biblical themes. Well-waxed cupboards, carved with exquisite artistry, displayed silver plate and goblets of Italian glass. Tasseled scarlet draped the high frame of a narrow bed set against the inner wall. Woven mats, like the ones at Whitehall, lay upon the polished floor. Even the high-backed chair at the desk was enhanced with a plump satin pillow.

The inner chamber was dominated by an enormous bed, large enough for four grown men and hung with velvet in sumptuous red, embroidered with threads of gold. The posts and tester were densely carved with fruits and flowers. Curtains of scarlet were drawn across the windows to keep the room from being too bright for a convalescent man. Tom smelled rose oil and vinegar and pungent medicines.

Bacon lay in the center of the bed, propped to a seated position on a bank of feather pillows. He seemed much better after a night's sleep. Color bloomed in his cheeks and his eyes had regained their penetrating quality. He was dressed in a high-collared shirt of snowy linen with a shawl of fringed scarlet draped about his shoulders. A broidered linen cap was firmly tied under his chin, framed by strands of hair that gleamed with cleanliness. Ben must have washed it for him.

Faithful Ben sat beside the bed on the stool where they'd left him the day before. He had the writing desk at his feet. Next to him stood a small table holding a jumble of vials, cups, bottles, and napkins. He looked as snug and content in his everyday garb and soft slippers as he did by the hearth in their own chambers. He raised his eyebrows at Tom by way of a greeting.

Tom grinned at him. He liked to see his friends happy. Intramasculine *amores* were no astonishment to the son of a sea captain. As long as they kept themselves to themselves and didn't play favorites, there was no need for any fuss.

"What news from Newgate?" Bacon asked.

Tom offered a short bow. "Limner Goossens is bearing up as well as can be expected."

Trumpet pressed his lips together, as if biting back some retort. Good. Whatever it was, Tom didn't want to hear it.

Bacon's quick gaze caught the byplay. "Has she evidence that can help us?"

"I am certain that she does, sir," Tom said. "But —"

"I'm not," Trumpet interrupted. "I think she's playing you like a big, fat fish."

"She is not! She could never be so underhanded." Trumpet rolled his eyes and opened his mouth to reply, but

Tom glared him down. He appealed to Bacon. "She's afraid; how could she not be? She was assaulted by her cellmates and only narrowly escaped poisoning."

Bacon was gratifyingly shocked, as was Ben. Tom told them about the basket of poisoned foodstuffs, delivered soon after Clara's imprisonment. Had she been alone or with cellmates who weren't bullying thieves, she would be dead.

"She's frightened and she isn't sure she can trust me," Tom said. "I don't blame her. She believes that all she has to bargain for her freedom is whatever she saw that day. She won't tell me until I get her out."

Bacon said, "Three murders and two more attempted in almost the same hour. We must have her evidence, Clarady."

"I'll get it. I promise. I promised her too, and I keep my promises." Tom was tired of being pecked and pulled at by temperish creatures, like a lump of suet hung in a birdcage. He caught Bacon's eyes and held them until the other man blinked.

Ben said, a trifle sharply, "It's a simple enough question, Tom."

Tom swallowed a growl of frustration. They didn't understand: nothing was simple with Clara. Even as he stood in Bacon's elegant bedchamber, he could taste her mouth, smell her hair, and feel the shape of her breasts under his palms. His senses were possessed by her weight and scent and silken touch, and yet there was more to her than beauty. She was complicated. He couldn't just ask.

Bacon said, "You might remind her that she's safer out of Newgate than in."

Tom shrugged. Even he had managed to think of that obvious argument.

Bacon smiled, oblivious to Tom's ill-balanced humors. "I have been busy as well. I've been thinking. I still cannot remember who pushed me, or even if I was, in fact, pushed. Though I believe at this point that we can stipulate a push. I am fairly certain it was someone I know. A Gray's man. Therefore, most decidedly not a Spaniard or a Frenchman or an invisible Jesuit."

His eyes twinkled. Was Tom supposed to laugh? He was being treated like a simpleton. He held his face calm, as if he was merely awaiting a reading assignment.

Bacon went on, "I've been pondering the question of what I have in common with Tobias Smythson, James Shiveley, and the Fleming." He frowned. "Do we know the man's name?"

"Caspar Von Ruppa," Tom said.

"You managed to learn that much from the limner, at least."

Tom bit back a retort. Why bother? He'd only earn another scolding from Ben.

Bacon said, "Smythson, Shiveley, and I are, or were, ancients of Gray's Inn. Von Ruppa was a stranger. Smythson and Von Ruppa were stabbed; Shiveley and I were pushed down stairs. Smythson and Von Ruppa were killed out of doors. Their deaths may have been incited by some feature of the moment, such as an argument. But the killer lurked, waiting, on my staircase and on that of James Shiveley. Those two acts were planned."

"Francis." Ben reached for his hand.

Bacon shook his head. "I'm all right. Thanks to you all. I owe you gentlemen my life."

He included Tom and Trumpet in a smile of gratitude that mollified Tom's ruffled feelings somewhat. It wasn't Bacon's fault that his life was lately overstocked with emotional turmoils. His angel was in gaol. His best friend had turned into a girl. His mentor was in love with his tutor, who was one of the most infuriating and brilliant personages he had ever met.

Bacon continued his summation. "Although this requires some speculation, we may assert the proposition that Shiveley was murdered. We are led to this assertion because the Fleming was killed, presumably by the Catholic conspirator who received and removed his pamphlets. The Fleming could not have been killed by Shiveley; therefore, Shiveley was not the conspirator. So why was he killed?"

"Mr. Bacon?" Trumpet sounded very young, and to Tom's ears, very girlish. No one else noticed. "I think my uncle killed the Fleming."

"Welbeck? Did he?" Bacon's gaze turned inward for a moment. "Is he our conspirator?"

"Yes, sir."

"You knew this before?"

Trumpet shrugged. "He's my uncle."

"So he is." Bacon accepted that excuse without further question, to Tom's relief. He was on tenterhooks every time Bacon's attention turned toward Trumpet. How could anyone believe that winsome moppet was a boy?

Bacon asked, "How certain are you?"

Trumpet shrugged. "Certain enough. I found a pair of bloody cuffs. He didn't come home Saturday night. When I woke up Sunday morning, his things were gone, his saddlebags with most of his clothes and money. His horse is gone too. I checked the stables."

"And there's this." Tom took the clay mold from his purse and handed it to Ben, who passed it to Bacon. "I found a set of these inside a hollowed-out almanac."

Bacon clucked his tongue. "Waste of a good book." He turned the disk in his long fingers, examining it carefully. "Fascinating. Do you have a shilling piece handy, perchance?"

Tom found one and gave it to him. Trumpet drew a false coin from his purse and passed it over as well.

"Fascinating." Bacon laid the three items on the coverlet to compare them. He tried each shilling in the mold, testing the fit. "Well crafted." He passed the three pieces to Ben, who tucked them into his writing desk, apparently assuming they were to be kept as evidence. Tom frowned at the loss of his shilling.

"The Fleming's death is accounted for, then," Ben said.

"My uncle is a murderer." Trumpet sounded forlorn.

Bacon's brow furrowed. "There are degrees, recognized even in the law. The Fleming may have objected to his payment. He might have seen that the coins were false. He was a large man, strong and threatening. Welbeck may have been defending himself."

Trumpet looked somewhat comforted. "I don't think he killed Mr. Smythson, though."

"Why not?" Bacon asked.

Trumpet explained about his uncle's demonstrations of grief and anger over the failure to bring Smythson's killer to justice. "Why bother?" he concluded. "If it was just me."

"Hm," Bacon said. "Slender evidence. Yet I'm inclined to agree with you. It doesn't fit. The crypto-Catholicism and its corollaries do fit. Nathaniel Welbeck was a man who enjoyed learning other men's secrets and playing roles, like an actor on a stage. Receiving contraband from abroad, counterfeiting: these would have seemed clever games to him. He would relish conducting such business under the noses of his fellow Graysians. The thrill of danger was sufficient motivation. He had, I believe, no real desire to unthrone our queen." He held Trumpet's gaze. "I do not believe your uncle poses any genuine threat to the state. However, Lord Burghley will have to be informed of his involvement here. It will not be safe for him to return to London for some time."

Trumpet nodded.

"In his defense," Bacon said, "consider this: the moment his exposure became imminent, he fled. A man of masks, he chose to hide himself. He did not kill again to prevent discovery. He might have murdered you, for example." He smiled cheerfully at Trumpet, who looked thunderstruck by the idea.

Bacon continued to explore his new theory aloud. "If he were planning to abscond, why linger to have the limner arrested? And why send her that basket? Why loiter at Gray's, waiting for me to rise so he could push me down the stairs? If Welbeck had learned that Smythson was aware of his seditious activities, I believe he would simply have vanished earlier. He would not have followed him to the tiltyard to murder him so near the crowds at the tournament. Nor can I imagine Smythson confronting him in such a location and provoking him into a rage. That part makes no sense to me."

He fell silent. He turned his gaze to the coverlet, his eyes roaming sightlessly across its surface while he thought. Tom could almost hear the joiner's felted mallets tapping as pieces of marquetry snicked into place in his mind.

The lads made faces at one another. *What now?* None had any ideas to put forward even if any had the nerve to interrupt Bacon while he was thinking.

They didn't have to wait long. Bacon began nodding his head. Soon a slight smile appeared on his lips. Another moment passed and then he raised his eyes. "I've been looking at the problem of Smythson's murder from the wrong perspective. I was distracted by my lord uncle's suggestion that a Catholic conspiracy was the cause. Although —" He broke off with a chuckle, his light eyes dancing. "Without the Catholic business, I would never have been charged with this investigation. That was a bit of bad luck for our killer."

Ben said, "You were bound to discover him."

Bacon shot him a fond glance. "I was. Eventually. Two threads have been tangled together here from the start: Welbeck's dramatic machinations and Smythson's murder. We have teased out the first thread. Now we can examine the second.

"Then you think someone killed Smythson on purpose," Tom said. "But why?"

Bacon held up a finger. *"A contrario.* I am now convinced that Smythson's death was an accident."

"He was stabbed more than a dozen times!" Trumpet cried. "How could that possibly be an accident?"

"It was an accident in the sense that it was unplanned," Bacon said. "The excessive violence suggested frenzied rage or panic, arguing against a case of simple theft. I failed to ask myself why a murder committed to prevent the discovery of a Catholic conspiracy would require such violence. Surely it would have been planned and a less histrionic method employed? And a more private locale. I ignored that odd detail when I should have given it my full attention on the grounds that it was so odd."

"We couldn't imagine how Mr. Smythson could inspire anyone to a frenzy," Tom said.

"You couldn't," Bacon said with a touch of his old hauteur, "but I should have. Especially after we discovered that a frightening menace, one that might inspire panic, was prowling those lanes south of Whitehall at the critical juncture: the Wild Men from the Earl of Essex's pageant."

"Those costumes were fairly hideous," Ben said.

"And we know they were chasing someone," Trumpet added.

"And they were cup-shot, according to their friends." Tom wouldn't care to meet one of those burly retainers, lion-drunk and looking for trouble, in those shadowy alleys, even without the fearsome costumes.

"They made a tale of it," Ben said. "Laughing about it later with their friends. *I've got a bone to pick with you, Counselor.* Remember?"

"Precisely," Bacon said. "That was a central bit of evidence that I foolishly regarded as peripheral. Assuming that the crimes centered on Catholic conspirators at Gray's, I was inclined to brush aside these little irregularities. I failed to examine the initial premise. A classic fallacy."

"It's understandable," Ben began.

Bacon wagged his finger again to cut him off. "Not for me. I won't make that mistake again should I ever be presented with another problem of this nature."

"But the Wild Men weren't the ones that were killed," Trumpet said.

"They were not," Bacon said. "This is what I think happened: Smythson was possessed of more than knowledge concerning Catholics at Gray's. He was also the chief counsel for a very wealthy and litigious man."

"Sir Amias Rolleston." Ben grinned. "Everyone wants a piece of that pie."

"It is a large and succulent pie. I might be interested myself, if most of his suits weren't juridically routine and patently baseless. Really," Bacon said, his words gaining speed, "it is far too easy these days to drag one's neighbors into court on frivolous grounds. Half the populace is waging law against the other half. It enriches the courts but impoverishes the nation."

He broke off and smiled sheepishly at the lads. "But I digress. We know that Smythson was expected at my lord uncle's house that afternoon. It is not an implausible assumption that our killer followed him, hoping for a private conversation. Perhaps he thought he could persuade Smythson to give him some small portion of the Rolleston cases. A brief or two; a foot in the door of a wider practice. But on his way, he attracted the attention of the Wild Men, who proceeded to amuse themselves by teasing him.

"For men such as those, an old grudge against lawyers would be enough. They chased our man through the lanes, taunting and menacing him, until he feared for his life. He may have simply stumbled into Tobias Smythson hobbling along. In his terror, he must have believed himself to be under attack and responded in kind. Perhaps he was blinded in some way, by panic or sweat dripping from his brow."

"His hat might have slipped over his eyes." Tom demonstrated with his own hat.

"Quite plausible." Bacon gestured to Ben, who passed him a silver goblet. He took a few sips and handed it back. "Where was I? Ah, yes. I suspect that if our man had been taken up by the authorities at that moment, with his terror writ plain upon his face, that he would not have killed again. And he himself might have been allowed to live. His violent deed had been done in self-defense, or so he thought. He would have been expelled from Gray's and disbarred from all English courts, but he might have kept his life.

"Instead, as the days turned into weeks and no punishment ensued, he grew more comfortable with his deed. Bolder. He'd stolen two fat purses from Tobias Smythson along with the letter to Lord Burghley. He knew about the conspiracy from the letter. I suspected at the time that a page was missing: he must have kept the one that laid out Smythson's suspicions about the counterfeiting. He had money, both false and true, and the means to gain more through blackmailing the counterfeiter, if he could watch and wait and discover his name. He must have felt quite successful until he heard rumors that I was prying into Smythson's death."

"Stephen." Tom clenched his fist.

"Not necessarily," Bacon said. "*Rumor volat.* Gossip is endemic in closed societies. At any rate, Smythson's letter and its contents provided our killer with a method of deflecting my attention. To my discredit, it succeeded. And there the matter would have rested. Smythson's murder would have gone unpunished, as well as Shiveley's, but for the antics of Nathaniel Welbeck, who did not have the sense to suspend his operations."

"I doubt that he could have," Trumpet said. "Looking back, I think he'd been expecting those pamphlets for months. There wasn't time to send a letter to France."

"Another stroke of ill luck for Smythson's murderer," Bacon said. "Had the Fleming been left alive to return to his own country, I would not have been inspired to reconsider the evidence presented in Shiveley's death."

"Yes, you would," Ben said. "We had the pamphlet I took from his sack."

"That's right. I'd forgotten. And that development was made inevitable by our unwilling witness, the beauteous limner." Bacon gave Tom a wry look. "Although, if she had been pox-marked or elderly, we would not have had the pamphlet either."

They fell silent. Tom was grateful for the chance to work through the sequence of causes and effects in his own mind. He felt as if he were back in Cambridge, slogging through a formal argument. Only this subject matter struck closer to home than Cicero's *De Oratore*.

"God works in wondrous ways." Bacon broke the silence. "Each seemingly disparate element was a vital link in the chain. Our job was to connect them properly."

Tom scratched his beard. He was due for a shave. "The murders were done from fear, then. First, fear of the Wild Men. Then, fear of discovery."

"Fear was the efficient cause." Bacon held up a finger like a lecturing tutor. His didactic pose was undermined by the fringed shawl and the neat little cap. Ben gazed at him with affection. "The final cause is greed. Or envy, perhaps, would be more apt. Our murderer lusted for money and status, the pursuit of which prompted him to follow Smythson. That murder, so far from having evil consequences, gratified his greed by advancing him to a larger purse. Smythson held a high position in this Society of ambitious men. His death opened a gap. Filling that gap opened others, so that his death indirectly benefited many men. Myself included: I gained a Reading, a desirable plum that ripens only twice a year. The murderer pushed me down the stairs to take my place as Reader as much as to prevent me discovering his identity."

Tom was flabbergasted. He could imagine no punishment more dire than being forced to expostulate in public on a statute of the law. To kill for the privilege was an act unfathomable.

"We still don't know who Smythson's killer was," Trumpet said. "My uncle wanted those things too: the Readership, the Rolleston cases. We only moved into chambers with a hearth hot enough for a crucible after Smythson's chambers were vacated and the previous tenant moved out."

"Mr. Bacon's hypothesis narrows the range of possible suspects, though," Ben said. "Only ancients need be considered."

"And benchers," Bacon corrected. "A well-performed second Reading can provide the boost a bencher needs to raise himself to a judgeship."

"Fogg!" Tom slapped his hand against the bedpost, setting the fringe around the tester swinging and making Bacon jump. Ben glowered at him. "Fogg wrote the writ that put Clara in Newgate."

"He did not," Bacon said. "We settled that yesterday. But we can't rule him out. His secretary might have written it. However, Mr. Whitt is correct: we have narrowed the field."

Tom tried to list the ancients in his head, working his way around their table in hall. "It's still better than twenty men."

"We can reduce that number. Most barristers have no interest in Reading. The expense and the burden of study are considerable." Bacon sighed. "If the Readership was his goal, pushing me down the stairs might well succeed. I can't Read now. I've sent a note to the bench asking for a postponement until August."

Trumpet said, "Whoever is chosen next had best be on his guard."

"Unless it's the killer," Ben said.

"Who will it be?" Tom asked.

"Treasurer Fogg is the most likely candidate, in my view," Bacon said. "He's due for a second Reading, and he has been campaigning vigorously for a seat on the Queen's Bench."

Tom tried to remember everything he knew about Sir Avery, mainly from seeing him at the Antelope. "He has a foul temper. It easy to imagine him flying into a rage."

Bacon nodded. "A hot temper coupled with high ambition."

"Then he's our man." Trumpet shifted his stance, ready to go out and start doing something. "We should warn the rest of the benchers. We should have him taken into custody."

"Not yet," Bacon said. "So far, we have only supposition. I can think of two other men who are equally well qualified."

"My uncle," Trumpet said. "But if he's the one, we'll never know. He can live hidden for years among our Catholic cousinage in Derbyshire."

"His ambitions will draw him out of hiding eventually," Bacon said. "He'll yearn for a larger stage. Little effort would be expended in the apprehension of a man who killed a foreign smuggler in self-defense. When the current fever of conspiracies around the Scottish queen cools, his crimes may be entirely forgotten."

"I don't want it to be Mr. Welbeck," Tom blurted.

Ben and Trumpet laughed, but Bacon smiled. "Because then we'll never know for certain. I feel the same." He cocked his head, eyes twinkling. "There remains one fully qualified candidate."

Ben's long face rumpled in thought. He began shaking his head before he spoke, as if arguing with himself. "You can't mean Mr. Humphries."

"I do mean George Humphries. In fact, I find little to choose between him and Sir Avery."

"But he's — he's —" Trumpet began.

"He's an oaf," Tom supplied. "A nithing. I can't see him shooing a goose from his path, much less murdering a grown man in the middle of the street."

"Can't you?" Bacon said. "Geese are far more intimidating than mild Tobias Smythson. And don't forget: we surmise that Smythson's murder was in main degree unintended. I can easily imagine Humphries being driven into a panic by the Wild Men."

"Me too," Trumpet said. "My uncle often used to make fun of Humphries in the privacy of our rooms. He said the benchers would never elect him to Read. He doubted the man was capable of speaking sensibly in public for three minutes, much less for three days."

"True," Bacon said. "He has never been a serious candidate. The men of the bench represent the Society, as well as govern it. They must be men of standing, education, and family. They must be possessed of at least a modicum of social grace. Humphries has none of these qualities and his knowledge of the law is superficial to boot.

"He is also a man singularly incapable of insight into his own nature. I don't believe Smythson would ever consider employing him in any capacity, however persistently he might have asked. Sir Avery might have gained himself a piece of the Rolleston pie by persuasive asking. But Humphries can be deaf to other men's opinions. He has seniority, he has complied with all the overt requirements: to his mind, that is enough. He is also possessed of a deep-seated resentment that sours his perceptions. Are you acquainted with his personal history?"

"That his father squandered the family estates on frivolous lawsuits?" Tom asked.

"And that he alienated the whole county in so doing?" Trumpet added.

Ben said, "Everyone knows Humphries's story. It's a cautionary tale about the perils of litigiousness. We get an earful of it in our first year."

"As did I." Bacon smiled in a way that reminded Tom he had been a student once, not so very long ago. "Humphries believes the world of law owes him recompense for luring his father into penury. One other clue, perhaps: he was oddly eager to escort me to my chambers on Saturday night. He loitered near the door and attached himself to me as I left. Had the Essex party not arrived at that moment, I might well have met my Maker on that night."

Ben's face paled. "Thanks be to God there was gaming in the hall!"

Bacon laughed, tilting his head back into his plump pillows. "That's an amusing syllogism: gaming attracts numbers; there's safety in numbers; therefore, gaming increases safety." He drew in a long breath and let it out in a long sigh. "His intentions may have been innocent. He may even have feared for my safety and intended, in his awkward way, to protect me. If only I could remember who I spoke with on the landing. At times I can almost hear the man's voice, but it eludes me."

"You must rest." Ben glared at Tom and Trumpet as if they were putting Bacon's health in jeopardy on purpose.

"Soon." Bacon patted his hand. "I am satisfied in my own mind that we have reached the truth of the matter, aside from the essential datum of the murderer's identity. We have at least narrowed the field. But even if I could remember and the limner would speak, a sketch made by a Fleming whose current address is Newgate Prison and the memory of a man who has recently suffered a severe blow to the head might not be considered sufficient evidence to dislodge a senior member of an Inn of Court. I would be happier with a confession before witnesses: the more exalted the witnesses, the better."

"But how?" Trumpet said. "And where? And when?"

"You have a plan." Tom noted the smirk on Bacon's face.

"I have, indeed. Where? In the Banqueting Hall at Whitehall palace, before the queen and all her court. When? On Christmas Eve. How? In the spirit of Misrule, we'll use the masque for our unmasking."

FORTY-TWO

The following week sped past in a blur of activity. Not, strictly speaking, for Francis since he spent the whole week in bed, but for those whom he directed in writing and staging his new masque. It needed to be both witty and fresh so as not to bore Her Majesty, but it also needed to recreate the atmosphere of Essex's pageant so as to stimulate a fearful memory in the man who murdered Smythson, and thus provoke a confession.

The method was not unlike the old belief that a murderer would be exposed by fresh blood flowing from the wounds of his victim. However, Francis's version was based not on foolish superstition, but on the clear-eyed observation of human behavior under duress.

He fervently hoped it would work.

His first task was to write a letter of exquisite politeness to the Earl of Essex, begging him to forgive the impertinence of performing a pastoral masque so closely related in theme and setting to His Lordship's inimitable presentation on Queen's Day. He wrapped the letter in another of even more sensitive construction to his uncle, begging him to forward it if he considered it acceptable. Francis stood on the brink of restoration to the queen's good graces. He had no intention of undermining his path at this point.

The earl graciously responded by sending his secretary to call upon Francis in his chambers, where he was told the whole story, in confidence and for His Lordship's ears only. The secretary promised to ask the earl to send at once for the two retainers. Assuming they could still identify the man they had chased after so many weeks, their testimony would be a vital support for the case against him.

Protocol having thus been satisfied, Francis summoned his creative team. Thomas Hughes, whose play, *The Misfortunes of Arthur,* would comprise the centerpiece of the evening's entertainments, and Thomas Campion, a first-year student with a gift for composition, were assigned to the design and execution of sets and costumes. Francis felt secure enough confiding a part of his intentions to these two men since both were far too junior to be dreaming of Readerships yet.

Benjamin Whitt served throughout the week as an able lieutenant, a trusted confidante, and an unfailing pillar of support. He quickly learned to emulate Francis's epistolary style and took some of the simpler correspondence upon himself. He spent the better part of the week closeted in Francis's chambers, to their mutual refreshment.

Francis kept the lash applied to Mr. Clarady's back, urging him daily to obtain a statement from the limner. Francis found himself enchanted by the richness of nautical vocabulary, which he elicited from a stableman who had served at sea, and amused himself by speaking to the privateer's son in his native idiom. He fancied it kept the wind full in his sails.

* * *

If Tom was told to 'clap on more sail and put his back into it' one more time, he would overpower Ben and wring Mr. Bacon's scrawny genius neck. He swore to himself that he would not return to that Chamber of Taunts until he had Clara's evidence in hand.

And possibly not then.

He had Stephen to contend with as well, who kept hounding him for help with his costume. He was playing the Forlorn Prince in the masque. Tom had his own role to prepare for as a Wild Man. His dialog consisted solely of grunts and roars, but the fittings were time consuming. And the costume was itchy.

Tom wanted their performances to be memorable as much as Stephen did. He welcomed the dance rehearsals as a release for his rising anxieties. He even found Stephen's self-centered stupidity refreshing after being badgered at regular intervals by men with razor-sharp wits. But he had no time for foolery, and he couldn't explain why he had no time, so he took to rising at first cockcrow, dressing by the glow of the embers in the hearth, and taking his meals at the Antelope.

The only person of his acquaintance who did not make tormenting him a daily ritual was Trumpet, who was burdened almost to breaking with his own troubles. His uncle was missed; questions were asked. Welbeck had sent a letter that could be shown about, claiming an urgent call from an aged relative in Derbyshire. Even so, Trumpet was dancing as fast as he could to avoid being pressed for details or trying on costumes in front of anyone.

He and Tom had taken to spending their scant free time in Trumpet's chambers, feet resting on the warm bricks before the hearth, in companionable and much-needed silence.

Between dashing about town like a dowager's footman, fetching materials and delivering messages, Tom tried everything he could think of to persuade Clara to unburden her secret to him. Nothing availed. He had never in his life met a female so resistant to his wiles. Had his dimple disappeared? Had his curls wilted? Had his legs grown thin?

But no, she seemed fond enough of him still. She was willing to snuggle and listen to his poetry, which she claimed to admire. She was stubborn, that was all. He would get nothing from her as long as she remained in Newgate. At least his daily visits — and daily bribes — protected her from the worst of the prison's abuses.

His first plan for freeing her had been to somehow oblige Treasurer Fogg to unwrite his writ. Tom was prepared to threaten the man with cold steel if necessary, but he was nowhere to be found. His clerk finally admitted that Fogg had gone to Kent to visit his elderly mother. Tom considered this highly suspicious. Why should a mother need visiting at this precise moment, however elderly? Surely a man might visit his mother after Christmas as easily as before.

On Friday, men began returning to Gray's, filling the yard with restive horses and the hall with hungry travelers. Gray's had the honor of entertaining the royal court on Christmas Eve only every fourth year, alternating with the other Inns of Court. Even those men who preferred to pass the holiday in the peace of their country homes were not so careless of their careers as to miss an opportunity to spend an afternoon in the presence of the queen.

Tom's frustration mounted. Not knowing where else to turn, he confided the whole story to Mrs. Sprye over a pot of spiced cider. She gave him her full attention, anger drawing sharp lines from nose to chin.

"This can't be allowed to continue," she said. "Not that I'm convinced Sir Avery is your man, mind you. The sorry truth is I'm not convinced he isn't. He'll be back tonight, but this can't wait. That poor woman must be released at once."

She gave Tom a letter addressed to Justice Roger Jarman of the Old Bailey. Tom found the man dining at an ordinary near the prison and sent for a jug of claret for him to drink while he read.

"Hm," Justice Jarman said. He folded the letter and tucked it into his sleeve. "Mrs. Sprye makes a pretty case, doesn't she?" He smiled as at a fond remembrance.

Her letter did the trick. As soon as the judge had finished his meal, he walked with Tom to his chambers in Newgate and stirred up a bustle among his clerks that swiftly produced a stack of documents, signed and sealed.

Clara was released within the hour.

FORTY-THREE

Tom oversaw the packing of his gifts and escorted Clara home. She clung to him as they exited the prison, her steps faltering as if she had spent seven dark years strung up in a dungeon instead of a scant six days in a relatively clean and well-upholstered cell. He had lived in far worse conditions on his father's ship, and he was the captain's son. He felt somewhat abused by her lack of gratitude. His discontent would grow until his eyes fell upon her face. Those sapphire eyes! Those velvet lips! How could any man resist them?

He all but carried her up to her room, where, at long last, she produced a sketch of such graphic power that Tom was shocked anew by the raw horror of the act of murder.

He thanked Clara with a heartfelt kiss. He would have thanked her more thoroughly, but she wanted to be alone. He wasn't altogether unhappy to be sent on his way. Rescuing damsels was less satisfactory in reality than in song.

He rolled the drawing up and tucked it securely into his sleeve. His duty now was to go forthwith to Mr. Bacon's chambers and deliver this crucial and most damning piece of evidence. On the other hand, Bacon had treated him most unfairly in the past week, nagging at him with those irritating little nautical quips. He'd taken Ben away from him too, just when he needed support and guidance the most.

Tom smiled wickedly to himself. Why spoil the effect of the master's masque?

FORTY-FOUR

Francis Bacon stood a calculated distance from the throne in the Banqueting Hall of Whitehall Palace. He knew the queen had noticed him and that she would summon him for a conversation sooner or later.

He was in no hurry. He loved Christmas at court. He and his brother Anthony had spent many a childhood Christmas Eve in attendance on their father, virtually at the queen's knee. The scene held a powerful nostalgia for him. In truth, he was glad to have a few moments to savor his restoration to his rightful place in society. His lord uncle had reviewed the progress of his investigation and found it satisfactory in the main. The Catholic conspirator, Nathaniel Welbeck, had been identified and his activities stopped. Smythson's murderer remained as yet unknown, but Francis had so narrowed the field that if his little ploy failed this afternoon, a turn in the Tower for each of his suspects would surely do the trick. Lord Burghley had persuaded the queen to allow Francis to return to court for this one day on a provisional basis.

He breathed deeply, inhaling the holiday perfume of cinnamon and cloves lingering after the feast. He hadn't attended the dinner, fearing to overexert himself so soon after his fall. He would stay through the masque to enjoy the fruits of his labors and then slip away home. Mingled with the aromatic remnants of a spicy feast were the green scents of rosemary and yew, shaped into wreaths or draped about the hall with satin ribbons. The walls themselves were made of canvas painted like an enchanted wood, with mossy oaks and flowering shrubs and bashful fauns peeking from the bracken. The ceiling was painted with suns and clouds and stars, day shading into night as the stiff-necked observer scanned from one end to the other. Lustrous hangings of gold and purple silk demarcated the stage at one end. Tiers of seats had been constructed along the walls for the audience.

The spectators were more marvelous to look upon than the decorations. Francis noted that he could easily distinguish the queen's inner circle from the outsiders. The *cognoscenti* wore stark black and white with accents of silver. Newcomers wore bright colors that competed poorly with the paintings on the walls and ceiling. He himself always wore black with white trimmings, and perhaps a touch of lilac on his hat. Easy, elegant, and expensive without being ostentatious. He might have difficulties with the social niceties sometimes, but his costume was faultless.

His attention turned toward the queen herself. Her Majesty was in splendid looks today. Her gown was black velvet, thickly encrusted with jewels and gold embroidery. Her ruff was a full eight inches of gossamer lace, deftly arranged in figure-eight pleats. It made her regal head seem to float upon a cloud of elfin tracery. One could tell nothing from her complexion, of course, given her liberal use of cosmetics on public occasions, but her eyes were bright and her mood merry.

She was flirting gaily with both Captain Sir Walter Ralegh and Lord Robert Devereux, the Earl of Essex, playing each against the other in a verbal sparring match. As their monarch and sole satisfier of their vast ambitions, she held them in the palm of her hand. But it was more than mere power that kept these vigorous, thrusting men dancing attention on an aging virgin. Queen Elizabeth possessed a full measure of the Tudor charm, a magnetism that added luster to her innate royalty as a golden pendant enhances the allure of a sparkling jewel.

Francis admired her immensely and felt a powerful affection for her, as deep as his love of England itself. He only wished he could find ways to please her without abrogating his commitment to the truth. Somehow, in his efforts to gain her favor, he always managed to put a foot wrong.

Ralegh and Essex nearly shoved each other down in their haste to go fetch something — a drink or a sugary tidbit — for the queen. She laughed at the sight and took the moment to survey her hall and watch her subjects at play, a smile of contentment curled upon her lips. Her eyes lit on Francis and she crooked her finger at him.

He approached her with the thrill of honored apprehension that always overtook him in her presence. He removed his hat and executed a deep bow. He was pleased to note no ill effects from the inverted posture on his still-tender cranium.

"Mr. Bacon," Queen Elizabeth said with mock alarm. "I believe you've been watching me with your quick, clever eyes. I feel quite exposed."

"You are cloaked in radiance and wisdom, as always, Your Majesty. Although I confess I was admiring the deftness with which you juggle your suitors."

She shrugged one shoulder, like a coquette. "It keeps my wits sharp and my spirits young."

"A sensible regimen, Madame. However, in you, I have no doubt those qualities will never fail."

The queen smiled her acceptance of his tribute. "My Lord Essex gives me to understand that a part of our entertainment this day has a dual purpose. A device of your own creation. A masque for an unmasking?"

Francis looked about, not wishing to be overheard. "May I approach more nearly?"

Elizabeth beckoned him forward. "I love secrets," she whispered, her amber eyes alight. "Tell me everything."

Francis felt a rush of gratification. He was conscious that the most important persons in England were witnesses to the comfortable intimacy he was sharing once again with the queen. He regaled her with his tale of crime and investigation, beginning with his reconstruction of Smythson's murder.

Elizabeth frowned, but not, for a mercy, at him. "I'll box Essex's ears for him. I won't have these idle retainers roving the streets, harrying my lawyers. He'll rein them in, or he'll lose them."

How wonderful to be so certain of one's potency! To know with absolute authority one's place in the world and to be fully empowered to occupy it. Francis had an inkling of the destiny that called to him, but feared there was little hope of his ever attaining it. He explained in detail his methods and his process of ratiocination. The queen did not seem bored, although her eyes did wander once or twice. Alert to the slightest fluctuations in her humor, Francis hastened his exposition, arriving at the nub: the unmasking, shortly to be performed.

"My device may not succeed," he finished, suddenly quite certain that it would not and that he would be humiliated in front of the whole court. Again.

"We shall see," said the queen.

Ralegh and Essex reappeared, each bearing a goblet and a napkin. Francis sidled away from the throne, but Elizabeth checked him with a gesture.

"Stand here by me, Mr. Bacon, to explain the features of interest in your Society's performances."

"Gladly, Madame." Francis regained his place at the queen's right hand, shooting a victorious smile at Ralegh, who was obliged to jostle in with Essex on her left.

A flourish of trumpets signaled the start of the first entertainment. The musicians in the gallery began to play a dance. Lord Stephen and Thomas Clarady leapt out of seemingly nowhere, bounding three feet above the ground, their long legs extended to the full. The crowd burst into delighted applause, the queen included.

Francis beamed. Gray's would have one success, at least. A strong start gained the goodwill of the audience, which might carry them through the masque, whether his device worked or not.

The dancers were as graceful as a pair of well-matched yearlings racing for pleasure across a bright field. Each wore a short tunic and silken hose. Lord Stephen was dressed in shades of green; the privateer's son in sky blue and yellow. Whatever their recent differences may have been, they performed their athletic dance with precision and an attitude of joy.

"They're magnificent," the queen purred. "Can such a pair of virile youths be dusty men of the law? I pray you, Mr. Bacon, tell me everything about them."

"They are first-year students, Madame, and thus perhaps not yet so very dusty. The man in green is Lord Stephen Delabere, heir of the Earl of Dorchester."

"A Puritan." She wrinkled her royal nose.

"The son is not, in my observation. Indeed, I believe his father's severity has led him rather toward the middle road."

"I'm glad to hear it. Catholics may be more dangerous, but Puritans are far the more tedious."

Francis was inclined to agree but refrained, lest he seem to criticize his own mother. He knew Queen Elizabeth was well aware of that lady's extremist beliefs. He knew she disapproved of them but suspected she would disapprove of unfilial gossip even more.

Informal conversations with monarchs were severely taxing. Sometimes the wisest course was a change of subject. "The other dancer is a boyhood friend of Lord

Stephen's: the son of a privateer. His name is Thomas Clarady."

"A privateer's son?" The queen hummed an expression of feminine appreciation that set both Ralegh and Essex on their toes. "Long legs and great loyalty: an irresistible combination. Wouldn't you agree, Sir Walter?"

"So long as the loyalty is less flexible than the leg, Your Majesty," he replied.

The trio began another round of flirtatious nonsense. Francis gave them half an ear as he watched the young men leaping and pirouetting across the floor. He was more than a trifle annoyed with Clarady for failing to deliver a statement from the limner before the afternoon's entertainments began. He still didn't know whether she had any statement to make. He thought back over the past few days and realized that he hadn't had so much as a glimpse of the lad since Wednesday. What had he been doing all week?

Dancing, he supposed, and fiddling with costumery. This was the fundamental difference between a gentleman and a member of the lower orders: a gentleman kept to his task until the task was done, and done to perfection.

"You don't like my dancing privateer," the queen said.

Francis startled and saw her eyes flash with amusement. She enjoyed catching her courtiers off guard. "I do like him, Madame." He offered her a rueful smile. "I do. He's as personable as he is comely. He's not lacking in native wit, and he displays a readiness to serve, when properly directed."

"But?"

"But he is distractible and oversentimental. More pertinently, I believe he may be withholding the capstone of my construction of proofs, which I would dearly like to have in place before the masque."

Queen Elizabeth laughed, not unkindly, at his confession of unconfidence.

The music rose to a crescendo as the dancers performed a series of somersaults that drove the audience to their feet, pounding their applause. The two men struck their final poses, arms raised, with wide grins aimed directly at the queen. Clarady's eyes slid toward Francis and took on an unmistakably devilish gleam.

The queen laughed heartily and applauded with her hands upraised so they could see. She tilted her head toward Francis and murmured, "You know, Mr. Bacon, I do believe he is."

* * *

Jugglers appeared to fill an intermission, allowing the audience to mingle before the next performance. Ralegh turned toward Francis. "Your gamble is likely to come to naught, Mr. Bacon. If you know which is your man, surely there are more certain methods of apprehension at your disposal."

"He claims he doesn't know," the queen said. "But that doesn't sound like our Francis Bacon, does it?"

Francis hoped she meant that as a compliment. "I believe that I do know, but belief is not certainty. I am loath to stain an innocent man's reputation with so dark a color as murder without more tangible proofs."

"Do you really think these foul crimes were committed for professional advancement?" Essex asked.

"Do you not believe that a lawyer can be ambitious?" The queen and Ralegh laughed, two adults versus the stripling boy.

Francis admired the way young Essex held his ground. "I merely seek to clarify the basis of the coming test. If ambition is the motive, then I place my wager on the murderer being found among the ancients of Gray's Inn. They have the farthest to climb and thus the most to gain from a ruthless gambit."

The queen said, "Ah, but it's the benchers that are always plucking at my counselors' sleeves, seeking serjeanties and judgeships. They're close enough to smell their prizes; their appetites are fully whetted."

"I'll take that bet, Essex," Ralegh said. "I wager that our man's a bencher."

The two courtiers shook hands. Ralegh begged leave to absent himself for a moment and drifted off into the crowd. Francis caught sight of him a few minutes later in animated conversation with Lady Elizabeth Throckmorton. He felt his stomach tie itself in nervous knots. His reputation was now at stake before the entire court. If nothing came of his unmasking, he'd be a laughingstock.

At least he could trust that the courtiers would maintain a clear line between the wagerers and the wagerees; between the court and the Gray's Inn men. None of these avaricious, novelty-starved noblemen and women would wish to queer their bets.

* * *

Thomas Campion next took the stage. He sat alone on a stool with his lute. The audience continued its loud chatter for half a minute, but soon he had their rapt attention as he sang "Beauty, Since You So Much Desire," a song of his own composition.

Another success. Francis loved music and wished he could enjoy the song, but he was fraught with anxiety waiting for his masque. He had arranged for the benchers to sit in the front stands on the left of the aisle and the ancients opposite them on the right. That way, all would be reachable by his Wild Men during the performance.

Treasurer Fogg sat arm in arm with Lady Penelope Rich, gossiping comfortably. They had obviously reached an accord concerning her debts to Sir Amias Rolleston.

Francis suspected the old gentleman would have to wait a long time to be repaid, but he wasn't surprised that Fogg had sacrificed his client's interests to curry favor with the lady.

Their current accord changed nothing. At the time the murders were committed, Fogg's ambitions confronted seemingly insurmountable obstacles. That he had now scaled those ramparts in nowise altered the past.

George Humphries sat with the other ancients, cheeks flushed with wine and excitement. He looked like a pettifogger, dressed in old-fashioned slops. Francis almost felt sympathy for the man's obstructed life. Almost. If Humphries was the man who had performed these heinous deeds, he deserved to hang, however pathetic his history and his wardrobe.

* * *

More thundering applause startled Francis from his thoughts. Thomas Campion stood, bowed, and walked off the stage to be engulfed by a bevy of young women.

The time had come.

Gray's men shifted the props and scenery for the masque onto the stage. A sneeze could bring the whole thing down, but it looked well enough from a distance. It wouldn't do for it to be too professional; they were gentlemen after all, not players.

Cornets rang out, commanding everyone's attention.

"Your moment has arrived, Mr. Bacon," the queen said. "Now we'll see how well you plot."

A tree made of painted pasteboard revolved on rollers hidden under its leafy stand. As it rotated around, Lord Stephen was revealed, standing with one ankle crossed over the other. He was still clad in shades of green but now had a short parti-colored cloak hung from one shoulder and a pair of pistols stuck in his belt. Francis was startled by that last touch. Where had he gotten pistols? From the privateer's son, no doubt. Trust Clarady to produce such a dangerous and unnecessary embellishment.

"I am the law-lorn Prince of Purpoole, a kingdom without law." Delabere recited his lines in a clear, carrying voice.

Ralegh leaned toward the queen, speaking familiarly across her lap. "Why does our law-lorn prince need to be so well armed, Mr. Bacon?"

"To symbolize lawlessness, of course," Essex responded.

Francis shrugged and shot a sly glance at the queen. "It can be difficult to prevent one's lieutenants from improvising in the field."

Queen Elizabeth laughed aloud and then covered her mouth with her hand as poor Lord Stephen was startled from his speech. She waved at him to continue.

He delivered a few stanzas explaining to the assembly how he had come to disdain the law and its practitioners. The law is cruel and unfeeling. No man may trust in it. Francis heard no snickering and saw no open yawns. The conceit appeared to be mildly amusing even to this jaded audience.

Mr. Trumpington, dressed as a woodland courtier in russet and spruce, strode onto the stage, accompanied by two others similarly arrayed.

The prince addressed him. "Tell me, Baron Scoffington, do you know how many lawyers are wanted to light a lanthorn?"

"Why, none, Your Grace, since the aim of a lawyer is to obscure rather than to bring light."

The audience laughed.

"I mean, how many must be engaged?"

Baron Scoffington shrugged. "How many coins have you?"

More laughter. Francis knew that signaled that the general mood was happy rather than that his jokes were clever, but he was satisfied nevertheless.

"But how many are needed to execute the action?"

Before the baron could answer, several Wild Men dashed in from a side entrance. "Lawyers are trespassing in our woods!" the one in front cried. Francis recognized Benjamin Whitt under the shaggy croppings of moss and twigs, and grinned. His friend's physique was more robust than one would imagine from his ordinary mode of dress. The Wild Man stalking beside him, growling fiercely, was probably Thomas Clarady, though his face was barely discernible under the layers of forest materials.

Soon the cry was general: "Lawyers! Alack! Alarm! Lawyers in the Kingdom of Purpoole!"

A bass drum rolled thunder through the hall as sheets of silver-white lightning — made of sheerest silk — streaked over the stage. The clumps of yew placed around the edge of the stage were shaken vigorously by their yew-colored bearers.

Many in the audience gasped. The mood darkened. Francis stole a glance at the queen. She was smiling. Good.

The Wild Men prowled about the audience, peering into faces. Wild Man Whitt loomed over Treasurer Fogg, growling and shaking his twiggy head.

Fogg shrank back, raising his hands in mock fear. "Oh, spare me, Dread Savage! I mean you no harm! I merely wandered into your kingdom by chance, pursuing this fair lady."

Whitt bowed to the lady. "See you advance no further into our realm, Counselor."

Lady Rich swatted him with her fan and he flinched and slunk away.

Francis could find no fault with Whitt's performance, but he wasn't happy with the result. Fogg had showed no signs of fear or animosity toward the Wild Man; but then, he wasn't the querulous type. Perhaps if the man had been

314

seated alone and if two of the Wild Men had confronted him simultaneously? Now the moment had passed. What a stupid idea this was!

The third Wild Man lunged, roaring, toward Thomas Hughes, who had volunteered for the role. Hughes shrieked in terror, provoking echoing screams from some of the ladies in the audience. Francis felt a shiver run up his spine and was pleased at the effectiveness of this bit of stagecraft.

Now Whitt and Clarady were prancing along the edges of the audience, chanting, "Here, lawyer, lawyer." Francis had acquired that bit of dialogue from the earl's secretary, who remembered it as a feature of the retainers' story. Their tone was menacing. One could have no doubt of their violent intentions should they succeed in capturing their prey.

A shivery silence fell upon the audience. Francis saw faces drawn with tension as the tall youths stalked the hall, stooping and rumbling and baring their teeth. Clarady thrust his hands toward one of the ancients, making snatching motions. The man shrank back until he pressed against the knees of the man behind him.

Clarady twisted suddenly and bent nearly double to snarl into Humphries's ashen face. *"I've got a bone to pick with you, Counselor."*

The drum pounded out an ominous roll. Humphries shrieked and sprang to his feet, pushing feebly at Clarady, who laughingly let him escape. Humphries quickly found himself surrounded by leering Wild Men, passing him from one to the other, chanting, "Here, lawyer, lawyer."

The audience laughed in relief from the tension. Someone called out, "Lawyer-baiting: a new sport for the Southwark stews." "Cheaper to feed than bears!" another voice cried, and the laughter rose to the painted stars high overhead.

But Humphries didn't hear them. His face was slack with panic as he tottered from one side of the stage to the other, vainly seeking a gap between his tormentors.

Clarady leapt out from behind Lord Stephen's tree and placed himself directly in front of Humphries. He reached behind him— for a knife? Francis felt a stab of sharp anxiety. He wanted no actual violence here in the Banqueting Hall. But no, what Clarady drew forth was a roll of paper, such as artists use for sketching. He unrolled it in a swift motion and held it before the eyes of the trembling barrister.

The effect was breathtaking. Humphries gasped and stopped so abruptly he rocked back on his heels. He stood panting and shaking his head. Clarady stepped to the edge of the stage to display the sketch to the audience. Everyone gasped as though on a single indrawn breath. Francis was as shocked as the rest. Why hadn't Clarady shown him the sketch earlier?

"Bring that to me," the queen commanded in a carrying voice.

Francis trotted down the aisle and accepted the sketch from Clarady with a severe frown, getting only a self-satisfied flick of the eyebrows in response. Perhaps he had been a trifle demanding, perhaps even a little brusque toward the lad in the past week. If so, he had now been paid in full.

He studied the drawing as he quick-stepped back to the throne. The limner had a superlative talent. She had caught Humphries in a moment of exaltation, kneeling over Smythson's blood-smeared body with his knife still wet in his hand.

As he handed the sketch to the queen with a bow, shouts from the stage drew his attention. "I didn't mean to!" Humphries cried. The Wild Men hemmed him in. "I'm not responsible! He should have helped me instead of blocking my way. It was an accident, I tell you!"

316

"Was Mr. Shiveley an accident?" Whitt's baritone voice rumbled like the voice of doom itself.

"They chose him instead of me. It wasn't fair! He had everything; I had nothing. Why should he be so favored?"

Humphries skittered toward the edge of the stage and then skipped back from the hissing audience. Clarady and Lord Stephen moved together to flank him. Lord Stephen reached toward him. Humphries jerked away, eyes wild. He dodged under Lord Stephen's arm and snatched a pistol from his belt.

"Look out!"

"He has a gun!"

Screams and shouts erupted from near the stage, traveling back in a wave, as those seated in front jumped to their feet and collided with those behind them. The panicking courtiers were hampered by their oversized ruffs and farthingales. Francis saw a roiling sea of silks and velvets falling from the risers, scrambling into the aisles, crowding against the wall. A pair of courtiers swung their fists at two of the Wild Men, who turned to defend themselves.

Humphries stumbled about on the stage alone, waving the pistol wildly over his head.

"Grab him!"

"Get that weapon!"

A shot boomed, echoing through the hall. Francis felt hotness streak past his cheek. He clutched his chest to support his faltering heart.

"'Ware the queen!"

Ralegh and Essex ran into each other in their haste to protect the queen, knocking Francis right into her lap. Essex dragged him to his feet and shoved him aside while Ralegh scooped the queen into his arms to carry her out of the hall.

"Mr. Bacon," she said over Ralegh's shoulder, "do not expect an invitation to dinner on New Year's Day."

Francis closed his eyes and pinched the bridge of his nose.

FORTY-FIVE

Monday morning, Tom, Ben, and Trumpet went out to the fields to practice shooting at the straw butts in the hollow out of sight of the Inn. The day was cold and overcast, and most of Gray's men stayed snugged up in their rooms, but the lads had had few chances for private talk since Christmas Eve, what with their various Misrule duties and the omnipresence of Prattling Prince Stephen at meals.

Trumpet spread a blanket on the ground, and Tom laid out his pistols, a bag of powder, a sack of balls, the cleaning rag and rod, and a bottle of oil. He and Trumpet each took a pistol and began to prepare them for firing.

"What's to become of Mr. Humphries?" Tom asked Ben.

Ben had gone with Mr. Bacon to the Tower, where Humphries had been taken direct from Whitehall. They'd assisted the sheriff in eliciting a full confession of his crimes, including his attempt to poison Clara.

"Once he started talking," Ben said, "I could scarcely write fast enough to keep up. Frank says it's the release of the pressure of secrecy. He's seen it before. He says it's like a dam bursting. Villains often long to confess, to alleviate the torment that preys upon their minds."

"They know they're about to face their final judgment," Tom said. "They want to spare themselves an eternity in hell."

Ben nodded. "He'll face his trial at the start of Hilary Term. There's no doubt about the verdict: guilty on all counts. They found Shiveley's keys hidden at the bottom of his chest along with a stock of counterfeit coins."

"Now he can dance the hempen jig alongside the Queen of Scots," Tom said.

"Don't be silly," Trumpet said. "Queens don't hang. She'll have her head cut off in the Tower yard, once Her Majesty makes her mind up to do the deed." She took careful aim, holding the pistol in her right hand, arm fully extended. She didn't seem to notice that the tip of the muzzle was wobbling.

Tom was getting used to switching pronouns when thinking about Trumpet. In public, she was he. In private, he was she. They'd let Ben in on the secret as they'd walked home from Whitehall after the excitement on Christmas Eve. So much had happened that evening, this fresh revelation barely earned a grunt of surprise.

Trumpet's shot missed the butt entirely. "It's this blighted pistol." She frowned into the barrel.

"No, it's you." Tom took the pistol from her and reloaded it. "It's too heavy for you. The barrel wobbles and you twitch your wrist before you pull the trigger. Try using both hands."

He gave it back to her then cupped her left hand under her right to support the wrist. His hands were half again as large as hers. The difference pleased him for no reason. "Try that."

She stood with her left foot forward this time and fired again. She was still wide of the mark, but the bullet raised a tuft of straw from the outer corner of the butt. She growled like a kitten and then asked, "How's *Clah-rah*?" She'd taken to overpronouncing the name in a pseudo-imitation of Stephen. Tom smelled jealousy, which pleased and alarmed him in a discomfiting mix. Things had been simpler when Trumpet had been only a boy.

Ben picked up the other pistol. He made sure the pan cover was shut and the dog pulled back, then took aim and fired. "This one definitely pulls to the right."

"Ha," Trumpet said.

Tom took the pistol from Ben, grateful for the distraction, and began to clean it. He was still sorting out his feelings in this area. "Clara is well. Or she was when I handed her into Lady Nottingham's carriage yesterday."

Clara's fears about losing her livelihood had proved groundless. Far from ruining her reputation, the talent displayed in her sketch and her intimate role in so thrilling a tale made her the most sought-after ornament of the season. After a hissing scuffle in the Banqueting Hall, the queen's friend Catherine Carey, Countess of Nottingham, had borne away the prize. Clara would spend the next month on her estate in Surrey painting miniature portraits of everyone within half a day's ride. She'd earn enough in that month to keep her for a year.

Trumpet sniffed. "By now she's found six new things to worry about. Will they despise her? Will they make fun of her accent? Will they drum her into the forest to be devoured by wolves?"

Ben chuckled. "She did seem rather inclined toward melancholic distress."

"She's a pick-fault," Trumpet said. "A blister. A harpy. Admit it."

"She's beautiful," Tom answered. "I love her madly." He winced as he heard the hollowness in his words.

Trumpet and Ben grinned at each other. "Such conviction," Trumpet said.

"Such devotion," Ben added.

"All right." Tom surrendered. "But she really is beautiful."

"That point was never in dispute." Ben took Trumpet's pistol and started cleaning it. He cast a sidelong glance at Tom. "How did your meeting go? With Frank and his lord uncle?" His brow was creased with worry. Time to let him off the hook.

Francis Bacon had netted Tom right and proper. He suspected Ben had helped him weave that net. Tom had been surprised by the proposal and a bit disgruntled by the conspiring behind his back, but all in all, he wasn't unhappy about the new arrangement.

Lord Burghley had received disturbing news from Cambridge that zealous Presbyterians were planning to hold a secret synod under the cover of commencement in July. His informant warned of plans for overt and possibly violent rebellion against the established Church. His Lordship needed a spy to worm his way into their confidence and identify the chief conspirators. Bacon had recommended Tom for the job. His payment would be continuance at Gray's Inn, guaranteed by a letter from Lord Burghley himself. Not even Stephen's father could undermine that support. He would finish the requirements for his bachelor's degree while he was at it, further bolstering his position.

"Frank was persuasive." Tom shot Trumpet a wry grin. "As per usual."

Ben blew out a sigh of relief. Tom clapped him on the shoulder and looked him square in the eye. "I'm happy. Honestly. It'll be fun, spying on the godly."

Ben scoffed. "I hardly —"

"Relax, *camerade*. I like investigating. It's lively and you meet all sorts of people. I've decided to become a barrister intelligencer, in special service to the queen. Someday. And this deal solves my main worry: that Stephen would get me expelled from Gray's out of spite."

"How was Frank?" Trumpet asked. "Whenever he mentions his uncle, he looks like a man with his breeches caught in a crack."

"I think he's on probation for something. He doesn't seem to be getting nearly as much out of this arrangement as I am. But you can't say no to the Lord Treasurer." Tom winked at Trumpet. "Think of the fun I'm going to have: weekly letters from dear old Frank, telling me what to think and where to shit and how to put my stockings on." They both laughed.

Ben shuddered. "Stop, stop!" He beetled his dark brows at them. "Call him Mr. Bacon, I beg you, even in your own minds. He wouldn't be happy knowing that you know that we — that he — that I've spoken to you about him in such familiar terms."

"We promise," Tom and Trumpet chorused with fingers crossed behind their backs. Ben groaned in frustration. It was his own fault. His every utterance had begun with *Frank says* for the past week. Even Tom had never been so besotted.

He was going to miss his friends badly, but he'd be twice damned if he would say it out loud. He took the second pistol from Trumpet, reloaded it, and extended his right arm. He sighted down the barrel and fired. The ball struck an inch to the right of the bull's eye.

Trumpet smirked at him. "See?"

"Huh." Tom squatted by the blanket and started a more thorough cleaning. There must be a bit of gunk stuck in the barrel. He glanced up at Trumpet. "What are *you* going to do, Lady Alice? With your uncle in hiding, you can't very well stay here."

"Can't I?" Trumpet grinned at Ben, who grinned broadly back. "With you running off to Cambridge, Mr. Whitt finds himself in need of a new chambermate."

"What! When was this little plot hatched?"

"This morning, while you were meeting with Mr. Bacon and Lord Burghley. I went up to your rooms to show you what Uncle Nat sent me and found Ben pacing back and forth like a caged bear. He told me about your meeting. He thought you'd accept the bargain, which would leave him without a chum to help him pay his rent.

We decided to team up and solve both our problems at once.

"I don't approve of this arrangement," Tom said. "In fact, I forbid it."

"Excuse me?" Trumpet held a hand to her ear. "Did I hear a pig fart?"

Tom bristled, shaking his pistol at the obstreperous trollop. The said trollop stuck her tongue out at him.

"Children, please," Ben said. "You know she has nothing to fear from me."

"She's not the one I'm worried about. I warn you, Ben: she looks completely different wearing only a shirt with her hair hanging down to her waist."

"She's still the wrong shape," he said equably.

"You won't like our chambers," Tom said to Trumpet. "They're drafty and the floors squeak. And there's this smell —"

"We're not moving into your wretched old rooms," she said. "Uncle Nat feels sorry for leaving me in the lurch. I kept my end of the bargain after all. He sent me the lease to his chambers listing me as sub-tenant. Under the name of Allen Trumpington, of course. Ben's going to move in with me."

"Nice, big hearth," Ben said. "And the kitchen fire is always lit. I'll save a fortune on fuel."

"Hm." Tom frowned, pretending not to like it. "I suppose I'll have to allow it." Their solution was brilliant. It would keep Trumpet in London until he came back.

He reloaded the pistol and passed it to Trumpet. "Speaking of fortunes, are you going to be all right? Money-wise, I mean? You can't very well write to your father for an allowance."

"I'll be fine." She flicked him a grateful smile. "Uncle Nat sent me a purse too — of real coins, not false. And I have a necklace of my mother's I can sell if I'm pressed."

She tried a new stance, right foot forward, and took aim at the butt. "I'm very resourceful."

Tom heard a world of loneliness under that simple remark. He caught Ben's eye; he'd heard it too. They nodded at each other. She was theirs now, and they would look out for her.

"Without me around, you'll do nothing but study," he scolded. "You'll grow fat and pale and weak from lack of exercise."

"We'll be formidable lawyers, though," Ben said.

"You won't last through Hilary Term," Tom said. "She's the most vexing, nerve-shredding, wit-rattling minx in all of Christendom."

"Why, thank you, kind sir." Trumpet's voice thrummed with that musical quality that got right up into Tom's midsection and played *glissandos* on his spine.

He growled deep in his throat.

She pursed her pink lips and blew him a kiss. She was playing him like a big, fat fish and loving every minute of it.

Tom would be vastly better off in Cambridge. A world of men dedicated to the life of the mind. A bracing challenge for his wits and a restorative vacation for his tangled feelings. No women; therefore, no trouble. He could hardly wait to leave. "Will you still be here when I come back?" He hated the plaintive note that crept in underneath.

"Don't worry." Trumpet adjusted her stance, facing the butt and balancing her weight on both feet. She supported her right hand with her left and sighted down the barrel. She tucked her tongue into the corner of her mouth and shifted the barrel slightly to the left, then held her breath and fired. The bullet flew straight into the bull's eye. She flashed a grin at Tom that made him feel happy from head to toe. "I will always know where to find you."

HISTORICAL NOTES

You can find maps of the places we go in this series at my website on a page called "Maps for the Francis Bacon mystery series:" www.annacastle.com/francis-bacon-series/maps-for-the-francis-bacon-series. Some are downloadable, some are links to maps I don't have rights to, including a delightful interactive map of Elizabethan London.

Bacon wasn't really banned from court, not in 1586 at any rate, although he did annoy the queen and his uncle with some importunate request around this time. The consensus was that he was too young to be granted the said request. He did make proposals to revise the common law, later in his life. He published a set of legal maxims in 1597 which were still being used by law students well into the nineteenth century. He worked on things for years before publishing, so it's not improbable that he was thinking about these things in 1586. The Queen's fury and his banishment from court are entirely my invention.

Sticklers will observe that I got the Reading schedule backwards: Lent was only for double readers — established benchers reading a second time. First-timers read in August. I made the switch to get Francis's reading closer to the season of Misrule. He really did give his first reading at Lent in 1588, however. Why this exception was made for him isn't known. Strings were pulled, but we don't know whose or why.

I like to use actual historical people whenever I can. Some are unavoidable, like the queen, her chief courtiers, and members of Francis Bacon's family. Others are minor figures, mere footnotes, now, in some book, but once the stars of their own lives.

Here's this book's roster of real persons:
- Francis Bacon
- Queen Elizabeth I
- William Cecil, Lord Burghley
- Captain Sir Walter Raleigh
- Robert Devereux, Earl of Essex
- Penelope Rich, née Devereux, Lady Rich
- William Danby, the Queen's Coroner. He makes a cameo appearance in chapter 2.
- Elizabeth Moulthorne, surgeon. I found her in Liza Picard's delightful *Elizabeth's London*. Tracing the footnotes yielded nothing more than her name, origin, and profession. I like her, though; maybe I'll try harder for a later book.
- Sir Christopher Yelverton. Member of an important legal dynasty. Heard walking up the stairs in chapter 9.
- William Philippes. Francis's close friend and assistant. He was the son of a Customs House official who probably lent Francis money in exchange for helping his son into higher social circles. Son's real first name isn't known, so I named him after his father. He was the brother of Sir Francis Walsingham's cryptographer, Thomas Phelippes.

Come visit my blog at www.annacastle.com/blog where I review history books and write posts about the fascinating things I learn that can't be put in the books, where Story is King. If you have questions or complaints, feel free to let me know at castle@annacastle.com.

ABOUT THE AUTHOR

Anna Castle holds an eclectic set of degrees: BA in the Classics, MS in Computer Science, and a Ph.D in Linguistics. She has had a correspondingly eclectic series of careers: waitressing, software engineering, grammar-writing, a short stint as an associate professor, and managing a digital archive. Historical fiction combines her lifelong love of stories and learning. She physically resides in Austin, Texas, but mentally counts herself a queen of infinite space.

BOOKS BY ANNA CASTLE

K eep up with all my books and short stories with my newsletter: www.annacastle.com

The Francis Bacon Series

Book 1, *Murder by Misrule*

Francis Bacon is charged with investigating the murder of a fellow barrister at Gray's Inn. He recruits his unwanted protégé Thomas Clarady to do the tiresome legwork. The son of a privateer, Clarady will do anything to climb the Elizabethan social ladder. Bacon's powerful uncle Lord Burghley suspects Catholic conspirators of the crime, but other motives quickly emerge. Rival barristers contend for the murdered man's legal honors and wealthy clients. Highly-placed courtiers are implicated as the investigation reaches from Whitehall to the London streets. Bacon does the thinking; Clarady does the fencing. Everyone has something up his pinked and padded sleeve. Even the brilliant Francis Bacon is at a loss — and in danger — until he sees through the disguises of the season of Misrule.

Book 2, *Death by Disputation*

Thomas Clarady is recruited to spy on the increasingly rebellious Puritans at Cambridge University. Francis Bacon is his spymaster; his tutor in both tradecraft and religious politics. Their commission gets off to a deadly start when Tom finds his chief informant hanging from the roof beams. Now he must catch a murderer as well as a seditioner. His first suspect is volatile poet Christopher Marlowe, who keeps turning up in the wrong places.

Dogged by unreliable assistants, chased by three lusty women, and harangued daily by the exacting Bacon, Tom risks his very soul to catch the villains and win his reward.

Book 3, The Widow's Guild

London, 1588: Someone is turning Catholics into widows, taking advantage of armada fever to mask the crimes. Francis Bacon is charged with identifying the murderer by the Andromache Society, a widows' guild led by his formidable aunt. He must free his friends from the Tower, track an exotic poison, and untangle multiple crimes to determine if the motive is patriotism, greed, lunacy — or all three.

Book 4, Publish and Perish

It's 1589 and England is embroiled in a furious pamphlet war between an impudent Puritan calling himself Martin Marprelate and London's wittiest writers. The archbishop wants Martin to hang. The Privy Council wants the tumult to end. But nobody knows who Martin is or where he's hiding his illegal press.

Then two writers are strangled, mistaken for Thomas Nashe, the pamphleteer who is hot on Martin's trail. Francis Bacon is tasked with stopping the murders — and catching Martin, while he's about it. But the more he learns, the more he fears Martin may be someone dangerously close to home.

Can Bacon and his band of intelligencers stop the strangler before another writer dies, without stepping on Martin's possibly very important toes?

Book 5, Let Slip the Dogs

It's Midsummer, 1591, at Richmond Palace, and love is in the air. Gallant courtiers sport with great ladies while Tom and Trumpet bring their long-laid plans to fruition at last. Everybody's doing it — even Francis Bacon enjoys a private liaison with the secretary to the new French ambassador. But the Queen loathes scandal and will punish anyone rash enough to get caught.

Still, it's all in a summer day until a young man is found dead. He had few talents beyond a keen nose for gossip and was doubtless murdered to keep a secret. But what sort — romantic, or political? They carried different penalties: banishment from court or a traitor's death. Either way, worth killing to protect.

Bacon wants nothing more than to leave things alone. He has no position and no patron; in fact, he's being discouraged from investigating. But can he live with himself if another innocent person dies?

The Professor & Mrs. Moriarty Series

Book 1, Moriarty Meets His Match

Professor James Moriarty has but one desire left in his shattered life: to prevent the man who ruined him from harming anyone else. Then he meets amber-eyed Angelina Gould and his world turns upside down.

At an exhibition of new inventions, an exploding steam engine kills a man. When Moriarty tries to figure out what happened, he comes up against Sherlock Holmes, sent to investigate by Moriarty's old enemy. Holmes collects evidence that points at Moriarty, who realizes he must either solve the crime or swing it for it himself. He soon uncovers trouble among the board members of the engine company and its unscrupulous promoter. Moriarty tries to untangle those relationships, but everywhere he turns, he meets the alluring Angelina. She's playing some game, but what's her goal? And whose side is she on?

Between them, Holmes and Angelina push Moriarty to his limits -- and beyond. He'll have to lose himself to save his life and win the woman he loves.

Book 2, Moriarty Takes His Medicine

James and Angelina Moriarty are settling into their new marriage and their fashionable new home — or trying to. But James has too little to occupy his mind and Angelina has too many secrets pressing on her heart. They fear they'll never learn to live together. Then Sherlock Holmes comes to call with a challenging case. He suspects a prominent Harley Street specialist of committing murders for hire, sending patients home from his private hospital with deadly doses or fatal conditions. Holmes intends to investigate, but the doctor's clientele is exclusively female. He needs Angelina's help.

While Moriarty, Holmes, and Watson explore the alarming number of ways a doctor can murder his patients with impunity, Angelina enters into treatment with their primary suspect, posing as a nervous woman who fears her husband wants to be rid of her. Then a hasty conclusion and an ill-considered word drive James and Angelina apart, sending her deep into danger. Now they must find the courage to trust each other as they race the clock to win justice for the murdered women before they become victims themselves.

Book 3, Moriarty Brings Down the House

An old friend brings a strange problem to Professor and Mrs. Moriarty: either his theater is being haunted by an angry ghost or someone is trying to drive him into bankruptcy. He wants the Moriartys to make it stop; more, he wants Angelina to play the lead in his Christmas pantomime and James to contribute a large infusion of much-needed cash.

The Moriartys gladly accept the fresh challenges, but the day they arrive at the theater, the stage manager dies. It isn't an accident, and it is most definitely not a ghost. While Angelina works backstage turning up secrets and old grudges, James follows the money in search of a motive. The pranks grow deadlier and more frequent. Then someone sets Sherlock Holmes on the trail, trying to catch our sleuths crossing the line into crime. How far will the Moriartys have to go to keep the show afloat? And will they all make it to opening night in one piece?

Made in the USA
Coppell, TX
12 January 2021